DEMIMONDE

Halli Starling

Halli Starling Books

Interior illustrations and cover © Željka Dobras
Design by Zeljka Debeljak
https://www.artstation.com/dzeljka

Edited by Laura R. Samotin
https://www.laurarsamotin.com/

CONTENTS

Also by Halli Starling

Wilderwood

Twelfth Moon

Ask Me For Fire

A Brighter, Darker Art

When He Beckons

The Way We Wind

Always There For You

Coup de Coeur

Venor

(The Werewolf Novels, Book 1)

Pose for Me

(coming summer 2025)

Verto

(The Werewolf Novels, Book 2; coming late 2025)

Book 3 in the Oracle, Tailor, Curator

INCARNER

CONTENT WARNINGS

- Horror elements, including gore and blood

- Violence against animals (committed offscreen, described in the aftermath in some detail)

- Discussions of sex and gender

- Discussions of magic and the occult

- Religious musings and considerations

- Demonic and angelic imagery

Author's Note

FOR A FULL ACCOUNTING of the research done to write this trilogy, please see the Author's Note in COUP DE COEUR. But for this book and the third in the trilogy, I had to delve into more...let's say *esoteric* spaces. There are only a few books on John Dee and his work, and they are heavily academic in nature. I've included that information in the "Sources and For Further Reading" section at the back of the book. For the darker themes and elements moving forward, I was heavily inspired by tales of the macabre; the twisted ones that sometimes let us peek at a truth far more frightening than we could have imagined. There are stories in darkness, too, and they are worth examining; even if it is so we might better understand the darkness inside our own hearts. Please mind the content warnings and take care when reading.

****

A few continuity errors have been corrected in the new version of COUP DE COEUR. The most glaring one being Ethaniel and Vincent's familial relationship; they are half-brothers who share a mother. Any errors in the final books are mine and mine alone.

FOLIO ONE:

UNBOUND

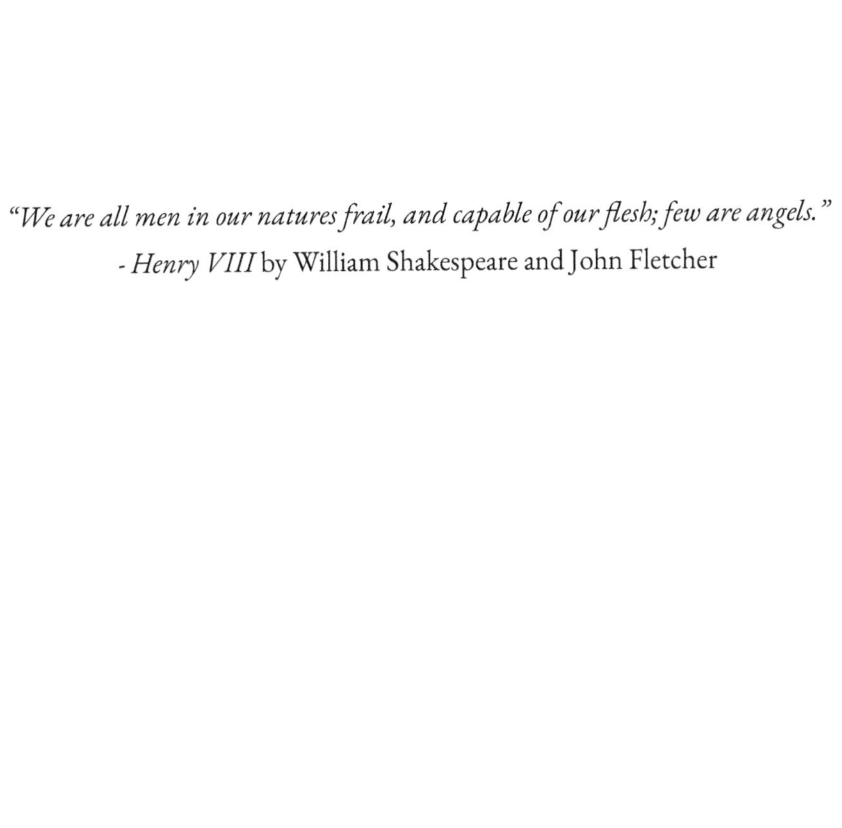

"We are all men in our natures frail, and capable of our flesh; few are angels."
- *Henry VIII* by William Shakespeare and John Fletcher

CHAPTER ONE

"He wasn't talking to angels, the crazy fool. No angel would lie, especially so smoothly. But for all my insistence that the voices he heard and the shapes he saw flickering in the flames were nothing, with all the fervor he held John would believe nothing less than that the Divine spoke to him, and moreover, heard him. That angels were whispering directly into his ear. Only his.

The hubris of such a thing.

I spent the first months attempting to dispel this from John's mind, but he held fast. They were angels, they must be! They couldn't possibly be anything else because he was a righteous man, appointed by God to bend the ear of the court and the Queen. John did not want to hear my careful explanations of the dead's trickery. For all he trusted that I also heard voices in the shadows and saw things in the fire, he refused to believe in their maliciousness, their greed, their avarice. The dead desire what they've lost, or what they never had, and what John wanted was to interpret their words and use them for Queen and country. And when scryer after scryer failed to assist him, he turned to a necromancer.

He found me.

He thought me a cozener. And I was, and still am. But what John wanted was as much as the dead would give him, and I never once lied to him about their dark desires.

–From the diaries of Edward Kelly, or Edward Talbot, around the autumn of 1582

CHAPTER TWO

CALIX

Calix stared down in horror at the hand holding his. He knew that hand, its neat nails and the fine bones lying just below pale skin. He had held that hand many times, fingers laced together, or his fist balled up in its warmth. He'd even traced the knobby wrist bones and veins flushed blue and green with his lips and tongue.

It was Lawton's hand, but the grip of it was all his mother.

"That's impossible." Aubrey's tone was hushed, awed, as if torn between prayer and hysteria.

They were frozen in place, hovering over Lawton's prone form, too stunned to move. Calix wouldn't tear his gaze from Lawton, even at Aubrey's words. If he'd been possessed of such self-awareness in the moment, Calix would have thought that they painted quite the tableau, their knees and backs locked in crouches, their faces masks of disbelief, shock, and, for him, grief.

The only thing he felt right now was cold truth seeping through his bones. Staring down at Lawton's lupine face and matted shock of red-orange hair, Calix knew it was true.

Somewhere, his rational mind let him examine Lawton for a hard moment, measuring the angle of his shoulders, the twist of his hips. Lawton's airs and stance were not masculine or feminine, and Calix had never held people to those strange societal standards anyways. It might be Lawton's form, but everything about him screamed *other*.

Mother

"Darling," Lawton said, reaching out for Calix once more. "It's me. It is."

"This isn't doing anyone any favors, blasted cold," Ethaniel said. The comment snapped Calix back into the present. *The vault. The phylactery. All the magical objects thrumming with life and power. All his mother's secrets buried beneath her crypt.*

Calix heard the chatter of his teeth and winced, but nodded, rising slowly with the aid of Ethaniel's strong hand under his elbow. This was another set of hands he knew, but not well, even though he wished to learn of them more. All this thought of hands and faces and cold stone vaults made the air rush into him too quickly, his lungs filling until they burned, and Calix coughed, eyes watering.

"Easy, easy," Ethaniel hummed in his ear. "Aubrey?"

Something passed across Ethaniel's face and Calix got to watch the play of it up close. It was calculated; not so expressive to set off Calix's worry, but certainly not placid. Whatever Ethaniel was communicating to Aubrey, he clearly meant to keep it in safe waters.

The hands clutching his – damn those fingers to hell and back – were frighteningly strong, to the point where Calix thought he might have a bruise. *So odd, knowing she would never bruise him except in death, while in life Lawton's hands had left bruises, purple and mottled green, yellow and blurry at the edges, and always where Calix had asked for them.*

"I've got him," Aubrey said as he appeared on Lawton's other side. "Let's get inside the house."

Calix's mind wandered during the short walk back into the blazing warmth of the kitchens, where the tiles under his shoes were familiar. A loose stone here, a crack there, the sound of their shoes echoing hollowly around them. He knew every inch of this house, down to the corners prone to cobwebs and the title of every book in the library.

Or, he thought he'd known it. It wasn't as if the vault had been a secret, but he'd rarely been allowed inside. And he certainly hadn't gone in there since his mother's death, terrified that he'd see her ghost in the shadows of the rock niches, or her fingerprints in the dust on the shelves. All of it played him for a fool. Just a boy who had never fully grown up, and had never forgotten his mother's love.

As they staggered into the parlor, Calix found no relief. He felt only exhaustion deep in his bones–deeper, even, down to the empty spaces between bone and sinew and muscle where she lived. There lingered the scent of hay and lavender and how the summer sun felt on his shoulders. He stared at Lawton's face and saw his friend (his *lover*, the only person he'd trusted and hated in equal measure, sometimes changing between breaths), but he also saw her. It made something crack in his sternum, horse-kick strong and terrifying.

"Calix."

A warm, gentle touch guided him by the chin until he was looking up at Aubrey. Ethaniel was on his right, Lawton (his mother) across the way, and there was Aubrey. Tall and almost leonine in his beauty, and so intelligent and strong. Calix's vision swam with Aubrey's visage.

"Calix." Aubrey now knelt in front of him, steadying himself with a hand on Calix's knee, the other on Ethaniel's. Calix wanted to close his eyes and sink into both of them; it was a much better choice than what reality was offering. "Are you certain about this?"

Beside him, Ethaniel sucked in a sharp breath, as if Aubrey's question was somehow improper. It didn't matter, that impropriety. The person sitting primly on the emerald velvet couch could be no other. "Yes," Calix managed to rasp out, his throat burning with the effort. "It's her."

"Just a piece." Lawton's own voice was higher now, airier. *Your mother's voice. You know it, even if it has the sweetgrass notes of Lawton's tone buried beneath.* "I'm so sorry for disturbing you, my love. But I couldn't let that *thing* in. It needs to stay where it is, trapped in that book with so many other slivers of consciousness."

Red flashed across Calix's vision. "The book! Where is it?"

"It's here. Aubrey has it." Ethaniel's voice was a balm over his nerves, but it wasn't enough. Calix felt the strange need for *more*. He *wanted* more, in fact, the desire for the nameless thing blood-hot and unshakeable. He needed and wanted their comfort and care, yes, but also their touches. He didn't want Lawton's hands on him, he wanted – needed – them. Desperately. Calix couldn't be sure if those were his thoughts or they were born of panic and fear, but right now it did not matter.

Beside him, Aubrey and Ethaniel were conversing, twin looks of worry creasing their faces, making them both appear older. Calix only heard a roar in his ears, a constant roll of thunder that seemed to mimic the frantic beating of his heart.

"I'm so sorry, my love," his mother said again. "I should return your friend to you. When you've rested and you're ready, we can talk."

"What in the hell..." Aubrey was on his feet immediately, bending over Calix and Lawton, his gaze sharp on Lawton's face. "Did you see that?"

Calix shook his head while Ethaniel replied, "No. What did you see?"

"I swore I saw..." Aubrey stepped back and rubbed at some invisible spot just under his collarbones, as if it pained him. Determination set Aubrey's face into a stony mask and Calix found himself shuddering under that gaze. Or perhaps he was shivering from shock. Distantly, he could recognize the feeling; his entire being shuttering itself from reality. He'd experienced rather similar sensations after oracle episodes in the past. He'd need a dark room and quiet soon, but there wasn't time for that when his frustration and confusion were mounting so rapidly.

"Dammit!" he cried out, leaping to his feet, feeling all the more unmoored. "Mother, why? Why would you do this to me?" He curled his hands into Lawton's shirt, resisting the urge to shake him. "I demand an answer! You owe me that much!"

Lawton's glassy gaze rolled up to Calix, and like a fog lifting, he saw his friend return. That spark that was Lawton flashed, then settled. "Calix?"

Lawton's voice was gravelly with pain and disuse and it rattled him even more. "Lawton? Thank God." Calix gripped Lawton's hands and searched for any essence of his mother — her scent, her touch, anything — but it was as if she'd slipped away as quickly as she appeared. All that was left of her were mausoleum-gray dust and memories of field sunsets and nothing else.

"Let's get him back upstairs," Ethaniel said from his side. "I'll take him. Stay with Aubrey, Calix."

"No, I want to go with him." But even as the protest left his lips, Calix felt the weight of the day's harsh truths keeping him rooted to his spot on the sofa. Some part of him didn't want to be near Lawton. He'd only just wrapped his head around Lawton's betrayals. And yet, he needed to be near his friend; if some part of his mother lived on in Lawton, Calix wouldn't stand to be parted from it.

A hand came down on Calix's knee, strong and warm and yet as unbendable as iron. Aubrey's glass-green eyes pinned Calix in place as surely as his hand did, so Calix stayed. "I think a bit of separation might be best. Only for now, only until we have a better understanding of what happened." Aubrey flicked his other hand at the book, which was on a small table across the room. "I've questions for that...*thing*."

Yet for all the strength and iron in Aubrey's voice, Calix saw worry settle in a little furrowed patch between Aubrey's eyebrows. He was as unsure as the rest of them, but Aubrey was strong-willed enough to not be obvious about it. Calix admired that about the man, among many other things. It was as pure and simple as the admiration he had for Ethaniel, for the tailor's care and caution as he helped Lawton to his feet and quietly said, "I'll be back in a few minutes. Please don't touch that blasted book before I come back."

They were both so much stronger than him. Talented and dedicated and careful. Meant for each other.

The shock to his system — of the past few days, of the moments stolen and shared, of a careful life shattered so pristinely it could have been that glass from two weeks ago — was too much to bear. A sob escaped Calix's lips and he closed his eyes. It was easier to succumb that way, so he couldn't see anything but the velvet black of a world he desperately wanted to close himself away from.

Aubrey said nothing. He didn't have to. Calix let himself be gently guided down, until he was half-sprawled across Aubrey's lap, his face smashed into soft trousers and a softer sofa, both quickly soaked through with his tears.

Everything was too much. It was all too much. His house of cards collapsed, its foundations spread to the four winds. But Aubrey let Calix have his sadness and his pain, and instead of trying to erase it, he *embraced* it. He held Calix close and ran callused fingertips through his hair and gave him space to grieve. And a new foundation on which to stand.

"Oh, my darling boy. There you are."

In the darkness, in the deepest recesses of Calix's mind, she came to him. The other times had been dreams – fluffy, floating things made of down and lavender petals. Soft memories, good ones. Things that, upon waking, left Calix feeling cared for and a bit sad at the same time.

This was not one of those times.

Through the darkness, his mother's voice came to him, an echo against unforgiving stone. He could feel it now, how the walls closed in and the ceiling pressed too close to the top of his head. This was a box, a trap. But was it one of his own making? Even now, in the dark, Calix couldn't tell if he'd built this box, if he'd constructed this thing to keep him safe. Or if he'd let someone else build it around him.

"Calix."

Calix looked up into his mother's face. She was whole, lovely and warm and exactly what he needed in this moment. Seeing her now, feeling her presence, drifting in the scent of lavender and hay, Calix could feel peace.

But the lies, the half-truths, and the betrayals lay heavy on his tongue, iron-sharp and as hot as a blacksmith's furnace. It came back in a rush and with it was a sensation of emptiness. He needed to know why.

Calix reached up for her, took her hands in his, and guided her down until they sat face to face, like they used to when he was little and she held up different flowers and herbs and shared her knowledge with him. When his mother was finally seated across from him, her gentle smile a balm to his raging, wounded soul, Calix asked.

"Please tell me why. Why the lies, the secrets? Why would you hide the vault, the real one, from me? Why not tell me about the soul phylactery?"

Lily's smile dropped and with it, she took a bit of his heart. The stinging in his chest began to build; a hive of hornets buzzing between his ribs. "Darling, you must understand. We Oracles are rare. Treasured. But none of that..." Lily shook her head and looked down at their joined hands. "None of that matters in the end. All the wealth in the world can't protect us from our own minds. It's why I was always open about our magic and the world's troubles. Eventually, it all becomes too much."

Something about her words struck a chord in his heart. Surely she wasn't saying what he was beginning to understand. It couldn't be. "Speak plainly, please. I can't bear all these half-riddles anymore."

An expression he was familiar with – a slight flicker of her eyes, the downturn of her brown simultaneous with her mouth, the thumb and index finger of her left hand rubbing together – made Calix's stomach churn. She was hesitating, weighing her words in that way she had when he was a child and she wanted to be honest, but not so brutally.

"The full truth, Mother," he said softly as he reached for her fluttering hand. "I'm not seven anymore and just learning of the death of poor Lady."

That got him a slight smile. "Lady was a good dog. I hated telling you she was gone."

"And again, I'm not seven anymore. Whatever you're keeping secret..." Calix trailed off, so torn between needing to know everything, and desperate to hide from what would only bring pain. "Just say it. Whatever it is. I won't think any differently of you or my childhood or anything else. I swear."

Lily's eyes welled and her grip on his hand tightened. Calix steeled himself. When she finally spoke, it was with a weight heavier than any anvil or anchor. "The madness we experience as Oracles isn't a sudden surge. It's a slow slide, like time slipping through an hourglass. It's a trickle sometimes, stronger on certain days than others. And it starts years ahead of the worst of it." Lily gave him a sad smile. "I *knew when you were five that I was on a shorter leash than most. There's no collected guidance for us, Calix. No book of knowledge or advice on how to keep your mind out of the claws of your own powers. Things become...wobbly. Uncertain. Translucent sometimes, then blinding the next. So I started making plans. Safeguards. For you, for your inheritance, for the house."*

Calix's throat went dry but he needed her to keep talking. He needed to know. "The vault?"

Lily nodded. "The vault. I know I lied to you about the objects in it being dead. But I didn't lie about why I kept them."

She squeezed his hand hard. Harder than she might have in the past. Calix was tempted to brush it off as the tension hanging in the air, all those pesky unanswered questions sitting heavy between them. But something in his mother's touch felt off, although he couldn't describe it if pressed. It was only a moment of doubt, of pain, after all.

"You were studying them," Calix said. "If not for your own academic curiosity, then why?"

Lily leaned in more, a strange light in her eyes. That bit of warning flaring in his chest sparked hotter now. But he couldn't pull away, not at their precipice, not at his moment of understanding. "To understand them, Calix. To understand their inherent magic so I might see the threads of the world and pull back the curtain. Magic is so much more than what we know it to be. Enchanted embroidery and fussy little light shows to attract customers? It is so, so much more, my darling. To understand magic is to know it, and if I could know it, I could use it." Lily took his other hand, squeezing that one as well. The pain arched up his arms and his instinct was to reel away from her touch, but he couldn't. That odd light in her eyes spoke to him, called him home, and Calix wanted nothing more than to sink into his mother's embrace and be warm and whole again.

He'd missed her terribly. And now she was here, in this strange dream space they could share.

Forever.

But he had to ask. They'd come this far. "To use it for what?"

"At first, to keep my madness at bay. To build protections for my mind when the world teetered on some brink I didn't want to walk along. The pull of it…" Lily shuddered, and Calix felt it go through him as well. *"The pull of our powers is seductive. It will walk you up to the edge of a cliff with no bottom in sight and ask you to jump with only faith to keep you aloft. And in my darkest moments, I heard voices. Calls and echoes of others. They wanted me to join them, to embrace what I was with no trepidation. But you, my darling boy, you kept me sane for far longer than I might have had otherwise. So, I studied and I experimented. I tore at the threads of magic in each of those objects and I wrote everything down because I knew you would find my work one day and need it, too. Tearing apart magical objects so I could understand the building blocks of this…this force in our world, and use that knowledge to protect you. A scientific approach to a thing we simply accept as true in our lives. And the things I saw, what I learned…"* Her smile was soft now, like the rest of her expression. *"Calix, there are worlds out there. More than what we can see or feel on this plane of existence. It's no paradise, but it is possibility. I didn't intend to find them, but I did. You may find answers there."*

Dear god.

The revelation of what his mother had done – how she had gone into the great, wide unknown in order to protect him – broke down the last of his barriers. He let her pull him close, as if he were a boy and she the doting mother shushing his whimpers over a skinned knee, and he listened to the rest of her story. He had no other choice.

He had to know.

"And when I could feel the end drawing near," Lily continued, her voice now a whispered hush coiling directly in his ear, *"I bought the soul phylactery and tucked away a bit of myself there. Just a spark. Only enough to allow us to talk like this, and to guide you. I didn't expect you to have others near when you found me. That was my fault, my poor planning. I don't know how to extract myself from Lawton, darling, but I'm sure you will figure it out."*

Lily drew his face up with a gentle hand and Calix was able to, once more, stare into those eyes he'd loved and trusted for so long. Gods, he had missed her. *"I don't know how,"* he said. *"What will happen to Lawton? To you?"*

"*Whatever it might be, know I'm here for you, Calix. I always will be.*" *Her grip on his jaw tightened and once again, Calix felt the strangest impulse to pull away, put distance between them. But why would he? This was his mother. It made no sense.*

"*I know you are, Mother. I know. But understanding all of this is…*"

"*Painful,*" *Lily finished.* "*I wish I could have spared you all of that. I wish you hadn't found my secrets the way you did. And I don't know what trouble that book will cause you, but I do know that you aren't alone. And I'm so very glad you have friends with you. They seem to care for you. Hold tight to that.*"

Calix nodded. "*I will.*"

Chapter Three

AUBREY

"Aubrey."

Aubrey sucked in a deep breath and carefully looked over to the bedroom door. Ethaniel had been so quiet; Aubrey hadn't been aware he was there until now. "I keep wondering what we're to do next," he said, running his palm across his temple. Ethaniel made a noise in response and Aubrey remembered — very vividly — how Ethaniel had noticed that little gesture right away and marked it as silent sign of Aubrey's distress.

"You can't stay up with him all night," Ethaniel whispered as he walked across the rug in stockinged feet. "I can feel that odd ache in my bones after using up so much of my energy. I can only imagine how you feel."

Aubrey gestured him forward, getting a grateful smile in return, so he waited until Ethaniel curled up on the other side of Calix before saying, "I didn't know this level of exhaustion existed, to be honest. I'm only upright out of sheer spite." He nodded to the padded cot across the room, where Lawton slept. "And to keep an eye on that one. I didn't see any immediate physical ill effects from the...possession, I suppose we'll call it. But I don't think Lawton's mind had figured out how to handle its passenger quite yet."

Ethaniel reached for Aubrey's hand, knotting their fingers together and resting their joined hands on Calix's stomach. The younger man breathed evenly and deeply and Aubrey doubted anything save a parade would wake him at this point. There was only so much the body and psyche could handle, and the shock of the day...hell, the past few weeks, had simply been too much.

There were too many questions and not enough answers and the possibilities — good, bad, truly awful — were rolling around in his mind like marbles let loose across a wood floor. And the one possible path toward a solution was, for one reason only, completely off the table.

Aubrey had to ask anyway.

"The Cunning Folk didn't write much about possession," Aubrey said softly as he rubbed his thumb over the sensitive skin between Ethaniel's thumb and index finger. "There were a few documented cases in history before the Church got involved. But their methods were crude and often permanently harmful."

Ethaniel raised an eyebrow at that. "And possession itself isn't permanently harmful?"

"Well, at that point, either the entity would consume you from the inside out, or the mercury poisoning from the so-called treatments would cause your kidneys to stop functioning. Neither was terribly optimal."

Ethaniel's pained expression said quite a bit. "Well, that's horrible."

"As I said, *permanently* harmful." But Aubrey had to chuckle. "I used to swear some of the things they did had to be documented incorrectly, that's how terrible their treatments could be. But no, we simply didn't understand enough about the human body and the nature of magic. It was raw then, not refined like now. And imagine what it might all look like when we're just bones in the ground."

Ethaniel made a noise at that, pitched so low that Aubrey almost questioned his hearing. "Is it, though? Doesn't refined mean..." His jaw tensed, the muscle jumping. "Doesn't it mean more civilized? Studied? Pondered over and processed and then handed out to the masses? And if it really was, would this have happened?" Ethaniel broke their contact to gesture at Calix. Other unspoken questions lingered in his eyes, deepening them to pools of pain and longing, and Aubrey immediately connected the dots.

All of this has happened, and it is likely bringing up memories of his sister and how she disappeared before she came into her magic. Why did you say such things? You could excuse your runaway tongue through exhaustion and trauma, but it wouldn't alleviate your guilt. And Ethaniel knows you too well. He knows you spoke carelessly.

"You're right," Aubrey said. "It should be all of those things. For the betterment of society, open to all. And like so many things, magic is kept back behind iron gates of money and power and authority. I shouldn't have said that, Ethaniel, and I'm sorry. I didn't..." He cast his gaze sideways to fix on the polished cherry wood dresser. "I was careless with my words. I hope you'll forgive me."

Ethaniel sniffled and scrubbed at his face with both hands as a groan escaped him. "No, that's on me, Aubrey. This is all a bit too close to home for me, as I'm sure you've deduced. Magic running amok and secrets kept too closely and all that utter shit." He looked down at Calix as the younger man shifted, eyes fluttering slightly as he slid deeper into sleep. "Calix's predicament is not like what happened with my sister. I can't help but be prickly when this subject comes up. But I am sorry as well."

Aubrey smiled at him, hoping to coax one out of Ethaniel, too. "Look at us. Already much improved over our last attempt at arguing."

Ethaniel's eyebrows went up and his mouth twitched, but he didn't smile. But oh, he wanted to. Aubrey enjoyed getting Ethaniel to open up to him, to unfurl and bloom in the light of his attentions. It wasn't hard, since Ethaniel absorbed compliments and coy, teasing remarks and the occasional bit of sarcasm like water soothing a parched throat. He really was lovely. Easily pliant once he trusted you, and Aubrey couldn't believe he'd gotten a second chance at earning that trust.

And if he'd earned that trust, maybe there would be more. He was eager to have Ethaniel once again, soft and sweet and, if memory served true, thick and rich like honey on Aubrey's tongue.

"You're horrible," Ethaniel said, wheezing with silent laughter as he curled his fingers into Aubrey's collar and hauled him close, managing to snag his mouth in a kiss without so much as jostling Calix.

"I am, you know," Aubrey whispered between mad little kisses that felt like fire.

"Sorry?" Ethaniel's grip on Aubrey's collar tightened. "Don't keep apologizing."

They slowly let go of each other, mindful of Calix between them and Lawton across from them, and Richard down the hall. The house lay still and quiet with only the splatter of rain across thick windowpanes to remind Aubrey of this time and place.

As Ethaniel settled against the headboard of the bed and closed his eyes, Aubrey watched the rain skate across the glass. The windows here were wide and low, not like what one got in the city. These windows were meant for warm spring afternoons and sticky summer nights, for flinging open to let in any hint of breeze or in hopes the air might hang heavy with the scent of loam and honeysuckle. Life at a place like this would have been different than his own. Likely more orderly and calmer, without the daily lessons on healing herbs and the cycle of hope and rejection that had come with understanding his abilities. They'd only broached the surface of Calix's powers and his mother's teachings, but Aubrey suspected Lily Addington had been much more accepting of her son's magic than Aubrey's father had been of his.

And then there was that book. The one now lying on a table in the furthest corner of the room, wrapped in a scrap of gray muslin and looking so insignificant. After all, what harm could a book do?

What harm indeed.

Aubrey waited until Ethaniel's breathing had slowed before gently extricating himself from the bedclothes to pad over to the book. The *weight* of it was a singular thing, its own pressure system that opened like a waiting maw the closer he stepped to where it sat.

He was so bloody curious.

"Tell me, Talbot," he said softly, hand hovering over the book's slightly tattered cover, "how did you come to be trapped in such a thing?"

Tell me everything, Aubrey thought as he stared at the book. Sentient objects weren't completely unheard of, but Talbot's essence seemed mostly intact. And since the man had died in the 16th century, how was that possible? Time alone should have eroded him, let alone all the darker forces he and John Dee had been *experimenting* with, for the sake of Dee's fervent obsessions. It was beyond baffling. It was worrisome, on a scale for which Aubrey had no match.

Aubrey swiftly recalled what he knew about Talbot. He was assistant to John Dee, Elizabeth I's court mage, until Dee fell out of favor due to his increasingly erratic moods and steadfast conviction that he could not only talk to angels, but he was one of Heaven's Chosen. It had been a baffling thought born out of what was clearly some kind of madness or illness. He had seen examples of Dee's journals, pages filled with illegible scrawl, symbols Dee claimed were actually the language of the angels–the Enochian language, out of which Dee and Talbot also supposedly constructed an entire school of magical thinking. It was absurd and borne out of religious fervor and, in Talbot's case, the deep desire for money and riches. Talbot was a con man, but...

The silence that followed didn't test Aubrey's patience one bit. After all, he was a patient man by nature, and his line of work only benefited from that...often trying bit of his personality. The day's modern marvels and wonders also increased the speed of things - the assembly line, the electric light, the adaptation of magic into mundane systems. Even the Collectio used a magical organizational system that hadn't been possible without newer, lighter metal shelves on which to hold all the artifacts. (Alon had even begun tinkering with *floating* shelves, a concept that both frightened and elated Aubrey.) But patience was as old as the gnarled roots of a tree, and he was content dug deep into the earth until the truth was allowed to surface.

Finally, the book rasped, "You knew my name. Reminded me of who I was."

"You didn't know?" Aubrey asked, instinctually leaning closer. But he wasn't about to give this thing a chance, any chance at all, to do something in retribution for the failure that now sat astride Lawton's mind. So, he kept his distance yet.

"I knew, but whenever I would remember, it would slip past me once more," Convergence said.

Aubrey rubbed his chin. He wasn't going to go as far as negotiate with this thing, not on his own at least. But he was oh so terribly curious. "So, you recognize Talbot."

"I do."

"Do you possess his memories, or are you *him*?"

"Memory is a tricky thing," Convergence replied, a sharper edge to its tone now. Aubrey couldn't conceal his grin; impatience came along with a tendency to spill secrets without meaning to. "I am him. He is me. If Talbot's is the strongest personality amongst all the poor souls trapped inside these pages, then doesn't it make us the same?"

Aubrey snorted. "You're no Sphynx, so your riddles don't mean anything to me."

The book gave a hoarse chuckle. "And you're no mere mage." The temperature of the very air around him seemed to chill, and if Aubrey were a more religious man, he might have wondered if a ghost had brushed its finger down his spine. "You are *fascinating*," the book hissed, the sound blurring some line between pain and pleasure. "So much power. So much conflict." The air grew colder still, and Aubrey began to scan his surroundings. The longer the book had been with them, the more aware it had grown, and while Aubrey was originally only concerned with the weight it pressed upon Calix's mind, he was now a tad more worried for all their sakes.

"I'm not easily intimidated," Aubrey said, crossing his arms and staring daggers into the book's cover. "So, whatever it is you mean to hold over my head, do it. If you know what you think you know, that is."

Another chuckle, this one deeper. Darker. The candles on the mantle above the roaring fire flickered, sputtered, then went out. "You gave me back my name, so I won't press that far." The fire immediately dwindled to no more than a single spark of flame. "Yet. Why don't we trade? I always did love a good trade."

That made Aubrey smile. "I always did enjoy a good quid pro quo myself."

"*Excellent.*"

"But I go first." Questions stacked one on top of the other in his mind like a rickety pile of blocks. But the one on top was of utmost importance. "What do you want with Calix?"

Convergence stayed silent long enough that Aubrey thought its passenger might have changed its mind, but then it said, "Haven't you seen his mind, little hedgewitch? It burns *so brightly*. It's the most beautiful thing I've ever seen, and I used to speak to the dead."

Aubrey eyed the book once more. Talbot's writings, of which few had survived a massive fire late in his life, had made their way to the Collectio early in Aubrey's career. It had been the first time he'd heard of Dee or Talbot, and he'd spent months fixated on any information about either he could find, fascinated. Magnus, his supervisor, had warned him off that path given the lack of primary source documents, but Aubrey couldn't help himself. Talbot hadn't entirely been a con man; he had been quite the necromancer in his day, capable of raising the newly dead from their graves to settle property disputes amongst family members, and as he did so, his fame rose too.

Fame...or notoriety, Aubrey thought. *And isn't that what you really wanted, Talbot? To be known, to be seen, to be respected? And when your powers scared people, you chose money as your king instead. Why try to change minds the hard way, when money could solve all?*

"Why Calix?" Aubrey said, stepping closer. "Because of whom he is?"

"Because of *what* he is!" the book crowed, gleeful and almost mocking. "I waited so long for someone like him to come along. No one has ever reacted to me like he did. I was there, and then he was, too, and our minds tumbled over each other like lovers in the dark." A noise escaped Convergence, another hiss, but this one made Aubrey contemplate the slowly rebuilding fire mere steps away.

"After all," Convergence continued, "a mind like his is as precious as any treasure. Imagine what he and I could do together. What we could *all* do together. And you have an enemy closing in on your gates. Hesitation is for the weak."

The gnawing thing in his chest was building to a red-hot anger, frustration and fear and a fierce possessiveness over Calix and Ethaniel. This thing was devious, and clearly happy to have someone to talk to, now that it seemed to have regained a sense of self. Dangerous, yes, but also something they could use to their benefit. Aubrey needed to discuss this with the others in the morning.

"Well, I think that's quite enough for tonight," Aubrey said, rewrapping the book in its cloth and shoving it into the satchel, then dropping the satchel into the closet and shutting and locking the door. And for peace of mind, he quickly drew a silencing ward on the closet door. It would last until morning, and hopefully give them all a chance to sleep.

When Aubrey climbed back into bed, he found Ethaniel curled like an octopus around Calix. He'd never seen anything sweeter, and it made his heart ache all the more for the grief he was about to greet them with the coming sunrise.

Chapter Four

ETHANIEL

Ethaniel awoke to find Lawton standing over him. He choked back a shout, but shot upright in bed, which jostled the others. "What the hell?"

"I'm sorry," Lawton said in that disconcerting voice Calix had identified as his mother; higher pitched and slightly nervous. "I was curious, and this body I'm...in was reluctant to move at first."

Realization – and panic – were a cold snap in his veins. "You...puppeteered him?"

Lawton's hands twisted together, knotting the loose front of his gray tunic. "I...I suppose it would seem like that."

"It definitely doesn't seem like anything else," Ethaniel said. That made Lawton – or, Calix's mother, as he should be thinking of it – frown. It was an odd, twisting thing that left Ethaniel's stomach feeling sour. If he were a religious man, he would have been calling for a priest immediately.

"I wanted to see you properly," the woman inside Lawton's body said. "Who, exactly, was taking care of my boy."

Ethaniel blinked a few times, let out a slow breath, then pushed his elbow out so he could nudge Calix awake. The man was going to *hate* this, but he didn't feel right keeping it from him, or from Aubrey. Secrets were partially responsible for the mess they were in, and there was no need to keep them now. "Calix. *Calix.*"

Calix mumbled and rolled over, closer to Aubrey and away from the elbow poking him in the side, but the movement jostled Aubrey, who awoke with a jaw-cracking yawn. "Ethaniel?"

"We have a, hmmm…a visitor," Ethaniel said. "I believe Calix's mother has –"

"Questions? Yes, I suppose I do," the possessed man replied.

That got Aubrey's attention immediately. Ethaniel was suddenly surrounded by Aubrey, one arm wrapped around his back, Aubrey's left hip kissing Ethaniel's thigh. The blanket of surety – safety – provided by Aubrey's closeness was enough to ease the anxiety scrambling his thoughts, but he doubted the pit in his stomach would close up any time soon.

Aubrey was tense, his body hard against Ethaniel, but his voice was as cool as silk as he said, "Well, I think we have some questions, too."

Ethaniel's gaze flitted between the two of them for a long moment before he leaned to the left to gently shake Calix's arm. When Calix cracked open his eyes and saw Lawton standing there, staring down at them, he blanched and immediately pulled back. "What's happening?" Calix asked in a near whisper.

Ethaniel exchanged a look with Aubrey. Calix would eventually learn to decipher their silent language. "Your mother," Ethaniel said, squeezing the hand that groped for his, letting Calix cling to him, "seems to be curious about us."

Poor Calix looked terrified as he came to understand the situation they were all in. He turned to Ethaniel with wide eyes and said, "I don't know what to do."

Ethaniel wrapped his hands around Calix's. His skin was clammy, almost too cold to the touch, so he pulled a blanket free from the bed and draped it over Calix's lap. Then he turned to Aubrey. "Could you start, Aubrey?"

"Of course." Aubrey's neutral expression, the kindness written in his gaze, made Ethaniel want to sigh in relief.

Ethaniel watched Aubrey turn back to Lawton. "I've got a rather simple question for you, ma'am. Why do this? Any of it?"

Lily's frown was a delicate thing. It brought to mind a similarly delicate woman, a forest nymph of power and unexpected resilience. Like Calix. "It wasn't on purpose," she replied, her gaze firmly caught on her son. "My unwavering hope was that Calix would find the vault and the phylactery. I saved my energy for that wonderful day we could be reunited so I could protect him and continue his training." She lifted Lawton's pale hand and placed it over his heart. "I wasn't expecting...this. He's so strong-willed and so..."

Lily paused, and as she did, the air in the room began to prickle over Ethaniel's skin. On instinct, he dropped the mental walls that kept his sight at bay, and when the room came back into focus, he gasped.

Lawton's body was an unrestrained tangle of magic, threads of gold and ruby and sapphire flickering steadily, as if mimicking a pulse. *A secondary pulse, for his passenger*, Ethaniel thought. But there was no magic where Lawton had been branded, the wound inscribed with the alchemical symbol for salt. There, Lawton was hollow, his essence as silent as a tomb.

"What is it, Ethaniel?" Aubrey asked, his grip on Calix clearly tightening, judging by the way his knuckles pressed through his skin.

"He's...I don't know how to describe it," Ethaniel murmured, awe and shock coloring his voice. "It's like nothing I've ever seen. There's a void near his heart, where the brand sits. But the rest of him is *dazzling*."

As soon as the words left him, the color and hypnotic patterns of magic coursing through Lawton's body dimmed. "I didn't realize," Lily said, pulling that hand over Lawton's heart into a fist. "He and I have yet to find a balance."

"What you're doing is wrong, Mother," Calix said, the words bursting out from his like a caged bird being released. "You can't simply...possess someone! You can't do any of this!"

"Oh, darling, it's all right," Lily said, stepping closer. Everyone tensed and for one hysterical moment, Ethaniel feared their collective anxieties would snap the bed in two. "But I understand. Change takes time. And it won't be for long, surely. I know you'll find a way to separate us and return me to my body."

At that, Ethaniel felt all the warmth drain from his body, leaving him cold and stiff. "Bring him back," he choked out against the rising panic trying to block his throat. "Let him be."

"Please," Calix whispered as he shrank back into Aubrey's hold. Aubrey had a good grip on him, thankfully, but it seemed like nothing to quell the way Calix shivered. "Please just...go. We need space and time to think. And I need to talk to him."

Lily's expression dropped into one of motherly sympathy, but Ethaniel swore he saw a spark of something else there, too. Defiant and headstrong. Willing to fight. He wondered if Calix saw the same, or if he was simply a son desperate for his mother's warmth and care. He couldn't blame Calix; it was often near impossible to sever the ties of family and blood.

"Of course, my love. My Calix." Lawton's body slumped, as if his strings had been cut, and he collapsed on the ground in a heap of limbs and fiery hair.

Calix scrambled out of their grasps and dropped to his knees, gathering up Lawton's thin frame to hold it tight against his chest. His breathing was uneven and Ethaniel's heart nearly broke at the sound.

He and Aubrey also went to the floor, surrounding Calix with all the comfort they could spare, trying to warm him with blankets and cushions and the heat of their own bodies. This he could do. He could be helpful. He could soothe and heal. He could comfort and lend his strength. But Ethaniel couldn't stop looking over toward the book, then back to Calix and Lawton.

Aubrey was the first to speak, just as Calix went limp against them, clearly exhausted to his core. "We're in the middle of others' machinations," he whispered before pressing a kiss into Calix's hair. "I think it's time we made our own plan. But we need time, and information." He drew a flat stone out of his pocket and handed it to Ethaniel. "Check on your uncle. I need to contact my mentor, Magnus, and see what knowledge he may have that can help us."

That panic, fluttery and fragile, pressed against Ethaniel's ribs once more. "What do you intend?"

"I don't know yet," Aubrey said, his tone so uncertain, so unlike him. Aubrey was never uncertain, never unmoored. But now he was as in the dark as the rest of them, fumbling for light and not caring about the source. Ethaniel worried they were on dangerous ground, and that even worse, a cliff was up ahead and they couldn't see themselves approaching the edge.

"All right," Ethaniel said as he took the stone. It was warm from Aubrey's touch, and he was reluctant to tuck it away. "Let's get them up on the bed."

Neither man weighed much compared to their strength, but the one thing that left Ethaniel with a lump in his throat was the tender way Aubrey stroked Calix's coppery waves before tucking a blanket around him.

"I'll stay with them," Ethaniel said. "I don't trust her."

Aubrey let out a deep breath before nodding. "Agreed. One of us should always have her in sight."

Ethaniel let his head thunk back against the wall, feeling all the more carved out. "Go. Take a walk, clear your head. We need your brilliance, Aubrey."

That earned him a slight smirk. "Just my brilliance?"

"Cad." But Ethaniel couldn't stop his smile. "Just don't go far."

Aubrey crossed the room in three strides just to cup Ethaniel's jaw with one hand. "I wouldn't dream of it."

Staring up at his lover, seeing the way those glass-green eyes went hooded and dark, sent a rush of emotion through him. Aubrey had been the only man he'd ever loved—a love so fierce and claiming it often left him breathless and reeling. Right now, helpless against him, Ethaniel felt it once more. He craned his head up and Aubrey's lips met his, sweet and honest. Ethaniel ran his hands up Aubrey's arms, meaning to comfort, but Aubrey held him closer and teased his tongue along the seam of Ethaniel's lips. He opened to him the way he always did, an invitation for whatever Aubrey wanted.

Because he trusted Aubrey. Because he loved him.

When they parted, Aubrey whispered, "We'll figure this out. I swear it."

All Ethaniel could do was nod and hold Aubrey's face in his hands, his thumbs tracing the sharp lines of his cheekbones as if to memorize them once more.

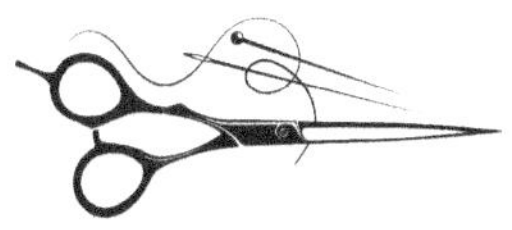

It was sheer curiosity that had Ethaniel dropping his sight to examine the patterns on the flat, dark green stone in his palm. He'd thought the stone black, so dark was its color, but here in the flicker of fire and lamplight he saw glints of a color that reminded him of pine trees. He'd seen pine trees while growing up, messy rows of slender trunks with bark rough enough to scrape your skin and needles growing only far above his head. The air would smell like them in the winter, resiny sap and crisp, bright, untouched snow stretching for miles that felt endless. Those days had felt endless, too, for a time, but nothing that quiet ever lasted in their lives.

He'd grown up far inland, toward the middle of the country where neighbors weren't connected by distance but cared for each other anyways. His father ran a small logging operation, and he and his sister Maria had spent every second of their young lives sheltered by those pine boughs while the mountains breathed through them. It had been a nice life, but not one without problems. Maria's magic hadn't been like his. Ethaniel's had been orderly, and how could it not have been, when his second sight was so full of dazzling patterns? But Maria hadn't stood a chance.

Ethaniel closed his palm around the stone and felt it warm to his touch. A spark of something tickled his mind and he let his sight drop. There in the darkness behind his eyelids was a single green line running north to south. Then another appeared, this one east to west.

Another and another and another, all so beautiful and so purposeful. The lines intersected again and again until a dense star made of light opened to him. Aubrey had said he only needed to think of Jeremiah, to picture him clearly in his mind, and the stone would try to find him. *It's a simple, singular object, for a simple, singular purpose*, Aubrey had said with a smile, his hand gentle as it wrapped around Ethaniel's. This was magic he understood.

Maria's face flickered in his mind and he forced himself to banish it as he brought up memories of Jeremiah. The stone couldn't contact Maria, but he didn't want to risk using up its latent energy. Jeremiah had, to his shame, become an afterthought in the middle of everything that had happened, and Ethaniel's guilt over that was clearly making him ruminate on his long-deceased sister; it had been a place left hollow after he had taken on Jeremiah's care.

"Hello?"

Ethaniel's eyes shot open and before him stood a hazy outline of his uncle. But instead of slippers and a housecoat, his uncle was wearing a smart-looking suit and hat. "Uncle?"

His uncle broke out into a big smile. "Ethaniel, oh my boy! I've been so worried. You didn't come home and I —"

Ethaniel winced, silently cursing at himself and his obscene selfishness. "I'm so sorry, Uncle. Truly. I didn't mean to leave the city without telling you, but it was –"

Time froze as a hand curled around Jeremiah's shoulder. "Jeremiah's been out a fair bit as well, brother. Have you told Ethaniel about the show you saw last night, Uncle?"

Vincent's voice was ice in Ethaniel's veins. "Vincent," he ground out. "Leave him be or I swear…"

Vincent chuckled. Ethaniel couldn't see his face, either because of the angle or because he had purposefully contacted Jeremiah and the stone actually *couldn't* show Vincent's face, but he didn't need to see his half-brother's smug smile to hear it, or to feel it burn like a lash across his skin. "Jeremiah and I have been catching up, Ethaniel. And I couldn't stand to see him suffering so badly."

Jeremiah grinned and Ethaniel felt sick. "He found me a cure, Ethaniel! Said it's some scientist's newest drug, it beats the consumption back. Can you believe it?"

Ethaniel's gaze went to Calix, who had fallen back asleep beside him. For one truly ugly, selfish moment, he wished it could all go back to how it had been. It would mean losing Jeremiah to an awful disease, but it would have kept his life predictable. Understandable. He could have had the quiet order he'd worked so hard for.

But the price would have been too great.

His fingers sought out the edge of Calix's sleeve as he said, "Jeremiah, would you mind letting me and Vincent talk for a moment?"

Jeremiah frowned but nodded, but was cut off by a cough Ethaniel had heard a thousand times. It made his soul go cold. "Yes, all right," Jeremiah wheezed, hacking again. "But do let me tell you about the magic show I saw last night!"

"As soon as Vincent and I are done. I promise."

Jeremiah disappeared from view just as a spark of purple energy shocked his palm. Startled, Ethaniel nearly dropped the stone, but he used the movement to jostle Calix awake. Calix blinked sleepily up at him, and Ethaniel jerked his head toward the now-visible outline of his brother. Shadows were all that suggested his brother's sharp features and wide forehead (a Harkness family trait), but it was enough to make Calix's eyes go wide.

Ethaniel was no actor, but he didn't need to focus hard in order to turn his attention back to his brother. "Back to blackmail me some more?" Ethaniel asked, his tone as even as he could make it with the volcanic heat of anger bubbling inside his chest.

Vincent chuckled. "Do I need to? Or were you expecting me to up the ante, so to speak?"

"Enlighten me."

Another chuckle. "Ethaniel, that ship has long since sailed. You had the chance, and now it's gone. If you want to make a deal, a different one, I'm going to need much more from you than a promise that you'll hand over that book."

Vincent's head turned...to stare right at Calix. "I want the Oracle too."

Calix sucked in a sharp breath but Ethaniel held steady. "Out of the question."

Vincent tutted at him. "Brother, do you understand what that book is? I suppose you don't, since you clearly haven't wielded its power." He cocked his head in thought. "Or perhaps you can't. Either way, it's a profane, sacred thing. It can't be out in the world, used by just anyone."

Ethaniel could hardly believe what he was hearing. Vincent had *always* been ambitious, but there was something needful in his tone. "It's not leaving my care. *Our* care."

"I was afraid you'd say that." Vincent put a hand out, palm down, and snapped twice. The thin connection between them from the stone started to stretch, as if whatever Vincent was doing was interfering.

What coalesced, seemingly from thin air, at Vincent's side was at first nothing but black shadow. Ethaniel could see it roiling and churning, and at his side, Calix groaned in pain. He glanced over to see Calix gripping his head. "I saw this," Calix whispered, horrified. "Right before I awoke. I saw a great beast..."

It was a beast. A massive black dog or wolf of some kind, its eyes a sickly yellow. It seemed to stare right at them through the wavering connection. Ethaniel's heart sped up. "Vincent. What have you done?"

"What I must," Vincent snapped back as he laid his hand on top of the beast's head. "What I must in order to ensure..." Then he broke off, chuckling. "Ethaniel, I want you to understand. To know what it is I'm...*we're* doing at the Golden Order. This isn't some flimsy excuse to sway influence, brother. It's so much more. Our family name could be restored. Do you know what that means?"

Ethaniel did. And he felt sick with it. "Our family doesn't deserve any grace, Vincent. How could you say such a thing, after what our ancestors *did*? The blood magic and necromancy and corruption and.... all of it!"

Vincent took that statement, one fueled by pain and loss and fear, with surprising aplomb. He was silent for a long moment, mulling. "The things I've learned since taking up the leadership role with the Order could make you change your mind. In fact, I know it would." Something like smoke curled around Vincent's legs, and even though Ethaniel couldn't make out the details, he didn't need to. Whatever Vincent was doing pulled on him, a single thread wound a little tighter around his soul. It was deeper than flesh and organs, deeper than bone; the magic his half-brother was coalescing spoke to Ethaniel like one might fall to their knees before the sight of a god.

"You have the book. I want it," Vincent said, his voice a deadly whisper, "and by helping me, you help restore our family name. That book contains power, brother. The forces of dark and light don't matter when the very essence of what makes us real could be at my fingertips. No more hiding, no more brushing off people asking if we're like our ancestors, those foul, wretched people who mucked about in graveyards, plying their trade amongst the rot and ruin of the dead."

And then Vincent's voice seemed to echo out and in his heart, Ethaniel felt real fear for the first time since Maria had disappeared. "We could be the rightful heirs we were meant to be. Don't you want that?"

Before his eyes, Vincent seemed to grow taller, broader, as did the beast at his side. Ethaniel could only watch, stricken silent in shock, as another beast appeared to Vincent's right. "But now isn't the time for droning. It is time for action." Vincent's gaze shot over to Calix again and he smiled while a shiver ran down Ethaniel's back. "I admit, I wasn't anticipating your Oracle's *fascinating* family history, but I've never been one to let an obstacle stand in my way. That estate you luxuriate in would make a fine base for the Order's growing operation –"

It happened so quickly, Ethaniel had no time to react, no time to stop Lawton from sprinting across the room with a hollow yell, and grab Ethaniel's hand in his. And then Ethaniel felt it.

Power.

Red-hot but like a shard of ice at the same time, spearing through him as one might lance a boil. Lawton, in Lily's voice, screamed one word, one clear note of "NO!" and Ethaniel was struck with magic so great it sent him reeling backwards.

The last thing he saw was Calix's worried face before darkness snapped his vision closed.

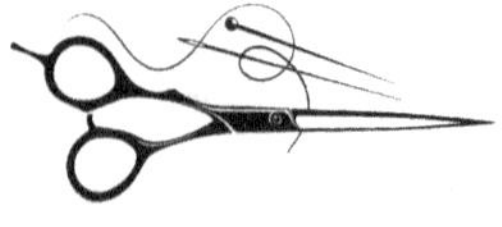

In the dark, in the silence, Ethaniel felt a hand slip into his. He knew immediately it was hers.

"I wanted to go into the woods, but it started raining," Maria said as she stared up at him. There were a few leaves in her hair and dirt across her cheek, but she was smiling.

*"I thought Father said you weren't supposed to go into the woods anymore,"
Ethaniel said. It was so strange – he felt his lips move, heard his own voice, but felt
strangely disconnected from the moment. As if he were hovering right behind the
step of a memory.*

*This was a memory. So why did it feel so real? Why could he feel her warm little
hand in his?*

And why did the next thing she said drive a rusty nail of fear into his heart?

*"But Father doesn't understand," Maria said, her smile still wide, her round
cheeks flushed pink as if she'd been out in the cold. "Carmen needs me. And she's
teaching me, Ethaniel! She's teaching me magic!"*

*His sister's eyes, so like his own, started to dim, as if someone had struck the light
from her very soul, siphoning it away. The whites turned gray, then black, and then
she was left with nothing but hollows where her eyes had once been.*

*Somewhere behind him, someone laughed. It strangely reminded him of the raspy
voice from the book —*

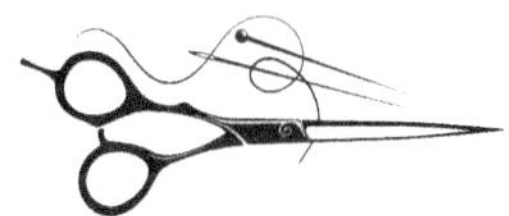

Ethaniel awoke when a warm hand passed over his brow. "What happened?"
he murmured as he fought to pull his eyes open against the pounding headache
in his temples.

"Nothing good." Aubrey's sonorous voice was an instant balm against the pain
in his head. "Seems your brother is plotting. Unsurprisingly." He frowned, his
scrutiny suddenly close. "But something else happened, didn't it?"

Somehow, Aubrey knew about his dream, if one could call it that. Something
slippery and sinuous curled tight inside his chest, and it was not a welcome feeling.
"How did you know that?"

Aubrey swallowed hard; his unease was making everything worse. "I
simply...did." In tandem, he and Aubrey looked across the room to where Calix

was sitting by the fire, watching Lawton sleep. Lawton had apparently collapsed again after Lily's outburst. They hadn't been alone, and all awake, since they'd come into the room hours ago. In the middle of the confusion and exhaustion, he and Aubrey and Calix hadn't been granted much time to discuss their next steps.

"Sharing some tenuous mental connection isn't the worst thing," Aubrey said as they joined Calix. Ethaniel took a seat at Calix's feet, and immediately there were warm, soft hands on his shoulders, rubbing away the tension.

"I'm guessing we have our resident grimoire to thank for this," Ethaniel said as he craned his head back to look up at Calix. The Oracle gave him a small smile in return, and it helped chase away the lingering malignance of the strange dream.

Ethaniel used to dream about Maria all the time, but it was never of the moments before she disappeared. That was new and...

"Disturbing," Calix said quietly, drawing a sharp look from Aubrey.

Ethaniel breathed out hard. "Took the word right from my lips."

"Well," Aubrey said after a long, heavy moment, "seems our little shared connection isn't some nebulous sense of each other's emotions or state of mind."

Ethaniel felt Calix's hands tense on his shoulders, and he patted one as if to comfort, even though his own feelings were a riot. "Surely it's not steadfast. It's probably because of that damn book. We should tuck it away again, not tempt Fate."

"Yes, please," Calix said as he slid his touch up the sides of Ethaniel's neck, strong fingers digging into the base of his skull. The pressure was *delicious* and exactly where he needed it.

Of course it was. Well, he wasn't ever one to look a gift horse in the mouth. He couldn't know for certain that Calix felt his satisfaction, but the way the younger man was pressing into exactly the right spots told him that was likely the case.

"What a strange thing," Aubrey said, his voice gone soft with wonder as he came to kneel before both of them, "to know how you both feel. It's like I've got two unique magic artifacts, one in each hand, but I can track them separately. Know them." Aubrey's beautiful hands came to rest on Ethaniel's knees, putting them face to face and as close as his folded legs would allow. "It should feel invasive, or alienating. But I feel…"

"Whole," Ethaniel breathed. Behind him, Calix hummed in agreement and before him, Aubrey smiled. "I should hate this. But I don't."

CHAPTER FIVE

LAWTON

It was a liminal space of gray and lavender, and he was weightless on an unseen tide. Lawton felt oddly safe, even while, far in the background of his mind, his nerves still rang with pain and panic.

He should have been frightened. And the arrival of another figure should have made him backpedal, as if to hide in the shadows that swirled around in his ankles.

Lawton had never met Lily Addington, but he'd seen plenty of portraits and even a few photographs, as those had come into fashion shortly before her death when Calix was sixteen. To Calix, she was someone who could do no wrong; as he told it, his mother was loving, yes, but also wickedly intelligent and independent. It was so obvious to him where Calix had gotten those traits, as well as his copper-brown hair and eyes.

"A pity we couldn't have met under more...lively circumstances," he said as Lily approached. Her long white dress flowed like water behind her, undulating hypnotically. He had to tear his gaze away, lest he be carried off by a pretty piece of fabric.

Lily smiled at him. "I agree. Calix wrote about you so often, and I never worried about him when he had such a good *friend* to take care of him while he was at school."

Her tone — soft. Her expression — gentle. Her posture — perfect, but also relaxed. But there was a barb in her words, a vicious thorn that Lawton could feel dig into his skin, like a burr hidden inside one's clothes. "Well, politeness and mutual *admiration* aside, I find myself curious —"

"Yes?"

"—how in the hell our little predicament came to be." Lawton crossed his arms, eyebrows raised. "Because when I last awoke, I was very injured and my head was a bit muddled, but I remember quite clearly I wasn't fucking *possessed*."

Lily shook her head, her gentle smile never once wavering. "Possession is a religious construct, my dear. I'm simply borrowing your form until I can get one of my own."

Lawton's mouth dropped open. It was so...so...*blatant*. He could almost admire it. But that didn't mean Lily's words were soothing; quite the opposite, really. A bevy of implications hit him at once, but the worst was realizing he may never have full control of his body ever again. That couldn't happen. "You planned this?" he asked, unable to keep the anxiety out of his voice.

The thought of sharing his body, his mind, possibly his *soul* with another for the rest of his life was too much.

For the first time in their conversation, Lily looked concerned. "Not to be executed quite in this manner," she said, wringing her hands together. The familiarity of the gesture, and the rising worry in his throat, made Lawton reel. Was it all his emotions knocking on the door, or were hers bleeding through?

"Explain."

Lily looked even more distraught at that. "It was a safeguard. A way to come back, so I might protect Calix. It clearly didn't work the way I'd intended. Soul phylacteries aren't easily broken." Panic welled in her eyes, and in his chest, and it staggered him. "I knew Calix would come back to Rosehill on his thirtieth birthday. Then I could reach out to him, help him —"

"Why would he come back at that time?"

She looked away. Lawton knew. He simply *knew* what was to come out of her mouth before she spoke. It made a chill settle in his bones. "The older an Oracle, the more susceptible they are to the magic of the world. At my thirtieth, I dreamed of a field. A massive field of swaying lavender, the scent of it heavy on the air. A place of peace, of serenity. A world just for me, some tiny bubble where I could live. I knew that some day, I could introduce Calix to it too." Lily shook her head, her copper curls gently floating on whatever invisible current of air teased the space in which they stood. "I studied for so long, Lawton. I studied the magic of this world, and others. And everything I found told me that Oracle powers ran in families, and that what was true for a parent, was true for the child. Like me, Calix would start to see his powers grow around that birthday, and like me, he'd start to see into it. Wonder about it. Dream of it."

Lawton didn't want to ask. He had to. "Dream of what?"

She floated to him as if clouds graced her feet, gently taking his hands in hers. "Of the *demimonde*. The half-world. The one between ours and others. It's a transitional place, and one of power. But it's seductive, and an Oracle can easily lose themself in it. I wanted to help Calix through that time, to keep him from following my path."

Lawton remembered Calix's grief, how it tasted heavy and mercurial on his own tongue when he would kiss his friend until the tears stopped. Nights and nights of quiet crying as Calix mourned his mother's death. *Suicide*, it was said, often with that secret, shivery delight society people took in the downfall of one of their own. *She drowned herself in a lake near the estate,* they'd say as they shook their heads and tutted, then went on to talk about the latest ball or romantic scandal. He'd heard plenty of talk about Lily Addington's tragic demise while lingering on the edges of smoky rooms and gilded dance floors, forced to tamped down on the urge to rage at their false sympathy.

"I made a mistake," Lily said softly, staring deep into his eyes. "I let the *demimonde* and what lingers there promise me things, and in return it said I could come back. I could keep him safe, even if I was gone."

This was all too much. His swagger and bravado now gone, withered and clinging to the vine, Lawton couldn't help but ask, "So you didn't take your own life?"

Lily didn't flinch, like most people would at such blunt talk. "Oh no, dear, I certainly did. But the promise was that I could come back, be there for him. Hence the soul phylactery. It told me how to make it, how to preserve it so Calix would find it one day and discover a bit of me inside. Just enough to keep him out of harm's way."

It all seemed so foolish, so shortsighted. But hadn't he done the same thing? Made a deal in exchange for what he'd desired the most—to not simply be in Calix's life, but to enjoy the power, the money, the influence as his own. No longer borrowing from a friend and burdening him. The burst of sympathy in his veins was a comfort, but a small one.

"I think I understand," Lawton said, finally letting himself hold her hands and bring them close to his body. "We mean to protect him, and instead, we made errors. Grave ones."

"I count myself fortunate it was you who came along," Lilly said. "If the phylactery had broken without a willing receptacle nearby, I would have been lost to the *demimonde* forever. A price I was willing to pay, but not what I had planned on."

Lawton reached up to touch the brand on his chest, feeling the raised wound as it dug into his collarbone. "Does this have something to do with our current predicament?"

The sorrow on her face deepened. "Yes. You were *salted*. Do you know what that means?" When Lawton shook his head, Lily gave him a sad smile. "It means you were turned into...what one might call unhallowed ground. Every person in this world, and in many others, has only one soul in their body. There are exceptions, certain religious and mystical practices that allow some to host spirits or other souls. But it's usually a very complicated magical process, involving years of study. A few mages have found ways to bring another into their body, but it's incredibly dangerous. There was one, centuries ago, a man named John Dee. But from my understanding, he invited in things that shouldn't tread in this world..."

She trailed off and like a moment earlier, Lawton could *feel* her thoughts, see them as clearly as a painting. The implications of what Lily had said rippled through him, but he couldn't begin to process more than one at a time.

"The Order stripped me of some...natural protections, didn't they? They *hoped* something like this would happen." Lawton looked down, the words stuck in his throat as if they'd been glued there. "Because why kill someone when you could torture them?"

Lily nodded. "They made you an open invitation to whatever untethered spirit wished to claim you as their own."

He could barely breathe. The panic, the anger, the sheer rage of it welled up in him until it was all he could see, all could feel. He'd been used, *violated*. "How dare they. How *fucking dare they*!"

And yet some small part of him knew he'd deserved it. Betrayal was a thing paid in silver and salt, apparently, and he was twice the bastard for it.

Lawton tried to pull away but she held him steadfast, suddenly much stronger than he could have ever expected. Her eyes blazed. "If you and I work together, we might be able to separate. And likely we'll need to do that, sooner rather than later, since our connection is tenuous at best. But I won't leave him again, Lawton. I won't."

The steel in her voice made him yank his head up and stare at her. He could feel deep down that Lily Addington was powerful. But she was ferocious, too, and clearly adored her son. Perhaps they *could* work something out. "Neither will I," he said.

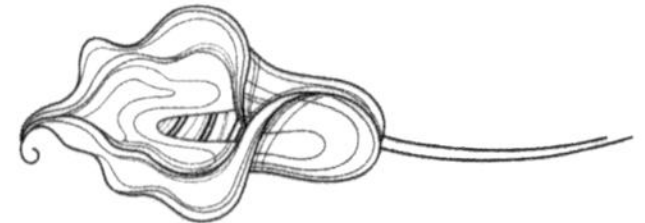

Lawton awoke on a bed decked out in velvets and satin, in a room that smelled like nightmares and wood smoke. But the four heartbeats he could feel pulsing at odds with his own were all unknown except one.

As he opened his eyes, Lawton whispered Calix's name; as if summoned, Calix appeared, the bed sinking a little under his weight. The relief on his closest — his only — companion's face was tempered by hesitation. It would have been grievous in any form, a knife splitting his skin, but Lawton had only himself to blame for the edge his friend's expression now took.

"Can you speak?" Calix asked, leaning closer. Lawton could feel Calix's breath on his cheek.

Lawton swallowed hard but managed to whisper, "Barely."

Calix looked away, to his right, and Lawton instantly felt unmoored. "Could someone...oh, thank you, Ethaniel." The smile Calix gifted someone else was another knife, slick and pretty, going right through his chest. Lawton had always liked that smile, gentle and even and so packed with meaning of the kind no words could properly convey.

Your love could power cities, Lawton, but what did your betrayal cost?

Lawton shut his eyes against the invasion, Lily's voice in his head making his temples throb even more. He felt her presence withdraw in the shadowed recesses of his mind, but she was still there, waiting.

A cool glass of water was pressed into his hand, and Lawton drank. He took in the sight of Calix, mussed but clean, beside him; the wavy-haired man Calix had called Ethaniel was hovering nearby, wringing his hands as he stared hotly at Lawton; and the museum curator, Aubrey, was observing from the far side of the room, unblinking and unmoving. Richard, Calix's man, was perched on the end of the settee, his youthful face a mixed mask of concern and anger. Concern was commonplace for the man but anger was new. Somewhere deep in his mind, Lawton could feel Lily's anxiety begin to rise. He couldn't name the source, couldn't guess at it even, but it was there anyway, crawling up the back of his throat.

The now-empty glass was whisked away and Lawton gave in to the bone-deep desire to close his eyes. The respite was brief, though, as Calix said, "It sounds like you, Lawton, but is it?"

I will disperse, Lily said to him, *but only for now*. Her words left Lawton wondering how long he would have control of his mind, his body until she returned. The unknown of it, the loss of control over something so intrinsic, made him sick to his stomach. "It's me," he managed to say, "but she's not gone."

"I didn't suspect as much," Calix said. A cool hand cupped his cheek and Lawton's head was turned toward his friend, so he screwed his eyes shut and focused on breathing. If he looked into Calix's eyes, he would see the pain he'd caused. It would be unbearable. "Well, I suppose I shouldn't be shocked."

Lawton couldn't help but open his eyes at the harshness in Calix's tone. Where he expected pain, all he saw was anger. Calix, *his* Calix, angry? Bemused, sarcastic, annoyed, tired – he'd seen all of that and more. But the sheer scale of that anger, hot and unyielding, shocked him to his core.

The only thing he could do was look away.

And apparently Calix wasn't the only one in the room with anger to unleash upon his head. So be it. "Your choices upended all of our lives."

Lawton knew that voice - it was from the man who had challenged him in the baths not days ago. Aubrey Lavigne, the museum curator. His inclusion in all this made sense, even if his presence rankled. "I'm afraid I'm out of petards on which to hoist myself," Lawton said between coughs as his voice came to life.

Aubrey's frown morphed into a glare Lawton had only seen in the eyes of the devout. Disapproval, certainly, but something like *malcontent* swam there, too. Well, he owed this man nothing, so Lawton refocused on Calix. But Calix looked just as angry. "What you did threatened all of us," Calix said quietly. His words, his tone, shivered their way down Lawton's spine, embedded in his flesh like glass.

He owed Calix everything. And he'd dumped it to the side, left it to rot in a field where their affections had once grown. Far below his own surface, Lily let out a small gasp and it ricocheted through him. His love, and that of Calix's mother, were slowly becoming intertwined; a very uncomfortable realization.

"What I did was for me," Lawton said, letting his mouth run before his heart could stop him. "You were never to be involved, darling."

"Don't call me that!" Calix shot off the bed and Lawton watched the other man wrap his arms around Calix from behind, his hands now sure and steady. And worst yet, Calix leaned into the touch, sought it out. He had been replaced, his pedestal now cracked and tumbling, if not completely in ruin already.

Lawton balled up the bedsheets in his fist, willing the fine material to tear, as if his own rage and self-hatred might make the threads screech in tandem with the factions warring inside him. But he had no chance to speak before the fourth figure in the room, Richard, rushed forward.

He felt the sting on his cheek before the sound of the slap registered. Lawton's head snapped to the side, his jaw worked against the pain, but no comforting hand was offered. No, he was left to ruminate on what that slap actually meant, and he couldn't say he didn't deserve it.

"You were always a viper," Richard hissed while the museum curator tried to pull him away, "and you were never good for Calix. How dare you. How fucking *dare you.*"

"Richard," Calix said, but the man was already bolting for the door.

When the solid wood slab slammed in its frame, Lawton could only nod and say, "He's right, you know. Though if I'm to be compared to an animal, I think a snake is a tad too biblical for a hedonist like myself." He kept his eyes locked on Calix—to make a point, yes, but to also help him ignore the way Lily's influence swam in and out of his mind, an amoeba of consciousness that prickled at him. "I suppose you have questions."

"A brash understatement," Ethaniel said from behind Calix, his arms still a protective cage around his friend, "but not incorrect."

"They can be asked while we put Lawton through his paces," Aubrey replied as he took up the space on the bed Calix had abandoned. "There is anger, yes, but we've more important things to worry about right now. You harbor another —"

Lawton smirked, but between the bruises and the slap, his face ached with every expression, so he swiftly let it drop. "That wasn't meant to happen, obviously."

"Well, of course," Aubrey replied in a tone that Lawton assumed he'd use with young children, "but it does compound our problems. So let's start with something easy, shall we?"

Aubrey pulled a monocle from his pocket, affixed it to his eye, and Lawton watched as the glass inside it shimmered like light through a prism. He gave the monocle four quick taps to its side, and Lawton found himself lured in, caught on the hook. His mind suddenly felt foggy, his head heavy, but he couldn't look away from that light. "Have you spoken to Lily?" Aubrey asked.

The words left his lips before he could contemplate them. "I did," Lawton said. "And what did she say?"

Lawton found himself telling them everything, from the way Lily had appeared to her worries over Calix to how Lily wanted her freedom. When the word *demimonde* left his lips, Lawton heard Ethaniel suck in a harsh breath and heard Calix murmur something comforting.

And yet he still couldn't look away.

"Well, I wasn't sure that would work entirely, but at least we have something to go on," Aubrey said as he put away the monocle. "Now, Lawton, I'm afraid you have a fair bit of ground to cover when it comes to apologies. But I'll leave it up to Calix whether you make them now or later. Either way, you'll be on your knees and begging." His smile was barbed, and with a snap of his fingers and a faint feeling of degradation, Lawton's mind cleared. "Ethaniel, shall we go down for tea?"

"I'll come with you," Calix said as he reached for Aubrey. "I don't want to right now."

"Calix —" Lawton tried to rise from the bed but his body, battered as it was, was unwilling. "Please."

"You're on my time, Lawton. And while you can't help us with the current problems we're facing, you can at least stay out of the way." Calix drew his shoulders back and straightened his far too-simple shirt before saying, "I won't make you leave Rosehill, but I will ask you to stay in these rooms. There's an ensuite washroom, and you'll have food brought to you. But please...stay out of the way."

Aubrey's steely glare, Ethaniel's frown, and Calix's dismissal were all tangled up together, and Lawton could only watch as Calix reached for both men. For comfort, for friendship, for anything and everything he used to give Calix and now might never again.

The door opened and shut once more, and he was alone.

Not alone, she whispered in the back of his mind. *We can help him, but I need to know more.*

Lawton swallowed hard. He knew this was the wrong choice, and yet her siren song was too hard to resist. *Tell me how.*

Stay close to them, listen, observe everything. And if you can get your hands on that book, do it. Don't hesitate for a moment.

CHAPTER SIX

The velvet throw he'd borrowed from his room was now wrapped tightly around Convergence, and with the book securely locked away in the study once more, Aubrey felt like he could breathe again. More troubles awaited them on the horizon, but he couldn't act without a plan. And they couldn't plan properly while exhausted and hungry.

While Ethaniel made stew and Calix took a turn around the bleak garden grounds with Richard, Aubrey settled on a stool in the kitchen and pulled out his last communication stone.

Ethaniel eyed him from the hearth, his expression a question. "Magnus...you trust him?"

Aubrey let out a hard breath. His history with Magnus was long and tangled, but there was only one answer. "Indubitably. He was the first and only person to provide opportunities for me in the city." Memories of harder, colder days, where loneliness crept in through the cracks and wind whistled through spiderwebbed windows, slipped back into place. Aubrey didn't enjoy lingering in his own past. "He's a little like Calix, now that I think about it. Wealthy and titled but largely doesn't take to the entitlements those things bring him. He's a good man. He'll help if he can."

Ethaniel seemed satisfied by this answer, his little secret smile all for Aubrey as he turned back to his potatoes and carrots. Aubrey returned the smile; just having Ethaniel near helped stem the swell of rising panic in his chest. Their plan seemed doomed to failure and yet Aubrey had to hold onto hope. He needed to, for Ethaniel and Calix's sake.

"You'll stay with me?" Aubrey asked as he held the stone in his palm and focused.

"Of course. Anything."

Aubrey almost let slip a "good boy", but figured this wasn't the time nor place. So instead, he smiled to himself before refocusing on the stone and pulling up the memory of Magnus. Dark hair slicked back, dark eyes that never missed a detail. The hawkish nose and strong chin. The brocade vests and starched collars, the scent of rosewater lingering.

Aubrey let his mind click into place, magnifying the memories until all he saw was Magnus. Heard him reciting poetry by the fire. Watched his hands flicker and flash as he composed sonnets with his magic, tattooed fingers and wrists blurry with energy and promise.

The glasses of wine they'd shared. The books. The long talks on dreary nights about the nature of their own being, and of magic and mystery and what lay beyond their world.

Yes, if anyone could help them now, it would be his mentor. The man who had silently taken up a fatherly role, though Aubrey had never asked for it and Magnus had never inserted himself with such a purpose. It had simply happened. Aubrey would have been someone else, somewhere else for certain, but Magnus had taken him in and given him the *trust* he'd craved for so long.

Magnus Magnus Magnus...

In the dark, a spark became a flame, which spun out into a pattern reaching across the miles. It penetrated air and stone, wood and light, and a moment later, Aubrey could smell the moss that had once grown around the stone in his palm. Its edges had been ground down, sanded and softened until it had no longer been itself, but something a human wished it to be. And within its very center, a tiny spark of whatever magic lay intrinsic to the natural world was awakened, and the stone knew how to speak to humans after that.

So Aubrey used it to speak to Magnus.

A hazy outline appeared. "Bloody hell," Magnus gasped, a long-fingered hand over his heart. "Christ, Aubrey."

Aubrey watched Ethaniel's eyebrows nearly jump to his hairline, but his love kept stirring. "Do you often yell like that in the Collectio? Perhaps when the rest of us are not around?"

Magnus scowled, but the effect was broken by the man's wagging finger, as if Aubrey were a naughty pupil. "You do not get to play sarcastic with me, Aubrey Lavigne, when you've been missing for *days*!"

"I left a note," Aubrey said. Magnus wasn't *always* prone to dramatics, but in this instance, he doubted anyone could blame the man. He *had* simply up and vanished, as if one had made him disappear into a magician's box. (They had a prototype of one such box in the Collectio until it had been, rather mysteriously, whisked away. Aubrey had mourned the lost chance to unravel the box's secrets.)

"A note?" Magnus actually stomped his foot at that, and a bit of his hair fell across his forehead. He blew it away and when it returned, he pushed it aside agitatedly. "Yes, I got your bloody note, Aubrey, but it wasn't enough! I was of half a mind to call the police!"

"I'm grateful you didn't," Aubrey said, stepping closer to the outline of Magnus the stone projected. "It's become...difficult, my situation. And far more complicated."

At that, all of Magnus's near-manic energy dissipated and who took its place was the scholar, the gentleman, the heir to a great fortune from his family estate back in India but who never wanted to profit without having done the work. This was the Magnus Aubrey loved most of all: fearless, a bit feckless, but ever so curious.

As Ethaniel watched on, Aubrey relayed the events of the last few days. The mention of the Golden Order had Magnus disappearing from sight racing across his office, only to return with a large tome in hand. "I knew they were up to no good," Magnus muttered as he flipped through the book. "Ah, here. Yes, yes, the rumor had been for quite some time that the Golden Order was an offshoot of the Rite of the Golden Hour, which can go back to the Rosicrucians." He looked up, ire marking his face. "According to some, anyway. And we all know how they ended."

"Indeed," Aubrey said.

From across the way, Ethaniel raised his soup ladle. "I don't," he said.

Aubrey broke out into a laugh, with Magnus watching on in confused mirth. He made short introductions and could see the sheer curiosity in Magnus's face, but this was neither the time nor place. "The Rosicrucians, or at least the original sect of them, disappeared after publishing their third manifesto around 1617."

At Ethaniel's questioning look, Aubrey said, "The story goes that whatever they discovered in blending Christianity, alchemy, and magic resulted in them opening a door to the *demimonde*, the place between planes. It's a transitional spot between our world and others, but when none of them ever returned, it was theorized that the *demimonde* wasn't a true doorway. You could go in..."

"But once there, getting back out is next to impossible." Magnus clucked a little at that, as if the idea of the *demimonde* offended him.

But across from him, Ethaniel went pale. It was subtle, but Aubrey knew him well enough. It would do him no good to prod about right now, but later he would ask and hope that Ethaniel trusted him enough to answer.

"It's never been properly proven," Aubrey rushed to say, "so, if you don't mind, Magnus, I need more...*we* need more than unsubstantiated rumors."

"Yes, yes, yes." Magnus turned a few more pages, then looked up, a triumphant grin on his face. "Oh yes, we have a winner, my friends. The Golden Order has been, by all our accounts, slowly buying up books from all over the city. Frieda, one of my little spies, had been tracking them at different auctions, but they seemed to grow wise to her game and began switching up their agents. The book buying grew rather manic toward the end of last year, as if they were searching for something specific."

"And now to the crux of the problem. At least one of them." Aubrey wrote down the word *Convergence* on a slip of paper, then held it up for Magnus to see. "Does that mean anything to you?"

"Do you want the dictionary definition?"

Ethaniel covered a snicker with his hand, but even with that mirthful noise, Aubrey didn't like how sallow his cheeks still looked. "It's the name the book gave us."

"Oh, dear." Magnus grew rather serious at that, and as Aubrey had expected, on went his tiny, gold-rimmed spectacles. "Books with names are one thing. *Sentient* books with names are in a class all by themselves."

Aubrey nodded. "And what do you know about Edward Talbot, John Dee's assistant?"

Magnus was quiet for a moment. When he eventually spoke, it was with a weight on his face like Aubrey had never seen before. "Quite a bit. Quite a bit indeed. But nothing I'm going to repeat it like this. I should come to you."

"It's a two-day journey on horseback, and that's if you ride fast," Aubrey started to say.

Magnus stopped him with a raised hand. "Trust that I will be there before nightfall. I only need to know where you are."

Aubrey paused. He hadn't discussed this with Calix, wouldn't have dreamed of what Magnus was suggesting to even broach it. He could track Calix down, but the longer they stayed connected through the stone, the weaker the signal would become. And he had no other way to get in touch tonight with Magnus; the stone expended its power with one communication, and took at least a week to rebuild the charge that powered its single utility.

Decision made, Aubrey wrote down the Rosehill address and showed it to Magnus. "Easy enough," Magnus said. "I'll have a bit of a walk to you from where I'll be coming in, but I'll be there before sunset."

Aubrey could only nod, a tad stunned. "All right. I'll let everyone else know."

"Excellent," Magnus said as he clapped his hands together, all worry vanished from his face. "Well, then. Tonight."

"Tonight."

"And Aubrey?" Aubrey paused, one foot on the ground as he'd made to stand from his seat. "Double check the wards on the place where you're staying. I've no doubt the magic's good, but if we're dealing with the Golden Order, there's no telling what they might throw at you. Best not to leave it to chance."

Magnus's outline disappeared in a cloud of smoke and when it swirled away, Ethaniel was staring hard at Aubrey. "You'd better go tell him," Ethaniel said, a look of disapproval on his face.

"I know." Guilt sat in Aubrey's chest, but in comparison to whatever it was Magnus knew, could possibly assist them with? A little privacy violation was nothing next to that.

"Now, Aubrey."

Aubrey raised his hands in mock surrender. "I'm going. Right now."

But Ethaniel's stern expression melted when Aubrey kissed his cheek on the way by.

"We're supposed to trust this man?" Richard was glaring at him, arms crossed as he leaned up against the side of the manor. "After everything?"

"Magnus is the only one I would trust outside this house," Aubrey said smoothly, looking from Richard to Calix but not stopping his perusal of the wards on the manor's brick exterior. "And I hope you trust me with this."

"Of course, Aubrey," Calix said without an ounce of hesitation. "Though I certainly have questions about how he's arriving so quickly."

"So do I. Magnus can be a...bit of an enigma," Aubrey said before giving him a smile.

"Can he?" Calix's tone teased and it sent a tendril of warmth curling through Aubrey. "Like someone else I know."

Aubrey didn't reply directly, only hummed a little before turning back to his task, flicking a finger against one ward's patterns. It reverberated like a plucked guitar string and in the feedback, Aubrey could see the foundations of its magic.

How fascinating. He'd felt something akin to this when Calix had saved him from the crypt defenses, which made complete sense, since these wards were also Lily Addington's work.

But this was...*extraordinary*.

Unlike absolutely anything he'd ever come across, including the odd magic on Convergence. Aubrey focused, diving deeper, letting his own magic push through the static of protection wards, repellant wards to keep out the unwelcome, and minor maintenance glyphs to entice the brick to stay whole a bit longer.

Deeper down he dove, pushing aside the mundane like cobwebs. Searching. Seeking. Questioning the strange bits of magic he was finding and then...black. Pitch-black like the velvet night of the sky, and yet not. There was an edge to it, musty on his tongue, and yet onward Aubrey pushed.

The darkness here was like the breath of the undying, and whatever source it had come from was *massive*. In the unlit spaces between pattern lines that zagged and curved, with no real logic guiding it along a forsaken path, Aubrey saw nothing. And everything he never wanted to see.

The darkness yawned, welcoming, and he could feel his consciousness slip from his body. *Not again*, he thought, snarling at the thing that challenged him. He was no hedge witch, no backwater sojourner plucking berries and making sticky pastes to bind wounds. He was no healer, but he knew how to find the source of nearly anything. So, he pushed further down, like falling into a pit, and at the very bottom lay something he never expected to see or feel.

Somehow, Calix's mother had woven a part of the *demimonde* into the base structure of the wards on this place. It went deeper than stone or wood and was far stronger than what he could have expected. Like the magic hiding the true vault from Calix, this was hidden, too, but this wanted to be found. It held its arms open for Aubrey and asked him to *please come inside*, ever so welcoming, the perfect host.

Aubrey pulled back, scrambling to get his mind away from that temptation, that place he'd never visited and only heard of and yet somehow was so desperate to explore. He pushed and pulled, running like one might through the woods with branches tripping you up at every step, yanking his mind and magic away until finally he was back in his own body, breathless and sweating.

And the moment he returned to this world, this plane, an idea began to form.

"Dear God, Aubrey, what happened?" Calix looked panicked from where he was pressed against Aubrey's side, his touch a comfort after such an encounter.

"I think we need a new plan," Aubrey gasped.

Magnus knocked on the front door of Rosehill at exactly six in the evening. With Lawton in and out of consciousness, an unease had settled about the manor, but they'd all been given a chance to rest and wash up, so Aubrey didn't fuss much about his own appearance. Magnus wouldn't care a whit, anyways; his mind was typically solving at least five problems at once and while his own appearance was spot-on every single day, he rarely paid much attention to that of others.

So, when the knock sounded, Aubrey knew exactly who it was. It startled everyone else, so Aubrey pushed himself up from his spot between Ethaniel and a dozing Calix, made a quieting motion to Ethaniel, and went to the door.

"Gorgeous place," Magnus said by way of greeting, his eyes cast toward the ornate stonework over the main door. "And Aubrey. Thank God."

Aubrey was crushed in a hug, which he gingerly returned. "I'm very curious as to how you got here so quickly, Magnus. But do come in."

Aubrey took Magnus's coat and hat, both done in a fine navy-blue wool, and walked him through the house to the small parlor set off the kitchens. Calix said it was his favorite room outside the library, and he'd quickly turned it into a veritable den of soft fabrics and gentle light, buoyed by the scent of good wine and woodsmoke. Aubrey watched Magnus take in the space, the sight of Calix and Ethaniel bent over one of his mother's journals, with Richard dozing on a nearby sofa, and said, "The last few days have been exhausting."

"I can only imagine," Magnus said. "From what you've told me, it sounds a fair bit dangerous, as well."

"Dangerous is an understatement." Aubrey crossed the room, feeling how Calix and Ethaniel watched his every move, and made introductions swiftly so as to not be distracted from the task at hand. Off in his corner, Richard was also keeping tabs, but Aubrey understood the caution; they'd been betrayed at every turn. If he hadn't known Magnus for so long, he would have hesitated to bring someone else into the fold.

Magnus took a seat and listened intently while the three of them (with helpful additions from Richard) told the story in its entirety. His mentor and friend paused every now and then to scribble down notes, and by the time they ended their tale with the strange connections their minds had made, Magnus's eyes were bright with curiosity.

"I have so many thoughts on this," Magnus said quietly, tapping his pen against his leather journal. "But mostly, I really want to see this damn book."

Aubrey chuckled. "I'm surprised."

"At me?"

"That you didn't ask to see it immediately," Aubrey said, earning him a knowing nod from Magnus.

"Well, I certainly couldn't burst in here and just demand to see the thing but..." Magnus trailed off, his attention snapping to the journal on the table. "What is that?"

With a nod from Calix, Ethaniel handed over the journal while Aubrey said, "Calix's mother was an Oracle, too. Despite current...circumstances, or perhaps because of them, we thought it prudent to go through all her writings and see if we might discover any kind of solution."

Magnus was uncharacteristically silent as he leafed through the small book, his touch careful and considerate. But with each page that passed, Aubrey could sense something in Magnus; his posture became more rigid, and his gaze had gone from curious to assessing to concerned alarmingly quickly.

"Magnus?" Aubrey said, leaning forward to get a better look at a page Magnus had stopped on. "What is it?"

When Magnus looked up, it was not to him, but to Calix, his stare pointed. "And your mother's spirit, or at least part of it, is now harbored in another? Is that what I'm to understand?"

Magnus turned to give Ethaniel a rather clinical once-over. Aubrey could see that sharp calculation in his mentor's eyes, bright and urgent, before Magnus said to Ethaniel, "You're a patterner, correct?"

Ethaniel hesitated, but Aubrey nodded encouragingly. "I am," Ethaniel said, smoothing his hands down his vest. It was the only piece of clothing to survive their slapdash run from the city. It was a pretty thing the fiery, dark orange of an autumn leaf in the sun, with intricate stitching in shining silver thread.

Magnus gestured toward the book. "Have you examined these patterns in the journal?" When Ethaniel nodded, Magnus leaned forward, his gaze blazing with intent and intelligence. "And what did you see?"

Ethaniel licked his lips. "Mostly nonsense. As if she'd tried to write a poem in at least eight different languages. Nothing connected, nothing made sense."

"Exactly!" Magnus leapt up and rushed around the coffee table to plop the book in Ethaniel's lap, other hand outstretched. "May I?"

It was always a delicate thing, trying to explain Magnus's magic to others. Aubrey knew he was paradoxical to his own family, but Magnus was an *enigma* and somehow a magnifying glass for the misunderstood. "Ethaniel is a patterner unlike any I've ever met," Aubrey said, coming to sit by his lover's side. From the chair to their left, Calix watched, enraptured, and a small flicker of pride lit Aubrey up from the inside. Pride of any kind was a sinful thing, according to his parents. But was it so wrong to use one's talents and know they might make a difference?

"He's an amplifier," Aubrey said, reaching for the most direct explanation he had. "Trust him. Trust *me*, Ethaniel."

Ethaniel mouthed, "I do," before giving Magnus his hand. "All right, what should I —"

"Brace yourself," Magnus said, before slamming their joined hands down on a page riddled with the lines of a pattern.

Immediately, Ethaniel's eyes widened and then, to Aubrey's shock, he felt that eye in his forehead react. Across the way, Calix sat up abruptly, his fingertips glowing.

"Fascinating!" Magnus said, his own face alight with academic glee. "Can you feel it, Ethaniel? Can you see it?"

Aubrey felt his own vision swoop, as if the world had been turned on its head and he was the only thing left standing right side-up. His stomach lurched, gorge rising, but he forced the nausea down, pushed it away to focus on the pull of his magic.

No, not a pull. An *answer* to Ethaniel's call. And beside them, Calix seemed to be experiencing the same.

Sourceless wind scuffed at all of them, teasing their hair and clothing, and all the while, Magnus and Ethaniel remained joined at the hands while lights and shapes played across their faces. Ethaniel's eyes, ever wider still, had gone luminescent with his power, glowing green and gold; Magnus's eyes had gone their usual milky white.

"Yes! Yes! Ethaniel, my boy, tell me..." Magnus swallowed hard. "Tell me what you see?"

"It's a door," Ethaniel whispered as a strange tone rang in their ears. Like a church bell but off-key, clanging away to signal something, herald something.

Call out for someone?

Aubrey started to cross to Magnus and Ethaniel, and then a voice, a gong of a thing, took over his mind.

Stop

stop

STOP

You must stop

It's a door without a key, no way to shut it once open

Don't go there

Or maybe do

the demimonde

THE DEMIMONDE

It calls for us, curator, it wants us

You won't let it

You promised me my freedom

The wind died. The sound faded. Aubrey's ears rang with it still, tremulous and horrific. And from the looks on Ethaniel's and Calix's faces, they'd heard it, too. After all, they were linked; why wouldn't Talbot use that to his own gain?

Perhaps they should start using it to theirs.

The book had slid off Ethaniel's lap and Magnus picked it up, gingerly shutting it before turning to them all. "It's a door," he said firmly. "She was figuring out how to create a door to the *demimonde*. The place between places." His gaze bore into Aubrey. "A place not meant for mortals. You know this."

"I do," Aubrey said, casting about for Calix, who had sunk to the floor, knees pulled up to his chin, brown eyes wide, fingers trembling where they rested on his thighs. "Calix? Do you have any idea why your mother would do this?"

Calix shoved a hand into his already mussed hair, making him look slightly manic. Aubrey still found him wildly attractive, but the obvious pain the man was in tempered that. "Towards the end, she told me she heard things. Voices. That her parents would whisper in her ear at night. And she kept to herself, always puttering about with things she said weren't for my eyes."

"The vault," Ethaniel said, to which Calix nodded his assent. "What was she looking for?"

"A way in?" Magnus asked. "Most don't even know the *demimonde* exists. But when a practitioner finds out, it often becomes a source of obsession. For an Oracle? I shudder to think how it might have gotten its claws in them. In this case, your brilliant, terrifying mother, Calix."

The door to the parlor opened and there stood Lawton. He was in fresh clothes, his hair perfectly coiffed, his spine as straight as an arrow. Dangling from his fingers was a silver amulet on a chain. "She told me where to find it," he said as Calix rushed forward, "and to let you know that's where she is." He put a hand to his chest. "Or, where most of her is."

Aubrey could hardly believe what he was hearing. One didn't go to the *demimonde*, and if somehow that had been achieved, surely they wouldn't *stay*. It was a world of failed dreams with claws and teeth, and from those failures had grown demons. Monsters. Abominations.

"Impossible," he said, even as Magnus turned a keen eye to him. "It's simply not done."

"Ah, the textbook practicality I do so adore in you, Aubrey," Magnus said, coming to Calix's side to inspect the amulet. "May I?"

Calix waved him forward, so Magnus took the amulet — a pretty thing of engraved silver — and ran a thumb over it. It popped open, like a locket might, and a tiny bit of fine red powder fell to the floor. Magnus seemed amused by that. "Oh ho, well, isn't that a find! I haven't seen that in many years."

Something tingled at the back of Aubrey's mind, but Ethaniel beat him to the punch. "Is that red divine?"

"It is indeed, my fair patterner. It is indeed." Magnus crouched and ran a finger through the faint trace of it on the floor. "It's very high quality, I can tell from the smell." He stood and held his hand out to Calix. "It's a powder made from a combination of herbs, known to help heighten concentration. Not exactly *illegal*, but certainly in the same space as opium."

Calix frowned, and Aubrey saw how he incrementally shifted away from Lawton; it made his heart hurt to see Calix in pain like that and immediately resolved to find them a distraction before bed. Something with warm hands and mouths and creating pleasure instead of enduring pain.

Beside him, Ethaniel sucked in a sharp breath, cutting his gaze over to Aubrey. "I'm surprised you can think such things at this moment," Ethaniel whispered as they watched Calix close his eyes and inhale.

"I can almost always find that frame of mind when the company is so alluring," Aubrey whispered back. "Am I incorrect in my thinking?"

Ethaniel's cheeks colored at that. "You know you're not," Ethaniel said.

"Good."

"How strange," Calix said a moment later. "It smells like honeysuckle. My mother used to smell like that."

Lawton cut through the chatter with a simple question. "Is this powder a hallucinogen of some kind?"

"It's more than that," Magnus said. "It's how you open doors in your mind and, if I'm right about what your mother was doing, Calix, it's how she cracked open a door to the *demimonde*."

Aubrey watched Calix round on his friend, suddenly very angry. "Where did you find this, Lawton?"

"In the library," was Lawton's answer, the words rushed, the tone soft as if Calix were a spooked horse.

"We've combed every inch of that space," Ethaniel said.

"Did we?" Aubrey asked, stomach sinking with the sudden realization. "We were looking in the wrong space, weren't we?"

Lawton motioned them forward. "I can show you, like she showed me."

Magnus looked *delighted*. He clapped his hands and said, "Well, lead on, dear boy. Do lead on."

They followed Lawton out into the long hall, then up the grand staircase, and as they trekked, Aubrey slipped his hand into Ethaniel's. "We'll figure this out," he said, trying to feel the truth in his own words.

"I hope so," Ethaniel said as they climbed, the worry in his face making Aubrey's heart clench.

Chapter Seven

CALIX

Calix had finally, *finally*, settled his nerves enough to stand being in the same room with an awake-and-aware Lawton, and then it had all unraveled again. Because of a thin blade, the one that had cut his hand as soon as he'd placed it on the false book Lawton had shown them.

Aubrey was leaning in, inspecting the hollow book and the blade that protruded from its back cover. Ethaniel was carefully wrapping Calix's hand in a bandage, his head bent, his hands warm on Calix's skin. Calix inhaled and knew Ethaniel would taste like the coffee he'd been drinking all afternoon, in between their moments of panic and madness.

"The amulet was in the book," Lawton was saying in the background. "And she said there was a place behind the bookshelves, but I pulled the book down and nothing happened."

"It clearly needed his blood," Magnus said, quietly, as if to himself. Calix watched Magnus and Aubrey crane their heads to look into the black space that had appeared in place of the bookshelf. It yawned ominously, an open mouth simply waiting for prey to waltz in. "I think she created some kind of...pocket dimension. A holding place entirely outside this realm, but not in another. Fascinating."

Magnus's words, as true as they likely were, made the pit in Calix's stomach widen. He felt sick. This was not the Rosehill he remembered, was it?

"This is still your home," Ethaniel whispered to him, and when Calix looked up, startled, Ethaniel gave him a sheepish grin. "I could sense your worry. I suppose it'll be like this for a bit, since our minds seem to be connected somehow. I'm sorry, I didn't mean to intrude."

Calix put his uninjured hand on Ethaniel's cheek. "Don't apologize. Truly. I appreciate the kindness, the thoughtfulness, more than I can say." He sighed and let his gaze drift over the packed bookshelves, letting the warmth of old memories seep in. The library was a beautiful space in the estate and even after so many years empty, the old ghosts of better times lingered here still. His mother on her favorite sofa, reading out loud to him while he sat next to her, his feet swinging in time with her rhythm. Then later, his visits for holidays and finding a tray of his favorite cookies and cider waiting beside that same sofa, his mother smiling as she welcomed him with open arms.

So many memories, so many of them warm and comforting. He didn't know if they would feel the same after all this.

"Do you think you can close it?" Aubrey asked Magnus, startling Calix out of his reverie. "We needn't explore this right now —"

"We absolutely must!" Calix said as he got to his feet. "Clearly my mother was keeping secrets, many of them, and those very secrets have threatened me and all of us." He stared over at Lawton, who was fidgeting and keeping his own gaze to the floor. Somehow, strangely, he could *feel* his mother's presence lingering there, like another layer just under Lawton's skin.

The anger, the frustration, the betrayal – all of it bubbled under his own surface, a pot left on the fire too long, and Calix couldn't take it anymore. Nothing was as he'd believed, and he'd been lied to, made a fool, and had his heart broken now twice in the span of a few days. And here were Aubrey and Ethaniel, strangers to him until recently, looking at him with concern, touching him carefully, making sure his heart and soul were safe.

Had he really been so blind? And since the answer was a resounding *yes*, could he trust his own judgment now or in the future?

So, Calix made a decision. He stared into that black void his mother had created to hide her secrets, and walked right into it. He heard Aubrey shout something in surprise, but it was immediately lost as his body was swept up in a wave of power so intense, Calix saw spots before his eyes. He could feel the power reaching inside him, seeking out *something*, but when he pushed back against it, it retreated.

All he could do was wait. He closed his eyes against the onslaught, and when his ears popped with some unseen force, he chanced a look around.

Bookshelves. Low, squat things cut from stone the color of deep jungle leaves spread out in a three-quarter circle across a slate floor. His footsteps made no sound as he crossed the small space, and as he neared the bookshelf furthest to the left, a plush green chair appeared. In it was a ghostly outline of his mother.

"I thought you might find this place one day," she said in a throaty whisper, as if she were hoarse from illness. "So, I recorded this in one of the times I was lucid."

That old grief rose up in him, polished and made anew by both her visage and her confession. "When you were lucid?" he repeated, walking forward and dreading every step he took.

Lily nodded. "I thought, at first, to simply leave you a letter. I was too weak, or so I believed, to secure a portion of myself here. But Edna knew what I was planning and —"

Calix gaped at her. His mother's dearest friend had known and hadn't warned him? It more than stung; it felt like a betrayal. He and Edna had been close, at one time; she like an aunt to him, especially after his mother's death. But she'd left for the west coast the moment the estate had been handed over to his care and, admittedly, that had hurt a great deal. They hadn't stayed in contact since, and the guilt of that inaction weighed on him now. "Edna! What in the hell was Edna doing helping you?"

The look she gave him was so sympathetic, Calix thought he might crumble under its weight. Perhaps he should have been offended instead, as if his mother taking pity on him was a thing too raw, too soul-numbing, to be acceptable. "Do you really not know?" Lily asked as she rose from the chair and came over to him. Her pale, ghostly hand reached up to caress his cheek. "Calix, surely it can't be a surprise that Edna and I were close."

A surprise? No, not quite. But to hear it put so boldly... Calix took a step back, removing her touch, and watched his mother's face crease with some unnamed emotion, one that hovered between shock and regret. *Well, good*, he thought bitterly as he looked around the room once more, *she should regret something.*

"Your...relationship with Edna is not my concern," he bit out, taking another step back. "I want answers, Mother." And he spread his arms wide. "Why this place? Why the soul phylactery? Why hide *all of this* from me?"

His words echoed around them, pinging off walls he couldn't see, ringing off the stone bookshelves and bouncing back to him. He sounded hollow. Sad. And wasn't that how he really felt, deep down? A shell of the man he'd thought he was becoming, betrayed by a friend and his mother in almost the same turn, and now the two of them were somehow bonded together in Lawton's body.

"What could be so awful that you needed to keep it from me?" Calix whispered, looking at his mother once more. "Was I so incapable? Did you trust me so little?"

"It was never that, darling," she said, looking stricken for the first time, her hands now clasped in front of her, her fingers twisting against each other. "As ashamed as I am to admit it, I was obsessed. From the very first time I learned about the *demimonde*, I knew I wanted to explore it. To visit, yes, to see it with my own eyes, but also to delve deep and discover its secrets."

And then Lily waved a hand to the side and a book was pulled from the shelves and floated over to them, as silent as the grave. "This was where I learned of it," she said as the book came to rest in Calix's hands. "I found it on one of my trips in the thin spaces, and it was the start of a journey I knew would likely end tragically. But I couldn't stop myself. The more I learned, the more I needed, and it fed on itself like the ouroboros. An endless cycle of acquiring information and artifacts, and delving deeper and deeper still."

The book was a pretty thing, bound in navy blue leather with a strange glyph in gold on the front. "What is it?" Calix asked, curious but not certain he wished to open it quite yet.

"The beginning of everything," Lily said, floating back to him. She put her hands on top of his and stared right into his eyes as she said, "It's where I wanted to take you, to get you away from the world you live in. The unfairness of it.

Knowing you'd be judged for who you are, what you are. And that nothing I could do in this world would stop your powers from driving you mad eventually, but somewhere else, maybe I could."

Then she looked away and Calix could almost feel her shame. Her misery. "I failed. I know that. I failed you and us. And in those last few months, I knew my life was over. I could feel the denizens of the *demimonde* reaching for me, their claws so sharp but their song too beautiful to ignore." She shuddered and it rippled through her, making her already paper-thin form waver. "Once they know you, Calix, they can find you again. It's the consequence of making yourself known to the *demimonde*. So I asked them for a boon. I asked for the knowledge on how to use a soul phylactery, and in return, I would give a part of myself to the *demimonde*. It was a bargain, but it was the only one I had to make. I was counting on you to find me, find this place, and be able to piece me back together. What's inside Lawton, and what's left of me in the *demimonde* should be enough."

But her tone wasn't as surefire and steadfast as her words.

The horror of what his mother was saying sank in. His mother wanted him to bring her back to life. To take the part of her inside Lawton and the part she'd bargained away and *resurrect her*.

Calix's head swam — with anger and frustration, pain and anxieties built upon a foundation of sand — but through it, he could see her truth, the deep, deep fear in her eyes. His mother had been terrified he'd slowly lose his tether to their realm, their reality, like she had. And she'd tried everything to save him and in that tidal wave of affection, she'd cursed herself...and him.

Lily's voice was sad, barely a whisper, as she said, "You won't make the mistakes I did, love. You'll wield the power better; I know it. This book contains a set of instructions on how to access the many realms outside our own, but you must follow the instructions to the letter. Each set of instructions won't unlock until you fully achieve the results from the previous one."

Calix nodded, tucked the book into his pocket, feeling dread even as he did so. He was still listening to her. Why? Then Lily looked down at their joined hands, pain evident on her face. "I wasn't strong enough to get past the *demimonde's* guardians. I tried to summon a guide, but the one that came never —"

A sound from behind him, like glass shattering.

A chill down his back, icy fingers skating across his skin.

Lily's eyes went wide. "Darling, you must go. You have what you need. And you won't be able to return here. But you *must go.*"

"What? Absolutely not!" Calix tried to yank away from her grip, but she held him, as strong as iron.

And what once was his mother's lovely face was now a gaunt thing of leathery skin and bones, empty eye sockets and lipless smile. "GO!" she roared, shoving him away.

Calix stumbled back, horrified at the visage before him, and as he lost his footing, two strong hands caught him.

"We're under attack," Aubrey said in his ear right before he was yanked through the portal.

"That, my friends, is a hellhound," Magnus was saying as Calix and Aubrey tumbled through the portal, "and I'm afraid there's more than one."

"Fuck," Calix felt Aubrey say as much as heard. His breath stirred Calix's hair and made him shiver.

"Hellhounds? Like demons?" Richard was pale, his fist clenched above his heart. Calix rushed over, worried the poor man would keel over. "Calix, this is mad."

I know. I know it is. I'm so sorry. But he couldn't say the words. Instead, he said, "Richard, take everyone else in the house down to the wine cellar and lock the door." Richard nodded but didn't move. "Richard. Please."

Richard seemed to startle awake at that, as if coming out of a dream. "Yes, yes. Of course." He put a heavy hand on Calix's shoulder. "Please be safe."

And then he was gone and Calix was staring at the others: Magnus with a small book in his left hand, his right hand moving in odd, almost unseemly configurations, his joints twisting in ways no bones should. "Your mother's protection runes are impressive," Magnus said, sparing Calix a glance, the golden light from his magic reflecting like firelight over his face, "but hellhounds are impressive in their own right. And tenacious. Check the western windows. They can't approach from any other direction."

Outside, the rain slashed at the window. A roll of thunder shook the house, and lightning danced in Calix's eyes, blinding him for a moment. He dashed to the window and saw nothing but blackness...and then...

An orange light, like a flame in the night. Then another. A third. A fourth. All emerging from the thick wood surrounding the house. The estate's walls were high, and if Calix focused, he could feel the latent energy laid down in every brick. More than stone protected Rosehill, and Lily had always ensured they were safe. Calix had known she was more than simply overprotective; she'd feared a mortal man as much as she'd feared otherworldly entities grasping her son and carting him off somewhere she couldn't follow.

"How many?" Magnus asked.

Calix swallowed hard. "Four. Four that I can see."

"Watch them closely, Calix, and tell me what they do."

Seconds later, those orange embers in the dark became figures. The lightning lashing at the sky illuminated them only in bits and pieces, but it was enough to drive fear into his heart. They were massive, hulking beasts made of what looked like shifting stone. As much as thunder rattled the glass under his hand, he wondered if their footsteps factored into the vibrations at all. They were easily as tall as he was at the shoulder, and when one howled, they all did.

He'd never heard something quite so terrifying in all his life.

"That sound," Calix gasped. Everything in him said *run* and yet he was standing there staring. "I think they're going to —"

He stopped talking when they all charged the wall. The four hellhounds were an incredible force meeting the brick and magic of Rosehill itself, two solid objects crashing into each other with no give and no take. The hounds barked and snarled, flashing gray-white teeth as long as his forearm and Calix thought *run, you fool.*

And yet he stayed. This was his home and he'd not be driven from it.

"Well, that tells me a fair bit," Magnus muttered. The energy gathering between his fingers, gossamer strings of gold and silver weaving together in patterns that made Calix dizzy, began to fill the entire space with light. "I have this. Check on Aubrey."

Calix whirled, only to see Aubrey across the room and also glowing, soft blue and green, the third eye in his forehead wide and unblinking. He, too, had a small book in his hand like Magnus, but his other hand rested on the library's eastern wall. "Help Ethaniel," Aubrey said, voice gone ethereal. "We'll remain here, repairing any holes made in the estate's defenses."

Outside, another howl went up. Another explosion of power, the demonic against his mother's protections. Something in Calix's veins sizzled, his body and magic reacting to that of his mother's.

Had he the time or ability, Calix would have marveled at Magnus and Aubrey's power. It poured from their fingertips and eyes, lit their skin from below. Two beacons of sheer magical force, it was awe-inspiring.

"What do I do?" Then Lawton was at his side and the moment broke and all Calix was left with was a panicked sadness. Such an odd pairing to feel beating like a second heart at his very core.

"Stay out of the way," Calix said, pushing past him to where Ethaniel was standing on the other side of the room, staring up at the shelves, unmoving. "And maybe ask my mother if she knows anything useful. Do you think you can handle that?"

He was being unfair. He knew it. And somehow, Calix couldn't bring himself to mind much in the moment.

He raced over to Ethaniel, who hadn't moved from that one spot. "Ethaniel? What can I do?"

But as Calix rounded Ethaniel, the man was still rooted in place. Worry flashed through him, and Calix came to stand before him. But Ethaniel didn't see him. Not with his normal human eyes, anyways. If Aubrey and Magnus were beautiful beacons of power, Ethaniel was a maze. A labyrinth. One hand he held, palm up, fingers twitching as a dark purple sphere of energy crackled and popped. The other he held over the books, those fingers dancing, as if he were reading the spines by touch alone, as his eyes had gone completely black. The sphere flashed, a brighter purple this time, and finally Ethaniel spoke.

"Hellhounds are essentially the barn mules of lower demons," Ethaniel whispered. "They'll do whatever their master commands, but unlike mules, they have no sense of self-preservation. They will, quite literally, kill themselves trying to carry out those commands. And where one dies, two more rise. For all they are a lesser demon, they're terribly hard to control." He flashed a grim smile Calix's way. "So, let's see if I can find a way to turn them back — ah, here we are."

And in the same space as a snap of one's fingers, Ethaniel's power winked out. The sphere disappeared. The light died. "I was hoping your mother would have a copy," Ethaniel said, sliding a book out from the second shelf.

Calix stared at the book. "That's a patterner's book."

Ethaniel smiled at him, but it was tight with tension. "More importantly, it's a primer. It's one of the books patterners use when starting their studies. It's also an incredible source of raw materials, which I should be able to use." Then, abruptly, he leaned in and kissed Calix on the forehead. "I'm so sorry, Calix. I didn't want it to be like this. Stay by Aubrey and Magnus, all right?"

Calix nodded and did as he was told, fighting back a helplessness that threatened to consume him whole. Outside the howling and yipping grew louder, competing with the thunder and wind and the slap of rain and the arcs of lightning. His world began to spin but he choked it down, pressed himself to the wall near Aubrey, and waited. Watching.

"Ethaniel?" Aubrey spared Ethaniel a glance, his face marred with confusion. "Ethaniel, what are you —"

"They're *hellhounds*, Aubrey," Ethaniel shouted, book splayed open in his hand. "I know how to deal with them!"

"Your emphasis is not an explanation!" Magnus shouted back, energy zipping between his fingers, flickering like so many fireflies.

"Then we'll all just have to survive for me to do so, then, won't we?" Ethaniel gave them all a grin, mad with something Calix couldn't read, and then his face was wiped of all emotion and his head snapped down to the book. Ethaniel tore pages from it and crumpled them in his hand, the paper sparking like tinder.

Simply from Ethaniel's touch.

Ethaniel's lips moved but Calix couldn't hear him. And the wind howled and the hellhounds snarled and the thunder rattled every bit of glass in the room and every bone in Calix's body. Pain lanced through him, sudden and sharp, in his left side, between his ribs. He hissed and slapped his hand over it, but another shot of pain hit him in the right thigh.

In the left arm, then the right shoulder.

In the neck, just below his ear.

Ethaniel's lips moved faster, and the embers in his hand turned into a flame, orange and red and purple and flickering as if caught in a breeze.

The pain was vicious now, single-minded but widespread through him. Calix cried out and fell to his knees, or perhaps fell to his knees as he cried out. He was losing track of what was going on around him, and everyone was turning into brightly hued blurs because of the tears in his eyes.

It was unstoppable, the pain. And he knew he was feeling every attack on the wards, every fang and claw, every chunk torn out that was replaced immediately by a rush of warmth as Magnus and Aubrey repaired them. Pain, then warmth. Pain, then warmth.

And in front of him, the flame in Ethaniel's hand split into four. The tailor, the man who kissed Calix with care and sweetness, looked so different right now. Fearsome. Powerful. Incredible. His eyes were still pitch black but his face had sunken, cheeks gone hollow, and there was a pallor to his skin that made Calix think of cold stone. Like the dead.

Calix had his hands dug into the thick rug, clawing his way to Ethaniel. He could make the pain stop. He could. He dragged his body closer and closer still, racked with pain, crying, aching.

He looked up just as Ethaniel looked down. The flames in Ethaniel's hand danced, waiting for his command.

"Go," he whispered, and the flame leapt forward, then rushed out the window. Glass shattered. Someone yelled Calix's name.

The pain crescendoed, then was gone. Calix was flat on his back, rain slipping in through the broken window, and Aubrey was hovering over him, dabbing at Calix's nose with a handkerchief.

"I would love to know what in the hell just happened," Magnus said, flopping down beside Calix and patting his shoulder.

As if on cue, Magnus and Aubrey turned to look at Ethaniel, who came to sit on Calix's other side with a heavy sigh. Calix caught sight of Lawton's orange hair across the room and knew his friend — and his mother — were watching, too.

Ethaniel brushed Calix's hair out of his face, his touch so gentle it almost hurt, and said, "I'm a Harkness."

"Well, shit," Magnus replied immediately. "That certainly explains it."

INTERLUDE

Vincent

Vincent watched as the summoner was torn apart by the very beasts she'd called forth. Such a waste.

"We could simply go after them," Cassandra said as she stepped away from the slowly spreading pool of blood. She didn't flinch when the toe of her shoe brushed the summoner's arm – or what was left of it – and the fingers twitched as if trying to grab her. Cassandra simply kicked the arm aside and took up a spot at Vincent's left. "A frontal assault. We were close at Lavigne's apartment, so bombarding any wards with as much as we have –"

Vincent held a hand up and Cassandra went silent. It was true that he could dedicate the bulk of the Order's resources toward the issue of the book he wanted. But Vincent hadn't crashed through the ranks to become like his predecessors — rote, old, insignificant when they should have been victorious. So he'd tackled the tedious first, spreading word of the Order through the proper circles. That was where young, pretty things like Lawton Adler had come in, murmuring into the whisper networks that sprawled to all ends of the city, courting influence. Sometimes fucking their way into influence. The methods hadn't really mattered; the results had been key.

He wondered if he'd tempted some idol of Fate and become his own Icarus the moment he'd made the book his passion. Suffice to say that a book of John Dee's writings would have been a lucky find, but the rumor had always been that it was more than a book of scribblings. That Dee's greatest work hadn't been attempts to contact angels (which didn't exist) or even his many musings on the existence of other planes and how one might travel there. Vincent had seen enough of those to recognize madness in the quill-scratch and smeared ink.

No, Dee's greatest work had been that very book. A soul trap, capable of harboring dozens of souls. A wealth of magical energy that could, if Vincent's studies held true and his conclusions were sound, open a door.

To anywhere.

Vincent realized Cassandra was still at his side, so he walked out of the chamber, fingers laced behind his back, gaze steady. Cassandra followed. The few people they passed in the black marble halls of the Golden Order kept their eyes averted.

He waited until they were securely in his office before speaking. "We need to find another way," Vincent said as he sat at his desk and drummed his fingers on its smooth surface. "They'll be expecting a frontal assault."

Cassandra raised an eyebrow at that. "I'm unsure what other way there is to attack."

Vincent let himself smile at that. There were more doors that went unseen than most realized. And he was betting the very intelligent Aubrey Lavigne would know this as well, but he doubted even that man would put it together in time.

"We find a door between here and there," Vincent said as he began to flip through his ledger. The list of names wasn't long; magical practitioners were a dime a dozen in the city, but specialists were tough to come by. At one point, he'd toyed with getting Lavigne into the Order, even if by subterfuge, but had realized rather quickly (and after a few successful reconnaissance missions by his spies) that Lavigne had moral fiber tougher than elephant hide.

"I'll handle the issue of the book from here, Cassandra," Vincent said after he found the names he needed. "I need a dreamer. Get me Isme Harkness."

Cassandra visibly blanched at that, and the paleness of her skin made her red coat look like so much blood. "A dreamer? Are you certain?"

Vincent gave her a thin smile. "And here I thought you'd question why the tailor, and yet here you are, white as a sheet at the mention of a dreamer." He leaned in, closely inspecting her. She was as well put-together as always, though the coat was new and a bit bold compared to her usual wardrobe. He idly wondered if she had a new romance in her life. Why else change what had worked so well for as long as he'd known her? Half the city was full of peacocks; it was a shame to think his trusted right hand might drown in the same pond as Narcissus.

Cassandra straightened, adjusted the lapels on her coat, and nodded. "A dreamer. Understood."

She made to leave, but stopped when Vincent said, "He's a Harkness."

"Sir?"

"The tailor. He's a Harkness."

Her dark eyes went wide at that. "An apostate, I'm assuming?"

"Not as much. From my understanding, he simply stopped talking to that side of the family at the behest of his father." He shrugged and turned back to his ledger. "But he won't have the protections of the family, and even if he has residual ones, Isme will know how to get around them. She should be able to...activate his latent powers."

Cassandra shoved her hands into her pockets and Vincent knew she'd have balled them into fists, the only display of nerves she would allow herself now that she had her orders. Threatening someone like Cassandra would never work; she was someone who had to believe in the cause, and fear was a tool of the weak and unimaginative. Yes, he could always have those who disobeyed thrown into the basement far below the Order's offices, but disappear too many people and you'd give birth to the very doubt you'd been trying to avoid.

He'd rather rule through what could be considered fairness, with a dose of coercion.

"Do this," he said with a purr in his voice, "and you can choose your reward." He knew exactly what she would choose, but it never hurt to dangle the raw meat on a stick lowered in exactly the right spot. Cassandra wasn't the type to casually talk about her family, but he'd had her followed enough times to know the exact gravestone she visited every week. Of course she wanted her sister back in the land of the living. And that glimmer of a promise would keep her steady at the wheel, so to speak. And she knew he had the family connections to make good on his promise.

Cassandra's right cheek jumped, as if she'd bitten down on it, but she didn't flinch. Only said, "Consider it done."

"You'll need this. Don't open it." Vincent pulled out a small cloth bag from his desk drawer and let it rest in his palm. It was no bigger than a dinner plate, but he could feel *it* squirming inside. Waiting to be free. "Tell Isme her half-cousin says hello."

Cassandra snatched the bag from his hand and walked briskly out of the office, never looking back. Vincent was finally able to lean back in his chair and turn to the large bank of windows, admiring the view of the city at night. He'd given away his last *ithliq*, so at some point he'd need to summon more. But that was a problem for another day. All that mattered was Isme would like the slimy little thing, and that would buy him exactly what he needed.

CHAPTER EIGHT

From the writings of *Edward Talbot, March 1, 1580*

It was as though winter itself knew something was wrong, as the sky was gray and the wind left to batter the shutters and doors of the small building behind John's home. He used to conduct his rituals in the dining area, but after his young son nearly stumbled into a summoning last year, John had this building constructed from an old barn for our purposes. There was no place to make a fire in the godforsaken thing, so I spent an entire afternoon shivering, watching John as he paced about, book in hand, trying desperately to contact the entity he swore was "on the other side."

I knew better than to interrupt. The last time I'd tried to assist, John had thrown a book at my head and ranted for several minutes about my ungratefulness. I didn't wish to repeat the situation, so I took notes. Watching him. Sneaking looks at his papers when John would occasionally wander to the far side of the barn to stare at the wall, his right hand casting random glyphs as he tried in vain to reach the thing.

John was convinced he was talking to angels. There are no such things. Despite his delving into the occult, John is a steadfast Christian, fervent in his beliefs, and no amount of knowledge will steer him from the path of his Christ. I know the truth, but if I cannot convince him to leave those beliefs behind... Well, no matter what the consequence, I'll not leave my own research to languish and rot.

By the time evening had settled around us like a cloak, John was manic. It had certainly happened in the past, but this time something was different. There was a gleam in his eyes, his cheeks pink with excitement (or perhaps madness), and he rushed over to me and shoved a bit of parchment in my face.

"Don't you see! Don't you see!" He proclaimed. "Edward, I've done it! I've finished the circle and now, now we can summon him!"

I tried to understand. John's moods were erratic at the best of times, and that is in comparison to my own swings of melancholy and despair. But the paper which he proclaimed to be the answer to all his labors was not anything significant. Or so I thought.

He had me set up the candles, chalk the circle, help him finish the runes. We stood just outside the circle, hands raised, as John chanted in his strange tongue that he swore came to him in a dream (but which I was certain was the product of too much wine and the consumption of a fine red powder I'd no desire to partake in). As I expected, the runes began to glow, then smoke; this had happened dozens of times before, a sign that the summoning was about to fail.

And then John stepped forward, his rolling speech halted, and he drew a dagger over his forearm. The blood hit the chalk and for a long moment, nothing occurred. Only the wind howling outside and the scent of iron in the air. The light that formed in the center of the circle began as a small cyclone, twisting and writhing, building and building into a crescendo, and as John danced in glee and smiled until the edges of his mouth stretched unnaturally, something formed there.

It was a creature of light and wings and fire, and it roared with anguish when it realized it had been ripped from its realm. John said it was an angel and that we should be in awe, cowed before its presence. There are no such things as angels. But celestial beings exist, and they are terrifying in their brilliance. I know this now because a celestial is what John summoned, and the moment it began to speak, my heart filled with dread. Celestial makes one think of the stars scattered about the midnight sky, but stars are the oldest things in our universe, and they could not exist without great fortitude and great malice.

Nothing good or kind lasts forever. Only the darkest seeds bear fruit.

While I watched on in fascination and horror, John attempted to converse with the being. Conversation was not what the entity desired, and it beat its wings against the confines of the circle, a mad light in its eyes as it turned its attention from John to me.

When it reached out a hand, beseeching, I became struck by its beauty, its ferocity. Now, I realize it had sensed my weakness and pounced, but in the moment, all I saw was that golden light.

"Come to me," it said, its finger curled, beckoning. "I've not met one who can raise the dead."

"What use am I to you?" I asked, backing away despite John's screaming at me for daring to insult the being. As if my steps were an affront to it.

"Curiosity," it sang in my head. The scent of summer flowers filled my senses. It was teasing me, luring me in, with the scent of home, a place I dearly missed. "You needn't be tied to this man. You could become powerful, be one praised as the savior of families, of kingdoms. Imagine a statesman who cannot die, a queen who cannot be displaced. Imagine what someone might pay for that."

Memories surfaced - of cold nights with no fire, huddled together with my siblings; of stealing bread from the market, running until my legs gave out and I flinched at every shadow, waiting to be hauled away by guards; of the disarray of John's ancestral home, and how the roof leaked and the windows whistled as the winter winds whisked by.

I pushed away from the table I'd latched onto for support, walked back to stand before the being, and stared hard at it. "Tell me more," I thought toward it. When it smiled, all I saw were fangs.

Chapter Nine

ETHANIEL

The greatest trick Ethaniel had pulled off successfully, for his entire life, was hiding the fact that he was a Harkness, a true one. He'd brush people off if they commented on the name, saying, "Oh, I'm of no relation", and most of the time, that was enough.

He was able to do that until he met Aubrey Lavigne.

Aubrey had never judged Ethaniel for his ancestor's mistakes, and Ethaniel had appreciated that deeply. But he'd also not been fully truthful with Aubrey, and therein lay the rub. Even now, as he gently set the pattern primer down and turned to the judgment of those in the room, Ethaniel wondered if this was the correct path. Maybe he should have stayed in the shadows. But it was far too late for that now, and even so, he would have never let anyone dear to him come at risk.

Ethaniel locked eyes with Magnus, who was staring at him with wonder. Calix appeared confused, and Aubrey looked concerned, both of which were expected. But Ethaniel sensed Magnus *understood*.

"Truly spectacular," Magnus said, leaning over Calix, as if to examine Ethaniel. It made something deep in his belly squirm but Ethaniel held firm. "I thought the Harknesses had been banished to the recesses. Scattered and adrift after some absolutely rotten bits of magic early on in the century."

Ethaniel knew the stories, had heard them as clear as a warning bell when his father had told them. *You're a Harkness, boy. You can't stay here. They'll keep calling for you, now that they have Maria. Get to the city, stay with your uncle. Make the patterns your priority. Don't come back.*

What his father hadn't said was the loudest message - avoid the thin spaces. Thick, old forests. Large bodies of water. Places long held sacred by his father's kin and many others because of how malleable they were. But graveyards and cemeteries were at the top of that list, and for good reason.

"My father's family is full of dark magic practitioners," Ethaniel said, every word forced up through what felt like a mouth full of sand, "and as soon as they started reaching out to me when I was about fifteen, he moved us west, to prairieland surrounded by woods that were constantly being logged for timber. A place where thin spaces between realms couldn't survive or would be disrupted."

Ethaniel paused, taking stock of everyone's expressions, but all he saw was empathy. Calix's hand was on his knee and it was more than comfort; it was an anchor. Comfort was pleasant enough, but an anchor he could cling to in the desperate hours. So, he swallowed hard and took Calix's hand in his own before continuing. "The distance and the safety of the wide open helped, even though I often had nightmares about men in dark masks with feathers. But a few years later, when my sister, Maria, started showing signs of...preternatural inclinations, my father was ready to move again. He didn't get the chance to before she disappeared, so he sent me to live in the city, and that's roughly the same time Vincent came to the States from Spain."

"Did Vincent know about your family ties?" Calix asked.

Ethaniel nodded. God, he was suddenly exhausted and no wonder—the entire day had been one blur of hectic activity marred by fear. As Aubrey came to sit at his right side, Ethaniel let the other man's warmth envelop him, and when Aubrey's arm looped around his back, he gave in. "My mother would have told him," Ethaniel said as he tried to keep a bitter note out of his tone. "She once admitted to my father that she'd been drawn to him because of his patterning abilities and she wasn't quiet about her fascination with magic. I think quite a bit of it was tied to the fact that she had no magical talents herself. So, after my father left her, she'd clearly found someone else to latch onto, someone powerful enough for her. Vincent's no Harkness, but he has some abilities."

Calix cut his gaze over to where Lawton sat by the fire and his whole face went tense. Ethaniel heard the unspoken; Calix was surely thinking about how much Ethaniel's mother sounded like Lawton. But Calix didn't say anything and it left Ethaniel worrying for him all over again.

"You are a fascinating man, Ethaniel Harkness," Magnus said, "and apparently I need to amend my theory on magical bloodlines."

"I'm afraid to ask," Ethaniel muttered, which made Aubrey snort.

But Magnus was a cheeky bastard and only grinned. "A conversation for another time, surely. You saved our hides, and I think that deserves a drink before we start talking particulars."

"Or three," Aubrey replied.

Ethaniel let Aubrey get him to his feet, then offered a hand down to Calix, who took it with a grateful smile. "Actually, Magnus, if you don't mind," Ethaniel said as they all straightened their clothes and Calix began to sweep up the glass with a handkerchief, "I'd like to talk to Aubrey and Calix for a moment. Could you take Lawton to the kitchens?"

"You could be direct and say, 'Keep an eye on him'," Lawton replied, his tone oddly flat despite his words. "It's not as though I have grounds to be offended."

Ethaniel waited for Calix to nod, and Magnus, ever magnanimous, guided Lawton by the elbow out of the room and instantly began to regale the man with a *very* detailed retelling of the talk he'd just been to on evolution.

When they were gone, Ethaniel said, "I really don't wish to be in this room anymore."

"More than fair. Give me a moment." Aubrey strode over to the shattered windowpane, placed his hand upon it, and it soon began to glow a gentle blue. Ethaniel watched as the glass began to vibrate, almost rolling like an ocean wave under Aubrey's palm. The rain outside hadn't ceased but the thunder had, and the magic that was *Aubrey* coursed through him. It was exacting, a scrutinizing gaze he was so familiar with, but it held heat as well. Ethaniel closed his eyes and let it cover him, coat him, suffuse his very flesh in what felt like the golden rays of the sun. It was breathtaking. Beside him, Calix sucked in a breath and Ethaniel knew he felt it, too.

They were connected. Not permanently, if he had to guess, but bound by magic and circumstance and a bond that felt like the most important thing in the world in this moment. But even more to that point, the ugly truth was they hardly knew each other; their bond had been forged in fires most people never had to jump through. Would they still be the same on the other side? Or should he simply enjoy it for the time being and hope, at the end, that he still had their affections?

"I can hear you thinking," Aubrey said in his ear as Calix led them through a few halls and up a small flight of stairs to a fresh guest room. Calix's bedroom was larger by far, but it had been tousled and lived-in for a day and for Ethaniel, it reeked of memories and magic. The room Calix let them into, the door firmly shut behind them, was well-appointed, with a large four-post bed done in a near-black mahogany wood, the tassels of the throws and pillows like gold and oxblood-red confetti strewn about the top. The wallpaper complimented with a muted cranberry, and the desk on the far wall was the same wood as the bed.

But the view....

"I thought a change of scenery might be nice, and now with the moon out, you can see across all the fields," Calix said softly as Ethaniel went to the window, dragging Aubrey with him. Aubrey's touch was as grounding as ever, but there was an energy to him, like a current under Aubrey's skin, that made Ethaniel shut his eyes for a moment.

"It's lovely," Ethaniel said. He could feel them, knew they were there, but turning around right now was the hardest thing he'd ever done. And yet, he did. Turned to face whatever they might be thinking right now — about him, about what he'd done, who he was from and *what.*

Calix broke the silence, but not to admonish. Instead, he huffed out a sound a bit like a strangled laugh, then sat down hard on the bed. "I'm sorry, did you...Ethaniel, did you send those hellhounds back to their master?"

Ethaniel blinked in shock. "How did you know?"

Calix tapped the side of his head, dislodging some of the hair he'd been pushing out of his eyes. "I could...I could sense it. Not exactly what you did, but the *intention* behind it. And I saw this flash of their eyes, and there was something reflected in them..."

"A woman," Aubrey said as he sat down beside Calix. "Dark hair, blue eyes, red dress. Their summoner, if I were to guess."

Ethaniel nodded, only a little shocked. Their shared connection seemed to be growing stronger, and while they'd guessed it had been because of Convergence, or Talbot, or whoever the hell he or it was, who really knew? Magic was still an imperfect art at best, flinging paint about in the dark and hoping to make something pretty or even useful. There were plenty of magical scholars (he'd read many of them, and swiped books from Aubrey during their initial time together so he could keep more up to date on the theories). Ethaniel had spent enough time in bars patterners frequented to also learn from their chatter. People were always inventing new tools or toys utilizing magic, discovering old runes or writings.

Maybe what linked them was the book. It only made sense, even if it felt slightly mad.

"My father never knew it, but I..." Ethaniel cut off, tugged at his collar. "I'd been curious when the Harknesses sent their first letters, but my father had caught me writing them back. That's when he told me the depth of their misdeeds. But after Maria disappeared, I had to know. So, when I got to New York, I studied. I went to talks, I read books on the realms and the *demimonde*, I even learned the family history."

"You wanted to find your sister," Aubrey said softly, to which Ethaniel could only nod. "No one would say you were wrong for that."

"Even if the information I was absorbing was made of the darkness that likely took her?"

Calix rose from his seat to take Ethaniel by the hand, bringing him back so he stood before them. When Ethaniel looked down at them, he saw no judgment. Questions, certainly, but no judgment. "That information saved us today," Calix said softly as he ran his hand up Ethaniel's side. "You fought darkness with a tool.

The people after us use darkness for their own gains. You used it like you use patterning magic. You are far more skilled, Ethaniel, than either of us."

"I think he's far more skilled than both of us combined, and then some," Aubrey said as he stood as well.

Ethaniel was hemmed in between them, warm and safe and nearly delirious with exhaustion. Calix's touch was nearly undoing him, unspooling him like so much thread, while Aubrey's ran over his arm, up his shoulder, and then to his cheek. "Please don't say that," Ethaniel said, voice thick. "I didn't like having to use it."

"I know you didn't," Aubrey said immediately, voice as gentle as Ethaniel had ever heard.

Ethaniel looked over at Calix, who nodded and said, "And I trust both of you."

Ethaniel tried to smile, but all he could feel was that fear pounding against his ribs, making his heart beat too quickly. And worst of all, the exhilaration that had suffused his whole body when he'd turned the darkness against itself and sent the hellhounds back to their master, hungry for flesh.

It had almost been too easy.

"You have to promise me, both of you," Ethaniel said, his gaze flicking between them, "that you won't let me get carried away. That you'll —"

"That we'll keep you from the edge?" Aubrey asked, his fingers now pushed into Ethaniel's hair. A thrill went down Ethaniel's spine in spite of himself, in spite of the worry he'd crafted for himself. "Of course we will. But I know you, Ethaniel. It won't get that far. You are too kind of a man to ever be tempted. Or to turn out like Vincent."

Ethaniel turned to Calix, looking for something similar, hoping to see its truth written so clearly on Calix's boyish features, but what he got was a kiss. It was better than a promise.

The bodies pressed against him, the lips against his, made Ethaniel shut his eyes and groan softly, and that was all it took. Aubrey gently but firmly tipped Ethaniel's head back and pressed his lips to the hinge of Ethaniel's jaw, while Calix abandoned his mouth.

Ethaniel made a noise of protest, but Calix shushed him and said, "You've no room to complain when there are two people trying to thank you for your bravery."

Ethaniel felt Aubrey's smile against his skin and bit back one of his own. "You're both terrible," he said, meaning none of it.

While Calix tried to wrest his buttons from their fastenings, Ethaniel took the chance to run his hands over Aubrey's shoulder and down Calix's ribs. When Calix hissed and pulled back, everything ground to a halt.

"Were you injured?" Aubrey asked.

Calix winced but shook his head. "It was painful when the hellhounds were attacking the wards, but I assumed that was because they're tied to me."

But when Calix twisted his upper body, he sucked in another sharp breath. Ethaniel wasn't about to let him suffer, so he gently guided Calix to sit on the bed and together he and Aubrey helped Calix pull off his shirt.

The man's pale skin blossomed with dark purple bruises, their irregular edges wavering over his skin. It was only when Calix touched the slight dip at his hip did Ethaniel see what looked like teeth in the bruises.

"Calix," Ethaniel breathed, kneeling to get a better look. "I heard you in pain during the attack but I had no idea —"

"My mother always said the wards were tied to our blood, but I hadn't thought she meant that literally." Calix frowned, then dug around in his jacket pocket to hand over a small book to Aubrey. "And then there's this. Books seem to be a source of trouble for us."

And as Calix explained in full detail the conversation he had with a bit of his mother in that strange space behind the bookshelves, Ethaniel's heart sank even more. The *demimonde* was not unknown to him, but it was a place considered foul by his father and revered by the Harknesses. A place of great danger and temptation, or one of power and possibility. Of course, his family would want access to it; they were power-hungry monsters whose desire to sink their claws into any magical source was well-known in magical communities and scholarly circles. They were pariahs, but always somehow managed to wheedle their way into influence.

Aubrey carefully looked over the book before speaking. "We need more information," he said as he turned the book over in his hands. It was a simple thing, no larger than a journal, and as Aubrey examined it with his monocle, he continued. "It's definitely powerful, but the magic on it is weak right now. The way I see it, we have options. Which, rather strangely, was not the case when we rose this morning."

Ethaniel was flabbergasted. "You see potential in our situation?"

It was the little half-smile that told him Aubrey was up to something. The man's capacity to find new routes through old problems was stunning. "I do. We have Magnus. We have Talbot, who was known in his day as a practitioner of darker magics. Thankfully, we can trust Magnus and I'm certain Talbot will do everything in his power to lead us to what he wants. It helps to be ahead of someone trying to circumvent you." He cut his glass-green gaze to Ethaniel. "And we have a Harkness. On top of access to your mother, Calix, no matter her form. That's a lot of magical fortitude."

But Ethaniel didn't like it. He got to his feet, every step as if it were weighed down by cement, and when he stopped to stand before the window, he realized Aubrey was right. It wasn't a path he would have chosen, and he knew enough about his family's magical prowess to be afraid...but for them?

Ethaniel turned to look at them both. Calix was sitting on the edge of the bed, his bare torso bruised and his fingers twisting in his discarded shirt, beautiful and kind and so, so tortured. And Aubrey was beside him, intent on them both even as his gaze was on Ethaniel; even sitting there, Aubrey made his heart beat harder than it ever had in his life.

Ethaniel came back to them, his chest aching but his mind clear as he said, "What would you have me do?"

Calix gave him such a soft, vulnerable look, one of trust. The kind of trust Ethaniel wanted desperately and was terribly afraid of. "Stay steady with us, Ethaniel. We won't let the darkness take any of us. I promise."

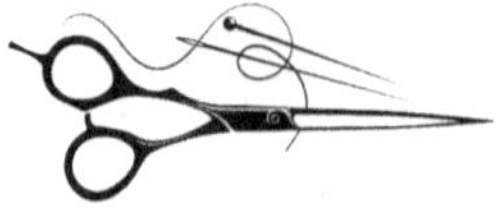

Magnus was proving to be as intelligent and resourceful as Aubrey had always said; the head of the Magnificus Collectio had bid them good night before setting off to write a letter to "an old friend nearby, someone who may be able to help us."

Richard had offered to stay in a room with Lawton for the night, leaving the three of them to climb into the bed of the red and gold guest room and finally try to sleep.

With Calix curled up at his side and Aubrey pressed against his back, Ethaniel let himself drift down in the thick blackness of sleep. As he closed his eyes, Ethaniel tried to slow his breathing, quiet his mind, but found himself holding tight to Calix instead of relaxing.

It was all so much. It was *too* much. And the one thing he swore he'd never do — lean into the power of his blood, let alone use it — weighed heavily on his mind.

Ethaniel shifted, ignoring the way the seams of his shirt scraped over his skin. It was clearly of fine make, for it had come from Calix's vast closet, but Ethaniel's nerves felt as though they were on *fire*. What if the power he'd reached for earlier, the power that had turned the hellhounds back on their master, was taking root? Would it happen that quickly?

Would he fall victim to the dirt-and-blood ways of the Harknesses? Would he become a grave vulture, hovering over the recently dead? Would he be able to hold onto himself?

Ethaniel's thoughts tumbled, a roil of worries and fears. He shifted again, but this time, a warm hand landed on his hip and squeezed.

"Quiet your thoughts," Aubrey said softly in his ear. He slipped his fingers under the hem of Ethaniel's shirt, the touch feather-light, his palm warm where it rested low on Ethaniel's belly. "Be here now."

Beside him, Calix tossed his head and sighed. "You'll wake him," Ethaniel whispered over his shoulder, rolling over just enough to see Aubrey's smirk. "Did you see him? His bruises, Aubrey…"

That hand left his hip to cup Ethaniel's chin, pulling him for a kiss. "I know," Aubrey said moments later, their mouths still so close. The temptation of Aubrey's lips, and the comfort of the entire wonderful, beautiful man, was right there for him to take.

If he had to be a little selfish, then so be it.

As carefully as he could, Ethaniel rolled over so he and Aubrey were face to face, and the moment he was on his other side, Aubrey kissed the breath from him. Their passions had been quiet of late, with the last few days feeling like painful eons, but Ethaniel knew Aubrey's hunger. It spoke through those lips sliding across his, hot and alive like the tongue in his mouth, and it used Aubrey's hands to mold Ethaniel's body into whatever Aubrey wished.

"Perhaps we should…take this to another room," Ethaniel panted in the scant moments he had between Aubrey's kisses. "I don't want to wake him."

"As if he's not seen it before," Aubrey murmured as he now loomed over Ethaniel, one hand planted on the pillow by his head.

Ethaniel could see down the loose neck of Aubrey's pale gray shirt, to where sparse hair dotted his chest and trailed further down to disappear below the waist of the soft trousers he'd borrowed from Richard. The sight of Aubrey's skin, the feel of his body pressed so close to his own, made Ethaniel suddenly dizzy with want.

Beside him, Calix rolled over to face them, but his eyes remained shut tight. Ethaniel thought for a moment the man might be trying to feign sleep…but was that so rotten a thing? Knowing Calix, if he were feigning sleep, it would be to give him and Aubrey a chance to *reconnect*, as it were. Their younger paramour, for all his station and wealth, was a uniquely soulful, unselfish man.

"Come," Aubrey said, slipping off the bed and extending a hand to Ethaniel. "If you're so distracted."

"Aubrey, no, it's not —"

But Aubrey was staring very seriously at him. It was a command Ethaniel was expected to follow. And if Ethaniel knew Aubrey, this was him asking for trust. For a chance to work on repairing their bond.

Ethaniel nodded and took Aubrey's hand. He didn't lead them far; Aubrey carefully backed his way through the room, his fingers wrapped tightly around Ethaniel's wrist.

"I knew as soon as I saw it," Aubrey whispered in his ear as he maneuvered them before the simple standing mirror in the corner, "and immediately I wanted."

The mirror didn't reflect much of the room; it was angled so it caught sight of the desk and wall behind them, but avoided any glare from the windows. Ethaniel gave him a questioning look, his expression reflected back in the pristine glass. "Wanted what?"

Aubrey hooked his chin over Ethaniel's shoulder and pressed a kiss to his cheek before replying. "Your trust. If I've earned any of it back, might I trade it in now?"

Aubrey pressed up against him, closing the space between them so tightly a slip of paper wouldn't fit there, and Ethaniel sucked in a breath. Aubrey's hardness rested on his lower back, a teasing touch that evaporated Ethaniel's will in an instant. God, Aubrey could play him like a fiddle and win against the devil with one simple tune, and he and Lucifer both would willingly follow in whatever dance Aubrey commanded from them.

"We're the only ones here," Aubrey whispered, his words dotted with kisses along Ethaniel's neck, his hands now tight on Ethaniel's hips. "I know your worries, Ethaniel. I do. Can I show you how much I believe in you? Your strength and your heart and all the wonderful things that make up who you are?"

Aubrey's words hit his soul and Ethaniel could only nod in return. "Very good," Aubrey purred in his ear as his fingers worked on the buttons of Ethaniel's pants. "Will you allow me to tell you what I see?"

Aubrey was a remarkable man. Ethaniel had known that from the moment they'd met. But what he realized as he watched Aubrey slowly pluck buttons from their holes and felt his touch lingering, sending sparks along his skin, was that Aubrey believed the same of him. That Ethaniel was remarkable. Special. And he wanted Ethaniel to know it, feel it, *believe it.*

The truth of it was a punch to his sternum, and as his breath left him in a gust, Aubrey's smirk turned into a soft smile. "Very good," Aubrey repeated. "I'm so glad you see it now."

Ethaniel shut his eyes and let Aubrey's touch ground him, the sweet, syrupy slowness of it, the gentle press of Aubrey's fingers into his flesh while his nails scraped trails along his sides, his hips.

"I always knew you and I were destined," Aubrey said, his tongue now tracing up Ethaniel's neck. Ethaniel had to slam a hand over his mouth to keep from moaning and waking Calix, earning him a nip to his earlobe. "Now, now. You and I can't connect if you don't watch me. Open your eyes, Ethaniel. Watch me take you apart."

It took effort, because Ethaniel wanted to melt against Aubrey and let him have his way, but Aubrey liked it when he obeyed. So, Ethaniel pried his eyes open and stared hard at their reflections. Aubrey, tall and proud and gorgeous behind him, his gaze sharp, his jawline even sharper, the angular planes of his face more perfect than any artist could create.

"You are so beautiful," Aubrey said, his voice slightly hoarse now. His words, his tone, rattled at Ethaniel's bars, shaking something loose in him he'd tucked away for so long. The last button on his pants was undone by Aubrey's clever fingers, and Aubrey shoved them down. "Can I see all of you?"

Ethaniel nodded, unable to speak, and Aubrey divested him of shirt and boxers, then added his own to the pile on the floor. When he came back to Ethaniel, naked and flushed, his green eyes gone dark with that hunger, Ethaniel gave himself over. Completely.

Behind them, somehow both distant and nearly in Ethaniel's ear, whispering right into his core, Calix sighed drowsily and flopped over onto his back.

"Does he...does he feel us?" Ethaniel asked, watching, enraptured, as Aubrey wrapped an arm around his middle, his hand resting over Ethaniel's furiously galloping heart. There was no shame or shyness in the way he stood before Aubrey, naked and hard and desperate. Aubrey wanted all of him. There was everything *right* about that.

How could something that felt so good be a sin?

"Perhaps," Aubrey said before yanking Ethaniel back with a vicious grin, "and if he does, then I can almost guarantee he feels how warm and sweet you are..."

Ethaniel nearly crumpled forward when Aubrey wrapped his free hand around his cock. "Fuck," he hissed, looking up. But Aubrey tutted at him, so Ethaniel forced his gaze back down. To watch. To watch Aubrey in the mirror, to watch his own face twist in pleasure as Aubrey began to stroke him.

He was on *fire*. He'd never wanted to burn so badly.

Ethaniel had no time or capacity to marvel at Aubrey's ability to do so many things at once. The coordination of the kisses he laid across Ethaniel's neck and shoulder timed with the easy strokes of his palm over his cock had Ethaniel writhing in pleasure, pushing back against Aubrey's hardness and angling his hips. A silent plea for anything Aubrey would give him.

"Behave," Aubrey admonished before setting his teeth in the meat of Ethaniel's shoulder. It made Ethaniel moan.

He was already such a *mess*. A whimpering puddle of flushed cheeks and twitching hips and aching core, begging for it. Ethaniel watched Aubrey raise an eyebrow, questioning, before sliding the hand over his heart higher. The heel of his palm now rested on Ethaniel's collarbone; his long fingers softly settled on Ethaniel's throat.

A promise to act only if Ethaniel asked, seeking permission for Ethaniel's trust.

Ethaniel nodded and Aubrey's smirk turned Cheshire. The fingers on his throat tightened ever so slightly. "So beautiful. So kind. So fucking *talented*," Aubrey said in his ear, his strokes now faster. Ethaniel's heart beat now with an urgency, his body bucking forward, chasing the pleasure of Aubrey's hand, begging for *more more more*. "I would have you like this every day, Ethaniel

Harkness. Desperate for me like I am for you. Moaning and sweating in my bed, under me, clinging to me, ripping the sheets from their moorings. I would bring you such pleasure, whenever you wanted. Do you know that? How much I desire you? Need you? I can taste you in my mouth like you never left, like we never parted, and all those months we weren't together, I pulled myself off thinking of you and your body and your brilliant heart —"

The flare of heat under Ethaniel's skin flashed, a bonfire set to roaring. He couldn't stop the moan that left his lips, nor his harsh whisper of Aubrey's name, and Aubrey groaned his assent – and his pleasure – into Ethaniel's neck. Aubrey's hips were set flush against Ethaniel's backside and Ethaniel badly wanted to thrust back, to give Aubrey something to grind against. But with no support other than Aubrey's strong arms around him, Ethaniel was helpless, washed along the tide of the pleasure Aubrey was pulling from him.

Aubrey's strokes sped up, his fist a tight channel for Ethaniel's cock, and Ethaniel was clinging to Aubrey, undoubtedly leaving indents along Aubrey's forearm. It didn't matter. It was all just flesh and sweat and incandescent pleasure, Aubrey's harsh breaths in his ear a rhythm Ethaniel chased with his own heartbeat and the stuttering thrusts of his hips.

"So good," Aubrey panted against Ethaniel's damp temple, "so beautiful. I would take my time with you every single day, unwind you until you were naught but unspooled yarn across the floor, then pick you back up and piece you together with my hands, my mouth, my body..."

"Aubrey. Fuck."

Aubrey traced Ethaniel's jaw with his tongue and Ethaniel had to look, to watch, as his lover (his partner, his other half, he'd always known it but now it was so *obvious*) locked eyes with him in the mirror. They were a sight, Ethaniel locked in place by Aubrey's strength, his body tight with desire, his hair falling in his eyes and sticking to his neck. He was controlled – *commanded* – by Aubrey. His body, his pleasure was at Aubrey's behest.

"Don't think," Aubrey whispered, voice strung tight with need. He'd worked his cock between the cleft of Ethaniel's cheeks, the friction a sweet drag that promised so much more if only Ethaniel could get Aubrey *inside him.*

"Next time, love," Aubrey said, each word a bite of promise and desire. "Take your pleasure now. Use me."

It unraveled Ethaniel, that desperation in Aubrey's voice, the lust beading on the broad chest and arms holding him in place. He did as Aubrey commanded and *let go,* spilling over Aubrey's fist with a gasp, vision whited out, his body one moment taut and the next limp in Aubrey's grasp.

Behind him, Aubrey moaned softly and his tight, controlled thrusts stuttered to a halt. Warmth spread over Ethaniel's skin and dripped onto the floor, loud despite their harsh breathing and soft groans.

"You are remarkable," Aubrey said after a long moment. He slowly let Ethaniel go, but didn't step away; instead, he gently turned Ethaniel around before sliding his palms along Ethaniel's jaw and kissing away what little breath he had left.

"Aubrey." Ethaniel was overwhelmed, too stunned and still-shuddering to put a sensible thought together. But from the look on Aubrey's face, he didn't need to. Aubrey understood what Ethaniel couldn't say.

Across the room, Calix groaned, then gasped, and fell quiet. They both turned to look at the younger man, who was now decadently sprawled across the large bed, shirt rucked up, pants pushed down, arms flung overhead. His limp cock was pressed against his thigh, and a streak of white speckled Calix's soft belly.

"Did he..." For once, Aubrey looked stunned.

Ethaniel could only laugh and tap the side of his head. "We're linked. It makes sense. Imagine what we just put him through."

Aubrey raised an eyebrow at that. "I certainly wouldn't mind." He held his hand up, examined it for a long moment, then locked eyes with Ethaniel as he licked Ethaniel's spend from his fingers. "The real thing is tenfold more glorious, though."

Once they'd cleaned up and settled back into bed, Calix immediately curled up between them, murmuring about how they'd woken him up and shrugging off their apologies with slow, drugged kisses.

"We should use this connection to our advantage," Ethaniel whispered over Calix's head. "There are rituals. We could try to strengthen it."

Aubrey nodded. "Family rituals?"

"Yes. They're not without danger –"

"No matter what we do, some danger is involved." Aubrey stroked Ethaniel's cheek with his fingers. The softness of his touch made Ethaniel shiver. "Sleep. We'll sort this out when there's daylight."

"And tea," Calix muttered, making them both laugh.

Chapter Ten

Morning greeted them with a gray exhaustion Aubrey could feel sinking into his bones. He usually slept hard after lustful exertions, but the lingering doubts and fears were plaguing his mind. Ethaniel and Calix were also dragging their feet the next morning, their soft steps and softer words of greeting the only real sounds as they all went through their ablutions.

They met Richard and Lawton in the dining room, where a simple, hearty spread awaited them. So did a pressed and neat Magnus, who looked every bit the head of a storied magical museum, even while wearing an apron over his deep navy suit and pouring coffee.

"I sent everyone home with pay," Richard said to them as they entered the dining room. "It didn't seem right, letting them all come back every day to who knows what."

Aubrey let out a silent breath of relief but didn't engage as Richard and Calix discussed how long it might be before the staff could come back (and while Calix tried to convince Richard once again to also stay far away). He let his gaze and his mind slip over to the question of the curly-haired man with a brand on his chest and a passenger in his mind. He trusted Lawton as much as he trusted Talbot, but trust wasn't entirely necessary when it came to using the tools at one's disposal.

While everyone began to eat, Magnus finally sat down across from Aubrey and said, "You and I need to go out into the field today, Aubrey."

Aubrey raised an eyebrow at that. "You want to leave the estate?"

"For a few hours, nothing terribly extravagant." Magnus dabbed at his mouth with a napkin. "I'd say we should all go but circumstances being what they are here, it's best we keep it to you and I. And the individual we need to speak to can be…well, peculiar. I'll explain on the way."

Magnus's surety struck Aubrey immediately; his supervisor wasn't normally the type to give commands in such a way. But he trusted Magnus, so Aubrey nodded and said, "If you think this person can assist us. You're certain they're not tied to the Order?"

Magnus actually laughed at that, hard enough to make the coffee in his cup slosh. "Oh, certainly not. Agrippa is of a singular mind and purpose, and it is in no way aligned with the Golden Order." Magnus shot a dark look toward Lawton, who wisely kept his eyes on his plate.

"Agrippa?" Ethaniel asked. "Like the physician?"

Magnus smiled at that. "The physician, the polymath, the legal scholar, and the occultist. Yes, that Agrippa. Frederich is a descendent. A truly fascinating person, but quite set in their ways. So I'm counting on our dear Aubrey here to charm them."

Aubrey's mind spun with possibilities. Magnus had never mentioned this Agrippa before, and he wasn't the secretive type. If this was something Magnus had kept close to the vest, there would certainly be a reason. "All right, but I won't leave this place until I'm certain the wards are solid. The possibility of harm is high enough when we're all behind locked doors and solid brick."

"I wouldn't have it any other way," Magnus replied. "And I think we should have a little chat with that book before we go. It's quite clear to me that the *demimonde* holds answers to all these problems, but walking through that particular door unprepared would spell disaster."

Silence hung over them for a long moment, hushed and gloomy. Calix was fiddling with his half-eaten eggs, pushing them around his plate. His face was wan and his spine a curve that made Aubrey's body ache in sympathy. And Ethaniel, always the supportive one, was busy running his hand up and down Calix's back. But watching Ethaniel and Calix turn toward each other, like flowers to the sun, only made Aubrey feel like they'd lost something. A chance for something – for peace, or comfort, or even the ability to live as they wanted.

All because of a damn book and the allure of a place no mortal should go. It seemed insane to keep pushing themselves with no end in sight. What if what waited for them was more pain? What if this tore apart the fragile, beautiful web the three of them had woven for themselves?

What if this book changed everything?

Aubrey finally spoke up, a rush of frustration rising like hot coals fanned into flame. "That fucking book. We've tried destroying it. We've tried negotiating with it. We've gotten nothing in return for all our troubles. And now we have a broken soul stuck in the body of an unwilling host, along with a fragment of a man trapped inside the book who clearly holds information wanted by a group with power and influence. I'm wondering why we don't simply throw it into the ocean and be done with the whole affair."

"That's certainly one solution," Lawton intoned, eyes still firmly stuck on his plate.

"We can't," Calix said, voice clogged with sadness. "We can't. My mother...if there's a way to bring her back..."

Ethaniel all but jumped up from the table and Aubrey had to put a steadying hand on his arm. "Calix, you can't be serious. That's...that's *necromancy.*" He waved a hand toward Lawton. "We have a big enough problem with this possession. But you can't...I didn't think you were going to go along with what your mother wants. My family did *horrible* things with their magic. Necromancy was only the beginning of that trail of sins."

"All magic is a tool in the right hands," Magnus interceded, seemingly unbothered by the rise in angst at the table. "Necromancy isn't inherently evil, just as protective wards aren't inherently good. Magic has no morality. It is simply a tool."

Aubrey let out a slow breath at that, but Magnus's words seemed to only inflame Ethaniel. "That's an incredibly irresponsible take," he shot back. "Centuries of using magic in human history and we still don't know where it comes from or even how to categorize it! Some things are simply not right, Magnus. Raising the dead is one of them. We might be able to separate Lily from Lawton, but the rest..." He trailed off before looking at Aubrey, his gaze pleading.

Aubrey hadn't meant for this to happen. Calix looked shocked at Ethaniel's impassioned words and he was gripping his fork so tightly, Aubrey feared the metal would bend and screech under the strain. He needed to bring their intensity down a notch. "I think we're all exhausted," he said as he placed a hand on Ethaniel's knee, "and tensions are high. Our priority should be securing the book and finding a way to sever the connection between Lily and Lawton."

"I would agree," Magnus said calmly, "but I'm not ruling out assisting Calix with bringing his mother back. She clearly went to quite a bit of trouble to secure as much of that path for us, and we might not need to rely on the *darker magics*, as Ethaniel refers to them." Magnus leaned over the table so he could look directly at Ethaniel, and said, "I understand where you're coming from. I do. My family has a fair share of magic users who let their thirst for knowledge lead them astray. But neither you nor I are beholden to the curse of our blood, young master Harkness. And imagine what the world might look like if we can bring Calix's mother back, so she might help him along his path to controlling his powers."

In one fell swoop, Aubrey's mentor and long-time friend had spoken aloud what this really boiled down to – saving Calix and preventing him from following in his mother's footsteps toward madness and death. Everything that had happened, from Calix's collision with Ethaniel only a few weeks back, to the apartment fire, the chase out of the city, and finally absconding to Rosehill– all of it was to help save Calix from a fate worse than death. A fate like his mother's. But now they only had more information, and more paths to choose from, instead of answers.

Calix's shaky breaths rattled in Aubrey's ears and with his heart beating far faster than he liked, he slowly got up from the table and said, "I'll be right back."

Talking was fine. Talking helped air out grievances and set plans into motion. But action pushed things along. Ethaniel would talk a problem to death, and

Aubrey sensed Calix was of a similar mind. What they needed was something more definitive than mere words.

Aubrey went to the secret drawer where Calix had stashed Convergence, unlocked the warding patterns overlaid on the wood, and plucked the book from its velvet blanket. The moment he did, Convergence was in his mind. He could feel Talbot's presence like a distant shadow, present but unobtrusive, and he pushed back with a show of force and magic to reinforce who was in charge.

The others here have questions, curator. Questions about their fates, as well as mine. They're only fragments, but fragments they will remain until someone releases them.

Aubrey had suspected as much. The strange, haphazard speech that had whispered into all of their minds wasn't merely Talbot's influence; his hypothesis might be true after all.

Test subjects, Talbot said. *From John, and others before. None of them are as strong as me, however. They don't have the clarity I do. They're mere whisps, floating on the gray lands –*

Aggravated, Aubrey pushed his magic back into the book, letting his frustration rise to the top and spill over. Power coursed through him, blue and brilliant, and he could feel the third eye on his forehead cracking open like a dragon waking from hibernation. His control was slipping, and he didn't mind. Perhaps that should frighten him.

Talbot growled something unintelligible, a beast cornered, and Aubrey smiled. *For once, do shut up,* he thought before turning the corner and returning to the dining room. But every chair was empty.

"We're in here," Ethaniel said from the doorway of the small parlor across the hall. "Things were getting testy and Magnus thought a change of scenery might be good. And Richard's out preparing the horses for your trip to wherever Magnus wishes to lead you."

Aubrey held the book up and Ethaniel nodded. "It's past time we set down some boundaries," he said before pulling Ethaniel close with his free arm and pressing their foreheads together. "I know," he whispered, mindful of the open door and Calix peering at them curiously. "We can figure this out. Remember who we're trying to save."

"Aubrey," Ethaniel whispered, "no matter what path we choose, there will be pain. Maybe from failure, maybe because of a lack of control." He swallowed hard and gripped Aubrey's arm harder. Ethaniel's brown eyes were intense, his mouth a grim line, and it made Aubrey ache to see him in such a state. "Promise me."

"Anything."

Another hard swallow. "Promise me what you did last night. I just need to hear it again…"

"I promise you," Aubrey began, but he stopped when another shadow joined theirs, another body pressed up against them. Calix was there with them, his hands shaking as he touched them both so gently. "I promise you, both of you, that I will be there every step of the way. That we won't work against each other, but with each other."

He felt their relief, their adoration, and their fears rise up, battering against his own, and it threatened to overwhelm him. Aubrey pushed it all back down. Their bond was fragile and new, but even spiderwebs freshly strung with morning dew could be incredibly resilient and beautiful.

"I like that metaphor," Calix whispered before he stared up at them. "Somehow I'm not surprised you're the poet in the group, Aubrey."

Aubrey chuckled at that. "I'm well-read, to be certain, but a poet? That's a tad too far."

Gently, he extricated himself from their embrace, hoping that by giving them a few moments to themselves, Ethaniel and Calix would take the chance. He met Magnus in the parlor, set the book down on the large table that now held a flurry of papers and notebooks, including Lily's journals, and sat down beside Lawton. The fire crackling in the hearth held no comfort for him, so Aubrey did what he could to appear far more steady than he felt–back straight, head held high, gaze imperious. Lawton was looking thoughtful and despondent at the same time and the way the man sat irked Aubrey. To be honest, everything about the man was more than irksome, but Aubrey could manage to be polite.

Lawton noticed him looking and graced Aubrey with a nod, so Aubrey approached. "Not to belabor the point," Aubrey said, "but this mess started because of you. I hope you're prepared to jump into the fray and help solve it. I'm casting aside the fact that you are still healing from a rather serious injury, since we both know that injury is from consequences of your actions. I'm not saying the Order should have resorted to torture, nor do I condone what they did. But your part in this may involve more than simply staying out of the way."

He watched Lawton's jaw work as he rolled around possible answers. Finally, Lawton looked him squarely in the eyes and nodded. "I'm aware. More than. I have some atoning to do. I never meant it to...I never meant any of this to happen, but it has, and I'll do what I can to help set it right." He shuddered suddenly and closed his eyes, his mouth going tight. Aubrey watched in horror as something *rippled* under Lawton's skin, traveling across his cheeks and down to wriggle and writhe until it disappeared into the collar of his shirt.

"Is that her?" Aubrey asked, pointing to Lawton's face.

"I...yes. She's restless." Lawton shifted in the chair, as if he'd sat on a tack. "She sees everything. Hears everything. And I don't have full control of my own body. It's disturbing."

"A vast understatement," Aubrey replied, but he couldn't help but lean in to take a closer look. Lawton was a pale man with hair like fire, and on further inspection, Aubrey saw strands of auburn in his orange-red hair. His lips looked fuller, too.

That cannot be a good sign, he thought as he straightened. Lawton seemed perturbed by his closeness, so putting space between them was wise. "Well, then, I'll keep my scolding to a minimum right now, since you seem to be dealing with your passenger." Aubrey pointed to Convergence and immediately, Talbot was trying to poke into his mind. *Little shit*, Aubrey thought viciously before he thrust magic back at Talbot, like an electrical shock from a poorly wired fixture, and the satisfying hiss Talbot let out almost made him chuckle.

"You need to talk to Calix," Aubrey said as he turned back to Lawton. "That's where you start. If Magnus and I are going out this afternoon, you have a prime opportunity."

"I know."

For whatever reason, Lawton's soft reply irked him. Aubrey was getting the sense that Lawton was saying he understood the severity of the situation he'd caused, but his words and tone lacked backbone. "Then a word of advice. Be very cautious how you go about apologizing. Calix has been through enough these last few weeks. He doesn't need you digging a finger into his wounds. Be honest, Lawton, for once in your life, and show some goddamn remorse."

Chastising done, Aubrey waited until Ethaniel and Calix came into the room. The flush on Calix's face had settled and Ethaniel's steps seemed more sure, so he took that to mean they'd come to some kind of agreement. He doubted this was the end of the tension, but the pathfinder in him didn't relinquish hope of finding another way forward. Their realm was full of magic not yet fully quantified or understood, and while he personally agreed with Magnus's line of thinking, he understood the pedestal on which Ethaniel stood.

When everyone was settled back in the parlor, Aubrey let the final strings of his power go slack. Holding power over a magical object was part and parcel for his work, but doing so on a *sentient* object left him feeling drained, as if he were losing something. Aubrey shook off the thought. They didn't need any more problems right now and his bodily weakness wasn't important. The exhaustion he felt deep in his bones was not unexpected, given what had transpired over the last few days.

With a rush of air cold enough to make them all shiver, Talbot's ghost image emerged. He looked the same as he had a few days prior, more hint of a human-type creature than something with distinct facial features. His long, sharp claws clung to the edge of the book, and where his eyes would be were twin points of flickering green flame.

Aubrey cast a look to Magnus, who was leaning forward, inspecting the figure closely. "Remarkable," Magnus uttered, "truly remarkable. Are you really Edward Talbot, John Dee's assistant?"

The head swiveled with a sickening lurch, so the makeshift eyes now faced Magnus. "Indeed. More myself now than before, though they still linger in the background, these ghosts of others trapped as I am." The twin flames in Talbot's visage flared brighter and Aubrey swore when he smiled, he saw fangs.

Magnus leaned closer, to the point where Aubrey put a cautioning hand on his mentor's arm. "Are you saying this is your prison? Who put you there? How did it happen?"

"So many questions," Talbot said, his words dripping with delight, like a criminal with the upper hand. The tone chilled Aubrey's bones, and yet some rational part of him knew there was nothing to fear.

Right?

When he glanced toward Ethaniel and Calix, Aubrey realized he wasn't alone in this strange, desolate place of anxiety. Calix had gone pale, his long fingers wrapped around Ethaniel's wrist in a way that, in another situation, might have been possessive or guiding. This was the tight-knuckled hold of someone teetering on the edge of an unknown, fearing if they took one wrong step, they'd plummet into the darkness. And Ethaniel's face was drawn tight, too. When Aubrey blinked and looked again, he swore he saw Ethaniel's face flicker with...*something*. A hint of bone white. The curve of an eye socket. The sharp hinge of a bare jaw.

Aubrey's heart sped up, his ears ringing.

And then it started. A whisper in his ear. No real words, only soft noise, like distant waves crashing against the shore. But something about the sound made Aubrey grimace and shrink away from Magnus and Talbot.

Talbot laughed. His claws clung to the edges of the book and he pushed forward against Aubrey's magic.

Into their world.

"Yes," Talbot hissed. "Yes. Give me more."

There was a shattering in Aubrey's mind, somehow both throbbing in time with his heart and sending his soul spiraling. His power flickered to life but it sparked and popped instead of flowing infinitely like it had since he was a small child. He could feel it surging forward to meet Talbot's strange energy, energy that was growing stronger.

He reached out, fingers trembling. He needed to touch it.

To converge.

"You promised me freedom," Talbot said, the words a whisper building and building into a crescendo louder than any symphony, any church bell tolling, any warning horn of a lighthouse before he would crash onto the rocks –

Magnus grabbed Aubrey's arm with a force far beyond his physicality and years. Aubrey saw Magnus's power, felt it snap over his skin and then dig in *deep*, cutting off Talbot's reach. Magnus took some of Aubrey with him as he amplified Aubrey's abilities to mend and heal, but there was a churning maelstrom at the core of his being. Aubrey felt as though his body was being pulled apart, stretched to infinity, to the ends of his abilities –

Magnus slammed the book shut and the blast of light was blinding.

When Aubrey's ears stopped ringing and he could see once more, no one in the room had moved save Lawton. He was now on his feet, his clothing rumpled and sweat beading on his brow, but his hands were steady as he held them above Convergence. Light danced across his fingers and dangled down, loose strings of golden energy. They twisted together to snap into a dome, one that encased Convergence where it sat on the table. Lawton was whispering something under his breath, snatches of an old language Aubrey faintly recognized. And as soon as Aubrey understood what was happening, he noticed the room was suffused with the scent of lavender and Aubrey swore he smelled hay and fresh grass as well.

But what broke his heart was watching Calix slip off the sofa to drop to his knees before Lawton and wrap his arms around the other man's legs while tears streamed down his face. Calix's sadness and loneliness beat against the back of Aubrey's eyes, thrummed in his head. It was all *so much*; to the point where he wondered if his seams would hold, or snap and leave him undone. He couldn't even find the energy or fortitude to move to comfort Calix, but Ethaniel managed to pry the younger man away from Lawton and lure him back to the sofa. Calix buried his face in Ethaniel's shirt.

Magnus was studying the entire tableau with an academic's eye as he softly said, "I thought we needed to use Talbot's knowledge to build our approach to the *demimonde*. But now I'm thinking otherwise." And his gaze lifted to Lawton.

Ethaniel spoke before Aubrey had a chance. "There has to be another way," he said. Aubrey could feel Ethaniel's turmoil roiling, buffeting against his own. "We can't rely on either of them."

"Rely? No, certainly not." Magnus tapped a finger against his chin, dark eyes snagged on the helpless look on Lawton's face. "But if I'm right, and I usually am, I'd wager Calix's mother knows quite a bit more about the *demimonde* than she's letting on." He waved a hand over the two journals of Lily's they'd spread out over the table. "We have pieces of a puzzle, gentlemen. But not the whole picture."

Aubrey raised an eyebrow at that; it was all he could manage while he fought to slow his racing heart. "I didn't bring you in to play the wizened guide, Magnus. But I'm grateful you're here."

Magnus scoffed at that. "Wizened, he says. Well, this *wizened guide* of yours says we should leave posthaste to see Agrippa. I'll explain more on the way, Aubrey, I promise. And while we're gone, I need our talented tailor to go through these two journals. The patterns Lily was laying down are incomplete, and from what she did manage to piece together, I can tell she was lacking knowledge of certain aspects. I think we can find those pieces. But you, Ethaniel, are the key."

Ethaniel looked at the journals like one might when trapped in a room with a snake. "I don't....I don't know if I can. The magic in that book is dark, darker than anything I've ever touched before. And the predilection of my family feels like it's lying on me like a shroud."

Oh, Ethaniel. You are so talented and yet so afraid of what you might become. You are so much more than your family's history and darkness.

When Ethaniel looked up at him, eyes shining with tears that refused to spill, Aubrey knew he'd been heard.

Slowly, quietly, Aubrey closed the journals, stacked them on the table, then pulled out the velvet bag containing his monocle and pressed it into Ethaniel's hand. "You are the only one I would trust with this," he whispered, "and we need answers. Please, Ethaniel. If not for me, for Calix. He needs us."

Ethaniel's breath rattled as it left him, but he nodded. "I'll do my best. But if I get any sense that these books will put us in danger, I won't push. I refuse to..." He trailed off, but Aubrey knew what went unsaid.

I refuse to follow in the terrifying wake of my family's legacy.

"Good man," Magnus said. "Aubrey? Shall we?"

"In a moment," Aubrey replied before going over to Calix, who had managed to curl his small frame into a large wingback chair. His face looked gaunt; his wrists too thin where he had pushed the sleeves of his shirt up. And he was staring at Lawton, who had all but collapsed to the floor in exhaustion, with a look torn between disdain and adoration.

Aubrey sank to his knees before Calix, took his clammy hands, and interlaced their fingers. "You, my dear Oracle, needn't do anything but stay by Ethaniel's side while we're gone. Let Lawton do what he must, but your priority right now is your own well-being. Physically, mentally, spiritually. Do you hear me, sweetheart?"

Waiting for Calix's answer felt like a moment and forever, but his voice was steadier than Aubrey expected. "I'm not leaving Ethaniel alone to unpuzzle the mysteries of my mother's research. I swear I won't. I would never."

"I know you wouldn't." Aubrey let go of Calix's hands only to cup his own around the other man's jaw and give him a good, hard look. He didn't want to leave the estate, fearful of what might arise in his absence, but he trusted Ethaniel and Calix to see through their task. And if he and Magnus were lucky, they'd come back with answers of their own.

"Be well, my dear earl," Aubrey said softly before swiftly kissing Calix and stepping away, lest he do something overly protective and borderline possessive like take Calix overseas and never let him near anything associated with his mother or Lawton ever again.

He and Magnus said their goodbyes and went out to the stables. Calix kept only a few horses, ones mostly used by the servants to cart goods back and forth from town, but any horse was faster than walking. The stables sat on the far south side of the estate, outside its imposing walls, so he and Magnus kept to the gravel paths that wound across the acreage, their shoes crunching against the pebbles.

Magnus was the first to speak. "Quite the predicament you've found yourself in."

Aubrey snorted at that. "And you jumped in right along with me."

"As if I'd leave you on your own to fight against anything, especially strange magic and unseen forces *and* a grimoire with a temperament like a hornet." Magnus ran a hand over his jacket, smoothing away wrinkles that didn't exist. "You do understand he's in grave danger, right?"

Aubrey stopped mid-step and heaved a sigh. He did, actually. There was a reason, many of them in fact, that Oracles were spoken of like long-lost deities. Feared, revered, reviled. As rare as the most precious of gems, and more dangerous than any storm. And most people didn't know they existed. They lived in worlds of occasional magic, meant for frivolity and never thought of as a tool. A purpose.

"Likely more than we can even grasp," Aubrey finally said. "And I hate it."

Magnus stared hard at him. "You're quite attached to someone you barely know. I won't harry you about this, but I won't stay quiet about my concern, Aubrey."

"I can't explain it –"

"AUBREY!"

The sound of shoes slipping on gravel, the pounding of feet, accompanied a bolt of fear that shot through Aubrey. Calix was running at them at full speed, his cheeks too pink, his brown eyes far too wide. Aubrey felt panic and fear...no, *terror*. Utterly overwhelming. Consuming.

He and Magnus parted on instinct and Calix dashed between them with a simple, bone-chilling two words.

"The horses!"

Aubrey was hit with a memory, the story Calix had told him, about when his precognition hadn't surfaced in time to save the horses he'd loved so much. *The screaming*, Calix had said with horror in his voice.

The screaming.

They screamed so much as they burned alive.

Aubrey whirled then gave chase. Maybe he yelled for Magnus, maybe he called out Calix's name. But the wind slapped at his face as he ran forward, hard and fast, and all he could hear was *the screaming.*

The screaming.

The screaming.

Chest heaving, his temples throbbing, Aubrey rounded the corner and came to a skidding stop before the large, well-kept stables. He could feel his eyes rolling in their sockets, trying to find the source of the noise that had taken up residence in his brain –

The screaming the screaming the screaming

– and when he blinked away sweat, or maybe they were tears, he could *see.*

The horses weren't screaming.

Calix was. Knees in the mud and hay, hands shaking, covered in blood *so much blood so much blood –*

– I told you there would be blood if you didn't let me free –

Calix raised his hands to Aubrey, his face a pale mask of shock and devastation. "What happened?" he cried, the words ripped from his throat as if he meant to tear his own vocal cords from their fleshy bindings. "What happened, Aubrey?"

Aubrey had no answer. The scene before him was inexplicable. Unexplainable. "Magus? Magnus!"

Magnus was at his side in a moment, panting with effort until he took in the sight of the horses torn limb from limb, the blood thick across the ground, the smell of offal and iron in the air. It was choking, that scent, and Aubrey had to drag a handkerchief from his pocket and hold it over his nose. Magnus seemed struck silent and could only stare as well.

The horses were a ghastly sight. Dismembered so brutally, eyes gouged out and presumably missing. But while he knew Calix would mourn the loss of those beautiful animals, it was Richard that would send him spiraling.

Richard was backed into the corner of an empty stable and gripping Calix's coat for all he was worth. His eyes, once a deep brown, were now only white orbs. *Sightless*, Aubrey thought even as he ran over, skirting the growing pool of blood (it was steaming, why was it *steaming*), and dropping to the ground beside Calix.

Aubrey immediately let his magic flare to life, searching for the cause of Richard's lost sight. He traced a sigil in the air, one he knew as well as his own body as many times as it had been drilled into him, and let the veil of his magic *drop*.

Healing was innate to his family, but for Aubrey, healing objects, repairing their frayed seams and shattered limbs, had been his calling. He *could* heal people, as he had with Lawton, as he had in the past. So, Aubrey remembered how that had felt, the joy, the freedom in it; realizing he hadn't been so completely not his father's son...and he felt that hot pulse once more, like blood running through his fingers.

His third eye cracked open, sleepy but indulgent, and a moment later, Aubrey was watching thin, snaking vines of sickly orange and green skate through Richard's body. Even the non-magical could be touched by magic's influence. Magic saturated the world through a thousand tiny cuts, and those with bigger, more destructive magics were feared...or respected. But the quiet ones, like him and Ethaniel, were the beating heart of magic. *Real magic.* And seeing Richard's tiny but bright magical center now poisoned, the heartbeat of it strange and unrhythmic?

Aubrey felt sick himself. And even more so, he could *smell* it, the foulness, like a festering wound. Someone had darkened the light inside this man, and had done so with malice. Panic started to well in his chest. He needed his books, he needed time, and he didn't have either of those things.

"It's some kind of poison," Aubrey said before running his tongue along the inside of his teeth. The poison's magic was foul enough to even bleed through to him. "It would have been done by someone very skilled in the darker arts of anatomy, or by a creature summoned here. I think Ethaniel would have sensed a summoning —"

"So would I," Magnus said from where he was crouched near the horses' remains, "so it was no otherworldly denizen. I'd stake my career on that."

Aubrey turned back to Richard. "Richard, can you hear me?"

Richard nodded, but tears were streaming down his cheeks, his sightless eyes unblinking. "I don't know what happened. The boy from town, Samuel, delivered a batch of hay this morning, so I brought it back to the house and started to saddle up the horses and then..." He shook his head. "It's dark after that."

Calix was gripping Richard's hands tightly, so tight Aubrey feared for Richard's circulation, so he carefully got them all standing. "We need to get you all inside. Magnus, do you have anything?"

"Just a moment." Magnus was now leaning so close to the remains that his long nose nearly touched what looked like part of an intestine. "I need a few samples."

Aubrey put one of Richard's arms through his and began to say, "All right, we're going back —"

The sight of Ethaniel running full speed at them stopped him in his tracks.

"My God, what happened?" Ethaniel asked as he charged up to the scene. "Aubrey? Calix?"

"We were attacked. Again." Aubrey craned his head to Calix. "Could you?"

"Of course." Ethaniel immediately began to run his hands over Calix, as if checking for wounds. His panicked alarm beat a tattoo under Aubrey's skin, making him flush around the collar. It was like suddenly stepping into a heated room after being in the cold all day, and the swing-shift of it made him dizzy for a moment.

"Aubrey?"

Ethaniel was looking at him, that panic twisting tighter, and Aubrey managed to nod and say, "Let's get inside."

The walk back into the house was quiet, and all Aubrey could think about was the poison leeching into Richard's system and the understanding that they weren't safe anywhere outside the walls of Rosehill.

INTERLUDE

You seem cowed, little cozener. Your fire is tamped down to a few pathetic embers. Why is that, I ask myself, when I can see you and your passenger's fervor?

Lawton shot upright in his chair, head on a swivel as he looked for the source. It wasn't Lily's voice, clear but weak and very feminine. This was…odd. Half-whispers that dove in and out, snatches of words that grated against the ethereal, vaguely sinister voice in his mind.

The book.

Of course.

In the frenzy of the last few minutes, the shouting and running about, Lawton had been left alone with the book. It was mere feet away, set on the large table nestled in the middle of the half-circle of sofas and chairs. Simply sitting there.

The very thing that had caused all of this to begin with. Well. How fortunate.

"Be mindful of it," Lily said to him as he kneeled on the floor, hands flat on the table on either side of the book's velvet-and-foil cover. "We need it. And it needs us. Who has the greater need is yet to be determined. Don't let it fool you, Lawton. We have the upper hand, but only because we've witnessed the chaos it can sow."

It was an odd thing to carry the spark of another soul in his body, but the longer Lily was with him, the more comfortable their arrangement became. He should have, by all rights, felt terribly violated. She'd taken advantage of his circumstance. Lawton touched the brand on his chest with a fingertip, tracing the ragged edges, feeling them snag and pull. It hurt, but in the way an old scar might ache with an oncoming storm.

No, Lily hadn't been the one to cause this problem, to make him feel as though he'd lost control of his own flesh. That was the fault of Vincent and the Golden Order. How could he blame the woman for stepping in to fill a void someone else had created?

"What should I do?" Lawton whispered.

What do you want to do? the voice from the book asked. *The world is full of possibilities. I can feel your ambition. Your desires. The desire for power, of course, but not just any type of power. Only the kind money and influence can bring.*

Lawton tensed at that. The voice wasn't wrong. But how did it know?

You assume me to be some magical artifact with a snippet of consciousness or intelligence tucked away, like a dormouse scurrying about the walls of a home. But this book is my prison, and I was put here by someone deeply jealous of my abilities.

The whispers swirled again. Broken. Frightening. And yet somewhere deep in his chest, Lawton couldn't help the convivial feeling that arose. Another being trapped, like him. He *knew* this book was the source of the calamity they'd been thrust into.

And yet.

"He's dangerous," Lily said to him. "But he has knowledge of the *demimonde.* Before my death, this man's work, and that of his master, held what I thought were the keys to the kingdom, so to speak. But patterns were never my specialty, and it took me years of work to decipher only a handful of pages."

Then Lily told him a tale about a man named Edward Talbot. A man who switched names as it pleased him, and as the situation warranted, so he might slip the chains of law and order when his petty thieving ways caught up to him. But then Talbot disappeared for a bit, only to return with great fanfare as he touted his services as a necromancer.

"He raised the freshly dead so estates might be settled. But Talbot sat in a strange no-man's land between those who deeply desired the use of his abilities, and those who thought him an abomination. So, he fled once more, and landed in the home of John Dee."

Like most people, Lawton knew a bit about Dee, but only the scandalous bits. The court mage to Queen Elizabeth I herself, Dee's talents for prognostication had been hotly debated when he was alive, and still were to the present day. Lawton had heard of how some students sat with Dee's papers and the snatches of journal entries in a strange language, spending days examining them with pink-cheeked fervor. But despite their academic celebrity today, Dee and Talbot had died in exile, shamed.

"Or did they?" Lily asked. Her eagerness was pressing on the boundaries of his mind and he found himself reaching out to the book once more. "It is supposition, but if Dee trapped Talbot in this book, there must have been a reason. It could be something we could use to our advantage. My son and the others spoke of part of Talbot's soul trapped inside. What if he is trapped, just like I am?"

Lawton felt her fingers digging into his brain, opening up his mind in a way that he'd never experience. It was if she had loosened bindings and for the first time, he was allowed to see it.

Magic.

His envy over Calix's abilities had waned over their years together as he saw Calix suffer the sensitivities, the headaches, the way nightmares hounded his footsteps. It had certainly left an indelible mark. But his jealousy was a thing renewed now, breathed back into glorious life as he saw what the world truly looked like.

Magic was in *everything*. It glowed and pulsed, tiny heartbeats glittering and throbbing and so, so beautiful he wanted to weep at the sight of it. The room he stood in, the house he stood in, was warded, yes, but the sheer breadth of the magic surrounding him left him feeling full. Whole.

"You see now," Lily said, so close, so intimate, as if she were standing behind him with a hand on his shoulder, "you see the beauty of it. These wards are my magic. They are tied to Calix as well. But the enemy is pressing against our gates, testing the strength of what I laid down years ago. At some point, it will fail. Everything I ask of you, Lawton, is to help Calix. I know you love him."

Lawton swallowed hard. He did love Calix. Some part of him burned to see Calix take up with another — *two others*, he reminded himself — but there were amends to be made. What if he could help them unravel the mysteries of this book, help bring Lily back, *and* help save Calix from the magic that would eventually drive him mad?

He'd never been one to linger with indecision.

Lawton reached inside the golden dome containing the book and, with a single finger, flipped it open. Immediately Talbot was there, clawed and fanged and staring up at him expectantly.

"You're trapped like she is?" he asked, still wary.

You know I am, Talbot hissed. *Though our circumstances are a tad different, it is the same desolate landscape where both our problems will be solved.*

"You both speak as if this *demimonde* is nigh unreachable," he replied.

Talbot seemed to shrug. *Not unreachable. Difficult, yes. The denizens who linger there do not suffer trespassers lightly, and there are guardians of other realms who patrol it. She ran up against a guardian. I can still see the stain on her, hear the strain in her voice.*

Lawton again touched the brand on his chest. "So, what do I do?"

"You wait," Lily replied. "You wait until Ethaniel begins his work, and then you use my knowledge to assist. You do everything you're told. That will let you save him, Lawton."

A clatter outside, footsteps and loud voices, had him looking up. *Withdraw for now*, Talbot said, and Lawton pulled away from the book, scrambling to get back into his seat and at the last moment, took one of Lily's journals with him. He should look like he was trying to help, because he was. Surely they wouldn't scold him for that.

"Stay vigilant, dear," Lily said softly. "Stay focused. Keep our goals at the forefront of your mind. And stay to the sidelines. I fully believe Calix will do everything in his power to find me, to bring me back, but he will need you. He doesn't know it yet, but he will."

Something tightened in Lawton's chest at that

As the others ran back inside with a bloodied, pale Richard slumped against Aubrey and Calix so worn Lawton worried he might faint, he knew it wasn't the time to interject. He stayed to the sidelines. He fetched hot water and towels as asked. He let Calix lean on him, and let that feeling buoy his own heart.

And he remembered to listen, to observe.

As the others eventually settled into a fitful afternoon of napping and quiet reading, Lawton let Lily take control for a bit, to let her pry open his mind once more so that the magic of the world could dazzle him again.

He'd always been a very good student, after all.

As night fell in a silent hush over the estate, he wandered. Dragged his fingertips over the rich wallpaper, along the edges of finely crafted chairs and tables. Let himself pull books from shelves and peruse them. There was a freedom in letting Lily reminisce, letting her drive his body for a bit. Every time she did, Lawton felt a little bit more from her. Her love and adoration for Calix was evident, bolstered by his own, but through her eyes and their connection, he saw more of Calix than he'd ever seen before.

There was freedom in it, yes, but also a deeper understanding of the man he'd called a friend for nearly two decades. When his own guilt and sadness threatened to creep in, Lily dashed it away with a hand.

"I could be angry at you, Lawton," she said as he sat in a chair next to the fire in the small parlor. "But you never meant to hurt Calix. You were wrong and you understand that now. You will do more than simply make up for past transgressions."

Lawton sighed and sank further into the chair. She began to recede, presumably to let him rest, and as he looked around the room and the discarded towels and bowl of slightly pink water long gone cold, he realized Lily's journals were still out.

So, he began to read.

FOLIO TWO:

RECKONING & RECLAMATION

"Even as a man ascending a steep mountain is lost to sight of his friends in the valley, so must the adept seem. They shall say: He is lost in the clouds. But he shall rejoice in the sunlight above them, and come to the eternal snows."

"Liber Porta Lucis" by Aleister Crowley, in The Holy Books, 40

CHAPTER ELEVEN

IT WAS NEVER A question of faith with John. He was a terribly devout man, the kind that lived and breathed and ate and shit his beliefs. They were intrinsic to his being, his existence. He believed so fully in his God, in angels and demons and minor saints and major sinners, that he never once doubted he was communicating with higher, holier beings.

The problem with belief is its blindness. Even learned men of science believe in a God at this time, and it disturbs me to watch them flit about with books of equations in one hand, and prayer scrolls in the other. "Well, why can't science have come from God?" they ask as their cheeks redden in indignation. And I refuse to argue my points, because it is pointless. They never hear the truth in my words, and continue about their lives in blissful ignorance. So be it.

I have come to this point of aggravation with John as well. No matter what I tell him, he refuses to hear the truth of it. Yes, angels and demons exist, but they are not beings made by God and Lucifer. These beings look this way because they are intelligent enough to contort their forms so we might believe what we see. Belief, again, is our death knell. We are led about by the nose by creatures not of this realm, but ones who are desperate to come to ours.

The first angel-like figure we summoned was beautiful and frightening at the same time. I heard it out, listening while John's fragile belief system fractured and he sat in the corner and rocked back and forth, a babe too old to be suckled but hungry for it still. For all his desires to see and speak with an "angel," the moment something looking like one appeared, John couldn't handle it.

I spoke with it instead. I recorded our conversation, and all subsequent conversations with the being, in one of my books. John eventually copied all of it into a book as well, which at the time seemed pointless. But I did find it odd that as my relationship with this otherworldly being strengthened, John's descent into madness began. He started to carry that little blue and silver book around with him at all times, muttering, talking, sometimes even singing hymns to no one in particular. But when he began to avoid my sessions with the being to barricade himself in his study — and not emerge until hours, or even a day later — is when I understood. Whether it was the appearance of the being, or something he'd uncovered during his solitary sessions with book and parchment and quill and patterns, something had broken John's mind.

His home, Mortlake, was never the same after that. But those tales are for pages deeper in, where they might hold both my rage and sorrow.

Ah, but the being. So beautiful. Golden and glowing, in fantastic robes of purple and gold. It wore a gold wreath on its head and had eyes so blue they made the ocean look dull. It told me its name was Lundrumguffa, but that was its true name in its world. On this plane of existence, it went by Uriel.

"But Uriel is the name of an angel in the Bible," I said, startled that it would so boldly proclaim such a thing.

But Uriel smiled with its sharp teeth and glittering eyes and sagely nodded. "So I am. And so shall I be. This is not my first time in your world, little necromancer. It will not be my last."

Over many nights, in the dark, in the quiet, Uriel and I spoke. John rarely included himself, and when he did, he kept a blindfold around his eyes, so the light of the being wouldn't "blind him". I could do nothing but scoff at that, but John was so far lost at this stage, what else was I to do?

And then one spring night, Uriel asked John a question that stunned us both. "What will you do with your book once it is finished, Master Dee?"

John's flush of guilt, and my pinched expression of confusion, only made Uriel laugh. "Do you know what it is he is working on, little necromancer?" Uriel's delight seemed to grow, to blossom and bloom, suffusing the air with a drunkenness I've never felt before or since. It was frightening. It was thrilling. And if I'd had the power of prognostication, as some Oracles do, I would have never let it get that far.

"It is a book unlike any other," Uriel continued, clapping its hands together, then weaving multi-jointed fingers together and wiggling them at us. "And it has a name. He named the book!"

I turned to John, stunned. Named books were dangerous. Even the most powerful of magic users didn't name their grimoires, lest the books take on their own properties or begin to awaken, to become conscious in our world. It was a thought that filled me with dread, and dreadful longing.

John began to weep, clutching his book tightly to his chest. "It has a name because it is everything!" he cried, despondent and sniffling. "It is my life's work!"

"But you didn't have to name it!" I cried back, horrified.

But John was insistent. Eventually, he divulged the name, much to my shock and Uriel's delight.

"I call it Aldaraia," he whispered. A penitent bit of harsh breath and a few words. How such small things could be the beginning of our destruction. Our downfall like that of Icarus, except we were never gifted wings. Only the right amount of information so we would walk willingly into oblivion.

"The word you mortals ascribe to the reading of the stars. How apt." Uriel's smile didn't abate and I began to wonder if it knew more.

I know now it did. Of course it did. It was a denizen of the demimonde, a harvester of magic and souls, preying on mortals who, like that ill-fated Icarus, flew too close to some greater, more fundamental truth, and perished because of their ambition.

What I did not know until it was too late that Uriel — angel, demon, otherworldly being of origin unknown? — was giving John exactly the information he needed to complete his patterns. Pages and pages of summoning patterns, to bring about creatures from all the realms. Power, in its purest form, at John Dee's fingertips. But the price was steep.

John paid that price happily. He fed Uriel small ones first. Dogs, birds, mice. When that didn't suffice, when Uriel refused John the answers he begged for, then John's obsession overtook him. The youngest house maid paid the price.

His stable boy.

The archivist John hired to document his library.

His own son.

All trapped in that book, all lending their life energies to John's madness, his magic.

And all the while, Uriel smiled with those fangs, those glittering eyes, and watched our destruction with outright glee.

—From the journals of Edward Talbot, Spring 1583

Chapter Twelve

CALIX

Another wounded friend.

Another plan gone awry.

Another piece of his heart shattered.

Calix's finely held control was slipping out of his grasp. They'd barely had a moment to *breathe*, let alone unravel the mysteries in which they were mired, and now Richard....

God, Richard.

Calix pressed his forehead into the wall, unable to watch through the doorway while Magnus and Aubrey wove magic around Richard. Magnus's power made Calix's skin prickle, so he used that excuse to step outside and try to refocus.

It was of no use. And he was starting to wonder what the point of all of this was. He'd held onto hope that, once he discovered his mother's plans, he could save her. Bring her back. Some part of him knew it was a risk, a large one, and that he'd have to make amends with Ethaniel's very blunt but understandable objections. He'd also held onto hope that in saving his mother, he could save Lawton. And after seeing the depth of his mother's plans, Calix had fully realized how deep her love went. She'd sacrificed everything in effort to save him, and in doing so, had doomed herself to a fate worse than death.

The dead he could mourn. How could he heal when a bit of his mother, the only person who had ever loved every piece of him, was trapped in a realm no mortal visited?

Calix lifted his head slowly when the door to Richard's room clicked shut. Magnus was headed down the stairs but Aubrey was at his side, looking more tired than even when they'd fled the city.

"He'll sleep for a good long while," Aubrey said softly as he gently steered Calix away from the door and down the hall. "Lawton's resting. Magnus is making contact with this Agrippa person, in hopes we can delay our trip. I'm not about to leave while the situation sits on the head of a pin."

Aubrey's hand on the small of his back was warm, a comfort when so little of that had been had of late. It made the deep, aching sadness in Calix's chest rise up, threatening to overflow. If he started to weep now, he'd never stop. Weeping would solve nothing, and he didn't have time to cave in on himself when the wolves – or hellhounds – were darkening his doorstep.

They needed to go on the offensive.

"I agree," Aubrey said as they entered the guest room they'd been using. "It's a bold move, but the only one I can see working in our favor right now."

Calix shivered. It was strange knowing the three of them could so easily pick up on each other's emotions and thoughts, like splinters of another's mind sticking into his own. It wasn't *invasive*, per se, but it was still uncomfortable.

Ethaniel was in the room already, sitting on the floor in the middle of the large Persian rug, bits of paper and several books scattered about in a semi-circle around him. He had a pencil stuck behind his ear and a smudge of ink on his cheek, and with his shirt half-open, Calix could see the lines of muscle in Ethaniel's chest shifting as he worked.

Ethaniel looked up and gave them a small smile. "How's the patient?"

"Resting. The same as we should be," Aubrey said as he crossed the room. He paused after a few steps and held out a hand in silent invitation. Calix took it, and Aubrey pulled him down to sit on Ethaniel's right, then he took up space on the left.

Calix took a moment to look over Ethaniel's work. Ethaniel must have felt him staring, because he held out one of his mother's journals and said, "I thought maybe there was a method in this madness. But it's just a mess of patterns that don't intersect. Most of them aren't even finished." He flipped to a page where a delicate drawing of a pattern resembling wide leaves had been sketched and then traced his finger up the lines. "Take this, for example. These lines are foundational for the command *expand*, which would normally be followed up with the object in which to expand. I use it as a mechanism to copy the same bit of embroidery, instead of creating it anew each time. But it then twists into this."

Calix watched as Ethaniel traced his finger down the lines that snaked and swirled, almost hypnotic in their dance across the page. "So, it's rubbish?" he asked. The pounding in his temples was starting to spread outward, encompassing the sides of his skull. His *hair* hurt.

The touch to the back of his neck left Calix shivering. His eyes fluttered shut, his lips parted, and he groaned in relief. Ethaniel only chuckled and said, "You should probably get some rest, like Aubrey suggested."

"Not while you two are up," Calix mumbled, but the sudden image of the plush guest bed with down covers and soft sheets turned his spine to liquid. He did need the rest. They all did.

Ethaniel sighed but didn't seem to have the energy to scold Calix, so instead he said, "It simply...doesn't make sense. And I can't help but feel as though I'm missing something." He kept rubbing the back of Calix's neck, humming in thought, and it lulled Calix into a drowsy state that felt *good*. For the first time in a while, he felt warm and safe and *connected*. To Ethaniel. To Aubrey. And even to his mother, who haunted these halls and the body of his former closest friend.

"Expand, expand," Ethaniel muttered. "What were you expanding? Why pair it with this bit that looks like a simple connector but doesn't produce a connection?" The touch to Calix's neck was now gone and Ethaniel lay back on the floor, pulling Calix with him. He obliged, mostly because being near Ethaniel was always a comfort but also because he wasn't about to let the man lay on the floor by himself.

Calix snuggled close, resting his head on Ethaniel's bicep. "I wonder if we'd get the truth from her if I asked her to explain what she was doing. We know she was trying to find a way to keep me safe as I grew older, but contacting entities from other realms and trying to bargain with them is so…antithetical to the person I knew as my mother." He sighed and shut his eyes, trying to be rational about this. They had a man possessed, another one gravely injured, threats at their door, and a book that seemed to be recognizing its own power as time passed.

And no real answers. No real understanding.

Finally, Aubrey spoke. "I have a rather…ludicrous idea."

Ethaniel snorted at that. "Here we go." He turned to look down at Calix, a slight smile tugging at his lips. "Aubrey might be the most rational, level-headed of us, but that also means when he comes up with ideas that stretch the limits, they tend to be quite spectacular. And yes, insane."

Aubrey had his head propped up in his hand as he lay on his side, putting him at a height advantage over Calix and Ethaniel. Calix could feel the man's energy—the intensity of it, the passion and intelligence. They were both so incredible, beautiful inside and out, and Calix was continuously stunned by their kindness and generosity.

"We could say the same about you, darling," Ethaniel whispered as he leaned down to press a kiss against Calix's lips. "You're incredible. With both of you at my side, I feel as though I can do anything."

Ethaniel's next kiss was tender and sweet, enough to make Calix wish to sink into the floor and sleep. He reached up to cup Ethaniel's jaw, but as soon as his fingertips brushed stubbled skin, pain flared in his hand. He hissed and pulled back, shaking his hand as if he'd been stung.

"Oh, my darling," Ethaniel said, leaning in to get a better look. "What happened?"

Calix found himself staring up at a skull, empty sockets mockingly sympathetic to his terror.

"Did you hurt yourself?" the skull asked, voice now hollow, rattling. The breath of the dead echoing across realm and dreamspace. All around them was a vast chasm of nothingness. Utter darkness.

Wickedly sharp teeth grinned at him, and when the thing unhinged its jaw, inside was a blackened tongue that darted out to lick Calix's across the cheek.

"So sweet. Tender. Your mother, mad as she was, knew you'd be eaten alive if you followed in her footsteps. She killed herself because she knew her failures well, and didn't want to stay around long enough to watch you succumb."

Calix shrank back, fear dousing his entire body with cold beyond description. He looked down at his hands and watched a blue tint wash over his skin. The same shade of blue as his mother's had been when they'd pulled her from the lake near the clearing. It rose quickly from his fingers to his forearms, then to his elbows, then up to disappear under his sleeves.

He stared up at the skull and immediately began to choke. But not with fear this time.

Water.

"Like the very water that she breathed in and let pull her under," the skull rasped as the thing's greedy fingers of bone clawed at his clothes. "I can give you salvation. Don't you want it? Don't you want to be in my arms, Calix?" The voice shifted and then it was like that of his mother's, sweet and alluring, and yet every sentence ended like the final drop of water wrung from a cloth.

"What if your fate was sealed the moment I gave birth to you?" The voice shifted again, back down into Ethaniel's slightly rough tone. "What if you're mine, no matter what? That more than magic and circumstance have brought us together. It's fate, sweet boy. Fate beyond our comprehension. Don't you want to be glorious in your magnificence?"

"You're not Ethaniel," Calix managed to say, shrinking even further back, scrambling away like a bug. "You're not."

"What if I am?" the skull asked. The being didn't move, but it didn't need to; its visage loomed, as dark and cold as anything he'd ever experienced. "What if this is my true face, pet? What if I cannot escape my family, just as you can't yours? What if I'm truly my mother's child?"

Calix blinked.

The skull was before once more, breath ghosting over his cheeks and carrying with it the scent of lavender and hay. "What if *you* are?"

While the skull talked, Calix tried to manifest his magic. Anything, anything to give him an edge so he might push away from this creature, or better yet, destroy it. He knew it wasn't Ethaniel or his mother–he *knew*. And while he'd never been haunted by the demons of nightmares to any great degree, he was also not a complete stranger to them. Occasionally, as his Oracle powers had grown, he'd hear bits of dead relatives float to him in that strange land between waking and death. He'd learned how to push them away, by words or force or magic. Magic was all he had right now.

The power built in him like a quiet warmth, and as the pressure in his chest grew, Calix had reached for his own power. What answered *burned*, a snap and pop of energy that he'd never felt before, but it was welcome against the cloying dark and the sensation of slowly drowning. It made him feel alive, slapped awake.

And when the skull asked that last question, Calix saw an opening.

He remembered his mother's words to him, the same ones he'd focused on when trying to save Aubrey and keep the door in his apartment from being torn to shreds while Ethaniel escaped with the book.

He closed his eyes and saw her face, whole and beautiful.

There's my boy. He could hear her now, even as his body fought the magic whipping through him. Even as the cold began to take him, and the skull laughed mockingly.

This world isn't safe for you.

You have the key, love.

Go back to the roses.

You'll know what to do.

You always have.

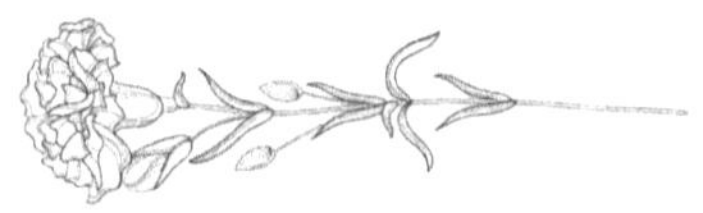

Calix awoke to the sound of glass shattering.

Across the room, silhouetted in darkness and surrounded by the glow of his magic, was Ethaniel. His arms were spread wide, palms to the ceiling, and above his right hand floated Convergence, its pages spread open. Above his left hand, twirling slightly as if they were dancing, were several large shards from a wine glass.

Something dark dripped down to the floor from between his fingers, and Calix saw dashes of red across the razor edges of glass.

"No!" he yelled as he dashed across the room. His limbs moved of their own accord, fueled by panic and fear and the hot lash of anger that Ethaniel would do such a thing —

The moment he reached Ethaniel, the door to the bedroom flew open and Calix was thrown back. He landed on the nearby sofa, the cushions taking most of the blow for him. Stunned, he looked up to see Aubrey, hand outstretched towards them.

"Calix, no," Aubrey said between harsh breaths. "You can't."

Aubrey circled Ethaniel to stand before him. Aubrey's clothes rippled with the wind whipping through the room. The wind carried with it the scent of blood and ozone and every hair on Calix's head prickled as he felt *something* split. There was a tear in the air, as if the seam of their reality had been sliced open by a scalpel.

Aubrey cried out in pain, but didn't reel away from Ethaniel. "I know you're in there, Ethaniel," Aubrey said. "Whatever has a hold on you now, you must free yourself. Come back to us."

Ethaniel's face, blank this entire time, now morphed into an expression of utter hate. There was no other word for the sheer venom of it. "I always knew there was so much kept from me," he spat, his voice nothing but the edge of a bloodied blade. "My father. Jeremiah. *You.* Everyone who ever told me I didn't dare tread that path of my mother's family. And look what you kept from me."

Something *slithered* out from that tear hovering between Ethaniel and Aubrey, making Aubrey reel back. Calix saw real fear on the man's face for the first time since they'd met, and his heart raced. If Ethaniel was opening a door to another realm, or the *demimonde*, this night would end in bloodshed and death.

The door slammed open once more and there stood Lawton. He was pale and sweating, but the strength with which he gripped the doorframe and the power that rippled from his body was not his own.

It's not the demimonde. Lawton looked over at Calix, a determined gleam in his eyes. Or in this case, his mother's eyes.

There are denizens there, monsters even. But that is not a door there, love. There's someone inside Ethaniel's head —

The thing poking out from the tear in reality whipped out at Aubrey, who threw his arm up to ward off the blow. Calix was already back on his feet, desperately reaching out with his own magic to try something, anything to help protect Aubrey.

He didn't need to. On Aubrey's arm was the outline of a glowing, golden shield, and the strange limb of viscous black energy bounced off it.

"Hold steady!" Lily, in Lawton's voice, yelled as she propelled Lawton forward, the ball of crackling power Lawton's hand growing.

The *thing* whipped out again, undeterred by Aubrey's magical barrier. Now Calix knew where he could help. Between the second and third strikes, he managed to push his way through the tempest of wind now pulling down paintings from the walls and upending furniture. And the moment he touched Aubrey's back, the third strike cracked Aubrey's shield and they stumbled back together, gasping.

But that moment of contact was all he needed. It was akin to being struck by Zeus himself, and as his body locked up, his mind *raced*. And with it came his magic. The connection he and Aubrey had established weeks ago, as they held off their attackers while Ethaniel escaped, answered his call. It sent him soaring, flying even higher than before, and Calix swore he could feel Aubrey's magic in his own body, connecting nerves and sinew and muscle, transforming them into a single being of twisting, sparking blue and purple energy.

As it built in him, he knew Aubrey felt it as well. The shield on his arm was no longer a simple, round thing, but a tower, a bulwark against the creature trying to force its way into their world.

And their combined efforts gave Lawton and Lily enough time to reach Ethaniel.

Lawton's narrow frame was bent nearly in half against the force of the wind, and his left cheek now bore a welt. But he, and Lily, never wavered. The moment Lawton laid a hand on Ethaniel's arm, the one holding Convergence, everything *stopped*.

The wind. The magic. The rift that was slowly opening in the room. Books and paintings and bits of furniture hung, motionless, in the air. But Calix could move and think, even if it was as if he were operating at half-pace.

Time had stopped.

At the center was Ethaniel, unblinking, while Lawton slammed the book shut, tossed it to the floor, and threw the ball of magic at it. The resulting burst of light stole Calix's sight and breath in one fell swoop.

And then everything snapped back into place.

Ethaniel was crumpled on the floor, hand bleeding, and Calix ran over. Panic clawed at his throat and all he could think was, *please no, not when I'd just found him, you can't do that to me,* in an unending loop during those few seconds it took to rush to Ethaniel's side.

Aubrey was there, too, practically upending the rug in his rush. Calix saw Aubrey's hands shaking as he reached out to check for Ethaniel's heartbeat and breath. Calix could see Ethaniel breathing, but he also saw the dark veins that skittered up the sides of his neck and across the backs of his hands.

The silence that built between them broke when Aubrey began to weep into his hands.

"I'm so sorry," Calix whispered again and again while holding Ethaniel's hand in his own, his other resting on Aubrey's leg. The pain on Aubrey's face, the dark veins on Ethaniel's body, and all the terror and torment of the last few weeks was simply too damn much. "I'm so sorry. I don't know how to fix this, but I know the Order will give chase if I take the book somewhere else. You and Ethaniel can go back to the city, you can pick up your lives, and Ethaniel can take care of his uncle and..."

Aubrey's cheeks were wet, but the hardness in his eyes betrayed his true feelings. The man had a backbone of unbending steel, and Calix saw it now, in all its glory. "Don't you dare," Aubrey said as he slowly straightened, not bothering to wipe the tears away. "Don't you dare say that. We wouldn't be here if we didn't believe in you and care for you. It would have been so easy to walk away from all of this, so simple to leave it all behind and wish you the best of luck. Vincent may have made this a family matter, and because Ethaniel is family to me, I'm not going anywhere. But you made it personal because we both fell in love with you so quickly. Because we care for you, Calix, and I know Ethaniel wouldn't mind me voicing that for the both of us."

Aubrey's hand touched Calix's cheek, turning his face to the left so they could stare into each other's eyes. "Do not doubt that for a moment."

The overwhelming sensation left in Aubrey's wake was something Calix had no words to describe. But he knew for certain that bringing up any plan that centered around him taking this on by himself was well put to bed. Aubrey would clearly hear none of it. An entire reality had shifted because of Aubrey's words and the emotions behind them.

Calix wasn't alone, and would never be again. He should have feared what that meant for the state of his heart, as soft as it was. But for once, he wasn't afraid.

Ethaniel slowly awoke and the dawning recognition of what he'd done showed on his face mere seconds later. Calix took him into his arms and let him cry — for what he'd done, what he'd lost, and what they'd gained. None of it was positive. And now Ethaniel's long-held fears were surfacing and all Calix and Aubrey could do was hold him and tell him he wasn't a monster. It snapped Calix in two to watch Ethaniel recede into himself, but the way Aubrey was looking at them made Calix confident they'd put up a united front to keep Ethaniel from losing too much of himself.

Vincent's war of attrition would not break them.

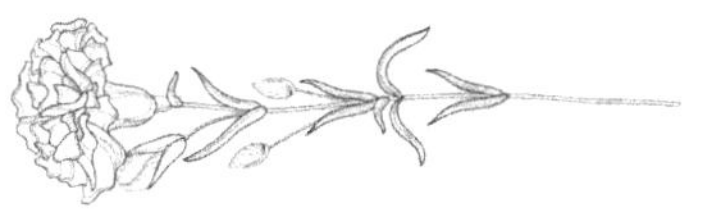

When things settled down and Magnus had been informed of the night's events, Calix finally managed to speak his mind. And this time, they didn't bar Lawton from the room, and Calix no longer feared the book or Talbot. He could fear his own mind and his dreams, but the book wasn't the culprit here. He'd known it as soon as he'd woken up.

"Someone was inside my dream. Twisting it to their own ends," Calix said as he watched Magnus perform a strange ritual with chalk and small polished stones around Convergence. The curator had said it was to dispel any errant blood magic, and Calix was fascinated. The man's magic was so effortless, as if he knew some secret not bestowed upon the rest of the arcana-wielding public. "But," he said, turning his attention back to the others, "I'm not sure who it was. I've had spirits, or I suppose bits of spirits, push into my slumbering mind in the past. It felt like that, but much more powerful."

Ethaniel was hesitant to meet Calix's gaze, and when he eventually did, the shame Calix saw there made his heart ache. "It was the same for me," he whispered, tugging the blanket around his shoulders tighter. "There was someone inside my mind, telling me I was weak to not use the tools at my disposal. That I would never live up to the family name, let alone be the one to clear away the tarnish if I didn't reach for what lay just below the surface."

Ethaniel held up his hands, turning them back and forth, examining the black-blue lines that were slowly fading. "I've never performed blood magic," he said softly, "and I never will again."

The statement felt like an anvil in the room, dropped from a spectacular height to crash into all of them below. But Calix understood. They'd both been unwittingly, unwillingly used by someone or something else.

"I can safely say it wasn't the book," Magnus suddenly said as he stood up and dusted bits of chalk from his trousers. "There are, as we suspected, other souls inside, but the book was merely the catalyst for whoever took over your minds." He pointed to the book, which now shimmered with red energy. To Calix, it felt like a warning. "I cannot shield dreams. I don't know that any of us can. But that one might know something. Talbot, or our resident possessor."

Lawton immediately shook his head. "I don't — she doesn't know how. Not against whatever it was." He went quiet for a moment, cocking his head as if listening. "Lily says keeping Ethaniel from completing the rift opening has drained her. That even if she could shield your minds, she wouldn't have the strength for it anytime soon."

"That puts all of us in much more danger, then," Aubrey said, his tone so matter-of-fact that Calix felt it whip across him like dry desert air. "We need another solution. Magnus, what about your mysterious Agrippa?"

Magnus frowned. "Unfortunately not. The realm of dreams is not studied very often, since it's one of the more dangerous lines of research. One must spend a lot of time in the minds of others in order to do so. Being linked to one person, let alone several, is tricky at best."

Calix felt a pang of panic go through him. "But we can hear each other's thoughts, feel each other's intentions sometimes. Surely it's not dangerous?"

Magnus sat down in the sole empty chair with a hard sigh. "I don't have answers for you on that, my young earl. There are so many aspects and facets of magic we don't yet understand. Every new endeavor, every new dive into a space where no research has been conducted, comes with great risk." He pointed to Convergence, which was bundled up once more in a dampening cloth made of dark blue velvet. "But I know someone who did the work centuries ago. I've read enough of Dee's papers to know Talbot was involved."

The room fell silent again, and with the silence came a kind of clarity.

Talbot might have the knowledge they needed, but it would want its freedom in return. That had been the plan originally, and it had been foiled through sheer bad luck. But now they understood the quagmire into which they'd trodden. If it was their safety up against a potential risk of what Talbot might do if they were to restore him to some semblance of life, versus handing Talbot over to the Golden Order?

"I agree," Ethaniel said quietly, making Magnus give him an odd look. "Calix was thinking about our best and worst case scenario here. And you're right. I need to put aside my fears and we need to use the tools at our disposal. So, I'd rather do that sooner than later."

Aubrey could only stare at both of them. "I'm not sure I'm hearing this correctly," he said. "The two of you want to pick the devil we know?"

Ethaniel reached up to run the back of his hand over Aubrey's cheek. "Don't act so surprised, darling. For once, I'm trying to not be so terrified that one slip could ruin me. I already did that tonight, not of my own volition, and we're all still alive. I spent *years*, decades even, fearing the worst if I were to put one toe out of line. And what good did that do me, other than take years off my life and put gray in my hair?" He turned to Calix, eyes blazing, but Calix could feel the pulse of his sadness speed up, crest, then slow down again. As if he were trying to keep his emotions in check. "I'm scared of what just happened and what it means. But I can swallow my fear if I have you two."

Ethaniel was going to shatter his heart. Calix knew that as sure as he knew they would survive this, but might not be the same on the other side. Ethaniel was already shifting, trying to adjust his reality and truth to make room for the utterly unpredictable. To open his heart and mind to the dark corners where shadows of his past, and his family's, lingered.

Calix bit his lip; then, decision made, he joined Aubrey and Ethaniel on the couch that was already too small for two people, let alone three. "I like the gray," he said softly, touching the hair near Ethaniel's temple. The resulting flush that spread across Ethaniel's face nearly melted Calix's heart. "And I agree."

Calix turned to Aubrey, who nodded, then to Magnus. "In the morning. None of us got any rest tonight. Maybe if we sleep in shifts?"

Magnus pulled a small vial out of his jacket pocket and held it up. The liquid inside looked like mercury. "I use this to help me sleep. It's nothing terribly powerful, but I think it could be a temporary solution." He passed the vial to Calix with a warning. "Only a small sip. Too much and you'll be out for days."

Calix drank, then Ethaniel, but Aubrey demurred. "I want one of us up and ready, just in case," Aubrey said, "and I won't hear any protests. That will give Magnus and me a chance to work on your mother's journals, Calix. I'll sleep when you're done resting. No sooner."

Calix knew there was no talking Aubrey out of a plan, particularly one of his own making. He and Ethaniel curled up on the bed together and the moment his head hit the pillow, sleep pulled at him, enticing Calix to sink down and in.

"We'll be here when you wake," Aubrey said, and Calix shut his eyes, trusting that was true.

INTERLUDE

Vincent

"What do you mean you hit a wall?"

Isme only stared at him, her glare punctuated by the tiny creature on her shoulder snarling at him. It had no eyes or nose, only a mouth full of jagged fangs and a smooth gray stone half-moon where the rest of its face should be. In the open space of the half-moon was a void, black as night. Vincent shifted his gaze away immediately; staring at the creature would make it feel threatened, and he did not want to deal with an *ithliq* chewing on his hand right now. If he blasted the thing to bits, Isme would raise hell. Also something he didn't want to deal with.

Finally, Isme graced him with an answer. "As I said, I hit a wall. The boy's mind is protected in a way I've never encountered. I wasn't able to fully penetrate his dreams, but I've seen enough." And then she fell silent again, her smile expectant. Because she knew he'd want that information, and she would only give it up for the right price. Clearly the little demon on her shoulder wasn't enough payment.

Few people would dare challenge *him*, but Isme had always been a different breed of Harkness. Ethaniel's sister, Maria, likely would have been of similar stock, but she'd disappeared before Vincent and the rest of the family could scoop her up off the doorstep of the rundown shack she was being raised in. Disgraceful enough for any child, but for one with a touch of magic in them – magic that could pierce through dreams and shift reality – it was wholly unimaginable. She may not have been Vincent's own blood, but he liked to think he would have been a good father figure to such a child.

With a sigh borne from long suffering of greater fools and lesser sins, Vincent clasped his hands behind his back and said, "What's your price for the rest of the information?"

Isme smiled, Cheshire-slow, and Vincent caught sight of her teeth. She'd filed them into points years ago, as a way to keep creatures like *ithliq* in line once they were in this realm. *They're like chimpanzees*, she'd said at a family dinner years ago, as they'd watched her first pet *ithliq* tear into a raw steak, *if you're going to smile at them, it better be because you're the bigger, meaner one.*

"I want the book when you're done with it. Once you've extracted information on the *demimonde* from it, I want what's left. Those little bits of souls trapped within. I doubt they'd make half a person all put together, but I want them."

The *ithliq* snarled again and she smiled at it, a parent to a child. Vincent couldn't help but be amused at her taciturn affections. "And if extracting the information from Talbot destroys the book? I have yet to determine if Talbot is merely keeping mum on the subject of the realms, or if Dee did something to keep him from accessing that information."

Isme hissed and in a blur of movement, she was suddenly before him. Her brown eyes had gone yellow, the pupils split vertically, her gaze boring a hole in him. They were playing a game of dominance, and he had no doubt he'd win, but Isme always seemed to get what she wanted anyways. It was one of the reasons he kept paying her.

"Then I want what's in that boy's mind," she said quietly. "Whatever is locked away there smells like the *demimonde*. Like dust and death and hope all at once, and I *want it*."

"He's an Oracle," Vincent warned, keeping his eyes on her. He'd let one hand drop to his side; his fingers curled in the first sigil of summoning. He wasn't about to get caught unaware and unarmed. "He won't be easy to keep contained."

She was still smiling. "Let me worry about that. Not all of us use blackmail and idle threats to keep our pets in line." Isme reached up to chuck the *ithliq* under the chin like one would a common house cat.

He could give up the earl. Batherton would make a nice trophy, but he wasn't the end goal here. Reaching the *demimonde*, finding the doors to other realms, and bringing their secrets back was worth more than the ridiculous amount of money he could charge for that information. Like so many before him, Vincent wanted *power*. But he knew his motivation, and that put him a head above the rest. He was no Feste, no Falstaff. Kingdoms meant nothing to him.

Real power was being able to wield the arcana of the realms and shift entire *realities*. He'd struggled for years to find a substitute for Maria after her disappearance, but she was once in a lifetime, a millennia. There was always another way.

Getting his half-brother to finally recognize what he'd been missing out on was key as well. But Isme had already laid the groundwork, pushing into Ethaniel's dreams as well and surfacing the magic he'd long buried. Blood was blood, and there was no vessel or spell or ritual that could contain the riot that was Harkness magic.

Ethaniel would see. He would. And Vincent would no longer need to seethe over how his half-brother, who had captured his mother's heart even an ocean away and a decade removed from sight, was not at his side. Not teaching him, guiding him, advising him in all the ways a brother should. No, once Ethaniel saw how much power his blood held, he would desire the world, just as Vincent did. And together, *together*, they would change everything.

"We have an accord," Vincent said. He quickly drew a binding sigil, laid his palm against it, and waited for Isme to do the same. The moment their magical contract was sealed, Vincent felt something in his chest *snap* into place. He couldn't help but smile at the sensation.

"Have fun with your half-brother," Isme said, her voice too high and flighty all of a sudden. Like a child who had just received their most-wished-for gift. "And don't say I didn't warn you. He won't come easily."

"No, he won't," Vincent said quietly as she opened a portal and disappeared. "But he *will* come. He won't be able to stop himself."

Chapter Thirteen

ETHANIEL

Ethaniel's dreams were peaceful this time, save for the chant flowing through his subconscious. The words Calix had relayed to them, his mother's message.

Go back to the roses.

You'll know what to do.

You always have.

Calix's mother seemed to like puzzles. The massive rose garden, dry and brown as winter lingered on the edges this far north, might hold a key. He and Aubrey needed to take Calix out there and see what they could find. But it felt like a fool's errand.

He should have dreamt of darkness and pain and blood, not the ghostly words of a dead woman whose soul, or part of it, was trapped in the cad known as Lawton Adler. They'd cast their own Greek tragedy with Calix at the center, and Ethaniel worried none of this would end well.

Lily Addington's words rolled around in his mind as he slowly opened his eyes and stared at the ceiling. Calix was curled up beside him, soft lips parted, his skin warm, his hair soft between Ethaniel's fingers. He knew he could wake Calix and lose himself in the other man for a short time; there would be time enough to push the thought of what he'd done down to the very bottom of his emotions, to the bottom of any understanding.

The problem was he *did* understand what he'd done. He'd fallen victim, unwittingly or not, to one of Vincent's schemes. The being who had pushed into his dreams had done the same to Calix, and Ethaniel was very aware that one

of his extended family had been the culprit. The magic had stank of Harkness
- hearthfire and moss and long decaying things. Necromancy and blood magic,
and at its center, a dreamer. One could find clusters of Harknesses all over the
world, and Ethaniel had long lost track of the names and locations.

And ultimately, it didn't matter who the dreamer was. What mattered was
protecting their minds from further invasion, and it seemed the only tool at their
disposal was a man who had once walked the path of a dreamer long ago. So back
they went to necromancy and blood magic and the world and word of Edward
Talbot.

That fucking book.

"Ethaniel?"

A warm hand, then a long arm, slid across Ethaniel's stomach, coming to rest
there with a weight that made him sigh. If he looked at Calix right now, the guilt
would swell so high he feared he'd never come back down. But if he didn't, he
would hurt the other man and that thought made Ethaniel's heart ache. So, he
turned his head to find Calix staring sleepily at him.

Calix smiled, and it was a genuine, heartfelt thing. Ethaniel put his bandaged
hand over Calix's, the sting of freshly torn flesh oddly welcome through the
turmoil in his mind. "You truly are something," he murmured, moving closer.

Calix furrowed his brow at that. "What do you mean?"

"So much danger. Hardly a chance to rest. And yet you still smile at me as if
you and I and Aubrey were holed up somewhere safe and lovely. Like the Spanish
coast." Ethaniel turned on his side so he could prop his head in his good hand
and let his other rest on Calix's chest. Calix went a tad wide-eyed at his proximity,
and it sent a tendril of pleasure arcing through Ethaniel's body. "I went once, to
visit my mother's family. Distant aunts and cousins. The whole neighborhood
was tight knit, so when my mother threw a party, everyone showed up, blood or
not."

His mother's face floated before him, pretty and vibrant, with the trademark
family nose. She'd never taken his father's last name, adamant that the Harkness
matriarchy stay alive and well. Thinking of her like this felt like an anvil on his

chest, and it was hard to let those thoughts scatter when their reality was so dire. But he did it anyway. Peace was a rather rare commodity in this house.

"I've not been," Calix replied. "I've never been further east than England. Which seems a shame, now that I think about it."

"It's beautiful there. Vivid sunrises and sunsets. Fruit you can pluck right off the trees. The air smells like salt and sand and wine and everything is so bright and bold, it dazzles the eyes." Ethaniel drew a finger down Calix's shirt. It was sadly devoid of adornment or embroidery. "I modeled my first patterns off the bougainvillea vines that grow on the houses. The house might be a tiny thing, but it would be absolutely covered in red and pink flowers and these deep green vines. I picked them every day, wore them in my hair and let their petals slip over my fingertips like silk..."

When Ethaniel thumbed at Calix's lip, Calix gasped and Ethaniel swore he felt the other man shudder. It was a good look on him, enhancing Calix's natural beauty with the headiness of all the ways they'd yet to explore each other.

And then Calix slammed his eyes closed and turned away. Barely an inch, but it was enough. Ethaniel felt rejection pang through him, even as Calix said, "It's not that. Not at all. I *want*...but with Richard in the state he is, and just down the hall, it feels inconsiderate at best."

Ethaniel nodded. He didn't move away, nor did Calix seem to want that, so he held Calix close, their limbs intertwined. "I understand. Of course. Have you seen him yet?"

"No." Calix's grip on Ethaniel tightened. "Magnus said he gave Richard something to keep him asleep for a long while. I know those who lose their sight can maneuver with little difficulty once they've practiced it, but this isn't some blindness made of illness or bodily weakness. It's magical. It must be. The outer grounds aren't warded, anyone could have snuck up to him and..."

Calix paused, then sat up so abruptly, he nearly yanked Ethanial along with him. "Calix? What —?"

Calix turned to him, suddenly frantic. "Did we check Richard for needle marks? Remember, at the bathhouse? It was likely that attendant who left the stinger for me to find and prick myself on. What if Vincent's tried that trick again?"

"Shit." But Ethaniel was up on his feet, too, and following a harried Calix down the hallway, shouting for Aubrey and Magnus as he went. Heavy footfalls echoed against the lushly wallpapered walls, and the magical sconces flickered as if in response.

Calix was already at Richard's bedside, and Ethaniel noticed he kept his gaze away from Richard's face. There was a soft cloth over Richard's eyes, in case the light was too much for him when he woke. Calix took Richard's pale hand in his, not looking toward the door when Aubrey and Magnus followed in behind Ethaniel.

Ethaniel quickly explained Calix's idea, which made Aubrey worry his lip between his teeth. "I hate to prod the poor man while he's...like this," Aubrey said.

"We must. Stingers and other tools of dark magic tend to leave more than a few pinpricks behind," Magnus replied while taking a seat on the other side of the bed. "Calix, help me?"

With careful hands, Calix and Magnus checked Richard's arms and shoulders, down past his collarbone; and when Richard's loose shirt stopped their pursuit, Calix leaned in to whisper something Ethaniel couldn't catch. He turned to Aubrey, his head pounding and his heart practically ripped in two, and said, "I have a horrible feeling."

Aubrey laid his arm over Ethaniel's shoulders, pulling him close. Aubrey was a furnace on good days, and today his warmth felt like a balm across Ethaniel's aching body. "About anything specific? Or about this entire situation?"

When Ethaniel looked up at him, Aubrey reflected nothing back but genuine worry, but worry focused through adoration. And that, more than anything, ripped him open. "All of it. But..." He looked away and Aubrey tightening his grip only made Ethaniel want to whirl away. He should want to be with Aubrey, with Calix, and yet their proximity somehow made it worse.

Guilt.

Guilt over what had just occurred. Over what he nearly did. Over getting them into this mess to begin with, by pulling Calix into his sphere. By not sussing out Vincent's involvement sooner.

Guilt, guilt, guilt. A pot overflowing with it. The air rife with the stench of burned dreams and lost opportunities. And now he was watching a man be disassembled, button by button, as the consequences of his failures were thrust into the harsh light of day.

Aubrey hissed but didn't pull away. "Ethaniel, I forbid it," he said, voice low so the others might not hear. "I forbid you to think that way."

Ethaniel scoffed, but it carried no heat. "Forbid me? I didn't think you were keen on fool's errands, Aubrey."

"You are *not at fault.*" Every word was a blow to his ribs, his heart. Couldn't Aubrey see? Surely he *knew* Ethaniel had been the instigator in this. Surely.

"I said stop." Aubrey's voice carried now, and the others look at them with questions on their faces, written plain as day. "Well, if you won't..." Aubrey turned to Calix and Magnus and said, "Ethaniel here believes he is at fault for our predicament. I say it's utter bullshit."

"Agreed," Magnus said smoothly, even as Ethaniel's face burned with the sudden attention. "And to elaborate on Aubrey's point with the bluntness of an outsider, such thinking will surely get in the way of your ability to help solve this situation. You cannot do that to yourself, Ethaniel, but more importantly, you cannot do that to them. You have a responsibility to see your brother's plans stopped. What use are you to the others if you cannot leave these thoughts behind?"

The truth of what Magnus was laying bare before him gave Ethaniel a woozy sense of *deja vu.* As if he'd been here before, in this very spot, standing before a reflection of himself that he didn't have to face and yet had it held up for examination anyways.

He had been here before.

"Look at what you are!" Vincent yelled. "You're a Harkness, Ethaniel! No amount of mundane lumberjack blood is going to wipe away that truth! Any drop of

Harkness is like power condensed. You are as capable of escaping that truth as you are likely to fly simply by stepping off a building. Your truth lies beating through your heart, pounding through your veins, and making your patterning possible! Take the chance, Ethaniel. Stay at your mother's or don't, but you cannot escape this."

"Magnus," Aubrey bit out, but Ethaniel waved him off, his words thick with emotion, but he shed no tears. It was past time for that.

"No. He's right, Aubrey. I have a responsibility in this. And I haven't been holding up my end."

Aubrey immediately stared at him, his gaze calculating. Ethaniel might as well have been standing on one side of a set of golden squares. *Time to weigh the measure of my heart, if not my deeds.*

"Ethaniel, I don't like this," Aubrey said, those glass eyes narrowed in a gaze that felt like a gunshot to the chest. "I don't. But I won't stop you. I can, and will, however, worry incessantly and be a terrible nag."

Ethaniel kissed Aubrey's cheek. "I wouldn't have it any other way." Then he squared his shoulders, swallowed down his fear like a fine brandy, and held out his hand to Calix. "May I look him over?"

Calix's brow furrowed. "Ethaniel?"

Ethaniel tried to smile, but he felt the corners of his mouth pull into a grimace. Dammit. "It's similar to how I found you two after we got separated, after the fire. A bit of patterning, a bit of old knowledge, and the power here." He gently pulled Calix to standing and pressed their joined hands together over his heart. "Running hasn't gotten me anywhere, and it's made our situation worse. Let me help."

Magnus swiftly fetched the few supplies Ethaniel needed while he took one of Richard's shoelaces from the pair beside the bed. Then he turned to Calix. "Do you have any object that means something to both of you? It could be anything mundane, as long as it's small enough to have a shoelace tied around it."

Calix nodded immediately, messy brown and chestnut waves flying. "I'll be right back."

While he ran down the hall, Ethaniel stretched the shoelace between his hands and instructed Aubrey to rub charcoal on his fingertips. "Are you sure? Ethaniel, my worry will never cease even when you're not doing dangerous magic." Aubrey leaned in, his gaze watchful, his mouth a soft curve of sorrow. "No one will think less of you for living as you have. For

being —"

"A mild-mannered tailor and patterner?" Ethaniel shook his head, reached up to touch Aubrey's cheek with his thumb. He left a trail of charcoal behind. "You know the kind of defenses the shop had. Some part of you must have known that was no average pattern. I made writhing red tentacles come out of the ground and threw a man into a bin. No pattern could do that."

"No, I suppose not." The resignation in his voice made something inside Ethaniel clench. As if bracing for a hit. Aubrey would never, not physically. When Aubrey kissed him this time, Ethaniel let himself get swept up in it. In the promise it held, in the warmth and love.

They both knew some lines could be crossed exactly once. And if they were both honest, Ethaniel had crossed it when he used his family's magic to defend his shop all those years ago. Some part of him had always known, and it was a bittersweet irony.

Calix came back a moment later with a pocket watch. It was a pretty thing, pure silver and dotted with garnets. "It had been my mother's, and she gave it to me. I gave it to Richard five years ago, on his thirtieth."

"I'll be very careful with it, I promise."

Calix smiled. "I know you will. But please be careful for your own sake, Ethaniel." His hands were soft as they held Ethaniel's face, the thumbs tracking over the dark circles under his eyes. "Please."

"I've been very careful my entire life, love. Look where it landed me. Afraid of my own shadow, afraid of stepping one tiny bit over the line. A line I drew, by the way, because of my fear." He gestured toward the sleeping Richard. "I can help him. If I can find out what was done, Aubrey and Magnus can help me undo it.

Maybe. I don't want to get your hopes up, darling, but I'm going to *try*. I have to."

"You are one of the bravest souls I know," Calix whispered before stepping back into the waiting embrace of Aubrey, while Magnus hovered nearby.

"Just in case, my friend," Magnus said as Ethaniel began to focus on the watch. "Consider me a pail of sand should the fire get out of control."

Ethaniel closed his eyes and waited for that *snap* of magic. If patterning was about intent and connection, then theoretically, this would be easy. But nothing about the last few days had been simple or easy, so as a tingle began to form in his palms, spreading down to his fingers and routing back, around the loop of shoelace, Ethaniel forced his eyes open to stare at Richard.

The guilt could consume him, or he could use it. Focus his magic there, imagine his guilt drying up like mud in the summer sun, then cracking, chipping away, until all that was left was pure *energy*.

The pocket watch now floated in the space between his hands and the very room seemed to tremble as Ethaniel reached for that little space inside his chest, close to his heart, where the true essence of his power lay in wait. It greeted him like an old friend, as if to say, *I knew you'd be back one day.*

Perhaps Vincent had been right all along.

Ethaniel took all of it, every shivery tendril, every pop and flare of magic, and pushed his intent in, forward, then down. His vision flashed white for a moment and he heard someone suck in a harsh breath, but he let the magic go forward, undeterred from his quest.

"Go," he whispered, and through the pocket watch his magic was focused, a single straight line of teal and silver (the teal his, the silver from the watch, their energies bonding, forming a connection, pushing and pushing and pushing Ethaniel's intent) into Richard's chest. Ethaniel's vision opened up, a bit of harsh daylight after a dark room, and he found he could scan Richard's body, like that German scientist who had invented the x-ray a few years back. But this was far more efficient, and accurate, than any grainy image of a skeletal hand.

He could *see* the blood in Richard's veins, the sluggish but steady beat of his heart. When Ethaniel moved his vision up to Richard's face, everything nearly ground to a halt. There was no spark of life, no tangle of black knots like he would expect from a spell. Any spell meant to damage left behind a trace, something he could dig his fingers into, and like unraveling a mess of yarn or thread, slowly pluck apart until the entire thing unspooled.

This was a void, placed squarely between Richard's eyes, and eerily reminiscent of the tentacles he'd used to protect the shop, this thing had spidery limbs that stretched out, to the backs of Richard's eyes. The void had its own rhythm, a heartbeat of danger and darkness that was spreading like spilled ink. This wasn't blindness. This was a parasite, a disease, one that would rage through Richard's body, slowly stealing his life until nothing was left but a husk.

Ethaniel, hands shaking but his will firm, followed one of the tendrils out, letting his magic do the work. If he was a Harkness, he would live up to the name by perverting it, reversing any damage his family did and, with any luck, obliterating their influence. He could do this. *He could.*

The tendril snaked out, weaving and moving at odd angles that made his queasy, but it didn't take long for Ethaniel to find the source of the disease. A single point, as dark as the void growing behind Richard's eyes, but it was in his ear. Possibilities flashed through his mind, and then Ethaniel remembered Calix's suspicion another stinger had been used.

"They went through his ear," Aubrey said, his voice so steady, so present. Like a firm weight at Ethaniel's back. But he could feel the horror in Aubrey's soul. Their connection seemed to be growing by inches every day, but every inch made a difference.

"Aubrey," Ethaniel said, staying as still as he could, "you'll want to look at this properly. Not just through what you're detecting with our...ahem, rather unique bond, let's say."

The temptation to shut his eyes in relief the moment Aubrey touched him was strong, but he had to hold off. Anything could disrupt the delicate connection he'd made with Richard and that *thing* growing inside his skull. Because behind the darkness, Ethaniel sensed a consciousness. Some form of sentience behind what looked like an infection. Aubrey had told them about the strange darkness inside Lawton, and he wondered if it was similar magic. As far as anyone knew, including him, illness was just that. The illness ravaging Jeremiah's lungs, the gangrene rotting away the foot of the man who lived next door to the shop, the unknown virus that had infected several aboard a merchant ship last summer.

Nature running its course. But what if that wasn't always the case?

Ethaniel slowly extended a hand to Aubrey, who instantly took it. Ethaniel heard Aubrey say something to Calix, but the words were muffled through the focus of his magic. A moment later, he felt Calix take up the spot at his right. Their magics, so different from each other and yet complimentary to his own, began to suffuse through the connection he had with Richard.

On the bed, Richard groaned softly, a sound of pure pain, and Calix's hand tightened on Ethaniel's shoulder. "It's all right, love," Ethaniel heard Aubrey say. He couldn't divert focus away now, but he hoped Calix felt his empathy, his sympathy, and his desire to fix what had gone so wrong.

"I'm not sure this will work," Aubrey said as he slid his hand on top of Ethaniel's. "Joining with Calix's magic was something done under intense pressure."

"And yet we have to try," Calix said. "None of us know what we're doing. But I know Richard is in pain, and I can't have that. It's not fair to him."

Ethaniel shook his head, refocusing on the pulsing black mass responsible for eradicating Richard's sight. "Aubrey, I'm going to be your eyes, show you where this thing inside Richard is causing the issue. Calix, could you try to steady us? Keep our power in line while Aubrey works? I'll remain the anchor point for you both."

Calix sighed and Ethaniel felt that sadness well up in his own chest, as if Calix's pain was now his own. They were doing this out of desperation and need mixed with that sadness, a desolate thing that left him feeling empty.

"Focus on that feeling, Calix," Ethaniel said. "Focus on fixing it. Molding it in your hands like clay and giving it to Aubrey. I've always believed magic is about intent, and if we try to get too experimental with our process, I fear what might happen."

Aubrey's other hand cupped the back of Ethaniel's neck, and a shudder ran down his entire spine with that simple touch. Nothing about this situation was sensual, but it was intimate, and at once he understood what Aubrey was doing. Aubrey's intent was to heal, and he needed the fuel of their connection — from him and Calix — to help him focus.

Aubrey relied on love to heal. Love of the objects that came into the Collectio. Love of the people he'd learned to heal, even after his abilities manifested in a way that made his father reject him. Ethaniel let his eyes flutter shut for a moment, let Aubrey's warmth and magic wash over him, wrapping him in something that felt like *home*.

And beside him, he felt Calix's magic stir awake, and from its hibernation came another feeling, this one with wings and a song on the wind, and suddenly Ethaniel felt something new. *Hope*. Hope that everything would be all right. That in the end, they'd be together. Peaceful, safe, warm. Hope for them, for Lawton, for his mother and Richard and Magnus and even, startlingly, for Vincent. Calix had taken that anger and sorrow and molded it into a thing of delicate beauty.

"Oh," Calix breathed as their magics began to merge, glowing gold and blue and dusky purple, all the colors of a spectacular twilight before the fall of night. Ethaniel watched the lines of magic, glittering so brightly, run up his left arm from Aubrey's touch and when it extended out from his fingers, it hit the pocket watch. The watch spun a tad faster and the moment it did, Richard sucked in a breath.

"Easy, easy," Ethaniel muttered, both to Richard and Calix, whose fiery furnace blast of anxiety was like a spike to his heart. "Calix, can you..."

Calix placed his hand on top of Ethaniel's right, mimicking Aubrey's touch, and his power began to run through Ethaniel. He doubled down on his intent — untangling the black knot inside Richard's skull and slowly picking it apart — and thought about the patterns he'd been taught by guild members that were meant for *unraveling*.

Ethaniel thought about Richard's bravery and kindness. How he helped take care of Calix. How he'd selflessly stayed even as the danger grew. He thought about Richard's dedication, his quiet, steely will, and how unfair it was that such a man would be pulled into a scheme dreamed up by Ethaniel's own blood.

You're not a Harkness except in name, Vincent, Ethaniel thought as he clenched his jaw. *You were always jealous that the family magics skipped you, but you made up for it with your ego and bloodthirsty ambitions, didn't you?* He felt his anger rise, but instead of biting it back, he let it run free. He let that intent to fix what his brother had done swell up in him, a fierce tidal wave, and carve a path for Aubrey's magic.

The moment Aubrey's magic slipped over him, Ethaniel could have sagged with relief. It felt like he was being cleansed from the inside out. Given a new chance, another golden opportunity to fix what was wrong. And with Calix holding strong at his side, and Aubrey pushing into his mind, his very *soul*, Ethaniel let go.

Moments passed, long and bright and smelling of the sea and cold stone and the sky after a storm. He was adrift, lost in the way their powers merged, in the feeling of *completion*.

"I've done what I can," Aubrey said, sounding winded. He slowly dropped his hand from Ethaniel's, and Calix followed suit, and when the energy faded, Ethaniel felt empty. Tears welled in his eyes, with how powerful the sensation of hollowness was, and then Calix was touching him softly and Aubrey was whispering in his ear.

"You're all right. You're all right. We're here. We aren't leaving."

On the bed, Richard slowly sat up, peeled the cloth away from his eyes, and blinked at them. His dark eyes were no longer the hazy white of blindness, but nor were they back to normal. There was an odd tint to them, a sickly yellow that made Ethaniel's stomach revolt.

"The mass is gone," Aubrey said as he dragged himself to a nearby chair. He looked so worn and weary and it broke Ethaniel's heart all over again. "And I'll keep checking, to ensure it doesn't come back somehow. But you were right,

Calix, it was a stinger. It was some kind of poison, like nothing I've ever seen before. It...it carried a magic with it that I don't know how to reverse. I am, unfortunately, not my father's son."

The bitterness in Aubrey's words was dashed away as Richard scanned the room, jaundiced eyes rolling wildly. "Will it come back? My sight? I can see shadows, the three of you in front of the bed, but I can't make out details." He blinked and as he did, a few tears ran down Richard's face. "Will it come back?"

Aubrey winced, his beautiful face twisted like Ethaniel's heart was. "I won't stop looking for a way to bring your sight back. I promise."

"Thank you," Richard whispered before curling up on the bed, a child again afraid of the world that had told him monsters were real.

Calix pulled the blankets over Richard and they left the room to give the man a chance to rest. As soon as the door was shut, Aubrey sagged against the wall and said, "It was awful. Whatever that thing was on the tip of the stinger. It had a horrible flavor. I can still taste it."

Ethaniel's heart sank with suspicion. "What did it taste like? Iron, maybe?"

Aubrey nodded. "Indeed. Akin to how the air smells when you walk into a blacksmith's shop."

"It's blood magic. *Harkness magic*," Ethaniel bit out. "And who knows, maybe Vincent found a family necromancer while he was at it. My family has expertise in both. Old blood from a corpse, blood taken from some kind of rabid animal, it could be anything —"

Suddenly, Calix was standing before him, his finely boned hands soft on Ethaniel's cheeks. "Hush, Ethaniel. No more of that. Not right now." He glanced back at Aubrey before looking at Ethaniel with such fierceness and said, "You and I and Aubrey and Magnus have enough magic in our bodies to blot out the sun, if we wanted. We will figure this out."

When Calix kissed him, sweet and soft and so gentle Ethaniel wanted to swoon from it, he felt the world tilt a bit back toward normal. They might be trapped, exhausted, and worrying themselves into an early grave, but Ethaniel knew without Aubrey and Calix, he might have wound up that way.

For all his anger and sorrow, the allure of what lay in his blood was too present. From the time he was a child, it beat like a second drum, thrumming in his temples and hands and teasing him with glimpses of what might be. What he could become. *Who* he could become.

He might have. Without them, he might have given in. But with them, he was stronger. Better. Known and seen and loved and adored and touched in ways he'd had yet to fully realize or articulate and it didn't matter because they were here with him.

CHAPTER FOURTEEN

AUBREY

They trudged out to the rose garden, the mud pulling at their boots, the rain relentless on their heads and backs, and each of them mired in their own thoughts. Today had felt like an eon, and Aubrey was quite sure at this point that even eternity had an end, unlike this day. This week. This last fortnight and then some.

And none of it he would trade for any other reality of any other realm, because that would mean losing those closest to him.

His thoughts stopped as their path did, with Calix coming to the center of the rose garden, his gaze assessing. Then he pointed to his feet, specifically the brick circle under them. "I had always wondered," he murmured, cocking his head and looking all the more like a curious puppy. Aubrey would never stop admiring the man's ability to look so innocent–it was a gift he wasn't sure even Calix knew he possessed.

"Wondered what?" Magnus asked from under his ridiculously large umbrella.

Calix smiled. "My mother never told me what this meant. I discovered it on my own, during one of the many, many days I spent playing here. Pretending I was the Queen of Hearts after Alice's head." His smile dropped. "I had my first 'fit' out here. Just a small one. But I was standing here, staring at all the pinks and reds and oranges and yellows of the roses and the next thing I knew, I was on the ground, my hands scraped up from the brick, and the circle started to glow. It would happen on occasion in the future, when I was emotionally volatile, usually having a cry out here."

Aubrey leaned in to get a better look. The brick was unremarkable, washed out from the rain, the perfectly straight edges of each one bearing signs of erosion from time and weather. He pulled out his monocle and began flashing through the various lenses, but nothing unusual appeared.

Beside him, Ethaniel was tapping his finger on his chin and staring studiously at the circle. It was barely large enough for two grown men to stand on, with a core of slate at its center. "Your mother clearly liked her puzzles," he said. "I wonder…"

Overhead, a crack of thunder, distant but present, rattled at the sky, the very clouds seeming to shake with its power. "Lightning and roses," Aubrey said. "They mean nothing together. And I suppose we could dig up the entire fucking garden looking for whatever it is your mother concealed here, but we'd be wasting precious time. Vincent could attack again at any moment."

"And not even our dreams are safe," Magnus added. "A pity, too. I usually have such wonderful dreams, but they've been nothing but darkness since coming here."

"I'm so sorry, Magnus," Calix started to say, but Magnus waved him off. "Pish posh, young man. I'm only trying to interject a bit of levity in the middle of a grave situation. No harm done."

The four of them stared in silence at the stone circle. Aubrey felt his thoughts begin to congeal, oatmeal-thick and not nearly as pleasant. "She said you would know what to do, Calix. Perhaps we should simply go ask her."

"I've tried, many times," Calix said as he crossed his arms over his chest and shivered. The rain was now blowing in with a cold snap that threatened to bite through their coats and clothes, and Aubrey swore he felt a bit of dread carried in on it, too. "Over the years, as well as now. She seemed more than confident I would understand. But I don't, and this whole thing has us playing a game to simply stay alive."

Wordlessly, Calix turned, a growl on his lips and frustration making his face tight, his jaw tight; he shoved his fingers into his hair and pulled, and when he scuffed one of the outer bricks with his heel, the brick lit up.

Aubrey and Ethaniel looked at each other. Magnus was grinning, a mad hatter in the middle of such beautiful chaos. "Strong emotions," Aubrey said. "Perhaps that's the trigger."

But Calix was unamused. "What am I supposed to do, cry on each brick and say abracadabra? This is a fool's errand. We should get inside —"

The glow from the brick faded.

Lightning flashed between the roiling clouds overhead.

Aubrey's gaze snagged on *something* moving in the shadows that choked their surroundings. As soon as he spotted it — there and gone, no slower than a flash of lightning above — Ethaniel went tense beside him.

"What was that?" Ethaniel asked, looking from side to side. Immediately, Aubrey felt the pull of Ethaniel's power, the spark of it behind his teeth, on his tongue, like the sharpness of a passionate kiss born out of the embers of desire. Cobra-strike fast, and then gone.

Calix and Magnus stopped and looked around as well, and when the lightning flashed again, it was Calix who pointed into the darkness. "There, I think."

"Another trick of Vincent's?" Magnus asked as he drew up his right hand, thumb and forefinger pointing to the sky as a coin-size ball of power appeared between them. "Another part of his war of attrition?"

"No," Calix whispered as thunder cracked all around this. "This is my mother."

Rain was cold, dripping down the back of Aubrey's neck, sliding across his skin like so much ice. The rattle of bare rose branches, the scraping of thorns against other thorns. The quick heartbeats of those around him. Aubrey heard it all, felt it all and for a moment, suspended in time and breathless in waiting, he wondered what would come next.

The screaming face in his did not make him step back, but Ethaniel drew away on instinct, a recoil that sent him into Calix.

It was that scene played out again. In the vault, just on the other side of the rose garden. Ethaniel stumbling backwards. The soul phylactery slipping from his grasp and arcing away, the glass a shy glint in the dim light of that catacomb for dead magical things. The moment that shifted everything, again, for the fourth or fifth or seventeenth time since they'd all met and reacquainted and pushed into each other's lives with the same amount of common jostle as passengers in a carriage and the winds of change at their backs.

But they were not the same now. Especially Ethaniel.

Aubrey felt the heartbeat of his magic, smelled the ozone in the air, before Ethaniel let a single red tendril of magic flick off the ends of his fingers toward the gruesome apparition that now floated before them. It hit the thing square in the chest and it reeled back, an overspun top careening with centrifugal force and a scream of pure pain.

Another one appeared far too close to Aubrey for his liking, and his mind conjured up the ward before he could think about it.

"Stop!" he yelled out, the power gathering in his palm coming to life with a flash of blue. Aubrey felt the eye in the middle of his forehead blink, crack open, and then focus on the creature mere feet from him. But what could he do? He could compel the thing to stay still, but he had no mastery of the spirit world. On some occasions, he'd rarely believed such a thing existed. But here was a specter, gaunt and stringy, its hair matted to one side, the eye sockets mockingly hollow, the fingers broken nubs as if someone had smashed their hand to bits in anger.

The anger. Aubrey felt it balloon in his chest. Anger at this creature, this foul thing threatening him and those he cared about. Anger at their situation, at those involved who had unwittingly conspired to make their lives hell. Anger at his own inability to solve that which seemed to have no answer other than the terrifyingly obvious.

We need to go into the demimonde.

It echoed in his ears, around him, reverberated in every single bone in his body and Aubrey *knew*. He knew and he hated it and that fueled the anger even more and with each breath *burning*, Aubrey let the magic in his palm swell and swell again until there was a roaring blaze of blue in his hand and he yelled at the creature. "Advance no further! You are not of this world. You do not belong here."

No, we don't, came the whisper, bouncing around them. Aubrey realized they were surrounded by skeletal *things* that creaked with the wind and sang with a dirge worthy of the finest funeral. *But neither does he.*

"It's a test," Calix breathed, his eyes so big and round and had this been any other moment, Aubrey would have willingly drowned in them. "She used to do this, to test my control. Keep me on a true and steady course, because if I lost myself in my predictions, my dreams, I might never come back."

"This is her fear," Ethaniel said. The trueness of his words cut through Aubrey's wariness, putting a chokehold on the terror bubbling up in his throat. "It's a manifestation of her fear. I can...I can taste it. Smell it." He turned to Aubrey, face ashen. "She used blood magic."

"As insightful as all that is, we need a way out," Magnus said. "We can unfuck the puzzle later, as Aubrey might say."

The ghostly figures rattled and clacked closer, their gait one giant limp at a time forward. This close, Aubrey could smell the death on them and that particular burnt-charcoal taste of beings conjured from another realm. Creatures summoned from another reality always smelled that way. Summon a demon, defy the Lord, and down ye shall fall as the scent of brimstone hangs in the air and the Devil takes you with him.

These were no devils. They were manifestations of Lily's fear for her son.

"Let me," Calix said as Aubrey's thought lingered in all three of them.

And like he had in the study, he strode directly into the chaos before Aubrey could pull him back. Magnus was the one to grab Calix by the arm as they all shouted for him to stop, and the moment Magnus's hand met Calix's elbow, the entire world around them shifted. It was the only way Aubrey could describe the way the air sparkled, glitter hanging amidst time and space, their breaths loud in the silence that now filled the empty places between their bodies and their magic.

The creatures surrounding them also hung in the air: two, three, four, five feet off the ground, their limbs askew, their bodies mere ragdolls against the force that was Calix, and his magic *amplified* by Magnus.

The world rushed back at him, first the rain on his face, then the thunder and lightning rampaging overhead as reality came back in sync with time once more. Wind — no, *force* — pushed him off the gravel path. On instinct, Aubrey snagged Ethaniel by the coat before they toppled to the ground together. Breathless, reeling, but unharmed.

His ears were ringing, but he heard Ethaniel yell his name, saw him point toward Calix. Magnus had also been shoved away and he was staring up at Calix as well.

Calix *glowed*. A golden boy with a golden head of hair, some of it teased up in the wind that buffeted them all. He was hovering a few feet off the ground and with a flick of his hand, he cast the figures back once more. Jawbones shattered. Skulls fractured. Ribcages broke into pieces and scattered among the rose bushes.

No more mocking eye sockets. No more bared grins. No more ghastly creaking of bones. And in the middle of the tempest was Calix, a beacon of power. Beautiful and terrifying. His eyes, his skin, were shot through with liquid gold and Aubrey had to look away, so bright was his countenance.

And then silence, and only silence, as the wind died and the rain stopped and Calix landed on the ground and slowly came back to himself.

He gazed out at all of them, his brown eyes backlit with a fearsome light that made some part of Aubrey shiver in delight, and pointed down to the brick circle. "There."

Aubrey helped Ethaniel to his feet and pulled Magnus up as well, so they could join Calix around the brick once more. The slate in the middle had fractured, and when Calix pried the pieces away, inside was a small lead box.

"Let's get inside," Magnus said as he turned his face up to the sky. "I don't think this storm is done with us quite yet."

Lawton was waiting for them when they trudged back into the kitchen like a line of bedraggled kittens. He had a ladle in one hand and was peering into a large stockpot when they came in through the back entrance. Something smelling strongly of onion and chicken floated on the warm air.

Calix was immediately at Lawton's side, confusion written like a poem across his face. Aubrey watched him as he slowly peeled out of his wet coat and boots, suspicious of Lawton's motives but not about to insert himself in the moment. He knew Calix believed his friend could be redeemed, and perhaps the young earl was correct. There were books upon books of the stories of far worse monsters and their redemption in the archives of the Collectio. But he and Ethaniel had an advantage on Calix when it came to Lawton Adler—they'd never seen any of the good. Calix had a few decades of history with the man, and while he quietly thought Calix's open mind for people wouldn't be so open after they made it through this endeavor, Aubrey wasn't about to dissuade Calix from his tender heart right now.

He also hated to admit it, but Calix and Lawton had more than a past. There was real affection there. Real love and a bond. He and Ethaniel were new, exciting, but they didn't have that past with Calix. Hell, they'd only just found each other again after so many months of chilly silence. They didn't know Calix like Lawton did. And while he couldn't speak for Ethaniel, Aubrey knew he couldn't love that quickly. Admire, desire, adore, and feel strongly for, certainly. Love was a slow waltz into something both finite and eternal in his opinion.

So, Aubrey stayed quiet and watched as Calix took the ladle from Lawton's hand and pressed it to his lips. He tracked Lawton's gaze, how sharp, how focused it became as soon as Calix had come close of his own volition, and how it widened in surprise when Calix said, "She taught you this, didn't she? Mother used to make this for me when I was ill. The benefit of having a mother raised by wealthy eccentrics was being raised by a woman wearing a day gown in the kitchen and not fussing when her brocade wrinkled because of the humidity in the air."

But then Calix's fond expression dropped and morphed into something harder, colder, as he thrust the ladle back at Lawton, stomped over to snatch up the box from Ethaniel's hands, and return to Lawton. He extended his arm over the large pot of boiling soup, long fingers clutching the box so tightly, and said, "And apparently that's the same woman who thought it wise to play games with her son. Her only child, who she supposedly loved so much that she tried to protect him, but also built herself a trap door in the form of a soul phylactery. The same woman who was *obsessed* with a realm not our own, and whose obsession turned into an addiction that killed her."

Calix's words rang out across the stone floors, each one like an anvil dropped into sand, the truth pushing through all the distractions. He'd cut to the quick of it in one fell swoop, and Aubrey was viciously proud of him. Aubrey could feel Calix's fear, but it was fuel on the fire of his anger. The man had been betrayed twice over by those who claimed to love him. He had every right to that anger and more, but Aubrey could sense the leash Calix had wrapped around the neck of it.

And beside him, Ethaniel was tensing in response. Ethaniel hated it when people argued. Aubrey had observed him, more than once, tense up when someone near them in public started up a row. It created a storm of anxiety in him, and this was surely making his entire body react. Without turning his head, Aubrey sought out Ethaniel's hand and when warm fingers met his, he smiled slightly.

I'm here, he thought out toward them both.

Lawton had frozen in place, his face a mask of fear. Aubrey blinked a few times because he swore he saw deeper, darker shades of auburn take up residence in the man's flame orange hair, and swore he smelled lavender in the air.

"Don't," Lawton choked out and *ah*, there was Lily's voice. "Calix. You can't."

"I can't?" Calix narrowed his gaze and it turned his beauty into something more sinister. "I think we're long past the point of me listening to your sage wisdom, Mother." He lowered his arm a fraction, bringing the box closer to the pot. Aubrey's stomach twisted, but he didn't stop Calix. He couldn't. This was Calix's battle, and he'd charge in if needed...but Aubrey didn't think that would happen. "What is it? No tricks. Tell me the truth. Be honest with me, for once, because you couldn't even do that for me in life."

Lawton — *Lily* — was now clutching the front of his shirt, eyes wide with fear and shining with what were surely unshed tears. A tendril of doubt began to worm its way up through Aubrey's chest, from the pit of his stomach. They had no idea what was in the box, why it was buried out there, or why Calix's powers activated in such a way. They had more questions than answers, suppositions even, and that thread of logic was getting in the way of his emotions. As it should.

"Calix," Aubrey said. "Think about it for a moment. I know you want —"

"But you don't. Know, that is. Any of you." Calix whirled on them, his face gone soft once more, but with a pleading edge to his voice. "I have been lied to my entire life. By Lawton, by my mother. And because of those lies, I'm here, and I dragged all of you into this mess. I don't want to do this —"

And he turned back, arm extended once more, his hand immediately flushing pink from the heat of the boiling liquid in the pot. "But I will, because I think there's quite a bit more at stake here than my mother's pride and my friend's ego."

"You're right." The words were broken, drug over the jagged glass of emotion now roiling up through Lawton's body, as if it could take on physical manifestation. As if Lily's turmoil was nearly forcing her from Lawton. His hair went auburn, his voice higher, softer now, even his physicality willowier. It was startling, and disturbing, to watch. "You're right. I hid so much from you. I told myself it was because I was protecting you, but I see now the damage that did. But you can't destroy it, Calix. It's...it's a part of you."

Silence lay over them as Aubrey tried to fit the pieces together. Magnus beat him to the conclusion.

"She didn't." Magnus was now on his feet but didn't approach Calix or Lawton. "You couldn't have — that's impossible."

Lawton smiled over at Magnus, no humor in it. "You know it's not. I did it before I died. Souls are easy to work with when the person is nearing death or newly born. And it's not unknown magic."

"No, it is not," Magnus replied. "After all, you learned from the best."

Lawton inclined his head, but the words were all Lily. "Ah, I see you've also read John Dee's greatest work. Well, his greatest work after the one he created that's sitting upstairs."

The realization of it was like ice down Aubrey's back. And from the way Ethaniel softly whispered, "My God," he understood it in the moment, too.

Calix frowned and what looked like doubt crept across his face. "Someone had best explain that."

Aubrey sighed, but it was not a sigh of impatience. "Calix, your mother may be the only person *alive* in any form who knows how to separate a soul into pieces. She did it to herself when she knew her Oracle powers would be her downfall, securing herself in that phylactery, allowing her to possess Lawton. I doubt her intention was to possess someone, but rather to be returned, whole and alive, after you put together the pieces. And she did it to you when you were a newborn, so I'd wager that's what's inside that box."

He scrubbed at his face in disbelief, the shock of it all fitting together rattling around his system like a ball bearing. "And she learned all of that from John Dee's work, because that's how he made the thing we call Convergence. It's what he did to Edward Talbot. And I would wager it's why she documented her work but split it into pieces that seem to make no sense. To ensure it landed in your hands only."

Slowly, Aubrey stood up and walked over to Calix. His face was so pale Aubrey worried he might faint, so he carefully plucked the lead box from Calix's hand and set it aside. "Your mother was a very smart woman. And she ensured that only you could reproduce her work, but also reverse it. So that she could come back and protect you even after her death. Because some of her is inside Lawton, and some of her is inside the *demimonde*, and if you open that box, I can almost guarantee you'll know what to do in order to bring her back."

"I don't know if I can," Calix breathed. His entire body trembled – from fear, from shock, from exhaustion, and Aubrey longed to hold him. He felt that yearning inside Ethaniel as well. Their connectedness, as much of an accident of magic as it was exposure to an artifact like Convergence, was a positive they could focus on, as was the inevitability of the path forward.

Aubrey pulled Calix close and the moment he did, the younger man tucked his face into Aubrey's neck and sobbed. It wracked his frame but Calix's grip on the back of his shirt was tight, as if Aubrey were a tow line and Calix was holding on for dear life. A few seconds later, Aubrey felt Ethaniel's warmth at his back and welcomed him into the embrace as well. His Ethaniel. His Calix.

They would all get through this together.

"We're of no use like this," Ethaniel said in Aubrey's ear. "We should get him to bed."

"But the box..." Calix looked so torn as he stared up at them, tears tracking down his face. He spared a glimpse back toward Lawton–Lily–who was standing before the stove with his hands twisted up in the pockets of the navy apron he'd donned.

"A problem for tomorrow," Aubrey said in a tone that brooked no argument. "I'm done running ourselves ragged. We know what needs to be done. It can wait until the morning."

"I would agree," Magnus interjected, "and on that note, so we can all sleep soundly, I'm going to reinforce the wards as much as I can. You three have been run ragged by this and I..." When Magnus trailed off, Aubrey saw some flicker of emotion over his face.

A deep, resonant sadness.

"Well, I'll do what I can," Magnus said, a note of resolution in his voice that would assure anyone other than Aubrey. If it was something his mentor and friend thought important, he would say it, and after all that had happened over the last few days, Aubrey was more than satisfied with a bit of mystery, if Magnus wanted to keep it to himself.

Aubrey turned to lead Calix and Ethaniel away from it all – and away from Lawton and Lily – but she stopped them. "Wait, please," she begged as she put a hand on Calix's shoulder. Aubrey made to shrug her off, and began to, but the movement stretched Lawton's arm and his sleeve rose up.

"My God, Lawton, your arm," Calix said, turning to his old flame and friend with a horrified expression.

"It's nothing." Lawton's voice was back now, meek but unmistakable. He quickly pulled his sleeve down, but there was no unseeing what lay on his skin.

Ethaniel grabbed his wrist and Lawton made a pained noise but didn't resist. "What happened?" Ethaniel asked as he, now much more careful with his touch, rolled up Lawton's sleeve to the elbow. His pale skin was covered in what looked like branching scars, from the fine bones of his wrist and climbing up to disappear where his sleeve hid the rest of his arm. "These look like Lichtenberg scars."

Magnus was instantly before Lawton, turning the man's exposed forearm this way and that, then nodded. "You're right. But I don't think Mr. Adler got them from an errant bolt of lightning."

Lawton wouldn't even look up at them. "It's her," he whispered. "I don't...I don't think two souls, even one so fractured as hers and one as tainted as mine, are meant to be in one body. I noticed them the first night, but they'd disappeared by morning and there was so much else going on —"

His words dropped off, rocks from a sheer cliff, and the look he gave Calix was pleading. Aubrey felt a pang of sympathy for Lawton. He shouldn't, and by all accounts, the man had no right to his sympathy. He dealt it to those he deemed deserving. But something in that aching, empty stare made Aubrey whisper in Calix's ear. "I think he's quite concerned, Calix. Perhaps you could talk to him? Away from the rest of us."

Calix's tone was icy when he said, "Why should I? He's the cause of this terrible mess."

"He is, and yet, aside from your mother, Lawton has been in your life the longest."

Calix stared up at him, unmoved. "Time isn't the only method by which I can take the measure of a relationship. Or a man, for that matter."

When Calix didn't move to comfort Lawton, Aubrey stayed at his side, keeping an arm around the younger man's shoulders in a silent gesture of comfort. He could *feel* the sadness and anger welling up in Calix, a hungry beast eager for more, more, more, all the pain it could consume and then some.

"I'm going to reach out to Agrippa again, ask them to hold off on any potential visit," Magnus said finally, stepping away from Lawton and pulling out a small notebook from his jacket pocket. "I do not think it's quite safe for them to come around. However, I'm hoping that vast library of yours may have something about possessions, Calix. May I peruse your shelves?"

"Of course." Calix's congenial charm surfaced even through the exhaustion dragging his words through the proverbial mud. "I can take you there."

Magnus waved him off. "No need, no need. I'm not so old I can't walk down a few hallways, young man."

Aubrey managed to snag Magnus by the arm as he left the kitchen and pull him into an alcove near one of the small parlors. "How bad is it?" he asked.

Magnus sighed and leaned against the wall, his arms crossed over his chest. Aubrey had seen that look many, many times over the years, and it always came before a set of carefully weighed words. "Not good, I'm afraid. Possessions by an entity aren't wholly unusual, you know that. But this possession is a bit outside my field of expertise. Usually, possessions happen after a traumatic event. But Calix's mother did this to herself, Aubrey, and there's no other example of that I can think of, save the similarity it bears to John Dee's work."

Magnus paused and ran his fingers through his short black waves; Aubrey could practically hear the gears turning in the man's head. "And the box? You're certain...Magnus, that seems impossible. That she took a piece of her own son's soul and locked it away?"

"It wouldn't need to be a large piece. Hardly more than a speck, honestly, if Calix never noticed something was off or wrong. And I would love to be incorrect on this, but I truly don't believe I am." He shuddered. "It's an awful thing she did, in an attempt to keep her child safe from the magic in his veins. So that begs the question...did she do the very wrong thing for the right reasons?"

"I wish I knew," Aubrey replied. "But I am certain that Calix has every right to his anger. And I wish I could do something to give him a reprieve. This entire situation feels...rather dire."

"It does." Magnus pushed away from the wall and put his hands on Aubrey's shoulders. They were of a height, but Magnus was the more willowy-built, and he was a decade older than Aubrey. No longer a young man, but still in his prime. And his friend had never looked so stooped or tired, as if every new discovery of theirs pulled him closer to the Earth's core. "Take care of him, Aubrey. I've met no one quite like him, or your Ethaniel, and it's rare for any of us to meet one love in our lifetimes, let alone two."

Magnus's words make the hollowness in Aubrey's chest fill a little bit. A candle in the darkness. Of course he was right. "I am so sorry I got you involved in all this," Aubrey said quietly. "And now you're trapped here with us."

Magnus did smile at that, small but genuine. "I'd be very cross with you if you'd left me out in the cold, so to speak. You needed my help, I answered. I would never turn you away, Aubrey."

Aubrey wasn't one for casual physicality. For him, touch was as important as any other sense, but it was through touch that his own magic could create, destroy, or change. So when he carefully, slowly pulled Magnus into a tight hug, he wasn't surprised the man let out a small noise of surprise, then instantly relaxed when he realized Aubrey wanted that embrace.

"You're a good man, Aubrey," Magnus said before stepping back. "Go on. Go take care of them tonight. Lend them your strength, so they might carry on."

He let Magnus go, waiting until he had disappeared down the hall and around a corner before returning to the kitchen. Calix and Ethaniel were seated across from each other at a small table, a loaf of bread and three steaming bowls before them.

"Come eat," Ethaniel said as he pulled out the empty chair for Aubrey. "Lawton's gone off to bed, and I poked my head in to check on Richard. I think the entire house is exhausted at this point."

"It's as if the world were heaping its sins upon our backs and asking us to bear the load," Calix murmured, his eyes stuck on his bowl. "I may have thought many uncharitable things toward Lawton, but..." He swiftly looked up and gave Aubrey an apologetic smile. "I'm so sorry. We should eat and head to bed, I think."

Before he sat down, Aubrey paused to examine the lead box where it sat on the far counter. "We'll need to lock this away like we've done with Convergence," he said, carefully looking over the edges and corners of the box. Every line was seamless, to the point where he doubted even a butterfly wing might slip between them.

When he came to sit at the table, the scent of warm, simple food overrode any higher thought, and his stomach growled. Ethaniel couldn't suppress his chuckle. "It feels like breakfast was forever ago," Aubrey admitted before tucking in. "We won't get anywhere without sustenance."

But before he put a single spoonful of broth into his mouth, or a single bite of bread, he took Calix's hand in his left and Ethaniel's in his right and said, "Both of you. I want you to hear me. You two...there's so much I want to show you. The Acadia Gardens on the first night of summer, when they let loose the firefly rockets to light up the sky all in shades of purple and blue. The hydrangeas and lilacs at the Botanical Gardens in the city, how they perfume the air to the point where you think you've been transported into some fairy realm. The simple joy of watching the waves roll in at this one perfect cliff in Maine, one of my favorite places in the entire world. So, hear me when I say I will make those moments, and so many more, happen for all three of us. This moment in our history together is a terrible one, full of strife and seemingly endless. But it will end, and we will move on. Forward. *Together.*"

Aubrey kept his voice steady, and managed to hold tightly to them both, until Ethaniel dropped his hand to lunge over the table, grab his face, and pull him into a kiss that knocked the breath from Aubrey's lungs. He gasped into it, then melted, and the screech of wooden chair legs over stone heralded Calix's warmth against his back. Then there were fingers pressing into his side and the glide of lips against his, on his neck, and Aubrey knew it was a perfect moment he'd cling to for a very long time.

CHAPTER FIFTEEN

CALIX

They knew before Calix said it.

Ethaniel was bare from the waist up, hands on his lower back, his spine stretched in a beautiful line as he worked out stiffness from his body, but he looked over his shoulder at Calix and said, "You're going to see him, aren't you?"

Calix turned back from the door of the room they shared and nodded. "I need to. With everything going on, with everything that has already happened, Lawton and I haven't truly spoken. I need to. I simply do."

Aubrey slid up behind Ethaniel, his hands wrapped around Ethaniel's waist. That simple sight made Calix shiver. An ember of desire banked into a small flame. The shared beauty of them, the understanding in their eyes, the tremors of sympathy he felt from them...it stoked something low in his belly and made him ache at his very core.

Aubrey hooked his chin over Ethaniel's shoulder, watching Calix with bright eyes and said, "We're here if you don't want to go alone."

The thing that had felt lodged in his throat since they'd come to Rosehill — a knotted ball of anger and frustration and terror topped with the screeching need to take out all of it on himself — started to melt with that simple statement. Calix felt it vibrate through him, tension slowly massaged into something a little less dire. As if they might carve out a moment for the three of them in the middle of all this horrible darkness.

"I need to go alone, but you must know..." Calix swallowed hard, trying to reassemble thoughts and feelings into a focus he could use for a conversation that had been coming for years. The destruction of the bond he had with Lawton had been inevitable, a slow-moving train aiming for a cliff. They'd always been on this path; from the very day they'd met. Maybe it had been that imminence that made him look twice, made him stare as if Lawton was the most beautiful thing he'd ever seen.

Lawton grinning at him, giving him a cheeky wave from across the hall at St. Matthew's boarding school, his hair like flames in the late afternoon sun. Calix, standing there with suitcases at his feet, feeling lost and alone, had latched onto that fire. Lawton had captured and caged him from that very first day.

"You must know how much it means," Calix said as he crossed the room to them, his hands and arms and body desperate for them, his mind hungry for them. The pulsing yearning deep in his chest drove him into their arms, to press his face into Ethaniel's neck, to run his hand across Aubrey's jawline. To mark their skin with fever-hot kisses so he might imprint his touch on them.

So they wouldn't forget – him or this moment, or the ones they'd shared over time stretched immemorial and yet so short a span.

Ethaniel caught his mouth in a kiss as Calix tried to pull back, and he was sucked in again, yanked down in a whirlwind of grasping hands and damp mouths and the sensation of being *wanted*. Had he ever been wanted like this, desire so, *needed* in that clenching way that left him gasping? At one point, yes, he'd thought the bridge built between himself and Lawton was that very thing, equal in every way. But there had been nothing equal about their bond and in the back of his mind, Calix knew he was being used. But he'd used Lawton, too. For pleasure, for companionship, for the joy of sitting with someone as the sun set and a sweating bottle of gin was passed between hands that lingered and glances that grazed and burned.

"We'll be here when you come back," Aubrey whispered in his ear, his hand hot where he'd slipped it underneath Calix's shirt, then down to grasp his rear and squeeze.

Territorial, their Aubrey.

The thought came unbidden, but one look at Ethaniel told him it had passed between them as easy as the breath they shared between kisses. As if to prove the point, Aubrey sucked on Calix's pulse, firm but not bruising, and Calix arched into his touch, clawing at them both, groaning his pleasure to the universe.

"I won't...leave...if you keep doing that," he panted.

"Then go," Aubrey said not unkindly. A promise of *more*, if he returned quickly. "But remember whose bed you're coming back to."

And Ethaniel.... he was all longing, working his stubbled jaw as if the words were there but they wouldn't come, his touch lingering. They were both so lovely, and Calix saw them each as their own and together, but Ethaniel's mind felt wrapped around his. They didn't need words.

Ethaniel raised an eyebrow, his smile tucked away not without effort as he glanced down to where Calix was already hard. "Don't give Lawton the wrong impression, dove," he said, voice a mere rasp, dragging across Calix's brain and body like velvet.

"The words I have for him bear no love," Calix said quickly. "Trust me on that."

He managed to tear himself away, only glancing back once to watch them kiss, and when he closed the door on such a sight, the silence of the hallway waited for him. He loved Rosehill, loved its gardens and pathways and massive hearths and the scent of *home*. But now it was forever changed, and he would never see it in the same light.

The same was true for Lawton. And his mother. So many questions, and so many chances for betrayal.

Calix knocked on Lawton's door after a few seconds of staring at the wood and paint, wondering if this was the right choice. Footsteps on the other side told him it was too late to flee.

"Calix."

It was Lawton on the other side, and it wasn't. Some of his mother blurred the man's edges; his fire-orange hair was now shot through with gray and auburn, his bared throat and forearms marked by the Golden Order and his mother's presence. But the eyes were the same, so like his and yet not, their gold-brown dulled by exhaustion and stress. For a brief moment, Calix felt guilty; maybe somehow he could have pulled Lawton from the brink. If he'd checked on Lawton before going into the vault, would this still have happened? Would his mother's soul have simply petered out into the ether, forever gone? Or would she have found someone else to inhabit?

Perhaps it could have all been different. But from the day they'd met, some part of Calix had known their destruction was imminent, a glorious implosion of color and sacrifice.

Calix pushed past him, then waited for Lawton to shut the door before wheeling around. "Is she here?" he asked. "I want to speak with you, but not with her...intrusion."

Lawton licked cracked lips and pressed his hands to his chest, his thumb brushing over the knotted skin where the brand now sat. It had healed well, thanks to Aubrey's abilities, but it was still an ugly thing, mistakes and mistrust burned into Lawton's flesh. "It's only me here now," he replied softly, thumb worrying the mark, "and if she rises, I can push her away. She's as uncomfortable as I am with this entire situation, as I'm sure you can imagine."

All the fire and brashness and beauty of Lawton was washed out, and on some level, it horrified Calix to see his friend diminished so much. And then the anger rose in him again. He couldn't stop how his fists clenched, his shoulders tightened and Lawton, ever observant, surely noticed.

"Here to have it out with me?" Lawton asked, a curl of his usual tempestuousness in his tone now. "I deserve it. I know I do. But Calix..."

Calix backpedaled until the backs of his knees hit the sofa and he collapsed into it, the soft velvet giving a welcome cushion against the hardness of his tense body. Everything was so very wrong with it. All of it. And it would never be right again. The thought made him sick, and he couldn't help but shrink away when Lawton sank to his knees and curled over Calix's legs. Eyes pleading, lips trembling, hands shaking as he gently touched Calix with a reverence that reverberated through him.

"Calix," Lawton whispered, his hands now squeezing Calix's knees, "darling, please..."

Lawton moaned his pleasure to the empty night air, to the trees and the grass and the moon overhead as Calix took him in, his body wet and open, hands grasping, tongues tangled together. He was in a mood tonight, torn between begging for Lawton the moment they'd snuck out, desperate for the marks his friend and lover would leave on his neck. He wanted to look in the mirror and pluck grass from his hair and admire the imprint of fingers and teeth on his skin.

"You are exquisite," Lawton panted as Calix rose up and slipped down. "You beautiful creature. You woodland nymph sent to seduce me, draw me into your trap with your sinful body and your eyes that sparkle and your lips that speak of all the sins we've ever been told would send us to the Devil..." He gasped again as Calix sucked marks into his chest, their spines arching until they were one writhing mass of limbs and flesh and heated passion beneath a cold moon.

"I'm no devil," Calix whispered into his neck, smiling as Lawton's hands slid down to grasp his cheeks and pull, his fingers slipping to touch where they were connected. "I'm too sweet for that, remember?"

Calix opened his eyes and saw Lawton on his knees, his eyes dark and shining, and took those hands in his own and held them. Tightly, until his grip ached and Lawton sucked in a breath. But neither drew away.

"I've barely had the time to think on what I might say to you in this moment," Calix said. "How does one assemble a conversation like the one we should have, after everything that's happened?" He dropped one of Lawton's hands to gently touch the brand on his chest. "They did this to you?"

Lawton's jaw worked for a few seconds before he replied. "They have...cruel men at their disposal. Vincent isn't one to get his hands dirty, of course."

Calix tried not to suck in a breath at the mention of Ethaniel's half-brother. The man who had caused so much pain and strife. And yet... "But you worked for him. Despite knowing that."

"I only knew so much," Lawton replied, his fingers warm where they wrapped around Calix's, but he didn't try to pull Calix's hand away from his chest. "I'm not feigning ignorance, Calix, I truly didn't know…I only ever met the man once. Had only heard a few things about strongarm tactics, but it seemed so —"

"Outside of what you were being asked to do?" Calix raised an eyebrow at that. "Following orders, were you?"

He wasn't sure if it was the acid in his voice or his words that made Lawton rear back as if struck, but he mostly didn't care. As long as he made some impact, that was all that mattered. "I truly didn't know," Lawton replied, dropping his gaze to the floor, looking all the more meek for it. And that rankled something in Calix, a sensation that wormed through him, made him grit his teeth. "The Order, they have a mission. It all sounded so good and even and well-intentioned. They said the purpose was to make magic more accessible, to study it further, to take the research out of the ivory towers of academia and the dens of the rich and give *people* a chance to see it, learn it."

When Lawton looked up at him, his eyes shone, but the tears didn't stay still. They streaked down his wan, narrow face and dripped off his chin, splashed onto his knees and soaked into the carpet below. It wasn't the first time Calix had seen Lawton shed a tear or two, but these felt *honest*. Real tears, real regret.

It was the regret that infuriated him.

"And yet, you kept it to yourself," Calix said, trying to keep his tone level. "You kept this wonderful group with *such good intentions* to yourself. You certainly didn't bring me into the fold. Why, I wonder? Why keep something from your closest friend, your *dearest* friend, the man who warmed your bed when the occasion or mood suited?" Before he could stop himself, Calix grasped Lawton by the chin, their gazes locking onto each other like magnets. "Why is that, Lawton?"

Lawton's trembling breaths made his whole body quiver, but he didn't look away. *Well, bully for him, I suppose*, Calix thought viciously as Lawton whispered, "Because it was *mine*. Because for all the parties and dances and nights spent smoking in some bar filled with dock workers and men in dresses, I was *alone*. I came to the States for you, with you, but we were never so far apart as we were the moment we came ashore. You had other pursuits here, charity work and salons. Things money afforded you that I had no entry into. And I felt…*empty*."

Somewhere in the back of his mind, Lawton's words rang true. On some level, Calix understood. But yet the truth of what he was saying *burned*, because all Calix heard was, "So I wasn't enough. It was all well and good for you to call on me when you wanted a wealthy friend to parade around on your arm, or someone to make connections for you. Or someone to fuck when you were sad and lonely because I was at least good for that. And yet, *I wasn't fucking enough.*"

The words dripped venom. He hated it. He loved it. He felt retribution and anger and all the angles and terror of finally, *finally* speaking aloud the things that he'd kept buried for so long. And with one single sentence, years of denial burned away into truth.

Calix yanked on Lawton's chin, pulled him up by it, until they were eye to eye, until he could put his other hand on the brand on Lawton's chest and feel that heart beat so furiously under his palm, just under burned and knotted flesh that was too warm to the touch. So he could look the man in the eye, stare him down, and let him see the pain he'd caused.

His own face reflected back at him in Lawton's golden-brown eyes, and for a moment, Calix hated himself. He hated what he'd said, what he was doing right now. And he couldn't stop himself from spitting out, "Be honest with me. For once. Just once. Did you ever love me? Tell me the truth, Lawton."

More tears spilled down Lawton's face, but he didn't look away. "I always have," he whispered, the words like so much broken glass. "And I've always known I wasn't worthy of it. So I looked for anything to keep some wall between us, because if I tore it down or let you do it, I'd never be the same. I spent years loving you and basking in my jealousy for what you had." He swallowed hard, still snagged on Calix's fire-hot gaze. "You are the only person who hasn't turned their back on me. I rode to you after I escaped Vincent's hold because I hoped you'd still find some love for me even after what I did. I only hope you'll not completely toss me aside in the future."

Calix was ripped apart. Torn asunder. Shattered by Lawton's words, the honesty churning behind them, the pain fueling them. He had known this man since they were young boys, alone in a strange place full of headmasters with strict schedules and stricter rules. No friends, no family. Only each other, their beds side by side in a room that never warmed, despite the constantly burning fire. They knew *everything* about each other.

And at one point, he had loved Lawton like his own — a piece of himself, a limb, a lung, a shadow ever clinging to him, keeping him from the loneliness that haunted his footsteps. He loved Lawton still, despite it all.

"I am furious with you," Calix whispered, pressing their foreheads together and relinquishing his grip on Lawton's chin. "I am devastated by what has happened. But I will free you from my mother's grasp, and then we will see where things stand. It's all I can promise you."

The click of Lawton's throat as he swallowed sounded painful. "As long as you don't leave me completely," Lawton whispered back. He sounded broken, beaten down. It made Calix's heart ache for him, but did little to soothe the burning anger. It was a fire stoked by years, not by moments.

"All I can promise is we can do everything in our power to free you. I can't...I can't promise more than that." Calix leaned away, desperate for space, desperate for air and sense and reason.

Acceptance came with nary a sound. Lawton simply dropped his head to stare at the floor, and Calix had to take that as his answer. It might have been the most honest moment between them in all the years they'd been together. He stood, wiped his sweaty palms on his pants, and made to leave.

What else was there to say? The bond between them had never been stable or equitable, and now it bore a crack, the Golden Order the tool that had made it. There were other fundamental disagreements there, too, but the Order was the proverbial straw that had broken the camel's back.

"Calix, wait." Lawton scrambled to his feet, still clutching at his chest as if the brand pained him. "Please. There's so much more to say, and I want to."

"Now's not the time," Calix replied as he put a hand on the door, ready to leave. He wanted to be the only place he knew was accepted, despite his flaws and magic and being the swirling epicenter of the chaos in which they were all embroiled.

With *them*, he knew he was adored. Loved, even. On equal footing with two men who, by all rights and purposes, should be off on their own little romantic getaway, getting reacquainted with the valleys and hills and angles of each other's bodies, searing their memories with kisses.

"And if the time never comes around?" Lawton was too close now, sweaty and disheveled, a manic gleam in his eyes that made Calix shrink back against the door.

"That's for me to decide, Lawton. Remember? You're on my time now. A trust betrayed isn't reforged through tumultuous circumstances." Lawton pressed closer, forcing Calix to suck in a breath and hold his hand up. "I'm leaving now. Get some rest. Please."

"No!" Lawton slammed his hand on the door, forcing it shut where Calix had cracked it open. The sheer *weight* of his words, his voice, the presence of him behind Calix, had his heart beating furiously. "No, I...you can't. We're not done. I have more apologies to make and I need to —"

Without turning around, Calix said, "You need to let me go, Lawton. What I want is time. That is the greatest gift you can give me now. Time, and your cooperation so we can set things right. I cannot and will not spend precious moments with you when I could be with those who accept me fully. Without a price or promises, without fear of repercussions."

He could almost feel Lawton shrink back in shame, his anger quelled. "I'm so sorry. I don't know what came over me."

"Likely my mother, a bit of her. She never liked leaving an argument until it had petered out." Now Calix turned around, let his gaze snag on the tree branch-esque scars running up Lawton's arms and across his neck. He stared up into those eyes that flashed hazel and gold and shook his head. "You have as much control as you allow yourself to maintain. And you have the gift of time this evening to do so. I recommend you take advantage of it."

Calix yanked open the door and managed to not run down the hallway. Ethaniel and Aubrey were so close yet so far away, and it pained him to be away from them. If Lawton called after him, he didn't hear.

All he could focus on was the twin beatings of their hearts he could feel beneath his skin, their soft smiles and beckoning airs as Calix threw open the door to the guest room, discarded his shirt, and fell into their waiting arms.

"I want both of you. Tonight," he said between trembling shivers as Aubrey kissed his neck and Ethaniel ran callused fingers through his hair. "At the same time."

The pause in the air was palpable.

Calix let his eyes flutter shut as Aubrey nipped at the join of his neck and shoulder and Ethaniel's gloriously warm hands slipped over his chest. "Please," he begged, torn between sobbing and pleading and yet willing to do both if they would simply fuck the very breath from him.

"Jesus," Ethaniel breathed, "Calix, I...are you sure?"

Calix answered by hauling him into a blistering kiss, wet and sloppy and perfect, until Ethaniel's hold on him tightened and Calix could practically *feel* the possessiveness in it.

"That is a rather delicate balance," Aubrey cautioned, even as his hands wandered Calix's body, pinching and stroking and twisting the coil in his gut tighter and tighter.

Calix thought he might *burst* from the heat of it, the adoration and attention they were gifting him with. He felt seen and loved and exactly where he should be. Always.

"Our center," Aubrey said softly as Calix turned in Ethaniel's arms so they could kiss as well.

Ethaniel took his weight easily, his touch gentler but no less attentive, but it wasn't where Calix needed it. Where he was straining against his trousers, throbbing in them. He took Ethaniel's hand in his and dragged it down his chest, basking in the way Ethaniel rumbled something thick and wordless against his jaw when their joined hands touched his hip. Then lower still, until Ethaniel took the directive and slipped his fingers beneath cloth to blood-hot skin, until Calix was panting between the slick kisses Aubrey gifted him.

"I trust you. Both of you," Calix said while they took him apart by inches. "Please."

"Christ almighty," Ethaniel groaned while twisting his wrist just so, making Calix stifle a moan with his palm.

"That won't do." Aubrey lifted Calix's chin with a finger, the touch so sweet and so at odds with the fire in those glass green eyes. "Listen to me carefully, dove. Can you do that while Ethaniel plays with you?"

Ethaniel punctuated Aubrey's words with a vicious downstroke and Calix crumpled forward, crying out, unable to stop the sound. "Yes, God," he sobbed, clinging to Aubrey.

"Good boy. I want to hear you. I want to hear your pleasure, and I want your promise that if anything hurts or is even uncomfortable, you'll say so." Aubrey stepped closer and Ethaniel let Calix go, but pinned him in until his hardness was pressed against Calix's lower back, his lips on the nape of his neck.

He wanted them. Desperately. And he wanted to please them. He wanted to be good for them, to give them as much pleasure as they gave him. A beautiful loop of passion and care.

"I will," Calix whispered as he stared up at Aubrey's lovely face, as he let his hands travel over them, the texture of their skin imprinted on his fingertips. "I promise." He could feel tears welling in his eyes, overdue by so many days and weeks and sleepless nights and nightmares, but these tears were for *them*.

For the ones who had saved him.

They hung there for a moment, silent and golden and glowing, their hearts beating in time while their minds interlocked. Calix could *see* Aubrey's vision as it came to life: the three of them on the bed together, Ethaniel on his back with Calix astride him, his knees spread wide by a pair of long-fingered, clever hands while another set held his hips. Breath mounting, hearts racing, sweat sliding down his back while he cried his pleasure to the air as they both thrust inside him.

"You two are going to be the death of me," Ethaniel grumbled, making Aubrey laugh.

"But wasn't it such a lovely image?" Aubrey teased, which made Calix groan and pull him into another kiss. "One we'll make reality."

When Aubrey pulled out of their kiss, Calix's lips tingling, his body *singing* from the touch of four hands, he was nearly too distracted to notice the look Aubrey exchanged with Ethaniel. He could feel them, so deep in his mind, their presence overwhelming everything else, and with that single look between them, Calix simply knew.

You've done this before.

Calix groaned low in his throat, succumbing to knowledge, how it made him tremble. "Who was it?" he rasped, grasping, greedy for them both.

"I don't know," Ethaniel chuckled, nipping at his ear, his neck, his hands pulling Calix's shirt up while Aubrey's hands guided him to step back, back, back, until Ethaniel hauled him down to the bed. "I was blindfolded."

Aubrey grinned at them both, Cheshire and utterly pleased. "By his request, I might add. The third floor of the Minotaur holds many delights and as long as everyone consents, the trouble you can get into is *exceptional*."

Images danced in Calix's mind: flashes of skin; the sweetly curved indents from nails and fingertips; the red, panting mouths leaving bruises behind. Aubrey's hands were there as he curled in on himself, overcome. He was not at the edge and he was; he was teetering on some quiet unknown, the pleasure as pure as anything he'd ever experienced.

"We'll have to experiment with this mental connection more, if given the chance," Ethaniel said, squeezing Calix's thighs to draw his attention. "Not right now. You wanted something, and we mean to give it to you, dear thing."

Calix nodded. Frantic, desperate, not caring if he sounded like a dockside whore earning their tips for the night as he drew Aubrey's fingers into his mouth and moaned while they petted him into a shaking mess. Occasionally they'd stop to kiss over Calix's shoulder and he could lay his head back on Aubrey and watch them lazily tangle their tongues together, admiring how they touched each other with such passion and such care.

And with Aubrey pressed behind him, wonderfully warm and bare, and Ethaniel beneath him equally naked and gorgeous, Calix felt undone. One of Ethaniel's spools of thread left puddled in a heap, his body theirs to command. He wanted *everything*. He wanted to feel, to let go, to consume and be consumed, and he wanted it only with them.

So few had one real love in their life, let alone two. Having them to himself and at the same time felt like a stunning impossibility, and yet...

"Where'd you go?" Aubrey whispered against his mouth. "Did we lose you, dove?"

Calix shook his head, the quickness of it dizzying, and said, "Not at all. I'm only..." He tore away to swoop down and capture Ethaniel's mouth, to pluck a nipple between his fingers and *feel* how the other man bucked up into the touch, how his moan rattled them both. "I feel so good, you both must feel it, tell me you do."

"Every bit of it," Ethaniel whispered back as Aubrey suddenly rocked against Calix's backside, driving him down into Ethaniel more.

It was *shockingly good*. The friction, the heat, the sweat building between them. Aubrey's hardness slipping along his back, his ass, and Ethaniel's cock pressed against his own, trapped between their bellies.

"Just a taste, pet," Aubrey snarled, the sound biting and playful at the same time. "The real thing will take time, but you should know what you're getting into."

Calix's need was a drumbeat in his brain, his heart, under his skin.

Take me use me fuck me love me make it better even for a moment.

"He seems a tad desperate, Aubrey," Ethaniel said through a wide grin, one that only grew wider when Calix lovingly thought disparaging things about that expression. "Maybe you should help him find his center again."

Aubrey began to chuckle and Calix knew he'd missed something. "You two cannot tease me like that!" He was pouting, he knew it, but they also seemed to both enjoy it. Aubrey's grip on Calix's hips tightened, and Ethaniel wiggled down to place lips on Calix's chest and suck bruises into the skin there.

"I think we can," Aubrey said, his smile a physical jolt through Calix. "But maybe not quite so much this first time." Fingertips slid down, curved around the back of his thigh, danced up, then explored one cheek while Aubrey growled, "How long's it been, Calix? How long since someone claimed you here?"

One little touch in, and Aubrey's finger slipped across his entrance. Calix bit out a curse, shuddering with the force of his desire. He felt like a firework on New Year's Eve, one of those brightly colored little pops of light against a velvet night sky and they the fuse and fire to his display.

Despite it all, some shame crept into his voice as he said, "Months. Many months, lonely ones, and I let him —"

Aubrey dragged his fingertips across Calix's lips and whispered, "There's no shame in taking what you need, dove. Not for you, and not because of who you were with. It's all right."

Another look passed between Aubrey and Ethaniel, one Calix could feel spread out like a ripple in his mind, but all he heard was a promise of tenderness, of pleasure, and it left him gasping into Ethaniel's neck while Aubrey trailed his lips down Calix's spine. Ethaniel knew exactly how to soothe him, his hands sweet, his words sweeter, and Calix was soon floating in some hazy, lustrous space between them.

"Easy, easy," Aubrey whispered when Calix jolted at the sound of glass and the feel of something slippery and warm where he hadn't been touched in so long.

"As slow as you need," Ethaniel said before kissing the sense from him—what little was left anyways.

It was only the barest tip of his finger, but the realization Aubrey was *inside him* had Calix clawing at Ethaniel, reaching back to Aubrey, tossing his head to capture one of their mouths so he might latch his teeth there and suckle. He settled for the hinge of Ethaniel's jaw, worrying the skin until Ethaniel hissed but pressed his head down, closing any gap between them

Calix let his eyes shutter, let his body tremble and shudder, let his mind relax as Aubrey worked him open and Ethaniel murmured honey-sweetness into his mouth. One finger became two, the drip of oil debauched but thrilling, the slickness of their bodies enough to bring Calix to the edge again and again. But they didn't let him fall.

When Aubrey yanked him upright with a strong arm across his chest, Calix was helpless, left to watch as Ethaniel built himself a throne of pillows; his hips propped up, his cock gorgeously hard and slick and all he wanted was it inside, pressing, driving deep, driving him mad.

"You paint such pretty pictures in your mind, dove," Aubrey growled in his ear. "Look at Ethaniel. Look at how he pants for you. How desperate you've made him. How he clings to the bedcovers because he knows if he touches you again, he'll impale your soft, sweet body on his cock until you're sobbing with it."

"Aubrey, fuck," Ethaniel hissed, but Calix could clearly see how Aubrey's words landed. Ethaniel was flushed and sweating, his hazel eyes blown open with desire, and indeed, his hands dug into the covers, fingers twisting and clenching in a mimicry of what he wanted and needed so badly.

Another finger begged for entry inside him and Calix hung his head with a low groan, willing his body to open. "I want it," he whispered, desperately scanning Ethaniel's face, his fingers leaving trails in the sweat on his chest. "Aubrey, please. Inside me."

"Patience." But the word hung by a thread like a mountaineer might to a sheer cliff, and Aubrey held him all the tighter for it. The barest hint of pressure against his collarbone, his throat, left Calix keening. He had certainly played that game with Lawton, but never sober. And it had never been like *this*.

"Take pity on us both, Aubrey. Let me help." Ethaniel was wild-eyed but grinning, his touch *everywhere* on Calix's body, but when he reached under Calix's cock and balls to press in where Aubrey's fingers were buried...

Calix yelled wordlessly, startled, humming with pleasure, ecstatic with how fucking *filthy* this entire arrangement was.

"You asked for it," Aubrey teased, his teeth sharp on Calix's earlobe.

"I did, I did," he sobbed while spreading his knees wider, letting them in.

Their fingers moved at different rhythms, pressing into his walls, massaging and stroking and keeping Calix at such a height he thought he might never come down from. He was so *open* and *wet*, his entire body one throbbing pulse of need.

He was *incandescent*.

"Gorgeous thing. Let's get you into place." Aubrey shifted him around, his murmurs sweet into Calix's neck, and soon he was astride Ethaniel with that cock slipping against his hole and he was gasping and groaning.

"Gently, Calix. We don't want to hurt you." As calm as Ethaniel sounded, Calix could hear the strain in his voice, feel how he trembled. They both needed as much as he did, and the surge of pride he felt at that (*he'd done that, he'd taken them apart as much as they had him, they were a collective of scrabbling, clawing desire and it felt like nothing he'd ever experienced before, and he knew they felt the same*).

"I need you both to fuck me," Calix snapped, flinging an arm back to pull Aubrey in close while planting the other on Ethaniel's chest. "Get in me. *Now.*"

After a moment of silence, Aubrey whispered, "Anything our earl wants," and helped Calix sink down on Ethaniel's cock, his hands gripping and possessive, so hot they felt like a brand on Calix's hips.

They'd taken such care with him, it was nothing to let Ethaniel inside his body, to take him to the root and start to rock back and forth, using Ethaniel's shoulders for leverage. Calix saw Ethaniel's eyes roll back, his mouth drop open, so he kissed those slack lips until Ethaniel returned the kiss with fire and snatches of curses crushed between their mouths. All the while, Aubrey held Calix close, petting his thighs and playing with his cock, smearing spit and slick into his skin. Marking him. Claiming him.

"So good, so good," Ethaniel panted. "Aubrey, you'd best..."

Aubrey did know. Calix could feel the other man's focus, mathematically precise but so careful, some small part of him terribly worried about Calix's well-being. The realization of it made Calix sob, made him curl forward, presenting himself and the vision of Ethaniel buried deep inside, forcing Aubrey to snarl, "I'll make a mess of you both."

He was already full, not bursting with it but pleasantly so, until the blunt head of Aubrey's cock nudged against him, and Calix's vision went white. *This is what it's like to burn*, he thought as Aubrey slowly, painstakingly so, pushed inside. He felt Aubrey spread him, as if to get an even clearer look at how he was impaled on them both, and Calix shivered under the scrutiny.

"Pretty thing, taking us so well," Ethaniel said, strained, as Aubrey hummed in agreement. "I wish I could see it."

"You would like the view, darling," Aubrey purred, spreading Calix wider, forcing another sob from his throat. "He's glistening, so slick from us both, and —" Aubrey groaned as Calix tightened around them, forcing them both even *deeper*. "I wonder if he'd let me have him afterwards, let me run my lips and tongue over him, eat him like a peach until he fell into another orgasm."

Calix could barely stand it. The gorgeous filth dripping from Aubrey's lips, the sensation of both of them inside his body, their hands drifting, artless in form but perfect in function. One touch, and he would ascend to such heights.

"I'm not even all the way inside your body, Calix," Aubrey said in his ear. "I wonder if you can take the rest."

"Please, please, please," Calix begged, the tears streaming down his face more honest than anything he'd ever said in his entire life.

"You'll have me, dove, I promise."

The moment Aubrey was fully seated inside him, time blurred. Calix felt them move him, yank at him, grip him so lovingly, holding him between them, using him for their pleasure while pushing him to the absolute brink of what was possible. One touch, one single touch to his cock, and he would explode.

"Tell us when," Ethaniel panted, "though I can't guarantee we can both hold off much longer."

"It's better if he comes first," Aubrey whispered back, and Calix could only nod. "I think he's...he's ready."

Gentle fingers drew Calix's face down until he was staring into Ethaniel's eyes, pleasure-drunk and so beautiful. "Calix?"

He was *burning*, he was on *fire*, he was lost to the way they pulled him to the edge again and again and all he could do was beg, "Please, please, both of you, touch me," and let them whisper against his skin and stroke him until his back arched and he saw stars behind his eyes.

Dimly, through the waves of his orgasm, as he came onto Ethaniel's chest and their hands, Calix felt Ethaniel go still beneath him while Aubrey's hips stuttered. And inside his mind, Calix could sense their pleasure, too; how it rocked through Ethaniel like a furnace blast, while Aubrey finally, *finally* let go of his control and lost himself in Calix's body. The rush of warmth nearly sent him into another weak orgasm, but he could do nothing except pant against Ethaniel's neck and lay sloppy kisses along his jaw.

Overcome. Overwhelmed. Lost in the perfection of the moment, utterly unaware of the world and its troubles for the sweetest of moments.

INTERLUDE

Vincent

"Something's changed." Isme frowned, her thick eyebrows nearly a straight line across her forehead. "He was blocked off to me before, but now..." She touched the rippling air before her with a manicured fingernail. A bit of grayish liquid, like mercury, clung to her skin. "Well, isn't that fun."

Vincent could only sigh at her theatrics. This was getting boring, and worse yet, for every step his dreamwalker relative made forward, she seemed to be dragged two back. "I haven't all the time in the world, *cousin*. I have other outlets at my disposal."

Isme actually grinned at that, all those little shark-like teeth glinting in the dim light of the ritual chamber. "Bully for you, but I'm not speaking of the Oracle. I'm talking about your half-brother. The one you're so blindly jealous of."

Anger was an old friend of his, but it had been some years since he'd felt its sting. "Explain," Vincent said as he dug his fingertips into the table's glass top. The screech of his nails against the surface was deeply unpleasant.

She tittered at him, unbothered. "I'll be taking credit for influencing Ethaniel to our side, Vincent, but sadly I can't take all of it." Isme touched the air again, this time hissing as it steamed at her touch. "My, my, and using some of the *darker* family magics, too. I only influenced him in the right direction, just a little push. He damn near jumped off the cliff." Her fingertip was now blood red, near to black like ink. "A push or two more, and he might actually fall right in line with the rest of us *heathens*." Isme spat the last word like everyone else on the Harkness side did; a curse, a hiss from a serpent's tongue, the drip of poison from others far too used to flinging accusations and accosting those separate from the main horde.

Vincent stared at her. Thinking. Taking in the knowledge that his self-righteous half-brother, the one with all the family magic and none of the ambition, was dirtying himself so. He should be thrilled, and he was, but the suspicious part of him wondered if he'd overplayed his hand. If somehow, Ethaniel was throwing Isme off, trying to trick them both. But either scenario proved fruitful for him; if Ethaniel was trying to fool them, then he'd miscalculated his half-brother's cunning, and if Ethaniel was actually dabbling in the family magic, the justification didn't matter.

Harkness magic was opium. It was a tunnel down which, once traveled, there was no return. What lay in their blood had fueled kingdoms and covens, sorcières and occult librarians and researchers for centuries. The history of their family, matrilineal since the first written appearance in the fourteenth century, was long and storied and full of deeds still never spoken of, at least not in mixed company.

But the other curse of Harkness blood was the seeming randomness at which it assigned powers. Isme was a dream walker, able to poke and prod about a person's subconscious and weave in suggestions. She dabbled in other arts: summoning, realm diving, strange languages. Areas no ivory-tower scholar would dare to tread. Others in his mother's family were the same way, going forth into the darkness with nary a torch or lamp, only their wits about them. And then there were those like him; they had some abilities, mostly mundane, and many in the massive family clan had learned to work capitalism in their favor.

Vincent could admire their resolve, their way of making good of a bad situation. But what burned deep in his belly was the knowledge that he had little in the way of magic but a mind large enough for even the most complicated of rituals, and all the power along the parallel lines of his mother's family had gone to his half-brother and sister. But Maria was gone, disappeared into the ether one morning, and all that was left was the moping, unambitious, *supremely talented* Ethaniel. When he'd learned of Ethaniel's powers, his deep connection to the family magic, he'd thought the two of them could make more than waves. They could be a tsunami.

Partners.

Brothers.

Family.

But it was never meant to be, at least in Ethaniel's eyes.

Ethaniel stared at him as if he were a monster. Perhaps he was. Perhaps ambition and memory and desire without concession were what made creatures like him. But Vincent saw the world as it was, and knew that power came at a cost. You could pay it yourself, or like the moguls and princes and nobles of any age, make others pay it. It didn't defy logic why Ethaniel would run from his family's magic, for Vincent knew who his half-brother was. Too kind, too giving, too willing to pay the price himself and suffer rather than be the one capable of doling out riches to those who deserved them.

"Uncle Jeremiah is in New York," Ethaniel managed to choke out. "Father wants me there."

"Instead of here?" Vincent couldn't keep the sneer out of his voice. "Your father has not one iota of understanding –"

"Yes, he does!" Suddenly, Ethaniel was in his space, their faces inches apart, so close that Vincent could see the furious rise of anger in his brother's cheeks. A flush so like the one that bloomed on his own face when angry or ashamed. They were related by only half of their family tree, but were so alike in so many ways. He'd longed for a brother, ached for one — a friend, a confidant, someone by his side no matter what — and instead he'd been given this.

A man with no spine, no ambition, and no sense of survival. Ethaniel didn't have his clear-eyed view of the world, of its foul mechanisms and glittering gold. It was all there for the taking, and in a world of infinite possibilities powered by a force they had so little understanding of, Vincent knew it could all change for the better if power was shared. If magic was shared. If rituals weren't for the penitent but for the curious, if magic lights could illuminate cities instead of only the halls of the wealthy. If real power meant creating a more equal world.

"He does!" Ethaniel kept protesting, but each pass at the words sounded less and less certain. "He knows what Mother's family does. The crimes they've committed."

Vincent shook his head. "You have no imagination, brother! No view of the truth of the world, and it's right in front of you because God rolled his bone dice and said, 'That one. I'll give him the magic, and fuck everyone else.'" He stepped forward, trusting Ethaniel's soft heart to keep a fist out of his face. Ethaniel was rarely so riled, but when he spurred into action, it was like a train headed for a cliff. "You could change things, brother. You could help mend the brokenness we see every day. You could take your power and do so much good."

But Ethaniel only shook his head, his face a mask of pure sadness. "That's not how the world works, Vincent. I'm a Harkness. And I may not be educated like you, or ambitious like you, but we've both read the same accounts. The reports, the diaries, the grimoires. The Harknesses have never once, in their entire existence across centuries, done anything remotely close to what you speak of."

There was real fear in his brother's eyes, in the grip he now had on Vincent's shoulders, as Ethaniel whispered, "After all that, you must admit that some are simply not meant for greatness in the benefit of others. Only to the benefit of themselves. That's us. That's what being a Harkness means. And I refuse that path completely."

After that day, their relationship had never been the same. And after that day, Vincent began to change the family name once again. He threw it aside for his father's, the de Laines never rising above the station of pocket-poor partisan, and he was all the better for it.

With Harkness gone in name only, he could move through the shadows until it was time to reveal the truth. And with any luck, he'd have his brother at his side once more. Ethaniel was already tipping in that direction, tottering, arms wheeling, desperate for balance. Well, what better balance than the person you'd once trusted more than anyone? A bond could be rebuilt. But blood was blood, it was fire and forge and air and *life*.

They were both Harknesses, after all.

"I see cleverness in your eyes, cousin," Isme said as Vincent strode toward her. "Shall we make another business deal?" Her gaze scraped around the room, snagging on his various antiquities and landing on a simple brass box on his desk. "A chance for me to earn a bit of Cecilia over there?"

Vincent almost laughed at that. "Do you no longer need those little creatures, cousin? I thought their supply, and your hunger, was endless."

"Hardly." Isme plucked a very sharp silver hairpin from her satchel and began winding her red hair on top of her head. "Besides, you and I both know that if you're truly going after Ethaniel, you'll need more than a bit of dreamer influence." With a vicious stab, the hairpin was lodged in her hair, the effect slightly messy but somehow perfect. Exactly like Isme. She'd always been two sides of her own coin, a fascinating study of contrasts. In another life, perhaps it was them facing the world down as Harknesses bent on reform (and revenge), but here, now? He had only Ethaniel.

Vincent tapped his fingers on the box as he leaned back against the desk. He had her attention for certain. "I need you to go back into Ethaniel's mind one more time. Make him question his reality in one very specific way."

She leaned forward, eyes gleaming. "And that way would be..."

Vincent smiled at her. "I want you to show him a door."

Chapter Sixteen

ETHANIEL

He didn't want to touch the box that sat in the middle of the table, and he certainly didn't want Calix to touch it, either. But it seemed they were given no choice, particularly when Talbot was humming off-key in delight.

"It's like the phylactery in the vault," Talbot hissed, his lidless, eyeless sockets almost rolling in teeth-gritting anger. "I can smell John's influence on it. It feels...it feels..."

Talbot suddenly yowled and pulled back into the book, clawed hands grasping its edge. "What is it?" Magnus asked as he looked between them all. "Talbot?"

There was a beat of silence, long enough for Ethaniel's heart to feel horribly heavy, and then Talbot whispered, "It's his. His magic, his patterns, his rituals. It's his, and it isn't." Talbot pointed a finger at Calix. "It's yours. Your mother was a resourceful one, that's certain enough."

Calix hovered his hand over the little box and Ethaniel wanted to scream at him, *no, please don't, you don't know what it could be or do, and I refuse to put you in any more danger*. But he couldn't. Because right now, the two most dangerous things in this room were sitting on neighboring tables while an Oracle pondered it all. And that was to say nothing of the man sitting in the corner, watching them—the man possessed by the mother of one of his lovers.

It was a strange, cruel world, and Ethaniel desperately wished he could whisk them all off to a little house somewhere in the mountains, where the timbers would gleam golden and the sheets were crisp and white and the fire was always banked and the air smelled of woodsmoke and wine and *them*. Somewhere safe.

Instead, they had nothing but violence and fear and questions.

"Do you really believe that?" Aubrey's whisper in his ear was the barest of sound, but it went straight to Ethaniel's soul.

"In some moments," Ethaniel whispered back, reaching for Aubrey's hand. "And then there are moments like last night, and I remember who I am and what I value in this world."

He felt the pang of a heart nearby and looked up to find Calix staring at them, his eyes glossy with unshed tears. "We'll make it work," Ethaniel said, trying to cement his words with a truth he was still so unsure of. Not because of them, but because of what he'd done, and what he might yet need to do. He wasn't so removed from reality that his own transgressions were simple to brush aside.

Once a Harkness, always a Harkness. Vincent had said that to him so many times. But it had never felt true until now.

After a moment, Calix straightened, put his hand on top of the box once more, and looked over to Lawton. "Final chance, Mother. One more opportunity to be honest with me and everyone else here. What is in this box?"

Lawton's absentminded scratching at his arm – something they'd all noticed when it began, and now as it became more incessant – didn't stop even under their collected scrutiny. He scratched harder, hard enough to raise welts over the branch-like marks on his skin. Calix made no move to stop him. "I can't...she won't..." Lawton managed to mumble. Then he grabbed the arms of the chair in which he sat and snarled to the air, something flashing over his face that looked like an argument building. And then it was gone, and he was back to Lawton. "She won't tell me," he said despondently. "I think it's because she's ashamed."

Calix's face was frighteningly blank as he replied, "Well, then we'll need to find out on our own."

He pried open the box with a finger and let the stone lid clatter onto the marble tabletop. The glint of glass caught Ethaniel's eye, and he leaned in as the others did.

A perfect circle of jagged glass shards.

"Aubrey," Ethaniel said, a warning to something he had no name for in his tone. *Dread* wasn't even the correct word for it, but the feeling was similar. He pulled back but the other stayed, hovering, staring down.

"I've seen this before," Calix murmured.

"So have I." Tension marred Aubrey's brow, and Ethaniel's desire to wipe it away was bolstered by how Aubrey leaned back, almost curving his entire body away from the box. "I think we need to inspect —"

Pressure. Heavy pressure in the air. On top of his head, on his shoulders, in his legs. Ethaniel was locked in place, stuck firmly to his seat, only his eyes able to move.

He was helpless, unable to do anything but watch as everyone else in the room seemed to be stuck in the same fashion. Magnus looked perturbed, but Aubrey looked *scared*.

Calix was the only one able to move, evidenced by how he slowly stood, pushed back his chair with a careless hand so it toppled over, and waited. He looked...odd. Glassy himself, in a strange reflection of the blue sheen cast off from the wickedly sharp edges of the shards. And as he stood, the glass shards began to rise from the box, as if lifted by an invisible hand.

The pressure in Ethaniel's head, in his ears, on his body grew, weighing him down like an anchor. He could still breathe, still see, still hear, but all of that was eclipsed by the incredible *force* pushing him down. He silently begged for a reprieve, cast the thought into the ether...and realized neither Aubrey nor Calix answered him back.

Their connection was gone. He knew it immediately. Aubrey's eyes slid to him, a quiet acceptance sitting there.

Calix paid them no mind. He was staring at the glass that now floated before him, the pieces still in a semblance of a circle, but they rotated slowly, catching the light, sending slivers of it to bounce off Calix's pale face, the walls, their clothes.

"Mother, what did you do?" Calix asked the air as the glass pieces stilled. "What did you take from me?"

Time froze. It was an unsettling but terribly familiar feeling, just as it had occurred in the rose garden. Calix had called it a test; he'd seemed certain of it. But this felt much more dire, and important, than that.

The glass was sparkling, glinting, gleaming. Ethaniel found himself fixated by the sharp beauty of it, even with that incredible pressure holding him down. So he watched on, immobile, as Calix leaned into the glass, his nose inches from it. When he did, all the pieces rushed together with a blast of ice-cold air, forming a perfect sphere. Solid, shining, beautiful.

Time caught up with reality again.

The blast of cold air became bitter, but now Ethaniel could move, could think, could properly breathe, and he dashed forward just as Calix touched the sphere with his finger.

Somehow, it felt inevitable.

No amount of daring-do or bravery or good fortune could have changed it. It was as inevitable as a sunrise, as the tides coming in with the moon. As inevitable as death herself. All Ethaniel could do was watch as the sphere launched forward, crashed into Calix's chest, and the room filled with light.

Ethaniel threw an arm over his eyes with a cry, hearing the others yell out in response as well. His heart, caught solidly in his throat, felt like it might beat its way out of his body, and his stomach turned for no reason at all except that it was *Calix* in the middle of the danger, and the only one he knew would be affected by that little ball of glass and light.

"I'm so sorry, my son. There was no choice. Not if I wanted to come back and try to save you from yourself." Lily's voice echoed all around them, seemingly distant but also right in Ethaniel's ear. *No, his mind.* She was in his mind, a whisper of a presence that carried more than enough force of personality to be reckoned with, even in its dissipated state.

"I'm so sorry," she said again, shouting it, calling it out. "But it was the only way. You'll figure it out from here, I know you will. But I can't help you anymore if you can't find me through the door. In the *demimonde*. The longer I'm here, in Lawton's body, the more of me fades, and the sicker he'll become." Sadness hung in the air like fog, and it pulled on Ethaniel's soul. He could almost feel her tears, the tensing of her hands as she might have clenched the folds of her dress between her fingers in a tiny sign of distress.

"It will know you're coming, my dear boy. It will know, and it won't care that you know its name. Don't listen to its lies. It lied to me, it lied to John Dee, it lied to so many others. It sits on a throne of skulls and laughs when inevitably we all fail."

It all faded at once.

The sound. The wind. The light. Lily.

Gone. Gone. Gone. Gone.

Ethaniel opened his eyes, ignoring the tears streaming down his face as his sight adjusted. Magnus was a few feet away, curled up on himself against the wall, his hair sticking up in every direction, but he seemed whole. Ethaniel frantically scanned for Aubrey and saw him also nearby; he'd somehow managed to crawl to one of the low-slung velvet sofas and was huddled against it, his arms over his head. But he was breathing and Ethaniel saw no blood or wounds.

The moment he felt a surge of gratefulness at their well-being, it all sank to the floor when he realized Calix was reaching out to a few ghostly fragments of a woman. The barest hint of auburn hair, of liquid brown eyes, of a sad but proud smile. Calix's fingers snagged through it like one would try to grab torn fabric, and then she was gone.

Calix met his gaze with a shocking steadiness, marred only by the fact that his eyes were no longer brown, but bright gold. He blinked rapidly, as if clearing tears, then dashed over to Aubrey. Ethaniel wanted to do the same, but he couldn't, not before hauling Magnus to his feet.

"Are you all right?" Ethaniel asked him, searching for any little wound.

Magnus nodded, the movement stiff. "I...believe so. But Calix, he's...my God."

Magnus all but pulled him over to the others, and Ethaniel could feel the tremble in his hand. Or maybe his own hand was trembling. Maybe it didn't matter.

Ethaniel sat on the floor and pulled Aubrey close. "Aubrey?"

"I'm here," Aubrey croaked, sounding dazed. "What happened?"

They all turned to look at Calix, who slowly sat on the floor with them, his head bowed, his spine curved as if he wanted to disappear inside himself. "It's so much," Calix whispered. He sought out their hands and of course they took them.

The silence in Ethaniel's mind and heart was terribly lonely. Having them close, beyond the physical, had felt like a gift. And now they were gone. It had been stolen from them as quickly as it had been gifted. From the way Calix and Aubrey were squeezing his hands, he knew they felt it, too.

"His eyes," Aubrey said softly while Calix looked them over. "Calix, what happened?"

The key question. Trust Aubrey to always cut to it directly. Ethaniel had a billion questions rattling around in his mind: *We saw your mother, or heard her…did you? Where did the glass go? Who is this "it?"*

Calix's answer proved to be more than enough. For now. "She took something from me. She gave me information, put it into my mind like a puzzle piece, and then ripped it out when it was most convenient for her." Ethaniel waited to feel Calix's sorrow, remembered what they'd lost, and simply watched on as Calix continued. "She *toyed* with my memory, made me forget what she'd put there. She took a piece of me with it when she did it, and now…" He gently withdrew his hands to put them over his heart. "That's what was in the box. That's why I wouldn't have been able to find it until I was ready. Because this all hinges on me."

…like a puzzle piece…

…until I was ready…

Glass and lightning and roses and the power of an Oracle.

Ethaniel was startled out of his reverie when Lawton staggered over to them, his hand pressed to his cheek, blood dripping through his fingers because a single shard of that glass was embedded deep in his face.

"Dear God," Magnus said, leaping up to seemingly magic a handkerchief from thin air and press it near the wound. "We'll get you seen to, I promise."

"I certainly hope so." Lawton's voice was paper-thin and he began to tip forward, so Ethaniel helped Magnus settle the man on the sofa.

"Aubrey?" Ethaniel said, "We've need of your skills, love."

But Aubrey was staring at Calix, transfixed. He worked his jaw a few times, then, fingers shaking, touched Calix's cheek and quietly said, "You have to go into the *demimonde*."

No, you don't! You don't have to do any of this! Look what she did to you!, he wanted to scream. But he couldn't.

"I do." Calix's words were an anvil to Ethaniel's chest. "Not just for her. But for Lawton. To separate them. What I do with her...I don't know. But he should be free of her. It wasn't his fault."

"Awfully generous of you," Magnus muttered, wincing as he tried to triage Lawton's wound best he could.

"Not generous," Calix said with a shake of his head. "It's simply true. I know that now."

"We have no way there, even if we were to go along with this plan," Ethaniel said, desperation leaking into his voice. "Calix, please. This is madness."

"It's not, love," Calix replied, staring at him so steadily. So self-assured. "It's the solution to everything. To separate my mother and Lawton. To pull Talbot from the book, thus destroying the Golden's Order's plans." He looked down, twisted his fingers together. "And maybe it's how I find answers to all the half-hidden things just out of reach in my life. Questions about my magic. My future. Everything."

"Calix, Calix, Calix," Ethaniel whispered as he crawled over to him. "Please. There has to be another way."

Aubrey gathered him close, and Ethaniel should have felt relief at the touch. But nothing could stop the hammering of his heart, the rise of panic swelling in his chest; nothing could stop him from being swept under by the pain of it all.

Calix smiled sadly at them both, and with a shake of his head, said, "I know how to get there. I know how to read her journals now. That's what she took from me, the final pieces of the ritual to open a door. I can piece it together, with some time. But I cannot do it alone. Please tell me you'll help. Please be with me through this. Both of you."

Aubrey looked at Ethaniel, the pain reflected in those green eyes so like his own. They didn't need a mental connection to feel the same thing. Despondent acquiescence.

Ethaniel laced his fingers through Aubrey's, his other hand grasping Calix's wrist, and softly said, "Tell us what you need."

FOLIO THREE:

REBIRTH

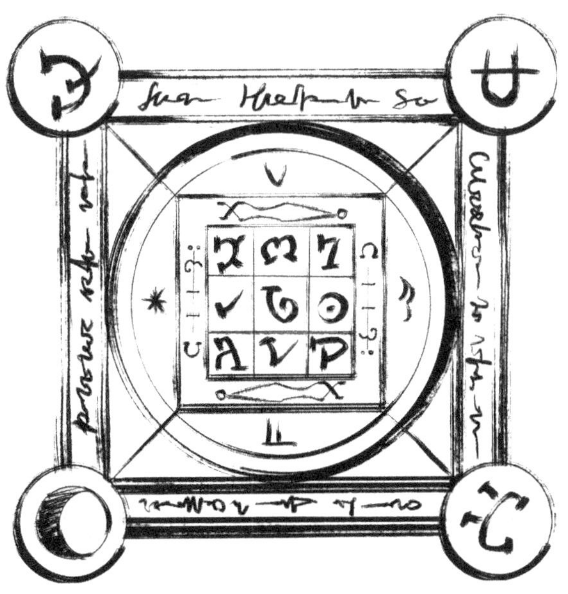

"He took what was mine — body, memory, soul — and made it his own. There were no devils, no angels. Only a demon walking around in the skin of an old man, cloaked in fervent prayer and fiendish slavering after power."
—Edward Talbot

CHAPTER SEVENTEEN

CALIX

His mother's hands were steady on his shoulders as Calix held a flickering ball of light in his palms. "That's excellently done," she said quietly as he stared in amazement at what he was holding. "You are a natural. I knew you would be."

They sat on the thick wool blanket she'd brought from home, the blue and red of it bright, almost clashing against the dull green of grass that had lost its summer luster. There were only a few leaves clinging to the branches over their heads, but their fading autumnal hues weren't what drew a smile from Calix.

That little ball of light was.

"How did you know?" he asked as his mother sat down beside him, her arm warm where it hugged him close around his middle. When she didn't answer, he said, "Mother? Are you all right?"

Calix broke his eye contact with the ball for a moment to see a few tears glistening on his mother's cheeks. She smiled at him before dabbing away the tears with a handkerchief. "I'm fine, love. Only proud. It's a strong emotion, pride. Especially when one sees their child accomplishing something so difficult at such a young age." When her smile faded, Calix felt something constrict in his chest. Not sadness necessarily, but something like it. He hated it when she stopped smiling.

"You're proud of me?" he asked, his gaze going back to the ball. Now that it had been in his hands for a few minutes, the light was growing warmer, a welcome balm against the chilly air.

"I am always proud of you, but there are moments in the existence of a parent where that pride becomes....incandescent." His mother held out her hand, her long,

delicate fingers outstretched towards him. "Now, you were able to take my magic from me and not only hold onto it, but control it. That was...well, it was perfectly done, my love." When she stared down at him, her face bore an almost serene expression. "Now let's see if you can give it back."

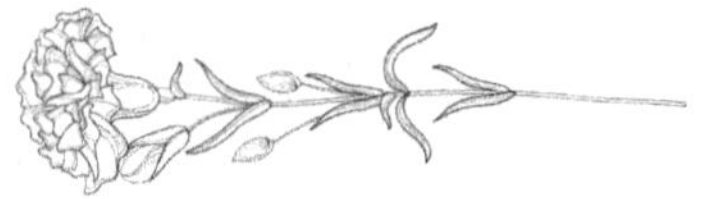

"Calix?"

Calix heard Ethaniel's voice, but it sounded like an echo. His name spoken across some vast chasm, and he could only hear it as a distant memory. Everything else was absorbed in what he saw all around him. It had taken time, several hours marching a line into a dark spring night, before he'd begun to notice flickers of color at the periphery. A tiny flash of blue or purple, green or yellow, and Calix would turn his head, trying to locate the source. And every time it eluded him.

So as the three of them and Magnus spent hours sprawled out across the floor of the small parlor next to the kitchen, his mother's journals and notes scattered between them, cooling cups of tea waiting to be consumed, Calix started to wonder if his epiphany after opening the box had been no such thing. What if he was wrong *again*? What if that burst of surety, that he could unravel her codes and writings, was incorrect?

What if there was no real end to this problem? No solution that allowed them all to escape unscathed?

Too late for that, his consciousness helpfully supplied as he thumbed through another small notebook. "I swore I knew...damn it," Calix said, tossing the book aside and burying his face in his hands. He smelled of ink and old paper, like the books he loved so much, but that scent lacked its usual comfort.

"You should rest," Ethaniel said as he pulled Calix close. His touch was soothing, taming the beast that was his frustration down to a slow burn. But burn it still did, and Calix doubted it would die out any time soon.

"We haven't the time," he replied, throwing a hand out across the books and papers. "All this mess to...what?" Calix raised his head and looked at each of them in turn. "My mother seems to have receded into Lawton, and we can't get her to answer after what happened out in the rose garden. And I have three extremely powerful magic users at my disposal, and all we have is incomprehensibility scattered with madness. It makes no sense."

"As much as I hate admitting defeat, I fear you may be right." Aubrey gave Calix a sad smile. "Magnus, dare we try to get your associate here? Would they be of any help?"

Magnus nodded. "I can certainly try, but I cannot guarantee a positive outcome. Agrippa is quite the hermit."

While they talked, Calix went back to scanning the pages once more, drawn to them in a way he couldn't describe but could only *feel*. There was the connection to his mother through the papers and journals, but that connection was deeper than old memories and thoughts preserved in ink. She loved to write, to document anything and everything as if their lives together were one big journey, and every discovery merited at least a sentence or two. And the longer he stared at the pages, as frustrated as he was, Calix swore he could feel her presence once more.

What would Lily Addington have done?

Calix let his eyes drift shut and tried to picture her. With every year, a bit of his memory of her faded, ghostly wisps that scattered like ash on the wind. Those first few years after her death, recalling her voice, her face, her scent had been easy, as she'd never been far from his mind. But it had been nearly twelve years, and now time had marched a line through his recollection, dissipating it in the most heartbreaking of ways.

That well of sadness he'd long learned to fill up with happier memories, better ones of better times, pressed down on him from all sides. He could feel the pressure, unyielding and massive, and all he could do was lean forward and try to breathe.

"Dove, I'm so sorry." Aubrey was at his left side immediately, his touch sure and grounding. Ethaniel hadn't let him go, so now he had both of them to lean on. Calix tried to refocus, to push the sadness back down into its hole, but the tears that ran down his face felt harsh, almost too hot to his clammy skin.

"Maybe we should take a break," Ethaniel said, gently tugging on Calix's arm as if to bring him to standing. "I think it's required after such strenuous mental activities."

"A man after my own heart," Magnus replied. Calix looked up to give him a grateful smile, which Magnus returned. "It sounds forced, I know, but in the face of such heavy grief and doubt, the restorative powers of tea cannot be underestimated, and I —"

A flash of color in his periphery again. Calix turned sharply to the left, his eyes roaming the wall and floor and oil paintings of pastoral landscapes framed in simple pewter. And as frustration mounted again and he began to turn away, *another flicker.* On the wall now, barely visible against the dark green wallpaper.

Calix quickly got to his feet, Aubrey and Ethaniel following after him with confused looks. "I saw something," he said as he approached the wall and laid a hand on it. As if the wall would spill its secrets and they could all be free of this mess. Well, one could hope, right?

"What did you see?" Aubrey asked as he also approached, his monocle already out of its velvet pouch.

"I honestly have no idea," Calix admitted with a shrug. "But it has happened a few times since I opened that box. I thought I knew how to finish my mother's notes, how to piece her puzzles together, and I was so sure I had the answers, and then it all slipped through…" He trailed off as that flicker happened once more, but instead of fading like a firefly's light on a July eve, it grew *brighter.*

Brighter and brighter still until a symbol appeared. Strange in form and almost nauseating to look upon, but look he did. Three sides of a square, drawn in bold black, darker than any ink he'd seen before, so dark it defied description. Then, a diagonal line from the bottom left inner corner to a few inches outside the open side of the square, where the line ended in a curve downward, like a hook. And written along the three lines of square were tiny runic-looking symbols. The entire thing was the size of Calix's palm, pulsing with light.

And *power*.

His mother's power.

It was *incredible*.

And as Calix stared, his focus became that wall. The deep evergreen wallpaper with tiny gold curlicues and other ornamental flourishes. A favorite of his mother's when they'd redone the house after she'd left England and brought Calix with her.

"Does anyone have a knife?" he asked. "I think we need one."

"I do." Magnus pulled out a pocketknife with a mother-of-pearl handle. Though calling it a pocketknife was clearly incorrect, because as Magnus flicked the blade open, the knife seemed to grow in size until the blade was the length of his hand. "Will this do?"

"Perfectly." Calix took the knife, held the extremely sharp tip against the wall, and drew a line down. "Ethaniel, Aubrey, would you pull on the paper?"

They did as he asked, and the paper parted like an onion skin. Calix pressed his hand to the wall once more.

"My God," Aubrey whispered as they watched the wall - every bit uncovered by the now peeling wallpaper - light up with arcane energy. He spun to stare, astounded, at the other walls. "Is the whole room like this, or only this wall?"

"I've no idea, but we need to find out." Because Calix was already greedily drinking in the symbols. Symbols that, as he stared hard at them, started to rearrange themselves. Pieces of that rune broke off to attach to another, while this rune unfolded itself into a circle dotted with what looked like stars.

The runes moved and shook and wriggled and the wall glowed brighter.

"We need to get this paper off the wall," he said, his grip now far too tight on the knife handle. "There should be more knives in the kitchen."

As Magnus went to fetch the knives, Calix and Aubrey worked to peel the paper back as much as possible while Ethaniel (the one of them with the best blade skills given his profession) ran the sharp knife in perfectly straight lines from ceiling to floor every few feet. Strips of paper curled away from the wall at his touch, and when Calix felt a gentle *push* of power against his own, Ethaniel gave him a wry grin.

"I'm only...suggesting it start to unravel a little," he said, making another perfect cut with the knife. "I do the same thing to thread when it's gotten all knotted up."

"He's *very* good at it," Aubrey said darkly, making Ethaniel blush and Calix bark out a sharp laugh. It *hurt* in the moment, knowing Aubrey was trying to lighten the mood a touch while they were falling apart at the same time. That he cared enough to see them fidget and smile and think about anything else for a few moments.

Magnus came back into the room, dispersed the knives, and they worked. Furniture was moved, paintings taken down, rugs rolled up as the entire space shifted in the matter of a few dozen minutes. And when all his mother's beautiful forest-green wallpaper was gone, heaped onto the floor like ribbons off a giant's birthday present, Calix stepped back and stared.

He could *read it*. All of it. Every single word. Could identify the triangles and diamond shapes. Could trace each line, and without thinking about it, read every single fragment.

None of it meant anything to him, but from what he could see, she'd inscribed a large ritual circle on each wall. And each of them practically vibrated with power.

And then he realized something.

She'd redone the *entire house* during his childhood. Every room. Every wall with new plaster and wallpaper and tile.

"What the hell?" Calix heard Ethaniel say as the others joined him at the wall.

Magnus leaned in carefully, his hawkish nose nearly brushing the wallpaper, then squinted. "This looks terribly familiar." He straightened to look over at Aubrey, who had come up on Calix's left. "Aubrey, why does this look familiar? What am I missing?"

But Aubrey looked shaken. Immediately, Calix put a hand on his shoulder, a question in his eyes as he asked, "Aubrey?"

Aubrey backed away from the wall so quickly that Calix stumbled after him. "God damn it. That *fucking book*!" he exclaimed, striding toward the door. "Talbot knew. He knew all along. He had to."

Calix reached out and the moment he touched Aubrey's arm, Aubrey came to a stop. It took a moment, but then he stared at Calix with such a deep sadness in his eyes that it made something in Calix's chest tie itself into knots. "You have to explain, Aubrey. Please."

"I know. I know." Aubrey sighed and ran his hands over his hair, which was slowly growing out now that they'd been away from the city for some time. From a distance, it looked like fine down, but up close, Calix could see the curl of each hair and he wondered what Aubrey would look like with it grown out. "I apologize. But I *knew* Talbot would try to trick us and I was ready for it. And then everything went to shit after your mother and Lawton and..."

Aubrey gestured helplessly around the room, and Calix could see how he avoided pointing directly at Ethaniel. He was quite sure everyone in the room did. For his part, Ethaniel glanced to the floor, the unspoken fear they were slowly adding to their collective worries thick in the air.

Barely gone a few hours and Calix already missed their shared connection. Worrying over Ethaniel and what might happen if he couldn't cauterize the strings of his family's power might be, if not easier, simpler, if they didn't need to speak everything aloud. If they could revel in those emotions, core-deep and raw as honey, once more.

Too late, his mind whispered as he took Ethaniel's hand and pulled him closer.

"Keep going, Aubrey," Ethaniel said quietly, his voice tight with emotion. "What about Talbot? Would he know something about the runes on the wall?"

"I should hope so," Aubrey said, none of the anger fading from his voice. "These are...well, at first they look like a bastardized version of *Sigillum Dei Aemeth*. From what I've read, it's the most well-known of Dee's summoning circles. 'The seal of God's truth,' supposedly." His jaw tightened and with it, so did Calix's stomach. "The very first successful sigil he and Talbot created. But the works detailing *what* they were summoning were lost, or, according to some accounts, burned by the Holy Roman Church. What little is known has been recreated, but there were vital parts missing…"

Calix felt the snap of a piece fitting into their ever-growing puzzle reverberate in his mind. "She figured it out, didn't she?" he asked in a whisper. "She summoned something or opened something."

"A door? Maybe." Ethaniel was staring at the walls now, with the same concerned look as he'd worn when Calix had peeled back the first strip of wallpaper. "It's so strange. I can understand this *somewhat*, but only in the way I can somewhat pick up context when a person speaks French. I can see a pattern form, but then it breaks off, picks back up, breaks off again."

Ethaniel's whole expression dropped. "Like it's been fragmented," he said after a deathly silent pause. "Like she broke it into pieces and knew her son would pick it back up. Because she loved him, and he loved her, and she trusted he would bring her back from whatever plane she's banished a piece of herself to."

The cold, hard reality of it felt like a backhand to his face. It all made sudden, terrible sense.

"She trusted I would find her, bring her back, and piece her back together. And that she'd be wiser from time spent in the *demimonde*. That she'd know how to…" Calix swallowed hard and tasted bile. "That she'd know how to save me from my own magic."

Heavy was the implication. He didn't need to say any of it aloud. Even without their bond, Calix could *feel* their emotions; maybe it was some aftereffect of their bond, or perhaps it was because Ethaniel was so expressive while Aubrey went still and stone faced.

"Is that your wish as well, Calix?" Aubrey finally asked. "To bring her back?"

"I don't know," he admitted, faster than he should have, but the time was well past for putting on any show. He had to be truthful, completely honest with them.

Because he didn't know.

"Do you think you can piece this all together?" Magnus asked as he slowly began to rearrange the papers and journals into some kind of order. "Is this what she took from you?"

Calix nodded and slowly walked over to sit beside the older man. "Yes, I think so," he replied quietly, voice gone numb with shock. "I think...no, I *know* this was her plan all along. And that I'd play right into it."

When he took a moment to blink away the hot, angry tears threatening the raw corners of his eyes, Ethaniel tugged Aubrey back down to the floor so they were all sitting amongst his mother's writings. "So we work until we find the answers, and we don't do anything moving forward without a plan. A good plan."

Calix so envied Ethaniel's steadiness, Aubrey's steadfastness. They were holding him up with everything they had and then some, and he knew they would bear the consequences of whatever happened as well. Anything they could do to keep the weight off his own back, they would.

He adored them. And it scared him and thrilled him in equal measure to realize he might actually love them.

"So we work," Calix repeated as he flipped open the first journal for what felt like the hundredth time that day. "And we go forward. Together."

CHAPTER EIGHTEEN

ETHANIEL

They stripped the wallpaper from every room with blades increasingly honed against their own sharply fading disbelief. It was a quiet kind of destruction, one that felt oddly welcome against the bleakness of the past days. They created piles and piles of curling, gem-toned paper Lily Addington had lovingly picked out that was now scrapped and lying about on the floor.

Ethaniel watched Calix as they worked, and with every wall they peeled, his expression grew more grim. He ached to comfort him, but knew if they all collapsed in a heap now, they might not finish the job. They *couldn't* afford any other outcome. From everything they'd come to understand through Lily's increasingly manic attempts at learning anything to save her son, and that son's warnings about how his powers would begin to go awry sometime in the next few years, Ethaniel felt panic form a knot somewhere between his heart and his throat. It sat there, uncomfortable and blood-hot, under his skin, and he found himself touching that spot several times throughout the fading light of day.

Aubrey saw him do it. Ethaniel didn't try to hide it, and he should have. Because as the day wore on and their arms ached from slicing and tearing, Aubrey kept brushing closer, his gaze wary, worried. But he didn't say anything, and for that Ethaniel was grateful.

They had enough to worry about as it was.

Because every room they stripped bore Lily's marks. The four rooms on the main floor — small parlor, sitting room, dining room, and study — bore those strange symbols. Different pieces of a large puzzle, but staring at them didn't make Ethaniel's eyes hurt. No, staring at them brought the symbols into deeper focus.

His magic was sparking to life. It buzzed and trembled under his fingertips, ran trails up his arms and down his sides, all the way to the roots of his hair and the soles of his feet. His own mind's eye was putting together the patterns, clicking things into place. He could match up the symbols, but he had no idea what they meant.

And when he pointed this out to Calix, all the younger man could do was stare at what Ethaniel had hastily jotted down.

"I think.... I think it's the start of an incantation. No, wait...a ritual," Calix said in a hushed voice, suddenly sounding so much younger. Not fragile, not at all. Simply...awed. And how could he not be? His mother might have been one of the world's premiere mages, had she not been an Oracle. And even then, if she'd found some way to stabilize her magic, she could have done just that. Risen to the pinnacle of success through the power in her veins and a bit of daring.

Look at what you are! You are a Harkness, Ethaniel!

Ethaniel flinched, pulling his hand back quickly. Aubrey gave him a sharp look and all he could do was shake his head and say, "It seems my half-brother lives in my mind only to cause pain." Thinking of Vincent instantly made his stomach go sour. "And while we're trapped here, he could be amassing some force to storm the place, for all we know."

"Given what I can make out from these runes," Calix replied, tapping one of the pages with a finger, "I don't think he'd stand much of a chance. These wards are more powerful than I realized. And they're only one part of what I can make out but..."

Calix quickly shuffled the various pages around, humming to himself every now and then while they watched on. Ethaniel caught it first. "That's the top of the sigil that's missing on the wall," he said quickly, pointing over to what they'd suspected was a half-finished ritual circle. "We'd thought it was left like that on accident, as if she didn't have the information she needed but this *matches.*"

He took the paper over to the wall and held it up above his head, so the point of the diamond shape was closed off and the runs matched up with the larger sigil on the wall. "The ratio is a bit off, but I bet if you closed the circle properly, you'd have a working spell."

"You're right!" Calix dashed over to him, eyes wide. Those eyes were now bright with recognition, the once brown irises now golden and glowing; Calix himself seemed to glow, too.

Aubrey was approaching as well, but his expression held a note of muted horror. Without a word, and before Ethaniel could ask what was wrong, Aubrey pointed to a small symbol in the outer circle of the rune. "You can't do this one first," Aubrey said, tracing over the simple circle with a horizontal line through the middle. "The sign for salt is in the third place. So this is the rune that should be awakened third, otherwise the symbol's secondary meaning activates."

It dawned on Ethaniel immediately. "That's the same symbol that's on Lawton," Ethaniel said. "Shit. You're right, Aubrey. We have to find the right order."

"It means more than one thing," Calix replied, as if to himself. "I can't believe I didn't see it."

"It does mean salt, or stop, in certain spell languages," Magnus said. "But when it comes to Dee's work, the little we know of it anyways, is that he used the rune in a different sort of way. He was one of the first mages to document his experiments with magic runes and circles, and in some ways, he changed how we interpret our magic now. Salt was a highly prized commodity in his day, so Dee took inspiration from that. The few letters of his I've read spoke of this in detail. So, he eventually...for lack of a better word, *taught* his runes a different interpretation."

When Magnus stopped, Ethaniel felt something twist in his belly.

Fear. Anticipation.

"Mages like Dee used salt to *dispel* magical workings," Aubrey finished for him. "So, if we did this in the wrong order, your mother wrote these runic circles with both meanings in place. To stop, yes, but also to obliterate. So we have one chance at this, and if we're wrong, we lose."

"Everything. We lose everything," Ethaniel managed to say. "That's...terrible. Why would she do that?"

But Calix was staring at the pages again, his eyes flitting back and forth so quickly, Ethaniel wondered how he wasn't dizzy. And when Calix put his hand on a page and slid it to match another, the pages began to glow gently. Gold, like his eyes. Like his magic before the restoration of his memory and, if they were right, part of his soul.

Perhaps those things were one and the same.

"Is this the last of the journals?" Calix asked as he shifted more pages around.

"It should be," Magnus said before taking a seat with a heavy sigh. "Calix are you...can you understand her spells?"

"Give me a bit of time," Calix replied, "and then yes, I think so."

Ethaniel watched, spellbound, as Calix began to match up symbols and lines, making connections where it appeared there were none. And Ethaniel's magic flared with it, as if every piece that clicked into place awoke something in him, too.

Their magics merging. Dancing. Their steps perfect and even. Flowing.

Ethaniel took up a place at Calix's side and began to help him move pages around. As they worked, the world fell away; the hazy darkness of twilight bled into something softer. Ethaniel felt as if he were in an oil painting, all shape and color but his form was bleeding into Calix, and Calix into his. Their fingers brushed, their hips and wrists and arms. They drew lines of light across the paper and leather and ink, making connections where the average eye wouldn't find them.

They didn't need to grasp about for the connection. It was there, *waiting*, begging for someone to come along and make them whole once more. Ethaniel's world narrowed, then widened, then narrowed again as pieces became parts, and the parts became a whole.

Minutes passed. Maybe an hour. Ethaniel felt full. Too large for his own body and yet so intimately linked to Calix. He'd been wrapped around this man, inside his body and mind more than once, in all sorts of wonderful ways, but when their magical essences melded together, suddenly Ethaniel could *see*.

He saw the walls the way Calix did. He saw the power there, beckoning, crooking a finger at them and asking for completion. His whole body felt suffused with light and warmth, but on the edges of his mind he felt its sharpness, too. There was a bite to that magic, an edge to Calix's power that he wasn't entirely sure Calix knew about. He could see it, though, clear as day but still far off in the distance. As if he were walking up a very tall hill and only at a certain point could he see an edge, and so the awaiting plummet to the depths below felt miles away. Not a danger.

Not yet.

He realized, with a shock of cold, that he was seeing what Lily had feared. And suddenly he understood her a bit better.

"My God," Aubrey said in his ear. The softness of his lover's voice sent welcome tingles down his spine, and he instinctually leaned into Aubrey's warmth. A hand spanned his back, gripped him by the waist, while the other came into view and pressed a palm to the pages. Aubrey's magic flickered into view; at first a bit of blue flame, and then a flash, bright as sunlight, and the pages began to *heal*.

Edges vanished, and the pages merged into each other. The image growing and growing, until Calix gasped and said, "Aubrey. You finished it."

So he had. Their powers slowly, quietly diminished. Ethaniel let his mind rest, let his body slump forward until Aubrey caught him. "Sorry," he said with a smile. "I forget how exhausting it can be to merge like that."

"Well, we've not had near enough practice at *any* kind of merging," Aubrey teased, drawing a weary chuckle from Calix. "You were all thinking it. I know you were." But he waved a hand over the now complete drawing. Before them sat a massive set of concentric circles, the runic symbols drawn in each ring so tightly packed it would have been impossible to make out each individual command.

Except Aubrey, in his power to heal artifacts and objects, was able to make the symbols different colors, and combined with Ethaniel's patterning, make them fit against each runic circle on the walls.

"It's a lock," Calix said. "A very complicated one, but I think we can fit them together now." The smile he gave them was bright for once. "You two helped me solve it. I truly don't know how I would have done it otherwise."

"Not nearly so efficiently, that's for certain," Magnus said. "You would have figured it out, Calix, but Aubrey and Ethaniel just so happen to have abilities that line up very nicely with yours."

"At least for this," Ethaniel replied as he sat down beside Magnus. His whole being ached with exhaustion. "But is this..." He sighed and looked down at the now-single drawing before them. "Is this it? Is this how we open a door to the *demimonde*? Four rings to this lock on the page, and four ritual circles to fit into? Is there a significance to the number?"

"Four was an important number to many religious and arcane scholars of the day. Even now, it's used as an anchor in castings," Magnus said. "I'm sure it holds some significance to Dee as well. Him, or Talbot, or both."

"And to answer your other question, Ethaniel, this is precisely how we open the door." When Aubrey paused, Ethaniel could see the weight of his words before he spoke them aloud. Aubrey's frown carved deep lines around his mouth, so Ethaniel took his hand. "I was merely thinking...now that we have the pieces, we need to go back to Talbot. He can confirm a great number of things for us," Aubrey said as he sat on the floor at Ethaniel's feet and leaned back. "It's in his best interest to do so, and it may be our only chance to get honest answers from him."

"Maybe," Magnus replied, "or he could simply lie again. Or try one of his little mind games."

"I don't think he will. He needs us more than we need him." Calix seemed steadier than Ethaniel felt, though the dark circles under his eyes told another story. "I think we need to plan, and then sleep, and then tackle this in the morning. Exhaustion doesn't do us any good."

"He has a point," Aubrey said. "As much as I hate losing time, we don't know what we're walking into with any kind of door into the *demimonde*. And we have an expert in our midst who needs us to go there for him."

"We're actually going to hold up that end of the bargain?" Ethaniel said, surprised. "I'm not one to back out of a deal, but Talbot's given us nothing other than grief this entire time. He tried to manipulate us, trick us, and use us. I don't see us benefitting from trusting him in any way."

"That's the problem," Calix said. "If we go back on our word, who knows what he might do? And honestly, I'd rather trust his word over my mother's. Anything she's written on the *demimonde* is tainted. She's proven herself to be a liar and manipulator as well. Her intent isn't any purer than Talbot's. I'd rather pick the devil we know has the information over the one who went mad trying to obtain it."

There was a dark truth in Calix's words, even if Ethaniel wanted to argue with him about intent. Clearly his mother's was the "better" intent, right? If she had been doing all this in an attempt to save her son, versus Talbot, who only wanted to save himself?

Right?

A sharp intake of breath had Ethaniel looking over to see Calix quickly wiping away a tear. "I'm so sorry," he said as he took Calix's hand. "We won't let anything happen to you."

"You can't promise that," Calix replied, his voice choked with sadness.

"We can, and we do," Aubrey said as he got to his feet and held out a hand to them each. "So let's agree to that right now, Calix, because Ethaniel and I aren't going anywhere. And I doubt you'll get Magnus out of here with anything more than an act of God."

"And considering I believe in many gods, that's quite the pact," Magnus said.

Ethaniel shot Magnus a grateful look for the bit of levity, but the man only shrugged and gave a wan smile in response. They gathered up their things and silently trudged back to their rooms, Aubrey pausing outside Richard's door with a soft knock, then, after a beat, entering and clicking the door closed. They'd all taken turns tending to the poor man, but it hadn't escaped Ethaniel's notice that Aubrey silently took up Calix's shifts more often than not. Richard hadn't been one for company, unsurprisingly, and the few times Ethaniel had spent with him, he'd been congenial but clearly exhausted.

Richard was one more person for whom they needed to make things right.

Ethaniel trailed after Calix as he went to stoke the fireplace in their room, but stopped a few feet shy of touching when he saw the tight bunch of Calix's shoulders, the grip he had on the iron poker.

"I want this to be over," Calix whispered, punctuating his last word with a thrust into the orange embers. Logs shifted with a scratch of bark and a hiss, more embers falling to the grate below.

"I know," Ethaniel said, helpless but to close that distance between them and wrap an arm around Calix's trim waist. "So do I. So does Aubrey."

He heard Calix's hard swallow, felt the shudder under his spine, the way it rippled. Calix was a bare tree branch rattling against the howling winds of a winter storm. And then Calix put his left hand over Ethaniel's, his heartbeat a distant thump Ethaniel could feel. He listened to its rhythm with the palm of his hand, awed at how connected he felt even without their mental bond.

It was a moment of quiet, cautious peace. It might be the only one they get for a while.

"Do you remember when I said I didn't know if I'd...if I'd bring her back or not?" Calix asked, pressing closer.

"I do."

"Well, I still don't. Necromancy isn't something I want to be involved with. Not for any of us. And Ethaniel...I only..." Calix set the poker aside and turned in Ethaniel's arms, until his arms were around Ethaniel's neck and they were so close. Calix's hair and golden eyes looked luminous in the flicker of the fire behind him, and he was so warm and inviting that Ethaniel couldn't help but lean down for a kiss.

Calix was immediately there, kissing back, soft and sweet but urgent. He walked his fingers across Ethaniel's temple, swept his hand down Ethaniel's shoulder, clinging, tasting of cold air and *magic*. And sadness. It was bitter on his lips, his tongue, and impossible to ignore even as Calix clutched at him.

He felt more than useless. *Helpless*. It was a horrible feeling. He wanted nothing more than to fix it all and go back to the city and the shop, but he was better for having these men in his life. It seemed like an easy plea to the universe and yet, here they were. *Trapped*. Beholden to forces so strange, so much stronger than them. They'd pledged to work through this together. Ethaniel badly wanted to believe that would truly be the case. But doubt was a splinter in him, buried deep, maddening under his skin. He was no Oracle, and he would never ask Calix such a thing, so he kept quiet, banishing the doubts to the deepest recesses of his mind.

As Calix curled into him, Ethaniel pressed his cheek to that golden-brown hair and whispered, "I only want us to find the time and peace to truly build something special. But that isn't the truth of our reality right now, and we know there will be decisions to make that will cause pain no matter what. But Calix..." He lifted Calix's face with his hands so he could stare down at him once more, desperate for connection. For meaning. "Whatever you decide, we're with you."

Calix's lips trembled and he pressed them together for a long moment before speaking. "I'm terrified," he whispered back. "I'm terrified of what might be. Of what I might lose. And the betrayals that have stacked up around me still hold nothing to the fact that I want my mother back. I have since the day she passed. But she took so much from me, in the name of protecting me, and I don't know how to separate all of it out."

"I know, darling," Ethaniel murmured, pulling him close once more. "I wish I had answers for you. But I understand."

He didn't need to say anything about Vincent. They all knew his half-brother's role in this. And in his mind, if anyone deserved to be ground into the earth until they were no more, it was Vincent. Calix still held love for those who had stabbed him in the back. He still had *hope* for their redemption.

Ethaniel knew better when it came to Vincent. And what he couldn't say aloud quite yet was that he knew Vincent wouldn't go down without a fight, and Ethaniel would be the one to give it to him.

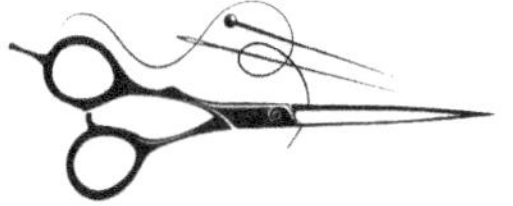

"You know. Deep down, you know something's missing."

Ethaniel opened his eyes to the color gray. All around him. Swirling about his ankles, swinging lowly overhead, pressing in from all sides. An endless space of gray, an imposing void of nothing, yet so overwhelming Ethaniel had to press a hand to his throat. As if he could relieve the unseen pressure with his palm.

"You know something's missing."

That voice again. An echo all around him, but also burrowed in his mind.

"Who are you?" he asked the gray space in which he stood.

Ethanial didn't expect an answer, and yet one came anyway. "Just an observer. I hover near the doors and wait."

At his feet, a pop of color. Blood-red and shifting restlessly, a shape forming out of the nothingness and into...something. Amorphous but a presence nonetheless, it cut through the air with the persistence of London fog, forming curling, snaking coils of color until it grew to nearly his height, but slimmer. The vaguest outline of a person.

And its presence grew, another weight on him, and Ethaniel reached out on instinct, his magic flaring. He meant only to create something solid to keep him from buckling at the knees, but the power he gathered in his hand flared, then burned. Like he'd put his hand right into an oven, but he could feel the heat and none of the pain. It was the oddest sensation, and Ethaniel backpedaled a few steps, clutching his hand to his chest.

"What the hell was that?" he asked the space and the shimmering figure before him.

"You haven't been a part of the demimonde for some time, Ethaniel. Not since you were a child. That's what you were feeling at first. That doubt, wiggling and squirming in the back of your mind." The figure drifted closer. "Doubt that you should be here, so close to a door, when your magic knows better."

"What are you talking about?" he asked in a whisper.

"You know."

"I don't." But the fear in his veins, chilling his blood, was no more a lie than his words.

"Well, some part of you does." Before he could move, the figure reached out and touched a single finger to his chest.

He was wracked with pain and bent over, screaming with it, digging his fingers into his scalp, dragging his nails down his face so that pain might distract him from the boiling pit of agony he'd become.

"Look," the figure said, yanking his head up by his hair. Ethaniel was crying, howling, almost inconsolable, but the moment he looked, it all stopped.

No more pain. No more anguish.

No more fear.

"Very good," the figure said, letting him go with a gentle pat to the shoulder. "Your Oracle will never get past the last seal without you. His mother had It, but he has you. How lucky he is to have a Harkness at his side."

Ethaniel could only stare at the door before him. A gently curving arc glowing silver-mercury, the edges of it hazy. Ethaniel could feel its endlessness, vast and yawning like the insides of Jonah's whale, waiting to welcome him in.

"He needs me to finish opening the door," Ethaniel whispered. Horrified. Elated. His blood now singing in his veins, overcome and ecstatic. He could feel that same thing bubbling up inside him, spreading out across his body. The increasing wonder of it. No pleasure had ever felt like…like…

THIS.

"Harknesses always come back eventually," the figure said as it began to fade into the gray. "Even the most stubborn ones do."

And then he was alone again, in that yawning space of endless gray mist. The archway glittered. It called his name by pulling on the power in him; it wrapped its fist in the threads of him and yanked.

Ethaniel stumbled forward, overcome. Desperate. Yearning. The rush of it — the magic, the mystery, the unnamed urge — pushing him forward until it was all he saw. The archway, and the nothingness beyond it.

Currents of light and energy crackled around him as he neared. The flickers of it became more solid, more real, and they began to weave strings of color, back and forth between him and the door. Building, building, building, until...

"There you are. I was wondering if you'd stay."

Ethaniel slowly raised his gaze to find something staring back at him through the archway. "Was that you a moment ago?"

If a shadow could laugh, it did so with liquid ease. The sound poured into Ethaniel's ears to rest somewhere between his heart and his stomach, leaving him feeling full.

"So you do still feel it. The call. The beckoning. Very good."

The shadow pushed at the confines of the archway, its head extended on an unnaturally long neck into Ethaniel's space, all while the little arcs of light popped and fizzled, sparking all manner of colors and making him wince and try to withdraw. But he couldn't move. He could only look up into the thing's face, where coal black eyes stared back.

And its voice... Resonant. Beautiful. Harmonious but with a grating edge, like a single, too-tight string on the neck of a violin. A hair off.

"You will stay and listen to me, loved one. Visitor of my soul, and mine of thee. I have waited for one like you for so long. And now I offer you the way forward. I can help you break open a door, one safe enough for you and your Oracle to pass through. One that will let you travel not only into, but also away from my plane. I can give you what you need."

Ethaniel regretted the words before he said them aloud. "And what do you need from me?"

It pushed again, against the very air, coming within an inch of Ethaniel's face. "I want you to help me put Lily Addington back together."

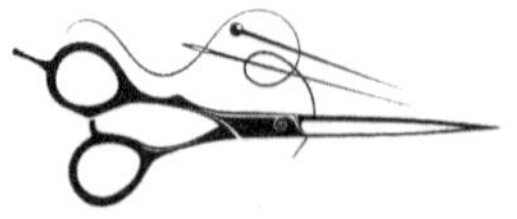

Aubrey and Calix found him hours later, bent over a desk, pen in hand, eyes bleary with exhaustion. He wanted to sleep. He *needed* to sleep. But it wouldn't come until he was finished. And he was so close now.

"Ethaniel," Aubrey said, hurrying over to him and dropping to his knees, taking the pen from Ethaniel's numb fingers. "My God."

Calix was already around the other side of the desk, gently taking Ethaniel's other hand in his own. His warmth was a welcome balm to Ethaniel's fraying mind. "Darling, what happened? What is..." He pulled Ethaniel's papers to him and stared.

"I figured it out," Ethaniel said, wincing. He could taste stale toast and cold tea on his own breath. "I figured it out."

"Ethaniel. Talk to me." Aubrey looked so worried, and it hurt his heart to see it, so Ethaniel squeezed his hand. But Aubrey shook his head and said, "No, none of that placating. Besides, you know it doesn't work on me. Please, Ethaniel."

Ethaniel slumped in his seat and let his head loll to the side so he could properly look at Aubrey. God, he was tired. Moving his eyes hurt, and trying to form words felt like dragging himself through quicksand. But after a few attempts, he managed to say, "The door. I can get it open."

Interlude

LAWTON

Lawton's gaze was firmly stuck to the ceiling as he lay on the far too soft bed. The house had settled after some flurry of activity through the early evening, but now it was so quiet, he could hear the wind rattle the shutters. There wasn't much he could do except lie here, useless and pathetic. His body was exhausted, but his mind was still moving, churning, *thinking*.

He'd worn himself out tracing the deep red-purple lines up his arms with his fingers, going over them again and again as if this time, *this time*, they'd fade with his touch. But he knew the truth; his body was sick, and the secondary bit of a soul stuck in alongside his own was eating away at him. She was fading, too. He could feel it, a vacuum of air where there'd once been plenty.

He'd almost gotten used to her over the last several days. But she was literal poison in his veins, tainting him with something that not one of the very smart, very talented people connected to Calix seemed to understand or even have a grasp on.

The lesson he'd learned as a child held true still: he could only rely on himself.

"Still don't want to talk?" he asked the candle-lit space around him. "Pity. I could use the company."

That faintest of heartbeats stirred, off-rhythm to his own; it sent a strange thrum of awareness through him. *I am here*, Lily said faintly. *It would be easier for me if you'd let me in.*

"I'm quite aware of what is easier on *you*," he snapped. "And since you've got me talking to you out loud, I suppose continuing to play the idiot in this tragedy is my fate."

The moment he closed his eyes, she was there. Just on the other side of a glowing archway. "Let me through, Lawton," Lily said. "We need to speak at length."

Lawton waved a hand at the archway, one eyebrow raised. "For the life of me, I don't understand why we can't just stay here." Lily opened her mouth, but he cut her off. "And saying 'because of the *demimonde*' is not the explanation you think it is. Quite the contrary. It's a bit of a pisser, honestly."

To her credit, Lily didn't even frown at him. She seemed invulnerable to his sour moods. And he certainly had plenty to be sour about, even without Calix hovering near his edges.

I heard your conversation with him. You seemed forthright in your apology.

Lawton snarled at her. "I hate it when you do that! Quit reading my mind! We're *in my bloody mind*, there's no need for the extra poking about."

That earned him a smile. Lily was a beautiful woman, even as splintered as her visage was. The cracks he'd seen across her skin, which early on in their connection looked like fine spiderwebs, had slowly begun to widen, deepen, and spread. The largest crack ran from her right temple, through her right eye, and down to her mouth. It had started to split, and in that space there was nothing.

Empty black. A void.

"Fine," he huffed, and stepped aside so she could enter.

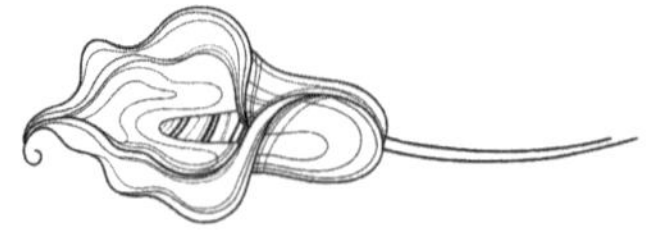

After the initial shock had worn off, Lily had explained it to him like this.

"We aren't sharing your body," she said, hands folded in her lap as Lawton paced. The furniture she'd conjured in his *space* in his mind was simple: two leather chairs and a table between them holding a fine china tea set. The scent of jasmine lay heavy on the air, and Lawton was never able to sample its heady sweetness without thinking of Calix. Their favorite restaurant had an outdoor seating area that practically burst with jasmine blossoms in the summer, and he'd shared with Calix many bathtubs perfumed with the stuff, the oil so thick it bubbled on the water's surface.

"How civilized," he said before sitting and waiting for her to pour them tea. "Quite a nice little setup you have here, Lady Addington."

"Lily is fine, dear," she said as she handed him a cup. The jasmine scent grew stronger and he closed his eyes and leaned forward into the steam. Somewhere, far along the horizon in his mind, he could feel his entire body throb with pain and exhaustion. But it was a distant thing, and the jasmine tea helped chase away the little bits that lingered.

"So what's this thing about not sharing a body?" Lawton finally asked after a few sips. "Because it certainly feels like we are."

Lily shook her head. Her auburn hair was so like Calix's, if a bit darker and lusher, and their eyes were identical. She was *clearly* the one Calix took after, even though Lawton had never seen an image of the former earl. "No, my dear, that's not possible. At least as far as I've been told. My body is long dead, and without extremely powerful magic, it will never rise. Even if it could be reanimated, a body isn't what makes a human who they are. Bodies are tools. We are sharing much more than that."

Oh. Well. Lawton didn't like the sound of *any* of that, and he was quite terrified to say the answer she so clearly expected out loud. "Do regale me," he said, throat suddenly quite dry.

The indulgent smile she gave him left him feeling all manner of ways, but mostly a bit like he was a naughty child who had pulled on a kitten's tail. Not to hurt, only to play, but still needing to be taught caution and care. A bit like a student with a very eager teacher. And the smallest bit like he'd felt when warming the bed of a certain heiress, at least twenty years his senior, and that was more disturbing to him than anything that had happened yet.

"We're sharing a soul," she said before leaning back in her chair. "You had a small piece of yours carved off by that symbol on your chest, leaving you open to those of us strong enough to manifest more than a bit of ghostly mist and cold air."

Lawton had heard the others talking in a similar manner. That the Golden Order, in their rather *creative* torture methods, had left him open and vulnerable to forces outside their world. (He eagerly left aside the concept of *other realms* for another day when things weren't so hysterical, or dire.) It had made sense on a certain level, but listening to Lily Addington speak so forthrightly about something that had changed his entire life felt deeply uncomfortable. Which was exactly how the truth felt most of the time.

"Right. Lovely," Lawton managed to choke out. He set aside his teacup so it would stop rattling against the saucer. "So had you not come along, I could have been...infected by something else?"

She shrugged. "Essentially. But I found you, or rather, the bit of me that was stoppered up and let go found you. It was good fortune for both of us. You won't have to deal with being puppeted around by some strange entity or vengeful spirit, and I can stay near Calix and help guide him."

Her words rankled, piling up in him like too many blankets stuffed into a drawer. "Unless I'm mistaken, you're quite dead and have been for some time," he snapped, ignoring the way he dug his fingers into the arm of the chair. "Calix speaks like you walked on clouds and did everything to give him the best opportunities. But I'm seeing a rather different picture."

"So defensive of my son," she murmured, and when he glared at her, she smiled. "You clearly love him. I'm glad he has you."

Lawton saw the memories, flashes of them but not like he was reliving them. *She* was. But he couldn't stop her; her pull was so strong, so steady, and she yanked and yanked on the cords of his memories, watching his history with Calix from the outside, with no context of certain events and moments that now made him cringe.

Lily saw it all — good, bad, ugly, kind, every bit of it. She watched Lawton kiss her son's forehead or cheek, take his hand, offer him wine or tea or a hug or pin him to a wall. She saw every time Lawton walked into a glittering ballroom, his arm casually tucked into Calix's, his new suit the latest fashion that could be funded by the endless Batherton fortune.

She saw *him*, and he shrank under her scrutiny to await judgment.

"I'm glad he has you," Lily repeated, and Lawton could hear no mockery in her voice. "He needed someone to take care of him and someone to challenge him. You gave him both."

"I fucked up," Lawton whispered. "I completely, utterly fucked everything up. I betrayed him."

Lily shook her head. "On a level, perhaps. In my eyes, your ambition outweighed your common sense. It's not a sin, Lawton, merely a mistake." She pressed her hand to her heart. "I can feel it. The weight of your soul. Yours is no heavier than his or my own. And now that we're linked in this way, perhaps I can help you restore your good name in my son's eyes."

Lawton leaned forward, waiting. He'd take any chance he could get to make things right with Calix.

He waited. And waited. But she didn't move. Eerily still, like a statue.

"Hello?" Lawton reached over, hesitated for a moment, then pressed a finger to her wrist. The image *shattered* at his touch and he jumped back with a yell, knocking his chair and the table over with how quickly he moved.

The furniture faded away, too, and was replaced in this strange, endless gray space, with a glowing archway. Lily Addington stood on the other side. "We share a soul, but I'm only a tiny piece of myself, and I cannot hold myself so close to you for long," she said, unmoved by his impression of a beached fish gasping for air. "This archway is what keeps us separate, so we don't merge into one. Think of it like a doorway into your mind, or one into mine. And since a doorway is a rather apt metaphor, I figured this made sense for a proxy."

Lawton slowly approached the archway. His nerves were on fire with every new revelation, but his worries couldn't keep his curiosity at bay. "So we can simply pass through this if we wish to talk for longer?" he asked.

She shook her head. "You can let me through on your side. You're a full, living person. You have complete power over your side. I don't have enough of myself pieced together to do the same. The archway is here to protect you, not me."

Carefully, he reached out with a finger to trace the archway. It tingled under his fingertip, but didn't cause pain. It was beautiful and fascinating and slightly terrifying. "But if I let you in, you can stay."

"For a while. And then you'll naturally overwhelm me and I'll need to recede for a bit."

The expectant look she gave him was so like Calix that it nearly ground Lawton's mind to a halt. But he knew that look well, and knew she was waiting to hear something specific from him. Well, he hadn't spent ten years at boarding school and another handful at Cambridge to be caught academically unaware. "I'm not one with magic," he said slowly, watching the archway's edges sparkle under his touch, "but I'm assuming this also means I can call you over whenever I want."

The smile he earned was bright and vicious. "Would you like to feel magic in your veins, Lawton? I can make that happen. You can use my powers, limited as they are right now, to even help Calix and his friends."

Lawton nearly snorted at *friends* but let it be. He didn't want Lily seeing how awfully jealous he was of the tailor with the broad hands and angular jaw, or the tall, lean museum curator with stunning eyes. He could stew in those feelings later. "So I could help them?" he asked. He already knew the answer.

"You could. You could protect them from those in pursuit. You could help Calix unravel the mystery I left for him. It's in his best interests, Lawton. The things I left behind..." Lily paused, her gaze going skyward. "I don't remember all of it, not all at once. But you will be able to help him. I'm trusting you will."

He wasn't fully aware of when he'd made the decision to let her through, but it took only a moment to let his mind relax and release whatever invisible barrier stood between them..

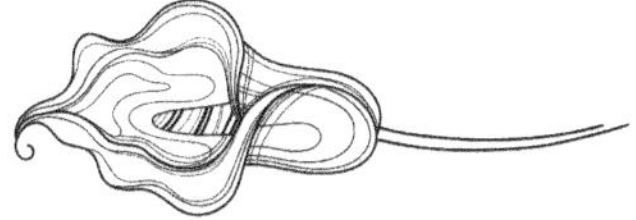

"You will need to keep safe once they open the door to the *demimonde*," Lily said not a second after she stepped through the archway. "The goal is for Calix to find me in the *demimonde*, bring that piece back, and start to put me back together."

It struck Lawton that Lily was relying on one sole truth: that her son loved her enough to want her back in his life. He knew Calix would give almost anything to have his mother back, even after all these years, but the quicksilver way clarity came to him in this moment nearly had him reeling. He hid it well enough, masking it behind a frown that didn't bely his true thoughts.

She might be stuck to me like a limpet, but that won't stop me from helping Calix. If he wants her back, I will see it through.

If he doesn't, I'll help destroy her.

"You say that as if it's as easy as popping down to the corner bakery for bread," Lawton said as he crossed his arms. "You're talking about going to another *realm*. A thing I didn't even know existed until quite recently."

"That's why you're going to give him this." Lily held out her hand and screwed her eyes shut in concentration, and Lawton watched something form there; he watched her already wispy form waiver even more, going translucent in some places. When she looked at him, he was staring down at the perfectly round gold coin in her palm.

"And whose passage am I paying for?" he asked, not sounding nearly as cheeky as he'd hoped. He itched to take the coin, some unspoken longing welling up in him.

Lily clucked her tongue at him and he yanked his hand back. "It won't hurt you, but I don't recommend prolonged contact with your bare skin," she said as she waved her hand and a bright yellow handkerchief appeared. She picked the coin up between folds of fabric and held it out to him. "Do not lose this. It is the only coin It gave me, and I was extremely fortunate to get one to begin with."

What she told him next was a story unparalleled to any he'd heard.

After years of study, experimenting, and failure, she had finally decoded the few writings that existed in their world from Dr. John Dee. A brilliant man. A madman. A well-intentioned scholar and practitioner of the arcane who had been ensconced in Queen Elizabeth I's court for years before his studies began to veer off track. He'd grown bored of prognosticating the Queen's minor issues with duchies and lords with too much coin and not enough sense, and had begun to veer into many things: alchemy, transmogrification, herbs, and summoning.

Summoning became his first love, his wife a distant second, his children mere afterthoughts. But he could never keep a summoned creature for long before the energy of its home realm called it back. He needed a way to leash these creatures, to keep them *here*. After a long, long search, an exasperated friend had recommended a man named Edward Talbot. His surname depended on the week, month, and if he was wanted by local authorities.

Edward Talbot. Wanted for, but not limited to: desecration of a corpse, practicing black magic, accused of fraud, receiving stolen goods, forgery, horse thievery, and necromancy.

Necromancy.

The word rang in Lawton's ears. Such a thing was *possible*?

"Talbot also had some deep connections inside the Harkness family," Lily said, her tone gone dark and wary.

"Harkness like..." Lawton jerked his thumb over his shoulder and she nodded. "Bloody hell."

"That's beside the point currently," Lily said before continuing.

Talbot was gifted, magically. Anything he put his mind to, he could make happen. And Dee had what he needed to keep fueling his own research into something he'd not told anyone else: he was quite sure that some realms held creatures the likes of which they'd never seen, and the *demimonde* was not just a land of shadows and half-truths, but a place where the shadows stalked and the half-truths grew as tall as trees.

Together, they slowly became nearly unstoppable.

Dee's trust in the Court fell, and the Court saw him as blasphemous. They parted ways rather tempestuously, which was to Dee's detriment because the Queen had been funding his lifestyle and research for nearly three decades. Dee was no longer a young man, but the fire inside him burned brighter with every inch toward a true summoning.

In 1582, they managed to summon a strange little creature, almost monkey-esque in appearance. It banged on the confines of its magical prison, screamed at the top of its lungs, and then disappeared. But they'd done it. A real summoning.

In 1583, what walked through their open door was unlike anything they'd ever seen. The odd oval face resting on a long neck. The four eyes, two larger on top, two smaller on the bottom, and a mouth full of fangs. Clawed hands with only three bony appendages that looked like fingers that had been twisted and knotted, almost vine-like. And the wings. Great, wide things made of bleached bone and deep red sinew, almost like a bizarre set of knitting needles had done the work then stuck around to create an even more frightening visage. The wings dripped with gold beads and snarled knots of copper, but Lawton doubted those shining bits were metal like what they pulled from the earth.

The creature was utterly alien and yet Lily hadn't feared it.

In his mind, Lawton saw it. Lily was gifting him this image, and the only way she could have done so was because she had seen it.

"I summoned it, following the instructions I pieced together over all those years," she said, her voice both proud and somehow small. Like shame was still there, underneath the surface. "It told me to call it Uriel."

The image grew bigger in his mind's eye and Lawton shrank back. Was this what true fear felt like? It was such an inhuman creature, impossibly tall and lithe and so frighteningly beautiful and so, so dangerous.

"It told me I'd find answers in the *demimonde* to help Calix as he grew older," Lily said, now wringing her hands together. "Oracles don't...we burn out so quickly. Our minds are so open to magical influences. And everything I did — the studying, the artifacts, the experiments — none of it stood up like Uriel and said, 'I have a solution for the problem you desperately want to solve.'"

Uriel had taught her so much about the *demimonde*, the place between realms. A transit station between the endless doorways far beyond the reach of any human. And that's where she'd find answers. "The magic of that place isn't like ours here, and Oracles exist in other realms. So, there must be something they do, or some resistance they have. That's what I wanted to find for Calix. To go through all those doors until I had answers," Lily explained. "And I never had any guarantees until Uriel put me on the right path. He showed me how to create a soul phylactery, how to carve off parts of myself so they'd activate when I died."

She floated over to him, sank to her knees before Lawton, and took his hands. "You must understand. Oracles go mad. We all do. Whether it's in the pursuit of knowledge, or the other realms begin to push on our minds, seeking a way in, a way to influence us...we all go mad. And I couldn't watch that happen to my son. I would do *anything* to keep him from harm. And I believed that my efforts wouldn't be in vain. That Calix — *my son* — would know what to do, and if he didn't, that Uriel would find a way to help him."

When he looked down, the coin was in his hand.

"Use it to help keep the door open. You only have to think about the coin when the door is open, and the being I know will come to your aid. And it will protect Calix while he's on the other side." The grief, the hope...all of it twisted up, now glimmering in her eyes. Lawton understood. The love she had for Calix rivaled his own, but she was his *mother*. She gave her life to try to help save him. He could do nothing but match her efforts. But still he wondered what lay in wait for them, at the end of the line.

Well, he'd always been a bit of a pessimist behind closed doors. And the doubt gnawing at him even now, even in the face of Lily's desperation, would keep from having the rug pulled out from under his feet.

"And what did this creature want in return?" he asked. His stomach was slowly souring, so much that he could taste bile at the back of his throat. But he had to know. Because Lawton might be inexperienced in making deals with some otherworldly creature, but he knew enough devils on Earth to make him wary.

Lily looked away, stilled her hands, laced her fingers together in front of her. When she looked back up at him, Lawton saw fear there. And triumph. He wanted to vomit.

"That once I had a body again, I would work to create space here for it and some of its kind," she said as plainly as one might ask for their dinner partner to pass the peas.

He shouldn't have been shocked, and yet his world wobbled a little. He stared at her, only managing to whisper, "That's madness. Do you know that? I have done some terrible things, but that is…" Lawton paused, rolled her words around in his mind. Then he thought better of asking where she would procure the body because the word *Harkness* rang through his mind again and again, drowning it out.

Lily may have loved her son. Adored him. Cherished him. But she was clearly still after her own ignoble, glorious end goal, and Lawton wasn't certain it included anyone else. Even Calix. So no, he didn't trust her. But if he was clever and quick, he might be able to outsmart her for just long enough.

"What must I do?" he asked, knowing she'd answer out of sheer relief.

Lily gifted him a smile so motherly it nearly got through his defenses. "Help whoever is on this side hold open the door. You can use my magic. It will take a great toll on your body, Lawton. And it will cut short what time I have left before I weaken too far to be of use."

"It's worth it." And for him, it was. He might be able to save himself and Calix at the same time, if he planned things right.

Interlude

Vincent

"Triumph smiles on us this day, cousin," Isme said as she rolled another set of *ithliq* eyeballs across the spell circle dusted with red powder. "The *demimonde's* guardians are getting restless. They can feel something shifting, even on their side of the door. Their vibrations carry over here, and there."

Vincent followed the point of her wickedly sharp nail to one eyeball, now hazy blue in death, where it had stopped next to a strange symbol. He'd watched her perform her ritual, watched as a sourceless wind blew papers around his office and pulled at their hair, their clothing. He'd watched her eyes go as black as the void of night itself, as her mouth grew fangs, as her skin took on a reddish hue. The power in the ashes she'd used had never been fully explored by one in their family, and here was his cousin yanking on the apron strings of another realm with naught but a few flicks of her wrist and a handful of eyeballs from her pets.

The symbol glowed, power incarnate; even now it flickered with gold and silver light. It and many others she'd carved into the ashes she'd laid down for the ritual had changed, morphing into different shapes. Many of them were incomprehensible to his mind, their limbs and twigs bending into forms that defied all natural laws.

They're not our laws, he reminded himself. *That's part of this point of this entire exhausting endeavor. To tread where others haven't. To find the wellspring of magic, no matter where it was tucked away.*

"Translate for me," he commanded.

"In due time," she replied, then dug a claw into the little pot of ashes at her side, held it to her nose, and inhaled. "My God, the *power*. It's a pity you don't have more cremated saints for me to work with. The things I could do..."

"Go raid a monastery then," he snapped. "What the fuck does the symbol mean, Isme? I'm out of patience."

And time.

Her head jerked up, almost on its own volition, and she stared at him with those bottomless, pitiless coal-black eyes. "I'll humor you this once, dear cousin. But only this once. If you speak to me like that again, I'll send my pets after you and take my sweet time dragging things from your brain until you're a husk."

Vincent was rarely afraid of anything. Mortal men were easy to fool, mortal women much more discerning. But Isme, after her years experimenting with only the darkest of Harkness magics, wasn't fully mortal or human anymore. He wasn't afraid of her, but he was aware of what she could do.

He settled back in his chair and waited. She only laughed, pleased, and went back to work. After a few long minutes spent biting the inside of his cheek raw, she finally stood, dusted off her hands, and said, "We've only a few hours. The energy is already gathering, waiting for them to open their own door. We'll need to parlay with a guardian to let us through, and then you can carry out whatever little plans you've got stashed away in that brain of yours."

Vincent stood and stalked over to her, using the movement to cover his surprise. "You don't want to go into the *demimonde*?"

Isme laughed like he'd told the world's most hilarious joke. "Oh no! No, absolutely not! I've no desire to walk there, Vincent." She smiled at him through a mouth full of those sharp shark teeth and a shiver ran down his spine. "You will go off into that strange place and get your book and Ethaniel and whatever else it is you seek. And I say good on you! It's so nice to have goals."

"You mock me," he snarled, fingers curling into fists at his side.

"I don't, actually!" she replied, her mirth high and deeply unsettling. "Because I have what I want. The ashes of Saint Cecilia, more *ithliq* than I know what to do with, and a cousin who will soon be one of the most powerful men in the world.

What more could a young, beautiful woman want from the upcoming century full of promise? I need an hour, and then we can start your ritual. With any luck, we'll be able to send you into the *demimonde* before Ethaniel and his friends get there. You can throw them a welcome party."

Isme patted him on the shoulder, dropped two eyeballs into his hand, and walked out of the room, humming to herself.

A few moments later, Cassandra entered. Other than to get her orders for the day, they went hours at a time without seeing each other. Cassandra clearly didn't enjoy being around Isme, not that he could blame her.

"Are you certain she's on our side?" Cassandra asked as she entered Vincent's office. When she spotted the red ritual circle, eyeballs scattered across its surface, one dark eyebrow went up but she said nothing else.

"My choices are slim," Vincent said as he sat back down and poured two glasses of bourbon from the glass decanter on his desk. "And she's...well, she's abominable, but she's family. She might go right up to the line of crossing into enemy territory, but she won't go over it."

"Won't risk it, or won't risk your family's wrath?" Cassandra took the glass he nudged her way, but only looked down at the slosh of red-brown liquid as she tipped the glass from side to side.

"Both. Isme's interests are not completely outside the family's realm of expertise, but she's more on the fringe than most." Even as he said it, the words rang hollow. The truth was, he was putting quite a bit of trust in one of the most explosive personalities the Harkness line had given birth to in quite some time. She'd always been odd, but Isme's mind was expansive, her magic unclassifiable in any regard.

"Besides," he said after a steadying sip, "she doesn't rule the roost. Ethaniel's mother does, and if Isme costs me this chance to pull him back into the fold, Esmerelda will banish her to some cellar somewhere. My cousin is many things, but she's not stupid."

Cassandra set the glass aside and leaned forward, her expression more intense than usual. "I don't mean to be... No, actually, I do. I do mean to be blunt about this. Are you *certain* you need to do this?"

Vincent couldn't stop the smile curling across his face. "Cassandra, are you *worried* about me? I'm touched." He chuckled into his glass, drank again, then set the crystal aside. "And since you've not asked before, I'll entertain the question. But yes, I do. For a myriad of reasons." He held up his hand and began ticking them off. "I want my cousin *back*. I want him whole and fully realized, of what he can do and who he can be. Because he is the only person who should be my right hand in a world gone mad with power and magical experimentation. I do not *need* him, but I *want* him at my side. I want to go to the *demimonde*, I want to see it with my own eyes. And I want to get my hands on that fucking book, because it is the only source known to us of how to reach the other realms. No guardian has ever been so forthcoming as this Uriel, and it has never responded to another practitioner the way it responded to John Dee and Edward Talbot. Dee touched something no one else has been able to replicate, and I mean to take it for myself and for the Order."

Vincent picked his glass back up, drained it, then threw the glass at the wall only for the satisfaction of listening to it break. Cassandra didn't flinch. Good. "And if you can't come back?" she asked.

"Not possible," he said, waving her off. "Between Isme and the guardian she summons, I'll have enough time. My understanding, from what I've been able to read, is that time doesn't move the same there as it does here. A second here could be a day there, for example. I'm prepared for whatever happens."

"And what about the price the guardian asks for?"

Oh, that he'd thought about quite a bit. And he was ready.

"You'll have to give something up, cousin, Some more than money. Something precious," Isme had said the previous night as she huddled over the books strewn across the cherrywood table in his study. *"Guardians are there to guard, after all. But almost anything can be swayed with the right price."*

She was clearly expecting him to ask what kind of things a guardian might want, but he simply shrugged and said, "Then I'll pay it."

That got her looking up at him, a curious light in her eyes. "Really? Well, color me surprised." Then Isme leaned forward, viper-quick, until she was nearly in his face, those strange eyes of hers boring into him. "What if it asks for blood? For flesh? What if it wants yours?"

He smiled at that. "What if it wants yours instead?"

She laughed. "Touché, cousin. Very good. I knew you were made of sterner stuff than most in the family, but you didn't even flinch. Didn't hesitate. You can't when confronted with a guardian of the door." She spun a book toward him, the runes dancing across the page before she waved her hand over them and they jerked, straightening out into words. "What if it wants not gold or artifacts, but time?"

Vincent took in the information on those pages with the same implacable fortitude as he did with anything else. The truth of it was laid bare on the pages before him, and nothing he did — no gnashing of teeth or bemoaning his fate — would change it. "Then it shall have time," he said before closing the book.

⁘

Two hours later, Isme had drawn her runes and circles, coated herself in some kind of sticky black ichor, and drawn shapes on his forehead and cheeks with her finger, leaving behind more of the black mess. While the substance dried and Isme had wandered off, her fingers dancing with magic that made his nerves tingle, Vincent sat alone in his office. Waiting.

But he'd never been good at sitting still. He found himself snapping the fingers of his right hand; an old habit, from before when he'd been able to feel magic more...intimately. He didn't have power, but he'd always been more sensitive to magic. More adept at understanding it, even from an outsider's perspective. Ethaniel had insisted he had power, tried over and over again to convince him that all he needed to do was "stay in the moment", but Vincent had always known the truth. He was without in a family full of powerful beings, and he'd always be on the outside for it. The bitterness had long turned to dust, and it caked every joint and crack.

Isme burst into his office, as rude and disregarding as ever. Only now she was practically covered in the black ichor. "I discovered that *ithliq* blood makes for the perfect arcane conductor," she said, practically giddy. "It's a bitch to wash off, though."

"Noted," he replied tersely. If she made him wait any longer, he was liable to toss her from the balcony, or have Cassandra do it, consequences be damned.

"The goal is to summon a simple guardian," Isme said as she went into the next room to walk the outside of the circle three times, her bare feet and hem of her linen dress already caked red from the previous ritual's dust. The footprints she left on his black marble floor wouldn't wash away easily, not with how she tracked the dust through droplets of ichor. "You will make an ask of it, and it an ask of you. A transaction. No strings. If it asks for anything *other* than payment to pass through, that will be on you to negotiate."

Vincent's thoughts ran wild, his nerves on fire with the anticipation of the moment. "This is why the world needs the Order," he said, triumph coloring his tone. He could taste it at the back of his throat, could feel it across his skin like a lover's touch. "If the Order were in charge of magical endeavors, studies would have been done. We would know so much more about magic and our world, their world, the realms beyond, all of it! We could know *so much*."

The moment fizzled out, and he walked over to the X she'd drawn on the floor in chalk. "There's so much we could know," he said, fixing her with a pointed stare. "You're about to benefit from all of my work, cousin. Don't forget it."

She gave him a fleeting flash of a smile, raised her arms, and began to chant. That same sourceless wind from before burst into being, more vicious this time, and left him breathing hard against it, wiping away tears with the back of his hand. It was cold, like walking into a blizzard without a coat. Through the maelstrom, he saw Isme's face shift, her jaw cracking, suddenly out of place and then back as if nothing had happened. Her eyes, fully black and round, going white, then red, then back to black. He watched her skin split along her neck, her arms, her hands, until blood dripped from so many shallow cuts but she never stopped chanting.

The sound of it raised — all around him, like a choir, an off-key harmony of a million voices, haunting and frightening — and overhead, something like a thundercloud began to form.

"Do not move!" Isme shouted into the wind, every word forced through the heavy breaths she was taking. "Let it come to you!"

Vincent watched in awe as it descended from above. A bone-white foot, frighteningly human but edges in shining scales of black and gold. Another foot, then a third, then diaphanous robes of purple and silver and more gold. So much gold that the glitter of it was nearly overwhelming.

And then he saw the void where its face would be, in its place was a sphere of crackling energy held between two rocky points made of pure alabaster. The head sat on top of a thin body, its four arms long, spindly things that fluttered like wings at its sides.

It was beautiful and horrifying and Vincent wanted to get closer to it.

A dreamwalker, a voice said. Not out loud, but in his mind. *Are you the one who called me?*

Isme looked stunned, even as bloody and dirty as she was. She stayed kneeling on the ground, her arms over her head, the only sound the *plop plop* of her blood onto the marble floor. "Yes," she whispered. "Might we know your name, guardian?"

Its head cocked to the side with the sound of rocks falling into the sea, then swiveled to stare down Vincent. He was in awe. He was standing before a god, a being of another realm so foreign from their own, and he wanted to fall to his knees and offer it anything it wanted. He'd never felt such fealty, such worship before. And for him, it wasn't weakness. It was *understanding*.

You may call me Descara. It is a name given to me by another of your kind long ago. And you... Descara pointed a long finger at Vincent. *Ah, I see. She was the one who summoned me, but on your behalf. A dangerous thing, to call a guardian of the door into your realm, even contained by this magical shell you've concocted. A clever thing, but not meant to hold me for long, I'm afraid.*

It jabbed its claw at the sphere around it, making the whole thing shudder. Something deep inside Vincent shuddered as well. But he'd practiced this speech over and over again, and nothing would keep him from its perfection. Or from seeing his goals through.

"I called you here in the name of reciprocity," he said, making sure his voice was loud and clear. "Entry to the *demimonde* in return for something."

Interesting, it said back to him. *Most who attempt to summon one of my brethren fail, rather spectacularly, I might add. Those who succeed typically launch into their demands and do not speak of payment in return.*

It blinked out of existence and for a panicked moment, Vincent could only strangle a scream of outrage. But it appeared again, this time just at the edge of its magical prison. Face to face with Vincent. It was impossibly tall, at least ten feet or more, but it bent itself nearly in half so their faces were level.

What do you have to offer me?

He glanced over at Isme, who was nodding furiously. "My time," he said as he pulled a silver pocket watch from his vest.

It was the longest pause of Vincent's life while Descara stared down at him. Then, very carefully, it traced a circle in the wall of its prison and popped it out like one would cut glass. It extended a claw and said, *Your offer is acceptable.*

Chapter Nineteen

AUBREY

Sleep was not an easy mistress to tame on even the calmest of nights, and tonight, Aubrey fought slumber with his entire being. Every time he opened his eyes with an exasperated huff, he found himself staring over at them.

Wondering.

If their fates were leading them down a path of destruction, he'd hoped Calix's Oracle premonitions would have given them some kind of sign, any kind. But the more he thought about it, the more he realized that the signs were all around them. Ethaniel's willingness to use his family's magic to save everyone else. Calix's mother and her betrayals. The loss of Richard's sight. The damage, the blood, the sweat, the stress. All of it forged together in a sword above their necks, and they were Damocles awaiting their doom.

But as long as he stood, Aubrey would not allow the worst of it to come to pass. He swore it again and again as he stared at the fan of Calix's eyelashes over his cheeks, at the waves of Ethaniel's hair. At how close they curled together, their respite made peaceful through exhaustion alone.

So, when they awoke and sluggishly pulled on clothes, gathered their things, and started to head downstairs, Aubrey stopped them with a simple, "Wait. Both of you."

Ethaniel gave him a curious look. "What's wrong?"

Aubrey swallowed hard. Of course, now would be the time his courage fled. "I simply..." He sighed, took their hands in his, and held them tightly. "Magnus let me know last night that he had one more chance to contact this Agrippa.

That they would be the source for answers, if we only could ask the right questions. That's what he's working on this morning, fixing one of the cracked communication stones I thought we'd used up. But it's a choice we have to make. We can either get answers from someone we don't know but Magnus trusts, but that would leave Magnus more drained of power once we open this door to the *demimonde*. Or we forgo the answers and charge in, and have Magnus at his full capabilities."

He watched the play of emotions across their faces, but Calix was the first to speak. "I think any answers are worth the risk," he said quietly as he ran his thumb over Aubrey's knuckles. "But that would mean —"

"That I have to step up more," Ethaniel said. There was no shift in his tone, no change in his expression. The man could have been talking about Sunday tea or the cost of thread. And that made something in the pit of Aubrey's stomach sink even more. "I can do it. But I'll need you to help me. To keep me from caving into other urges until I can find some equilibrium again." Ethaniel looked down to the floor and took Aubrey's heart with him. "I spent so long fighting against this– this *itch* under my skin. Like a living thing that I knew I couldn't ignore forever. So if I'm to use my family's magic, I want it to be because I'm protecting us. Helping us."

"Saving us," Aubrey said. Ethaniel only nodded in response.

He drew them close and kissed them both. Softly, slowly, with all the reverence and adoration he had stored in his body, his heart. And then he let them go.

Calix was the first to head downstairs, and while Ethaniel gathered his papers, Aubrey stayed back. He stared at the curve of Ethaniel's back, strong and proud in his simple blue shirt, and felt his heart break all over again. The unknown price of Ethaniel calling on Harkness magic — dangerous, addictive magic — was one Aubrey would willingly pay. He wasn't sure if he was the one who could jump in front of the oncoming train, however.

"I wanted to show you this," Ethaniel said as he turned and held out a piece of paper. "It's done. The ritual circle." As Aubrey took the page, Ethaniel rambled on. "I wrote several versions, all based on different summoning patterns I've used in the past. But I amplified them with Lily's notes. I made sure we won't be summoning whatever gatekeeper she ran afoul of, but this..."

He pointed to a set of runes that, at his touch, seemed to dance before Aubrey's eyes. Aubrey was not a rune speaker or spell writer, but when he focused, he could see where Ethaniel had broken several runes up into something new for his purposes. His mind wanted to reforge the runes, make them whole, but that was the healer in him. When he shook that off, he could somewhat understand what Ethaniel had done. It was brilliant work, better than anything he'd ever seen come out of the Collectio or any of the academic circles so invested in unspooling the mystery of magic in their world.

It left him a little breathless, once he put the entire picture together.

"You're able to open a door without summoning a guardian?" Aubrey asked, tracing one of the charcoal lines with his finger. "Ethaniel, that's..."

"Absurd, I know, but I think...no, I *know* it will work." Ethaniel took the page back, bit his lip, and looked up at Aubrey. "I know it will work. It has to. Magnus and I can hold the door open while you and Calix locate Lily's essence. If you take Talbot with you, he should be able to point you toward his own. At least, that's my understanding. But it's truly untraversed territory, so if there's any sign of a threat, of danger, you're to come back *immediately.*"

Aubrey's head was spinning. It was all so much, and so esoteric, and they were wading into dark, uncharted waters and that should have thrilled him. Had it been any other situation, any other group of people, he would have felt the sting of excitement. They were going into the *demimonde,* a place only known about in certain circles. What they might find on the other side could defy description and categorization. It could change the course of magic as they knew it. The course of history.

Aubrey was, instead, terrified. And his face must have shown it, because Ethaniel was immediately there, warm and real and wrapping his arms around Aubrey's middle, his face tucked into Aubrey's neck, and whispering things like, "It'll be okay. It will. I know it will."

He held Ethaniel close, closed his eyes, and let his mind rest for the few seconds they had.

"It's not perfect," Magnus said as they gathered around the little communication stone he'd placed on a small side table. "But I can get a connection through to Agrippa. We'll need to be quick, so I hope you're ready to talk fast and write notes even faster."

He waved his hand over the stone, which immediately glowed a gentle blue, his magic filling in the cracks that had occurred after Aubrey had used it. "Don't be put off by Agrippa," Magnus said, a bit of sternness seeping into his voice. "They're an academic and not used to people in general. Don't take their gruffness for a lack of care."

At Aubrey's nod, Magnus closed his eyes, held both hands out, and Aubrey let him in. The last bit of magic was Aubrey's to do, amplified through Magnus, and Aubrey focused on those cracks in the stone. Focused on making it whole and useful once more.

After a few moments of silence, Aubrey felt his power seep into Magnus. The image in his mind of the stone flashed, flickered, and became solid. He felt his third eye crack open only a little; it was an easy spell, particularly with Magnus at the helm. He could almost feel Magnus's nerves, the quiet energy that threatened to spill over into real panic (*what if it doesn't work what if I fail what if what if*), and then everything snapped into place.

"Magnus said I'd have visitors. Wasn't expecting...well, any of you."

If a voice could have wings and float, Agrippa's was the pinnacle. There was a musicality to it, rivaling the lilt of any lounge singer or choir, and it had Aubrey opening his eyes.

Before them stood a faint vision of...someone.

Some thing.

Aubrey shook his head at that passing thought, knocking it away like one would a bothersome fly. But he wasn't entirely wrong, and he could tell from Ethaniel and Calix's expressions that they were just as surprised.

"Well, don't waste Magnus's efforts by gaping," Agrippa said, swiping back a lock of their snow-white hair. "Magnus, did you not warn them?"

Magnus shot Aubrey a guilty look. "I didn't think it was my place, Agrippa. They know about your relations, but — "

"Well, piss on it," Agrippa bit out, crossing their arms over their chest. "Yes, all right, get it out. All the staring, and then we can move on."

Calix was the first to respond, much to Aubrey's shame. He was the professional here, wasn't he? "I know you," Calix whispered, stepping forward. "Or...someone like you. How is that possible?"

Agrippa gave him a wry smile. "Given what Magnus has told me about your connection to magic, my boy, I can only guess one of my brethren came to you in a dream?" When Calix nodded, Agrippa chuckled. The sound was like a dozen bells sounding at once, in perfect harmony. "I'm also guessing they had wings or extra limbs. The price I paid to stay in your realm was to leave those pieces of myself behind."

Agrippa held out their arms, forearms revealed by sleeves pushed up to the elbow. There were scars, thick and ropey, all along their bare skin. Aubrey could only stare, even though he knew it was utterly rude. "I'm so sorry," he managed to say, but Agrippa didn't look sad or aggrieved, only shrugged. "But you're..."

"Not human? Well, from what Magnus tells me, none of you are exactly paragons of straight-laced humanity."

"Agrippa, please," Magnus replied, pinching the bridge of his nose between thumb and forefinger. "We can talk all about how you came to our realm later. When several lives aren't at stake."

"Yes, yes, fine." They waved an elegant hand at them, pushed their long white hair back away from a finely boned face, and smiled. Their mouth, Aubrey noticed, was full of fangs. "A very long story short, I left the *demimonde* when someone opened a door for me many years ago. I bargained part of myself to stay, and since then, I've been inspiring certain scientists and mages with bits of information. The one I was most fond of I named myself after." Agrippa sniffed and continued. "A story for another time. Magnus was very correct in calling on me to explain how that infernal place works. He's given me the basics, but I want to see how you're going to get this door open."

Aubrey had *so* many questions, but now wasn't the time. He gave Magnus a look that promised a stern tongue-lashing later, particularly because Magnus had only ever mentioned Agrippa in terms of their magical knowledge and their work in keeping certain artifacts safe. So much of that made more sense, and yet very little, in this new light.

Ethaniel stepped forward with his pages of ritual circles for Agrippa to peruse, and they spent several long moments peering at them. "Yes, yes, that's...well, that's certainly something I haven't seen in quite some time." They straightened and gave Ethaniel a look that sent chills down Aubrey's spine. He wanted to pull Ethaniel closer, protect him from such scrutiny, but Ethaniel awaited Agrippa's judgment with a stiff spine and bright eyes.

"My, my...a Harkness that hasn't fallen afoul of their dark urges," Agrippa finally said. "It's a delicate line you walk, little patterner."

Ethaniel looked over at Aubrey. "I'm well aware."

"Good. Then you won't mind me correcting some of this." Agrippa quickly drew a few runes in the air. "Copy those down exactly, and replace your second, third, sixth, and twelfth runes in this order. Your spell wouldn't have failed, but it would have opened the door a bit too wide for my liking, and I prefer to keep my casting as tidy as possible. Plus, we don't want any bleed-over from the *demimonde*, or any other realm that decides to be cheeky."

While Ethaniel and Agrippa worked with Calix watching on, Aubrey pulled Magnus aside. "Magnus."

Magnus licked his lips and gave Aubrey a grin. "Yes, yes. Go on."

Aubrey's mind felt too full, so full that all he could manage was, "Are you fucking serious?"

Magnus laughed at that. "Entirely so, I'm afraid. Agrippa's existence here is a *very* well-kept secret. There's only a few people who even know about them, and even fewer who have worked with them in any great capacity. I wasn't going to break that trust, even for you, my dear boy. I know you have questions, and I promise that we will visit Agrippa in their little enclave once this is all done." He nudged Aubrey's shoulder with his. "I've told them much about you over the years. I think, from afar, they've counted you as a confidant, even if that relationship was purely one-sided. Don't be angry at them."

"I'm not," Aubrey said, "I'm not angry at either of you. I'm just so surprised you were able to keep them a secret all this time."

Magnus threw his head back and laughed. "Oh, Aubrey. You always need that last word, don't you?"

Aubrey didn't get the chance to reply, as Calix was waving them back over. "I think they figured it out," he whispered as they drew near.

"Your patterner is very skilled," Agrippa said as they gathered back around the table. "Even the errors I would expect another practitioner to make weren't there, by and large anyways. Must be that Harkness blood."

Beside Aubrey, Ethaniel stiffened, and Aubrey put a hand on his back for comfort. "Yes, well," Ethaniel said faintly, "I trust that we're done here?"

"With the circle, yes," Agrippa replied. "But Magnus said you had questions. Let me make this very simple — you will have limited time in the *demimonde* before the guardians realize you're there. You'll need to be quick and quiet. Ethaniel, when you take Calix through the door —"

Aubrey held up his hand. "I'm going through with Calix."

Agrippa only shook their head. "No, I'm afraid that won't work. Magnus will need your mending abilities to hold the door open. He's said many times you're quite adept at turning those abilities on their head, using them in ways he never anticipated. He'll need your magic to keep that door open as long as possible, and your Oracle here will need the patterner's magic to recognize the arcane signatures of those you're seeking. There won't be any vaults or traps, but only endless miles of gray expanse that you could traverse for the rest of your lives and never find what you seek."

Panic clawed at Aubrey's throat. "I have to go with him."

"You certainly *can*," Agrippa replied with a slightly imperious air, "but it's not what I would recommend. You're going through without the permission of a guardian, who are notoriously hard to deal with in any regard. Few have even interacted with beings from other realms, especially humans. Not having permission affords you a very small window of time under which you can remain undetected. Once a guardian is aware of you, it will chase you back to your door, seal that entry shut, and it will never be usable again." They paused to scratch at the side of their face and Aubrey saw an iridescent shimmer.

Feathers.

Their face, along the jaw and, as Aubrey looked closer, around the hairline, was covered in feathers. They were impossibly hard to see in the faint image of Agrippa conjured by the still-fractured communication stone. But they were beautiful, and the sight of them only piqued Aubrey's curiosity even more. And it still wasn't enough distraction from this sudden change in plans.

"They're right," Magnus said, his gaze darting to Aubrey. "We'd be fools not to follow the advice. Out of all of us, Agrippa is the only one from that place. I trust they've got our best interests at heart."

"I'm touched," Agrippa said in the most even of tones, but Aubrey could see their gratitude in their eyes. "And yes, I would recommend following my advice."

"We'll be okay, Aubrey," Ethaniel said. "I won't let anything happen to Calix."

Aubrey swallowed his words and his grief and nodded.

"Well, with that settled..." Agrippa began to draw in the air once more, this time complicated patterns that looked similar to some scientific drawings Aubrey had seen in the Collectio's library. They were nearly mathematical in form and function, but beautiful as a whole. When he said as much, Agrippa chuckled and replied, "Where do you think your scientists came up with the idea? Not everything in your world started there, Aubrey. The origin of each realm has its own story, and none of them are identical, but there's more in common between some than others."

Aubrey turned, wide-eyed, to Magnus, who looked similarly surprised. "Right, well," Magnus said, "so how do Calix and Ethaniel go about tracking down little bits of lost souls in the *demimonde*?"

"The *demimonde* is a land of unchecked arcana, so you'll need to focus your energies. Take something with you that's connected to the person you're looking for–the more personal, the better." Agrippa paused in their writing, wiped a hand through the last rune they'd drawn, and replaced it. "Better. That should help you focus your energies a bit more, Aubrey. But yes, take something personal with you and focus on that. Is this person someone you knew well?"

"One of them," Calix said, voice cracking with emotion. "My mother. The other is...no, not well at all, but we have part of him trapped in a book."

Forehead wrinkled in confusion (or concern, Aubrey wasn't sure), Agrippa seemed to float a little closer. "You have part of him in a book? This is the same book Magnus mentioned?" When Calix nodded, Agrippa actually smiled. "That's going to make at least half your job very easy, then. Souls don't like to be separated from bits of themselves, so the person in this book will know where their lost part is as soon as you open the door."

"That's a relief," Ethaniel said. "Good to know that damn book has some use after all this."

"And it's another reason why you'll want your patterner with you," Agrippa said immediately. "Time and distance mean nothing in that place. But you, with your Harkness magic, have a deeper innate understanding of realms, even such an odd one as the *demimonde*."

Ethaniel looked stricken at that, and Aubrey put a placating hand on him. "But how will I know what to do?"

Agrippa's mouth was a grim line as they said, "Trust me when I say you will. There's no way for me to describe it."

"No, I think I understand," Ethaniel replied softly. "Something similar happened recently, as if an old, buried instinct kicked in and I didn't have to think about it."

Aubrey hated how true those words were, and how crestfallen Ethaniel sounded. But the reality of their situation was undeniable. And they could only go forward.

"You've done me a massive favor," Magnus said as they rounded out their conversation after a few more minutes of planning with Agrippa still present, before the spell faded. "Name it, and it's yours."

Something like sadness crept over Agrippa's face before they said, "Come for a visit, and bring your young mages with you. I might be a hermit out of necessity, but I'm not immune to loneliness."

"Consider it done." Magnus gave Agrippa a snappy salute and a smile before letting the spell fade into glittering specks on the air that disappeared when they hit the carpet. "Right. Well. Here we are."

Aubrey could only look at the three of them, lest he spiral into a ball of worry and fear.

After a moment, Calix ran off to find something of his mother's while Magnus promised to bring up a tray of "fortifying goodies" before the hard work began. While Ethaniel started on the ritual circle, his lines more precise even than any embroidery Aubrey had seen him bring to life. And Aubrey was left to pace and fret.

He made about a dozen passes through the room before Calix came back clutching a fistful of dried lavender. "From her very first lavender garden on the grounds here," Calix said. "She put a tiny preservation spell on them, so they'd keep for a while. It was one of the first spells she taught me."

"Poetic," Aubrey murmured as he passed a hand over the stalks, feeling the smallest spark of magic. "Outside of your presence, I can't imagine any other object would speak to her as much as this. Well done, dove."

Calix flushed under the praise and that splash of pink over his cheeks made Aubrey want to never, ever let him go.

"So…that's it," Ethaniel said as he stood from kneeling, dusted off his pants, and motioned to the large ritual circle in the middle of the room. "God, I hope I did this right."

They were immediately at his side, boxing Ethaniel in. However, Aubrey was the one to lift Ethaniel's chin with a finger, stare down at him, and say, "You have already done so much. Never, ever doubt your talent. Or your heart."

"He's gone all stern," Calix said. "I think he's rather serious, Ethaniel."

"I'm extremely serious," Aubrey said, even as he gave Calix a tiny smile. "That goes for both of you. Beauty and talent all wrapped up together. I am truly a fortunate man."

They stood in silence as the morning sun warmed the room, casting across their faces as if trying to brighten their moods. No amount of spring sunshine would keep Aubrey's darker thoughts at bay, but he knew he wasn't alone in this.

"I will do anything to protect you both," he whispered before kissing Ethaniel, then Calix. Calix was as sweet as ever, yielding and pliable. And Ethaniel was his rock, his foundation. If Calix was his sky and Ethaniel his ground, surely Aubrey could be the steady middle?

Surely they would make this work.

When Magnus came back, tea tray rattling with every step, they took their time. Magnus started to tell one of his favorite stories about a fresh-faced, extremely ambitious Aubrey, new to the city and the Collectio, and soon had Ethaniel and Calix laughing at all the times Aubrey had a spell go awry and wound up on the roof, frozen in place, or even one very memorable time, suddenly wearing Magnus's clothes and Magnus his. Given Aubrey was six inches taller and a few dozen pounds heavier, the image was particularly funny.

But the laughter didn't last, and with its disappearance came the resurgence of Aubrey's fears. He bit back at them, teeth bared, magic blossoming under his skin in preparation. He retrieved Convergence from the other room, and when he entered, Talbot's voice rang out.

"Finally!" he said. "Finally, I am on the path to freedom."

"Don't get ahead of yourself, necromancer," Ethaniel muttered. Aubrey saw Calix's lips twitch as if trying to hold back a laugh.

"We're retrieving a part of you," Magnus corrected. "I can't believe I'm scolding a book, but here we are."

The door creaking open drew all their attention.

"I heard a lot of moving about," Lawton said as he entered, looking more haggard every day. Today, the purple circles under his eyes looked more like bruises, and Aubrey felt a pang of pity for the man. "Is everything all right?"

Calix stepped up to his friend, as if to shield them from. "It's fine. We're handling the issue of my mother and this damn book in one fell swoop."

Lawton crossed his arms, the branch-like burns across pale skin almost gold in the morning sunlight. "And you weren't going to tell me when this was happening?"

"He's keeping you out of harm's way," Ethaniel snapped. "Be grateful."

"Oh, I'm grateful. But if my friend is charging right into this danger, I'd think someone would have told me beforehand." Realization flickered over Lawton's face and he looked down. "Unless secrecy was the point. Which is sensible. I'm not exactly a font of trustworthiness, am I?"

"You can stay," Calix said after a moment. He pointed to a chair at the far end of the room. "But do not stay if anything even seems dangerous. Do you understand?"

"I do. But can I at least..." Lawton walked over to Calix and very carefully put his hands on Calix's shoulders. "You're doing something incredibly dangerous, if my lack of knowledge of those drawings on the ground are any indication. Calix, I–I'm not asking for your forgiveness. I am, however, asking if you might embrace me, just this once, as your friend. Even if those friendly feelings are all on my side of the line."

Calix's face twisted with emotion and tension hung in the air for a shining moment until he said, "Yes, I...yes, Lawton."

The embrace was lopsided, Lawton trying to get close to Calix without Calix moving on his own. Not that Aubrey could blame Calix. There was quite a bit of hurt to heal yet, and they'd only begun to see the chasm between them from Lawton's actions.

Finally, Lawton stepped back and, looking all the more like a kicked puppy with words of thanks on his lips, slouched over to the chair and sat. Aubrey was only mildly rankled by his company, but Ethaniel practically bristled.

Magnus took up at the north end of the room, the page on which they'd transcribed Agrippa's runes ready for his magic. Everyone knew their steps in this dance, but as Aubrey watched Calix and Ethaniel take up at the south end of the room, doubt gnawed at him.

Maybe it was simply because they'd been through so much. Maybe it was the exhaustion. *Maybe maybe maybe.*

Magnus began to chant, began to channel his magic, and when Aubrey felt it brush up against his own, he let his hands drop and his mind *open*. That third eye, his companion since the day he was old enough to understand how he was different from his family, was a familiar presence. Like greeting an old friend. Aubrey let it take over, let Magnus's magic wash over him, pull him under.

He took that magic that wasn't his, watched for his moment, and when his mortal, human eyes saw energy begin to gather in the center of the circle, a vibrant blue-green and practically *humming* with otherworldly power, Aubrey let every wall but one in his mind drop.

The floodgates opened. Magnus was there, a welcome presence at his back and side and all around, smelling of citrus and incense and strong black tea, filling Aubrey's mind.

The portal flickered. Flickered. Again and again.

And then it opened.

Calix and Ethaniel looked back at him one more time, lavender and book in hand, and stepped through.

"Hold on!" Magnus said. "Keep holding, Aubrey! Stay with me!"

Aubrey gritted his teeth, his body going tight with effort. It was an immense amount of magic funneling through him, a twining of his and Magnus's. A joining. A fracturing.

If their wills splintered, if their powers waned, before Calix and Ethaniel were back...Aubrey snarled at the open air, the portal, the very *thought* of anything happening to them. He wouldn't let it. He couldn't let it.

He loved them too much to let anything happen.

Seconds passed, hazy blue and hot, growing hotter by the second as he and Magnus worked together to keep the portal open. There was nothing but gray beyond the portal, but Aubrey's mind was deliriously bright.

He was overwhelmed. Overcome. He could feel the energy begin to seep into him, pulling from his own body. The pain of it was real but not, in a drugged sort of sense that left Aubrey gasping.

"Hold steady." Lawton's voice was in his ear, a hand on his back. Aubrey couldn't whirl or snap in surprise, lest he drop concentration, but a large part of him seethed at Lawton's presence. "I told him I'd help when needed. You're overwhelmed, curator. Let me help."

That was Lily's voice in his ear now, her power at his back. Coursing through him. *Changing him*. In some ways, it was reminiscent of the moment Calix had merged their magics together, and in a flash, Aubrey's entire being was *flying*, transcending past any limits he'd had before.

He could *feel* the portal. He could feel its power, its promise. Seconds passed. Maybe minutes. Time had no meaning, wasn't even a concept where he and Magnus and Lily Addington, in Lawton's body, stood just on the other side of a land of endless gray.

But he felt it when Ethaniel cried out in shock and pain. He felt it as deep as his own marrow, in the roots of his teeth and hair, a shockwave of regret and sadness and sheer *agony*.

And the power snapped shut just as the portal did.

Calix stood before them, a bloody gash on his head, the book in one hand, the other clutching a scrap of blue fabric.

Aubrey raced over to him. "Calix! Fuck. Are you all right? Where's Ethaniel?"

Calix looked up at him, tears in those now golden eyes, and whispered, "He's gone."

SOMEWHERE IN THE DEMIMONDE...

SOMEWHERE IN THE DEMIMONDE...

THE MOMENT THEY CROSSED through the portal, Ethaniel knew something was wrong. His mind, already bogged down by a strange pulling, stretching sensation, couldn't keep up with the changes in scenery before him.

The gray, swirling mist obscuring ground darker than volcanic rock. The shadows of bare, ghostly trees in the far distance. The vast *space* in which he stood. A space that separated him and Calix by what felt like miles, and appeared to be only a few feet.

"I'm here!" he called out, waving his arms in the air so Calix might see him. And when Ethaniel reached out to take Calix by the wrist, the man's visage evaporated on contact.

"Ethaniel? Where are you?"

Heart pounding, Ethaniel wheeled around, gaze bouncing across the bleak space. It was all gray, all dark, and the hopelessness that suddenly weighed on him nearly took Ethaniel to the ground.

Was this it? The promise of the *demimonde* was some space that never ended and never saw color?

"A Harkness walks here again." Deep and resonant, as if pulled from the very cracked gray earth under his feet, came a sourceless voice. But unlike Convergence, this had *presence* and *weight*. As if someone had stolen the air from the space around him. And yet that feeling was so similar to when Convergence — Talbot — had shown its capabilities.

"All who touch this place bear its mark. It is the curse of this realm-space. Never-ending, and never beginning. It simply *is*."

A spike of pain went through him, starting at his temple and spreading out. Nausea rolled his stomach and Ethaniel flinched, but didn't try to back away. "Calix? Are you here somewhere? Calix, please!"

"He'll find you eventually," said the voice. Another lick of pain on the other side of his head and Ethaniel bit the inside of his cheek. It lasted only a second, but it was enough. "Oracles who come to this...ancestral home usually learn quite quickly how to shape the space of the *demimonde* around them."

Gritting his teeth, Ethaniel began to walk. He didn't want to respond to the voice. He *couldn't*. Something in him *screamed* of blood and pain and dark consequences if he did. He had to push on, find Calix, and get him back to the door.

The door.

Ethaniel wheeled, peering through the swirling mist, to see the door still there, still glowing a soft gold. But the edges of it seemed to spark and pop, like a flashbulb over a camera. They didn't have long.

"Calix! Calix, answer me!" Ethaniel called out. "I know you're there; you only need to think of me and answer back!"

"Perhaps you can bring him to you," the voice said, its presence even heavier now. It was able to dominate Ethaniel's mind, make him stop in his tracks.

"No. Whatever you are...no. I am not of this place," he ground out, closing his eyes so he could better picture Calix's smile and the deep honey-brown of his hair, his eyes.

"Oh, those eyes are realm-touched now, my dear patterner." The voice came closer. Ethaniel could feel its breath on the back of his neck. "The *demimonde* has a hold on him now. Just as it does on you."

"It *does not*," Ethaniel snapped. "I am —"

"A Harkness. Your blood is responsible for finding this place, for telling others of it. You are touched by it too. You cannot deny the pull of the dark."

Something shifted to his left. A brush of cloth, or maybe even fingers, against his shoulder. There was a figure here, some entity toying with him. A guardian, perhaps? Or some other denizen of the *demimonde*?

"Very good. Very smart of you."

A few feet to Ethaniel's left, a tear appeared. A single, bone-white claw sliced open the very *air* beside him, and then two bony, multi-fingered hands grasped the edge of that tear (that was impossible, air couldn't *tear*) and pulled it open, ripped it apart like the flimsiest Christmas wrapping paper so it could come through and stand before Ethaniel.

Ethaniel stopped counting the number of arms at six. At that point, it didn't matter how many arms the creature, the being before it had. Because a creature like it shouldn't exist and yet here it stood, towering over him, somehow staring right at him even though it had no eyes.

He couldn't breathe. Couldn't think. The impossibility of this being overrode some higher functioning in his mind, and all Ethaniel could think was, "I stand before a god."

"Not a god," it said, laughing despite its lack of mouth, as its main head tipped to the side. The smaller heads, two each on its shoulders made of what looked like pure black marble, resembled human skulls without the lower jaws. But the main head was a single oval, its edges broken and crumbling. "But a seeker. I walk these endless lands looking for my twin." Two arms on each side rose, and Ethaniel saw the spaces between the wrists and elbows were only glowing orbs of red. One set of hands folded over its chest, the others came to clasp in front of its elongated, bony torso. "You may call me Uzala. Path Seeker."

Ethaniel had a million questions. The creature's odd, disjointed nature came into focus as he stared, trying to sort his mind into some order, and he realized its long, tattered white robes and strange, pulsing orbs of red where joints and muscle would be on a human, were part of a map. Uzala was wearing a map. He could *feel* its energy like a pattern, and seemingly of a will not his own, he stepped closer, hand reaching forward.

"You are correct, of course," Uzala said, bending more arms in his direction. These came up from under its robes, seemingly attached to its lower body and not the upper. But Ethaniel still walked forward. "It is a map. A map of the doors between realms. A horrible affliction, a cruel tease, as a joke from one who walks these lands, too."

Ethaniel stopped, his hand inches from Uzala's robes. He wanted to touch. He *needed* to, and yet instinct still screamed in the back of his mind. "You are made of a map of doors you can't use?"

"Cruel, so cruel, was the one who did this to me. We fought a war in shadow and flame, over a door opened long ago. Uriel wanted it for itself, and I stopped them. We fought for so long that the one who opened the door was lost to the mists, and so was his chance to walk free."

Ethaniel dragged his gaze up the being's form to land on the large stone oval. As if he could look it in the eye. "Uriel? It did this?"

Heartbreak reverberated through his mind now. A long, deep sadness. "It did." Uzala pressed a hand to its robes, over a red orb where its heart might be. Drops of red slipped between its fingers to the ground, where they shattered like glass. "And now I have not one, but two Harknesses at my disposal. I might have my revenge yet."

Two Harknesses?

The hand on his shoulder was one Ethaniel knew well.

"Brother."

"Ethaniel."

Vincent circled his right and Ethaniel saw blood. A lot of it. Vincent smiled grimly and held out a hand covered in it. "Cousin Isme didn't hold up her end of our bargain. Fitting that I would get trapped here, and it would be in your company." He looked dull, almost gray himself, as if the *demimonde* were seeping in through his wounds. Even Vincent's eyes were dim, red-rimmed and bloodshot.

"I am keeping him alive for now," Uzala said. "But for that to continue, you must prove useful to me."

Ethaniel swallowed hard. This was not happening. It couldn't be. "And Calix? Where is he?"

The four skeleton-like heads all tipped up, the sound of bone on bone sending a horrible pain through Ethaniel's head. They stayed that way for a moment, as if scenting the air, then turned to face him. "He's nearby. Bring him here."

Ethaniel paused. If he could somehow get Calix here, then maybe Calix could escape through the door behind them. Maybe they could outrun this thing. He gave Vincent another look, and now he saw the fine slash across his face, and the wound dripping from Vincent's side. The blood was so dark it barely seemed to stain Vincent's black suit, and Ethaniel knew he couldn't wait. This creature clearly had its own motivations, and staying near it was a very bad idea.

Ethaniel began to step back, as if to put space between himself and Uzala. This Path Seeker. He wasn't sure if Vincent would understand, but he had to try. "I'll bring Calix here," he said, "but we're not useful to you in this state. We need to go back to our world, make a plan."

"You wish to bargain? Now? When I already have what I need?" If the creature could laugh, it would probably do so, but instead it lashed out with a bony hand and grabbed Vincent by the neck. Uzala lifted Vincent from the ground, its fingers curled around Vincent's throat as Vincent struggled and gasped and tried to pry its hand from him.

"Call your Oracle. Call him, patterner. Call him here and let you both be known to this place so you might truly understand your magic."

Uzala's voice was *everything*. It was in his head, his ears, his very body. Ethaniel felt its presence and was helpless against it. He sank to his knees, fighting the whole time but enjoying every second of supplication.

"*CALL HIM.*"

Ethaniel closed his eyes and thought about Calix, his tears disappearing into the gray mist.

"Ethaniel?"

Ethaniel could have collapsed with relief, was barely able to lift his head to see Calix kneeling before him. "Thank fuck," he whispered hoarsely. "Are you okay?"

"Are you?" Calix gestured to Vincent, who was still fighting in Uzala's grasp, clearly shocked at the sight. "Is that...Ethaniel, that's the man I saw outside Aubrey's apartment the night of the fire."

"Vincent," he croaked. "He's trapped here too, somehow. Calix, Calix, please..."

"Anything, Ethaniel. I'm just glad you're all right." Calix pointed over Ethaniel's shoulder. "The door's just there. We need to go back."

Ethaniel shook his head. "But Uzala..."

"Who?"

Ethaniel paused. "The creature that has Vincent, we have to..."

Calix frowned. "I see...something in the shadows, but no creature." He grabbed Ethaniel's hand and said, "We need to go."

Gods, he couldn't *think*. It was all so much. "Calix...go..."

Uzala leaned forward, all white robes and red, glowing orbs, and four black skulls now chattering their teeth against its shoulders of white marble and bone. There was madness in the air, and Ethaniel could feel it pushing into his eyes, his ears, coating his tongue and forcing its way down his throat.

But it hadn't fully dampened his own magic. Ethaniel could feel it still, a faint second heartbeat in his chest. If he focused enough, if he pushed with everything he had, he could block this creature long enough to save Calix. Maybe he was a Harkness after all, and maybe he could work that magic in his favor.

Ethaniel thought about all the things he'd taken for granted. All the things he'd lost. He remembered his sister's round little face and the way she'd smiled when she'd lost a front tooth. He remembered Aubrey's hands and Calix's smile and the way Jeremiah used to sit with him late into the night and show him a new pattern, their needlework glowing gently in the lamplight.

Ethaniel thought about all the things he loved and cared for, and he wrapped them around his heart. He wove it into the warding patterns he knew in his mind, his magic buffeted by the buzzing energy of the *demimonde* and he knew.

Harkness magic was of this place. Harkness magic was as chaotic and dark as the realm in which he now sat. It was always the family way. But it didn't have to be *his way*.

I can change the rules, he thought before, with one giant heave, he shoved to his feet and pushed Calix toward the door. "Run! Calix, now!"

Ethaniel spun in front of Calix, blocking him with his body, and when the last rune connected in his mind, the air in front of him shimmered. From a circle roughly the size of a dinner plate came a shield, one that grew and grew and grew until it blocked him completely from Uzala. Uzala immediately attacked, pummeling the shield with all the hands not holding Vincent by the throat, and when that didn't work, it dropped Vincent to the ground and heaved itself at Ethaniel.

The shield wouldn't hold long. "Calix, go!"

Ethaniel was desperate to keep Calix safe, and this was the only way he knew how.

The seconds passed as Calix stared at him. "I can't leave you! I won't!"

Ethaniel smiled, even as Uzala's fists began to crack through the shield. "Then you come back for me." Hand shaking, he reached out to take Calix's. "Take Convergence and go. NOW."

A piece of the shield splintered with a heavy *crack*, and when Ethaniel looked over, Calix had a hand pressed to his forehead, blood running between his fingers.

Calix knew he had no choice. He ran for the door, and Ethaniel had to trust he'd make it.

The shield gave out with one more mighty blow, and then Uzala was all he could see.

"Welcome home, patterner." Its laugh, victorious and bone-chilling, echoed around them. "I seem to be collecting your kin, and how glad it makes me to know that even the most disciplined Harkness cannot ignore the call of the *demimonde*." It waved one large, bony hand to the empty space at its right. "Your brother has finally sought you out, little one. Doesn't that make your heart sing?"

Ethaniel could do nothing else but stare in shock as a small form, no higher than his waist, appeared in the mists. She was still wearing the blue dress from the day she'd disappeared, still had the white bow in her hair that Ethaniel had carefully tied in her thick hair. He remembered how she'd smiled at him after looking at his work in the mirror, and how small she'd felt in his arms as he'd swung her around while she'd giggled.

"Come, child," Uzala said. "Don't you wish to see your brother again?"

Maria clung to the creature, a sickening mockery of the way she used to cling to Ethaniel's leg. Bile rose up in his throat as horror overtook his mind. "My God. Maria? How?"

Uzala leaned down to him, its neck now a long, pale column along which veins grew, purple and fat with gods knew what, and said, "Now, Ethaniel, is that any way to greet your long-lost sister?"

Sources and For Further Reading

Sources used directly in DEMIMONDE:

- *Enochian Vision Magick: A Practical Guide to the Magick of Dr. John Dee and Edward Kelley* by Lon Milo DuQuette, 2019 by Weiser Books

- *John Dee and the Empire of Angels: Enochian Magick and the Occult Roots of the Modern World* by Jason Louv, 2018 by Inner Traditions

- *The Queen's Conjurer: The Life and Magic of Dr. Dee* by Benjamin Woolley, 2001 by HarperCollins

- *Western Esoteric Masters Series: John Dee*, selected and introduced by Gerald Suster, 2003 by North Atlantic Books

- *Grimoires: A History of Magic Books* by Owen Davies, 2009 by Oxford University Press

I also highly recommend the Esoterica YouTube channel by Dr. Justin Sledge. Dr. Sledge "produces content relating to topics such as alchemy, magic, Kabbalah, mysticism, hermetic philosophy, theosophy, the occult and more using the best academic scholarship currently available." His videos are easy to follow and he has an incredible wealth of knowledge on these strange, mostly unknown and understudied theories, philosophies, and people who influenced our world. After all, John Dee was the man to come up with the phrase, "The British Empire"; something we use in common parlance to this day.

Acknowledgements

Massive thanks need to go to my cover artist Željka Dobras for the incredible work she has done for COUP DE COEUR and DEMIMONDE. I'm eternally grateful for her skill, imagination, and dedication.

Also huge thanks go to Laura R. Samotin for her cheerleading, early read, and editing skills.

To my friends who read this book early and kept me going, all my love.

And to everyone who picked up COUP DE COEUR and decided to stick around for the rest of the story – thank you.

About the Author

Halli Starling is a queer librarian fascinated by the occult and strange history. She lives in Michigan with her spouse, feline supervisors, and is always surrounded by books.
When not writing, she co-hosts The Human Exception podcast and plays D&D.

For updates on the final book in the trilogy and more, follow Halli on Instagram @hallistarling.
Website: hallistarlingbooks.com